Copyright © 2018 by Ra

All rights reserved. No downloaded, decompiled, reverse-engineered, or stored in, or introduced into any information storage and retrieval system, in any form or by any means, whether electronic or mechanical, now known, hereinafter invented, without express written permission of the publisher. For permission requests, write to the publisher, addressed "Attention: Permissions Coordinator," at the address below.

Typewriter Pub, an imprint of Blvnp Incorporated
A Nevada Corporation
1887 Whitney Mesa DR #2002
Henderson, NV 89014
www.typewriterpub.com/info@typewriterpub.com

ISBN: 978-1-68030-948-5

DISCLAIMER
This book is a work of fiction. The characters, incidents, and dialogue are drawn from the author's imagination and are not to be construed as real. While references might be made to actual historical events or existing locations, the names, characters, places, and incidents are either products of the author's imagination or are used fictitiously, and any resemblance to actual persons living or dead, business establishments, events or locales is entirely coincidental.

Praise for Mason's Impossible Prey

Mason's Impossible Prey is a great read that introduces readers to an exhilarating, thrilling, and heart-stopping journey that will surely leave a lasting impression.
—*Nicola Uy, Goodreads*

Loved every single chapter of this.. Have never been so interested in a book before and love the author for writing such an amazing book hope she keeps on writing books as great as this one
—*Ramlah, Goodreads*

This book, isn't just a typical werewolf/alpha book, if only better. This is a book that makes you laugh, cry and feel the pain and the happiness, the characters felt. Also, the scenes were so well-elaborated that I can imagine them well as if I was in the book. The character development was wonderfully done, too. You can see how much the characters have grown and learnt. Personally, I have read this book for more than 5 times, still, I still haven't got bored of it and I don't think I ever will.
—*Amy Wong, Goodreads*

I loved this book it was magnificent and I loved that it wasn't to fast paced:) you are an amazing author. It's so hard to find a good book as well.
—*Amelia*

The story is so great! One of the best werewolf stories. Mason's Impossible Prey is one of the cause why I want to read more werewolf stories! Mates and Heat are awesome! I'm a fan in wattpad.
—*Karen Ritz M. Custodio*

MASON'S IMPOSSIBLE PREY

RANEEM HASAN

This book is dedicated to my mom, Lina Nassar, who has supported my dreams and goals from the very beginning. I love you.

Trigger Warning:
The following story contains profanities and physical violence. Reader discretion is advised.

PROLOGUE

"Adam!" the eight-year-old girl shrieked, running towards her so-called friend and tackling him to the ground.

Adam cried out in shock when he stumbled. Tiana started to hit him everywhere, but the little boy only laughed hysterically at her attempt to hurt him.

"Geez, Tiana, calm down," he yelled as he tried to catch his breath.

"Calm down?" she hissed. "You want me to calm down after what you did?"

"I told you I didn't mean it," he said while trying to hold back a grin. "It was an accident."

"You liar! It was definitely not an accident! I saw you with my own eyes, Adam!" She pouted as she started to hit him once again.

Adam was about to push her off when Tiana was pulled from him by someone else.

"What is going on here?" Tiana's mom asked, her hands on her hip, while Tiana's dad carried the struggling girl in his arms.

"I swear I didn't do anything," Adam said while getting off the ground. "She went all crazy on me and pushed me to the ground."

"Liar!" Tiana yelled. "He took my ice cream from me and threw it on the ground." She pointed to the almost melted ice cream that was on the floor with a pout firmly plastered on her face.

"No, I didn't! It was an acci—" Adam wasn't able to continue when Tiana interrupted him.

"Stop lying, Adam!" Tiana tried to get her father to release her.

"Okay, okay, that's enough, you two," her mother cut in. "It's just ice cream, Tiana. We'll get you another one tomorrow." Her mother assured her with a small smile on her face.

Tiana was finally placed on the ground. "I want one now," she whispered while glaring at Adam.

"Sorry, honey, but it's late, and you both need to go to sleep," her father told her.

Tiana turned to him and scrunched her nose.

"He's sleeping over?" She pointed at Adam while Adam just smiled in excitement.

"Yes, he is. His parents will return to the pack house late," her mother replied.

"I don't want him here," she said stubbornly. Her mother gave her a stern look. She huffed in defeat and stared at Adam.

"Fine, only if you say sorry for dropping my ice cream on purpose," the little girl said while emphasizing the word *purpose*. Adam shrugged, then reached his hand out to her, smiling a toothy grin.

"Okay, I'm sorry for accidentally dropping your ice cream," he told her, trying to hold back his laughter.

Tiana's father immediately picked her up before she could tackle Adam to the ground once again. "Okay, off to bed, you two."

Tiana's parents led them both to Tiana's room and placed them in bed next to each other.

Her father gave her a look when she started pushing Adam off the bed, so she immediately stopped. They were about to leave when Tiana called out to them.

"Yes, sweetie?" her mom asked.

"Mom, can you tell us a bedtime story?" Her mom looked to her husband, and they exchanged a couple of words.

"I have some stuff to finish, but your dad can tell you one. Is that okay?" she asked.

The two kids nodded in agreement. Tiana's mother kissed them both goodnight, leaving her husband behind.

Tiana's father pulled out a chair from the corner, placed it in front of the bed, and sat on it.

"Okay, so which story would you like me to read, guys?" He looked at the books that were placed next to Tiana's bed.

Tiana thought for a while. "Daddy, we have read them all. Can you please tell us a story that we don't know?" she asked.

"Yes, can you?" Adam agreed with a smile on his face.

"Sure, why not? Let me think of one," he replied while thinking of a story that they never heard before.

"Can you tell us the story about the Black Shadow Pack?" Adam asked.

Tiana's father turned his head towards the boy. "Where did you hear that from?" he asked, raising his brow.

The boy shrugged. "I heard one of my friends talk about it at school."

Tiana's eyes lit up and eagerly nodded. "Please tell us that story, Daddy."

"I'm afraid I can't, dear. It's not a pleasant story to tell," her father told her.

Tiana's curiosity only grew along with Adam's, and they were now more eager to hear it.

"Please, pretty please," they both begged.

"Your mother will kill me if she hears about this," he laughed. "Well, this is based on a real story."

The two kids cuddled closer together and listened as he told them the tale of the dark pack named Black Shadow.

"There's this pack that lives not too far from here. It used to be a peaceful one, with happy and nice members. Little did they know that their alpha and their luna were not what they thought they were nor what anyone else thought."

Tiana's curiosity grew more and more as she listened to the story.

"The alpha and the luna had two kids: a boy and a girl. Everyone else thought they were happy, but they actually weren't. There were rumors that the kids were cursed and evil, especially the boy.

"The kids would do weird stuff and wouldn't communicate with anyone else, except themselves. They would isolate themselves from people. They were strange. Nobody knows what exactly happened, but when the boy turned thirteen, everything went downhill for the pack."

Tiana's father stopped, but the kids begged him to go on.

"Goodness, I'm a horrible father," he muttered to himself while shaking his head. He then continued, "On that day, the boy did something no one thought he would ever do. He killed his parents."

Adam and Tiana gasped. *Who would ever do that to their own parents?* they thought.

"It is believed that the kids planned it out, but it is also believed that the girl had nothing to do with it. Some say the boy did this to take over the pack and to be the alpha, while the others argue that something might have happened, which no one else knew about. After that, the boy took over and didn't let anyone else join the pack. He was known to be cruel and merciless towards all his prey.

"It's called Black Shadow Pack for a reason . . . because it is dark and full of mysteries, and no one knows what really happens in that pack and what really happened to the alpha and the luna," he finished with a sigh.

Tiana and Adam looked at each other, a hint of fright on their faces.

"What's the boy's name?" Tiana asked curiously.

Her father got up from the chair and tucked them in before replying.

"Mason Wood."

CHAPTER 1

I woke up from my peaceful sleep when I felt someone sit on the edge of my bed, poking my arm every once in a while. I groaned and pushed my head deeper into my pillow. *Who on earth is disturbing my beauty sleep?* I growled to myself.

"Wake up, wake up, sleepy head, sleepy head. That's not your bed," an annoying voice sang.

I groaned and immediately knew who it was.

Adam.

Didn't he already know that I wasn't a morning person and that I didn't like to be woken up? Well, clearly, I had to remind him because it didn't get through his stubborn head.

"Adam! Leave me be!" I growled at him, but he only chuckled.

"Come on, Tiana. It's time to get up," he said while poking my arm even harder.

"No! Why would I get up? It's summer break, for God's sake." I pulled my arm from his grasp and waved it around, hoping to smack his face.

"Well, we have lots of things to do today. Your mom wants us to go to the market and grab a couple of stuff for the party tonight," he answered.

I opened one eye when he mentioned the party. We had just graduated from high school yesterday. To celebrate, I, Adam, and a couple of friends had gone to a bar after the ceremony.

Today, my mom was hosting a party for us and for the rest of the pack members who had graduated.

"I'll get up in ten minutes," I muttered and closed my eyes, trying to get back to sleep.

I sighed happily when I felt him off my bed. I got comfortable and was about to welcome sleep with open arms when I suddenly jerk up and gasp for air. I was confused for a second until I saw Adam laughing his butt off, so much so that he was gasping for air too. I then realized that I was soaked in water, and my clothes were hugging my body.

"Adam!" I interrupted his laughter and immediately stood up. His eyes widened in fear but with a hint of amusement when I took a step closer to him. He gulped, putting his hands in the air.

"Hey, Tiana. You didn't take that seriously, did you?" he asked while laughing nervously.

"Adam! You are so dead!" I hissed and ran after him when he sprinted out of my bedroom door while screaming like a five-year-old. I growled and jumped on his back, punching his arm several times.

"Help! Help! There's a crazy girl on the loose," he screamed while laughing hysterically.

"How." Punch. "Many." Punch. "Times." Punch. "Do I." Punch. "Have to tell you." Punch. "Never." Punch. "To wake me up?" Punch.

Of course, Adam however just kept on laughing while trying to get me off his back. "You do know that your punches aren't affecting me, right?" he asked.

"I don't care!" I continued to throw lame punches at him. "You freakin' dumped water on me!"

"Okay, okay, I'm sorry. Just get off me!" He wiggled and tried to make me fall off his back.

I sighed and punched him lightly in the head, letting go.

He pouted and rubbed his head. "Geez, woman, you're so violent!" He smirked as he ran his eyes over my body.

I blushed when I saw my shirt became see-through due to the water. I looked at him and scowled, but he only grinned.

"Might as well clean up so we can go." He shrugged and walked to the kitchen. I looked around and saw no one was awake yet. Good, because I wouldn't want anyone seeing me like this.

Adam will so pay for this.

I rushed to my bathroom and took a shower. I then thought about high school and how time went by so fast. It was just like yesterday when I was in freshman year, and now I was done—done with all the drama and done with all the stress. I planned to attend college, but I still didn't know which university yet.

For the meantime, I wanted to enjoy my break while I could. I turned eighteen a couple weeks ago. That meant I'm an adult now and I could do stuff I couldn't do before. Don't get the wrong idea. I was talking about traveling the world. You could say my parents were always worried about me and they never agreed with the idea of me traveling to new places, but since I'm eighteen now, I could convince them that I could already take care of myself. Well, I hoped I could.

After showering, I put on some casual clothes, applied mascara, and tied my hair into a high ponytail before walking down the stairs.

Everyone was sitting at the table, getting ready to eat breakfast. My pack wasn't the biggest nor the smallest pack. But since we weren't that many, we all lived in the pack house, except for our alpha and our luna since they had their own house.

I went towards the big table and kissed my parents on the cheek.

"Good morning, sweetheart," Mom said.

"Good morning."

"How's my baby girl?" Dad asked. I smiled at him and glanced at Adam, who was across from us, and looked back to my dad. "I'm fine. Just someone woke me up in an unpleasant way."

Adams' eyes widened, and a smirk grew on his lips.

My mom turned to Adam and gave him a pointed look. "What did you do this time?" she asked.

Adam shrugged while glancing at me. "I didn't do anything. She just wouldn't wake up."

"He dumped water on me."

My parents looked at Adam while he just laughed. "I told you, she wouldn't wake up."

I rolled my eyes at him and sat down. Soon our breakfast was served, and we all ate. After we were done, Adam and I had to go to the market to grab the stuff my mom needed for the party tonight. My mom had insisted that she planned out the party and no one else. It's like she's planning a wedding or something.

I hopped into Adams' car, and once he got into the driver's seat, we took off. After an awkward silence, Adam decided to speak.

"You mad at me?" He glanced at me, then back to the road.

"No, just annoyed."

"Well, sorry about that," he chuckled.

"Just don't do that again, or I will do something you won't like," I murmured.

"Like what? Throw punches at me?"

"No, like cut Adam Jr. off." I grinned while he gasped.

"How dare you say that!" he said dramatically.

I chuckled and elbowed him in the arm. "Next time, think before you wake me up."

"Next time I'll wear armor," he said and I glared at him. "But there won't be a next time," he assured. I laughed a little, and he smiled at me before turning back his focus to the road.

After a while, we reached the market and parked the car before getting out.

"So what's the first thing we should get?" I asked Adam. He took the list that Mom had written down from his pocket and opened it.

"Food. She wants us to get food," he answered. I smiled at that.

Food! The best thing that has ever happened to me!
  Okay, before you think that I'm exaggerating, think again. Food is life.

"Then let's go!" I grabbed his hand, pulling him into the food section. I sighed happily and wiped a fake tear off while Adam just looked at me like I was crazy.

"This is my heaven," I told him.

"Yeah, I know. It explains the times when you attacked me over them," he chuckled.

We bought treats and drinks, then we chose some decorations. After a while, I became so tired. All I wanted to do was go back to bed and sleep, but clearly, that was not going to happen.

"Can we take a break?" I whined.

Adam shook his head at me and continued walking.

"Come on, Adam. I'm tired," I begged.

He gave me a knowing look. "No, we still have lots of stuff to buy."

I huffed and crossed my arms. "You're a guy! You're not supposed to like shopping," I pointed out.

He smiled at me and raised a brow. "Sexist much? Besides, who said I like shopping? It's just that you don't have any friends other than me to go shopping with."

I gasped. "What? I do have friends."

He shook his head. "Like your bed?"

Okay, maybe I didn't have many friends, but it was all this guy's fault. Whenever I tried to make friends, he would always ruin it, telling them I was weird and that I would go crazy on them. He would tell them a handful of lies.

"You're such a bully," I muttered under my breath, but of course because of our werewolf hearing, he heard it.

"Says the violent girl." We both laughed. Adam was the only friend who stood by me and never left my side, and for that, I was grateful even though there were times I just wanted to strangle him.

After hours of torture, we finally stopped to grab a bite. We had tons of bags, but I, being the lazy person that I was, made Adam carry them. He didn't mind, anyway.

Adam ordered our food while I sat and placed my head on the table. I was about to close my eyes for a bit but pulled my head back up when I saw from the corner of my eye a pack member who I barely knew sitting next to a boy while holding hands. I guess they're mates.

Not many people would find their mates, but for those who did, they were lucky. At least, that's what they all said.

I heard having a mate was the best thing that could ever happen to someone, but somehow, I couldn't believe it. I mean, yes, it would be nice to have someone who loved you deeply and who you could share your soul with, but I found that hard to believe. I didn't want a mate nor any guy. Not anymore, that is.

I was pulled out of my thoughts when Adam placed a tray of food in front of me and sat down. I lightened up, and at the right moment, my stomach grumbled.

"Dig in," he said, and I didn't need to hear that a second time to chomp on my food.

* * *

We entered the pack house, and my mom walked up to us with a smile on her face. "Thank you, honey. You too, Adam."

"You're welcome, Mom," I told her.

A couple of people took the bags from us and walked away, then we excused ourselves.

Adam and I walked up to my room. I took out the simple white dress that I had bought while we were shopping and placed it on my bed. Adam looked at it and furrowed his eyebrows. When I bought this dress, he was waiting outside the store, so it was his first time seeing it.

"You're wearing that?" He pointed the dress.

"Yes, is there something wrong with it?" I questioned, looking at him.

He crossed his arms over his chest. "Not really. It's just, it's too short," he muttered.

I raised a brow. *Here we go again*, I thought. Adam always complained about the clothes I wore. Whether it's too short or too tight, he would act like an overprotective brother.

"I know, but it's not that short," I stated and showed him the dress. "See?"

He shrugged and scratched the back of his neck. "Um . . . I'll just go. Call me if you need anything." He walked out of my room. I shrugged and sat on my bed while admiring the dress.

The party was going to start at seven and it was still three, so I had plenty of time to get ready. I decided to lie down and relax my eyes a bit.

* * *

I snapped my eyes open when I felt someone shaking my arms.

"Tiana, wake up."

I looked at the person and saw my mom standing with her arms crossed. "Mom? Is there something wrong?" I asked.

"Yes, there is. You have about an hour to get ready," she stated. My eyes widened. I turned to the clock and saw it was almost six.

I looked at her and got up from my bed. "It's okay, Mom. I'll get ready before the party starts."

She smiled and nodded before turning around, but then she stopped and looked at me. "Just don't be late." With that, she walked out.

I rushed to the bathroom and took a quick shower. I then applied less makeup and let my hair loose. After that, I wore the dress and looked at myself in the mirror. *I look good*, I thought to myself while smiling.

I checked the time and saw that I still had ten minutes left, so I got out and walked to Adam's room. I entered without knocking and saw him putting his shirt on. I wasn't embarrassed nor did I think much about it because he and I had known each other since we were babies. That meant I had seen him naked before and the other way around.

Once he was done, he looked at me and smiled. "Well, don't you look beautiful," he said, and I only chuckled at him.

"You look good too."

"Good? I look sexy," he stated, and I laughed.

"Sure, you do."

He gasped. "For your information, girls die to have a piece of my body," he said.

I rolled my eyes and sat on his bed.

He came up to me and sat next to me. "Well, thank you for the compliment," he said sarcastically.

I grinned and bumped my side into his.

He laughed while looking at me. "I meant it when I said you look beautiful," he said seriously.

I smiled at him and nodded. "I know. Thanks." I got up from the bed and walked towards the door, but not before turning around and looking at Adam. "Let's go before my mom gets us herself."

We made our way downstairs. There was food and drinks everywhere. The main lights were off, but there were colorful little lights everywhere, giving the room a party feel. Lots of teenagers were dancing to the music and eating away. I smiled and made my way to Mom and Dad and hugged them tightly.

"Thank you," I said.

Adam came up from behind me and said the same thing. "Yes, thank you. It's wonderful."

"Oh, it's no problem. Besides, the pack needed a break and some fun," my mom said. We nodded, and I kissed both my parents on the cheek.

"Have fun," my dad yelled through the music as we walked towards the dance floor.

"Let's dance." Adam grabbed my hand and pulled me further into the dance floor. We grooved for a while until we were tired. Then we decided to have some snacks, so we went to the food section.

We were about to eat when my parents came running towards us, and all of a sudden, the music was turned off.

My face turned into confusion, and I had a bad feeling that something terrible was going on.

"Mom, Dad? What's wrong?" I asked. They looked at each other, their faces filled with fear.

And what they said next made my heart stop beating.

"We're under attack."

CHAPTER 2

"What?" I asked in shock.

My parents' faces were red, and their eyes were watering. Adam's face held the same expression as mine, confused and afraid.

"Listen closely, honey," my dad said, loud enough to be heard amidst the screaming and running that was happening around us. "You and Adam can make it out. Run away and don't look back."

My mom nodded and started to push us both out the back door. I immediately shook my head. I was still confused and didn't know what exactly was going on.

"Mom, Dad, I'm not leaving without you guys," I said, giving them a pleading look. They stopped and looked at Adam and me for a moment as tears poured from their eyes. I felt my vision blur, but I blinked to prevent my own tears from falling.

"You have to. Save yourselves while you still can." My mom held my hands in hers. While this was happening, there was chaos outside. Growling and screaming were everywhere.

"Why can't I take both of you guys with me?" I asked, looking at my parents, hoping they would agree. "I can handle it."

"No, you can't. Your powers can only hold two people, and the other person is Adam. He will protect you no matter what," my dad said, looking at Adam.

Adam grabbed my hand and nodded to my parents. "Don't worry. I'll keep her safe." He dragged me to the back door.

I pleaded for him to let go so I could return to my parents. But no matter what I did, he wouldn't budge and he just kept pulling me until we were outside the back door. I turned my head, and my parents gave me a small smile while trying to hold back their tears. A tear fell out of my eye, but I wiped it away when I was no longer in their sight.

I started to shake my head when I heard the front door break and growls erupted in the air. Adam cupped my face in his hands and stared me in the eyes.

"Tiana, you need to calm down if you want to make it out alive," he said calmly. I nodded and breathed in and out. "Good job. Okay, now I want you to concentrate on your powers so we can get out of here safely."

I nodded once more and closed my eyes. I concentrated on all the energy I had left and on Adam's hand that was in mine. I opened my eyes and sighed in relief when I saw that I succeeded in making both of us invisible. Adam gave me a weak smile and nodded towards the woods. I looked back, and my eyes widened when I saw dead bodies everywhere and an unknown werewolf behind us. He wasn't aware of our presence due to my powers.

I glanced at Adam, and he tugged on my hand. "We have to move before your powers weaken, Tiana."

I nodded and looked back once more to see that the pack house was full of werewolves that were not part of our pack. Rogues.

Adam and I ran into the woods and as far as we could go before my power wore off and made us visible. We went behind separate trees and stripped out our clothes. After concentrating, I shifted to my small light brown wolf and grabbed my clothes with my mouth.

When I emerged from behind the tree, I was met with Adam's gray wolf. He tilted his head to the right, indicating we should move on and pass our pack's borders. I felt sadness wash over me just by the thought of leaving my pack and my family, but we had no other choice.

We started running towards the borders. Our furs danced with the wind, and our paws thumped on the ground, allowing us more speed as we ran. We came to a stop when we were close to the borders. By now, my powers had worn off and we weren't invisible anymore.

"Let's move before anyone catches our scents," Adam said through the mind link.

Ignoring the pain, we moved on and ran to who knows where. I wasn't worried about where we were going but what was to come. I couldn't let go nor forget my pack. Millions of questions ran through my mind: What happened? Who were those werewolves? What did they want? But the biggest question that lingered in my mind was if my parents were okay.

I was sure Adam was feeling exactly the same way. He also left his parents with no choice. I knew my parents weren't dead because if they were, then I would have felt the pain of the broken connection between us, but thank God I didn't.

After hours of extreme torture from running, we decided to stop and take a break. I went behind a tree and shifted into my human form and wore my clothes. I sighed and went back to where we stopped. It was already dark, not a single star at sight. I felt fear creep into my heart, but it immediately went away when I felt familiar arms wrap around my waist.

"It's going to be okay," Adam whispered. I turned around to hug him back, laying my head on his chest.

"Where will we go?" I asked. We had nowhere else to go. No one would agree to take us in their pack because we were rogues now.

Rogues were werewolves without a pack. They were known to be violent and bad, and that's why alphas would never accept them.

"I don't know, but no matter what happens, we have each other." He kissed my forehead. I relaxed in his arms and let a tear escape my eye. I didn't want to admit it, but I was scared. However, I knew having Adam by my side would make things better.

A yawn escaped my mouth. Breaking our hug, Adam looked around and pulled me under a big tree.

"Let's sleep for a bit. We'll continue tomorrow," he whispered, and all I did was nod. He rested his back against the tree, and I rested against his chest.

I closed my eyes and welcomed the darkness with open arms.

* * *

"Happy birthday, birthday girl!" I heard someone shout as I opened my sleepy eyelids. A smile crawled onto my lips when I saw who it was. My mom was standing beside my bed, holding a plate of pancakes which, I must say, looked delicious. My dad was by the door, smiling from ear to ear.

"Good morning," I said back.

"Come on, honey, get up. We have to get started," my mom squealed, and I just raised a brow.

"Get started for what?" I asked.

She gave me a look that said, "Are you crazy?" She then placed the plate of pancakes on my lap. "For your sweet sixteenth birthday party," she replied in a duh tone.

"You know you don't have to, right?" I said, smiling. "I wouldn't mind if it was just small."

My mom shook her head. "You only turn sixteen once."

I nodded and looked down at the pancakes. Yum! They were my favorite thing to eat for breakfast.

"Okay, you eat, and once you're done, get ready and come downstairs."

I started to eat once they left my room. Then I showered and wore a summer dress and did my hair.

While I was applying mascara, I saw someone open my door. I smiled when I saw Adam. He came to me and hugged me tightly. Pulling away, he smiled a toothy grin.

"Happy sweet sixteenth," he greeted.

"Thank you."

"Well, don't you look gorgeous today," he said while looking at my dress.

I faked a gasp and pretended I was hurt. "I'm always gorgeous!" *I pouted.*

He chuckled and shook his head. "Sure, you are, if that helps you sleep at night."

I was about to strangle him when I heard my name being called out. I huffed and walked downstairs with a grinning Adam behind me. When I made it downstairs, I was greeted with friendly smiles and happy birthdays.

I immediately smiled at the affection I was getting from everyone. I walked up to my mom and saw she was making food. Yum!

"So, what are we going to do in the meantime?" *I asked.*

"You can go to the mall with Adam and have fun, but make sure you are home before lunch because I'm making your favorite food," *she gushed.*

I squeezed the living daylights out of her. "Thank you so much," *I said.*

"You're welcome, sweety. Have fun!"

I nodded and ran up to Adam, who was eating breakfast.

"Eat fast so we can go to the mall," *I said. He looked at me and raised his brow.*

"Don't rush me, woman."

I smacked his head and sat down on the chair next to him while he just pouted and rubbed his head.

"God, you're violent," *he muttered, but I heard and just rolled my eyes.*

All of a sudden, I felt a slight pain in my upper back. It wasn't strong, but it bothered me. I didn't think much of it, though, and just ignored it. After Adam was finished, he washed his hands and we made our way outside the pack house.

After a couple hours, we decided to return to the pack house because I was not feeling good. The pain in my back grew, and my face was hot.

"Are you sure you're okay?" Adam asked with a worried expression.

I nodded. I must be having a little fever, nothing serious. But the thing was that werewolves didn't get sick often, and that's what worried me.

When we entered the pack house, everyone was sitting at the table, ready to eat their food. Just when I made eye contact with my mom, I fell to the ground.

I heard a loud scream and realized it was coming from me. I was in pain—so much pain. It felt like I was shifting for the first time again.

When someone first shifted into their wolves, it's painful and that's what I was feeling, but I already shifted a couple years back, so I had no idea what was happening.

Everyone ran to me. I just closed my eyes shut, hoping the pain would go away. I cried out when I felt the hurt in my back grow to the point where I felt like it was going to tear me apart.

I heard shouting and talking, which were just hurting my ears.

"What happened?"

"Is she okay?"

"Call the pack doctor!"

"Give her space!"

"Oh my God! This can't be happening!"

The last one caught my attention. It was my mother's, and even though she sounded shocked, she seemed happy, more like excited.

But I couldn't think more because I fell into the darkness right at that moment.

*   *   *

I snapped my eyes open and inhaled fast, catching my breath. I groaned once I remembered the dream I had. It was more like a flashback. That was the day when I first discovered my powers and became half angel and half werewolf. No wonder all my life I was never like any other wolf. I was always small and weak compared to the others, but then I discovered what I truly was: a hybrid.

I got my angel side from my mom. She's not an angel but her grandmother was, and it was passed down to me. My mom was so happy that I inherited the angel genes, but since my dad was a full werewolf, I was only able to inherit half of it.

Because of that, my powers were weak, and I couldn't use them for a long period of time. I could make myself and another person invisible. I could also heal people's injuries, but like the other one, there was a limit. My favorite was my wings. The pain I had that day was because my wings were growing, but due to me being a hybrid, they weren't that big and I could only fly for a while before I got tired.

I was snapped out of my thoughts when I felt someone behind me move, and that was when I looked at my surroundings. I then remembered the attack that happened yesterday. I sighed and got up from the ground and saw Adam blinking his eyes open.

"Morning," he muttered.

"Morning."

Getting up, he stretched his arms and ran his hand through his hair, looking up at me. "Did you sleep well?" he questioned.

I gave him a weak smile and nodded. "What about you?"

"It would have been better if a certain someone wasn't squishing me against the tree the whole night," he said with a teasing grin. I rolled my eyes at him, and he just chuckled. "Let's get moving. I'm hungry. Let's find a deer or something to eat," he said. I nodded, and at that exact moment, my stomach growled.

We went behind separate trees and shifted into our wolves. My wolf had been wanting to stretch her legs and run, and that's what I was going to do.

We started to run in our wolf forms and sniffed out anything we could eat. At the moment, we were in an unclaimed territory, so we had nothing to worry about.

After a while, we came to a complete stop when we saw a deer in the distance. I growled but not loud enough for the deer to hear.

I looked at Adam, and he was eager to attack.

"On the count of three, we attack," Adam spoke through the mind link. I nodded and waited while lowering my body so the deer wouldn't see me.

"One... two... three."

And right then and there, we leaped and ran towards the deer. The deer turned its head and started to rush as fast as it could when it saw us. I growled and ran faster. Of course, we were faster than the deer, but since it wasn't close to us from the beginning, it was ahead of us.

After a while, we were so close to our prey, but I felt the air around us change. Adam and I stopped in confusion, then realization hit us. We had crossed another pack's territory, and the worst part was, we were rogues.

"We're in claimed territory. We have to get out of here before we get in trouble," Adam said.

I immediately agreed, and we started to run in the direction we came from, but not long after, we heard growls and howls approaching us. Adam and I picked up our pace but stopped when we were surrounded by wolves.

We had no place to go. We were trapped.

"Maybe we could convince them that we meant no harm," I told Adam through the link. His eyes were dark, and he growled lowly.

"I don't think that will change their mind," he said in a dangerous tone.

Okay, now this was just frightening me.

"Why?" I asked in a careful voice.

He looked at me and came closer, shielding me from the other wolves.

"Because we are in the Black Shadow Pack."

CHAPTER 3

My eyes widened in fear. Black Shadow was the biggest pack in America, known for their cruel punishments and never showing mercy to rogues that crossed their territory.

That's it, we're dead.

I looked around to see if there was a way out, but there wasn't. We were surrounded by angry wolves that kept growling at us every time we made a single move. I couldn't see Adam's face because he was in front of me, but I could tell he was as terrified as I was. There was no place to run, no place to go.

"Tiana, do you think you can save us with your powers?" Adam asked in a hard tone.

I immediately tried, but it was no use. I didn't have much energy left because I didn't eat anything at all.

"I can't. I don't have much energy," I replied.

Adam growled lowly, causing some wolves to step closer to us. He was about to say something through the mind link but was immediately cut off when we heard loud growls from a distance. It soon turned louder and louder until a big wolf emerged from the trees.

The wolf had a strong vibe coming from it. My guess was that it was either the alpha or the beta. Okay, now we're screwed. Soon the wolf came closer and shifted into his human form, leaving his naked body on display. I lowered my head because no way was I going to see something I didn't want to see. I raised my head back up when someone from behind him passed him pants and wore it.

He stepped closer to us, giving us a deadly stare.

"Shift!" he growled in a dangerous voice.

Adam looked back at me and nodded, indicating we should listen to him before it all got worse.

We both shifted into our human forms, and I immediately wore the clothes that were in my mouth, ignoring the stares I got from the other wolves.

"You do know you're in claimed territory, rogues?" the man asked.

Adam grabbed my hand and moved in front of me once again. "We do," Adam replied.

The man stepped closer and growled lowly. "And do you know what happens when you cross our territory without our permission?" he questioned.

It was pretty clear he didn't like us at all. Nope, not one bit, but I knew the answer to that question. Everyone knew the answer to that question, and it was death.

Adam stiffened and squeezed my hand tighter. He nodded and didn't say a word. I gulped when the wolves came closer to us.

"You're lucky the alpha isn't here right now because if he was, then you both would be dead on the spot. For now, we're taking you guys to the dungeons." He looked at the guards that were behind us and nodded. At that moment, they came up to us and grabbed us by the arms.

I growled at them, and so did Adam.

"Let go of us!" Adam yelled. He looked at me, and his eyes were pitch black. His wolf wanted control, and so did mine. "Let go of her," he yelled again. He started to struggle and growl at the guards that were holding us.

I wanted to tell him to calm down before he got himself hurt by the racket he was making, but I was too late. The beta nodded to a guard behind Adam, and he knocked him out. Adam fell to the ground and closed his eyes as the guards started to carry him.

"Adam!" I yelled when they started to take him away.

I started to fight back. *How dare they hurt him!* I was about to curse at them, but a scream came out of my mouth from the sudden pain in my neck instead, and I fell to the ground.

At that moment, I knew my life was going to come to an end sooner than I had ever expected.

* * *

I slowly opened my eyes and groaned. I shook my head and moved my hands to massage my head but instead winced from the burning sensation on my wrists. Shocked, I looked around and gasped when I saw the state I was in.

I was in a small cell that screamed death and horror. The smell of blood wasn't hard to catch at all, making me want to gag. My wrists were tied up by silver, a werewolf's weakness, draining me of all the little energy I had left.

There was a small window beside me, which only allowed a little amount of light to enter the dark cell. It was so dark that I couldn't see what was clearly happening outside.

I sighed and lay my head back on the wall and tried to prevent the tears from falling.

I'm not going to look weak. I will die with courage and dignity, I swore to myself.

I closed my eyes but snapped them back open when I remembered something important, someone important.

Adam! I looked around and tried to make out if there was another cell close or in front of mine.

"Adam," I said softly. No answer. "Adam!" I called out loudly. Still no answer. "Adam, please answer me!" I yelled. No answer. I closed my eyes and put my head down but smiled a little when I heard his voice.

"Tiana?" he asked

"Yes, Adam, it's me. Are you okay?" I asked loudly for him to hear.

"I'm alright, just these chains are draining my energy. Are you okay?"

I sighed in relief. Thank goodness, he's alright.

"I'm fine," I replied.

"Tiana, I want you to know that we'll find a way out. I'm not going to let anyone touch a strand of your hair even if it's the last thing I do," he called out to me.

"I know, Adam. We have to find a way out of here." As I was finishing my sentence, hysterical laughing erupted in the air. I furrowed my eyebrows in confusion, and I bet so did Adam.

"A way out of here?" asked a squeaky voice, which I was sure definitely belonged to an old man. The voice was coming in front of me, which only creeped me out. "You both want to find a way out of here?" he asked again. "There is no way out. No one can escape this hell we are in." He started to laugh again.

Adam growled, and I just clenched my fist.

"Who are you?" I asked.

He stopped laughing and cleared his voice.

"You want to know who I am? I'm afraid I can't tell you that, but I will tell you that you both will die. No one has ever escaped him and neither will you."

I just gulped and shook my head. *Don't listen to that crazy man, Tiana.*

Adam growled. "Shut up! We'll find a way out," he yelled. And of course, the man started to laugh again.

"I've been in here for years, and I've never found a way out. I know the pack like the back of my hand, yet I have never managed to get out."

I bit my lip and sighed. He was right. Who could ever escape the most feared pack in America?

"You were in the pack?" Adam asked, confused.

If he was in the pack, then what did he do to be in the cells? I pitied the members of this pack for having a cruel leader, but I guess the members might be as cruel as the alpha.

"Oh yes, I was. They treated me like garbage. No one appreciated me," the man hissed. I furrowed my brows in confusion.

"Why are you here?" I asked. The man stayed quiet. Not a single sound came from him, and that only made my curiosity grow.

I was about to ask one more time when the doors slammed open and guards came into the dungeon, allowing light into the cells. I prayed they didn't come for us and then closed my eyes when they started to walk towards my cell. I started to pull my hands from the chain, only to wince in pain.

I opened my eyes and sighed in relief when I saw they opened the doors to the cell next to mine and entered it. A moment later, the guards were holding a struggling man, pushing him towards the doors.

"No! Please, I can't die! I can't!" The man's words echoed throughout the dungeon.

I closed my eyes shut, and a shiver ran down my spine. I breathed in and out, trying to calm myself down.

Only a miracle could help us get through this. That was the last thought I had before I blacked out.

* * *

I fluttered my eyes open and was met with the peaceful blue sky, not a cloud in sight. It was calm, and the breeze hit my skin softly.

My eyes widened. Where was I? The last thing I remembered, I was in the dungeons. I sat down and looked around. There was a small lake, and tall grass was everywhere. It was beautiful. This was the place where I go to relax and calm my mind, somewhere with no drama nor headaches.

I got up and ran my hands over my face. It still didn't explain why I was here.

"Hello?" I yelled. I started to walk around but found no one. "Adam!" I yelled. "Where are you?"

"Adam isn't here, honey."

I gasped and turned my head to the person that said that. I felt my eyes water at the people who were in front of me.

"Mom? Dad?" I whispered and placed my hands over my mouth. How could this be? How were they here? The last time I saw them was the day of the attack. It wasn't long ago, but I missed them so much.

My mom opened her arms, and I ran into them and hugged her tightly. A few tears slipped out of my eyes, but my dad immediately wiped them off. I hugged him too, and we soon pulled apart.

"How are you here?" I asked. They smiled at me, and each of them held one of my hands.

"It's a long story," my mom replied. My dad nodded in agreement and gave my hand a squeeze.

"Darling, we want you to know something," my dad told me.

I slowly nodded. My parents looked at each other for a moment, then looked back at me.

"You're dreaming right now," my mom said.

My eyes widened, and I pouted my lower lip. *So this is not real?* I guess it was too good to be true. It was nice while it lasted.

"But that's not the thing we wanted you to know," my dad spoke. I nodded once again, letting them continue. "We want you to know that no matter what happens, everything will be okay."

"How? I mean, it's impossible to escape the dungeons nor the pack. How will things be okay?" I asked. This was all too confusing.

"Tiana, trust us. There's a solution for everything." My mom placed her hands on my shoulders. "Just don't give up."

I inhaled deeply and nodded.

"But where are you guys? Are you okay? How are we even communicating in my dream?" I asked. There were so many questions in my head, too many that my head started to hurt.

"You will get your answers in time. Just be patient and remember to never give up." With that, they started to disappear into thin air.

"Mom, Dad, wait!" But it was too late. They were gone. But before my mom completely vanished, she said two words that made me face reality.

"Wake up."

* * *

"Tiana, Tiana, wake up."

I heard a familiar voice calling my name. I slowly opened my eyes and found myself sitting on a chair. My hands were free, but my feet weren't. I rubbed my wrists and groaned in pain. They were all red and bruised. Well, I guess that would leave a mark.

I tried to move my legs from the chains, but they wouldn't budge. *Great!*

"Tiana!" Adam called.

"Adam?" I snapped my head up "What happened?" I asked.

"They took the chains off our hands and tied them to our feet so we could eat what they gave us. It isn't much, but it will do. I woke you up because I wanted you to eat before they chained our hands again," he replied.

I looked around and saw a small tray with bread on it in the corner of the cell. My stomach grumbled at the sight of food.

"Thanks, Adam," I spoke.

"You're welcome." He sighed.

I reached for the tray and started to eat. It wasn't much as Adam said, but I was thankful they gave us something. The last time I ate was last night. I think that's the longest I went without food.

After I was done, I started to think of the dream I had. It seemed so real, like my parents actually communicated with me. However, that's impossible, wasn't it?

"I had a dream," I said.

"A dream?" he asked.

"Yes, and I saw my parents." I sighed. "It felt so real, like they were sending me a message."

"What was the message?" Adam asked. I ran my hands through my messy hair while thinking about the conversation I had with my parents.

"I didn't really understand, but they were saying that I shouldn't give up," I replied, "that there's a solution for everything."

"Yes, there is. No matter what happens, I'll be there for you."

I smiled at that. I could always rely on him.

"But if something does happen, I want to let you know something," he said in a soft tone. "I really shouldn't be saying this in the dungeons where lots of people might hear," he muttered to himself, but I was able to hear him.

"What is it?" I asked.

"Tiana, I—"

He was cut off when the dungeon doors slammed open. My eyes widened, and I gulped in fear when I saw the guards walking towards me. This time, they opened my door. I clenched my hands, and my heart started to beat fast. One guard came up to me and smirked at my scared facial expression.

"Tiana? What's happening?" Adam yelled.

The guard unlocked the chains and pulled me outside the cell.

"Adam! They're taking me!" I yelled back but winced in pain when the guard pushed me against the wall.

"Shut up," he sneered.

"Run, Tiana, run!" Adam yelled.

Once Adam's words registered in my mind, I did something that might get me into more trouble or might save my life. I hit the guard with my knee right where the sun didn't shine.

Poor guy might never have babies.

He cried in pain and fell to the ground. I started to run towards the door, but two guards were in the way.

I used the little energy I had left to make myself invisible. The two guards' eyes widened and started to search the room. When they got out of the way, I ran to the door, but my powers immediately wore off.

"She's over there! Get her!" one guard yelled. They chased me as I ran to wherever the hall would take me to.

I stopped dead on my tracks when I smelled the most delicious fragrant ever. It was the smell of woods and a hint of dark chocolate. It sounded weird, but it smelled delicious.

My eyes widened when I realized the guards were gaining on me, so I started to run again. But this time, I stopped not because of the smell but because I bumped into someone's chest. I stumbled back and realized the smell was so strong that it made my wolf purr in delight.

I slowly raised my head, only to be greeted by dark brown eyes staring at me like they could see right through me. My eyes widened when I heard what the guard behind me said.

"Alpha Mason."

Right then and there, my heart literally stopped, not because I was in front of the most feared alpha but of what my wolf kept repeating.

Mate.

CHAPTER 4

Mate—someone you're supposed to love, supposed to cherish, and supposed to stick with till the last breath you take.

Not everyone would find their mate, but the ones that did, they're lucky. Well, that's what everyone said.

I didn't want that, not now, not ever. To make the matter worse, the alpha everyone feared was my mate. How was I going to deal with that? Would he just kill me or let me go?

I stayed standing there in shock. He had strong vibes. No doubt he could scare someone with just his eyes.

I would be lying if I said he wasn't attractive, but I wasn't paying attention to that. What caught my eye was the way he was coldly looking at me, his glare filled with disgust and anger.

I gulped a bit when he stepped closer and growled lowly.

"Mate." He immediately shook his head and clenched his jaw.

"Why wasn't this rogue with you?" Alpha Mason asked the guards while keeping his eyes on me. He then moved his glare to the frightened guards. They weren't the only ones who were frightened; I was terrified too. However, my wolf was purring in my head and begging to be with her mate.

I closed my eyes and bowed my head down, trying to calm her.

"A-Alpha Mason, she was too fast, and we couldn't catch up with her," one of the guards replied.

The alpha growled loud enough for everyone to hear. "I ordered you one thing! One thing and you failed!"

I opened my eyes, and all the guards were looking down in shame. I gulped once again. *Mate or not, I'm dead.*

"Take the rogue back to the dungeon!"

I furrowed my brows in anger when he called me a rogue. Sure, I was one, but it wasn't like I wanted to be one.

"But, Alpha, you ordered us to take her to you so you can execute her," another guard said.

At that, my wolf whimpered. I slowly looked at the alpha and saw that his eyes were black. His wolf wanted out. He closed them shut and opened them once again.

"Take the rogue back to the dungeon, and I'll decide when it will take place," he said in a dangerous tone.

The guards came up to me and grabbed me. I tried to make them let go, but it was no use. Alpha Mason looked at me one more time with his emotionless eyes and turned his back, walking away.

The guards dragged me to the dungeon aggressively, and all I could think about was, *what will I do?* Surely, he didn't want me, and I didn't either. It's either rejection or death. My wolf wanted to take control so she could go to her mate. She didn't like the idea of being rejected or killed by her mate, but I didn't like the idea of having a mate in general, especially if it was him.

Once I made it to my cell, they pushed me in it, and I fell to the floor. They gave me a hard look and walked out of the dungeon. Well, looking at the bright side, they didn't chain me to the metals.

"Tiana! Tiana, are you okay?" Adam yelled.

I raised my head and sighed. "I'm okay, Adam," I yelled back.

"What happened? Why did they put you back in your cell?" he asked loudly.

I wanted to tell him why, but I couldn't tell him here where lots of prisoners would hear. It was weird how we kept talking to each other and not one of the prisoners told us to shut up. My guess was they were too weak to talk or there weren't many of them because all this pack did was kill.

"This isn't the right place to tell you. It's too complicated," I told him. I sighed and rested my head on the cold, hard ground.

"But are you okay?" he asked softly. If it hadn't been for my werewolf hearing, I wouldn't have heard him.

"I'm okay, Adam. Don't worry," I replied. I heard him sigh, then everything went quiet. My wolf wasn't speaking to me nor making a single sound. She was heartbroken, but all I could feel was anger. If he weren't planning on killing me, then I would just reject him. I didn't need a mate, especially not one that didn't have a heart.

I closed my eyes to calm my thoughts, but that only led me to a deep, deep sleep.

* * *

I snapped my eyes open when I heard laughter. It wasn't a happy laughter but rather an evil one. There were lots of people around me wearing dark hoodies. They were laughing while pointing at me. I furrowed my brows in confusion and tried to move, but slowly realized I was tied down to a chair.

I started to panic, but the silver chains absorbed all my energy. I closed my eyes and shook my head. What's happening?

Everyone started to calm down, and all the laughter stopped.

I sighed but immediately stiffened when I heard someone speak up.

"Open your eyes, rogue!"

I immediately opened my eyes and met a pair of cold, dark eyes glaring back at me. A shiver ran down my spine at the way he was looking at me.

"What were you doing in my territory?" he asked in a hard tone.

I gulped and clenched my hands.

"I didn't mean to cross your territory," I said while looking into his eyes.

"Liar!" he roared. "I'll ask you one more time. What were you doing in my territory?"

I lowered my gaze and then looked directly into his eyes. I was not showing him that I was weak.

"I told you, my pack was—" I was caught off guard when he growled loudly. He was furious.

He came closer to me, his face inches away from mine. "You decided to come into my territory, then lie to my face shamelessly. Let me tell you, mate, you came to the wrong pack," he said in a hard tone.

What was this guy talking about? I wasn't lying! Why was fate so horrible to me that it paired me up with someone like him?

Alpha Mason looked at a man and nodded. The man looked at me and smirked. He disappeared for a moment but soon came back. And this time, he was not alone.

He had Adam.

"Adam!" I yelled. He was unconscious, and that broke my heart. What did they do to him?

"Shut up," the alpha yelled.

I clenched my fist to prevent myself from calling him once again.

The man brought Adam closer and landed him down right in front of me. A tear fell out of my eye, but I sighed in relief when I heard him breathing slightly.

"Adam! Wake up!" I yelled.

Alpha Mason nodded once again while the crowd just cheered. The man who carried Adam shifted into his wolf and started stalking towards Adam. All the blood left my face, and my heart started to beat faster.

"W-What are you doing?" I yelled, but he didn't stop. "Get away from him."

He slowly walked up to Adam and growled loudly, causing the whole crowd to go wild. What's wrong with these people?

The whole crowd went silent after the wolf raised his large head in the air and lowered it immediately, biting into Adam's neck. My heart stopped, and so did Adam's breathing. I was left there looking at my best friend's lifeless body, and a tear fell out of my eye while I yelled one thing.

"Adam!"

*   *   *

"Adam!" I yelled and jerked my body off of the hard ground.

"Tiana? What's wrong?" Adam yelled. I looked around and saw that I was still in the cell. I breathed in and out, and rubbed my face with my hands.

It was only a nightmare. Thank God! It was weird that these days, I had been having lots of weird dreams, but what mattered now was that Adam was okay! Speaking of Adam . . .

"Nothing. It was just a bad dream." I sighed.

"What was it about?" he asked. I hesitated to tell him. I didn't even tell him about finding my mate.

"Nothing important. It's all over now," I replied.

"Don't worry, Tiana. Nothing's going to happen to you," he reassured.

I wasn't worried about myself; I was worried about him.

"Adam?"

"Yes, princess?"

I grinned at that. See the irony? He called me a princess, but I was in the dungeons.

"You were about to tell me something before they came and took me. What were you about to say?" I asked. It seemed like it was something important.

"Uh . . . it can wait. Besides, we have better things to worry about."

"And what's that?" I questioned.

"Whether they're going to kill us or not."

A shiver ran down my spine. Who would ever have thought that a mate would want to kill his mate? I was not really affected by it because I never really wanted one, but that didn't stop the feeling I had deep down inside—a feeling of betrayal and anger.

The dungeon doors slammed open, and I immediately pretended I was asleep. It might seem dumb, but what if they came for me, and when they saw me asleep, they would just decide to come later? Okay, that wouldn't happen. They would just aggressively wake me up, but it didn't hurt to try.

I kept up with the act and didn't move. My heartbeat started to go fast when I heard people walking towards my cell. My heart fell to my stomach when I heard someone open the door and walk in. Then I heard a gasp as something collided with the ground.

What is happening?

"P-Please let me go," a soft voice whimpered next to me. Dark laughter came out of someone's mouth, and the door of the cell closed, then soon after, the dungeon doors.

I waited until the coast was clear and opened my eyes. I found a girl about my age curled up in the corner, crying and whimpering.

Why did they put her here? I wasn't complaining. I did need company, and it looked like this girl needed help too.

I got up and walked towards her slowly.

"Are you okay?" I asked softly.

She snapped her head towards me. There was fear in her eyes. She shook her head while whimpering.

I sat in front of her, but she scooted as far away from me as possible.

"Hey, it's okay. I'm not going to hurt you," I told her softly. She relaxed a bit at that but stayed stiff.

"What are you doing here?" I asked. She sighed, and a tear fell out of her eye.

"I accidentally crossed this territory," she replied, and I immediately understood. We were on the same boat.

"What's your name?"

She glanced at me hesitantly before looking at her hands. "Kayla. What about you?" she asked.

I smiled at her. Well, at least I was not the only one asking questions.

"I'm Tiana," I replied while reaching my hands toward her.

She reached for my hand and shook it. "W-What are they going to do with us?" she asked.

I sighed and shrugged. "I really don't want to say," I whispered.

Her lip trembled, and I knew she was about to cry.

"Please don't cry! Everything's going to be okay," I reassured her. I knew everything wasn't going to be fine but it wouldn't hurt to stay positive. "We'll get out of here."

"Promise?" she asked.

"I promise." I nodded.

She nodded too and closed her eyes. After a couple of minutes, her breathing steadied, and she fell asleep.

I sighed and wondered if we would ever make it out of this mess, if things would ever get back to normal and we would be happy once again.

I closed my eyes and waited until I fell asleep once again.

* * *

After a couple hours, I snapped my eyes open upon hearing the dungeon doors open. I moved to the corner and put my head in my hands.

They aren't coming for you. They aren't coming for you, Tiana, I kept repeating in my mind. I calmed myself and my wolf, but it didn't help when the door to my cell opened and a voice echoed through the dungeon.

"Get up. It's time."

CHAPTER 5

"What?" I whispered.

The guard in front of me only smirked. He grabbed my arm roughly and pulled me up while I only winced at the pain he was causing.

"You didn't think you would survive, did you?" he asked and then chuckled darkly. "Let me tell you, no one gets away without punishment in our pack."

I growled and tried to let him let go of me, but his hold was too strong.

"Let me go!" I kept repeating, but that didn't stop him from pulling me outside the cell. While he was dragging me, I saw three guards trying to get ahold of a struggling Adam, making me growl in anger. He kept yelling and growling for them to let us go, but that only made more guards come up to him.

"Let her go!" Adam roared.

"Shut up, pup," one guard sneered and continued to pull us towards the dungeon doors. I looked back and saw a guard was holding a scared Kayla that was on the verge of tears.

Once again, I tried to set myself free by pulling myself as far away from them as possible or by whatever movement that would make them let go of me, but that only made the guard holding me growl loud enough to echo around the dungeon walls.

"Stop it, or I will kill you myself if I have to," he yelled.

My wolf whimpered in fear while I just looked down to not anger him any further. This guy had some anger management problems.

They dragged me once again, and from the corner of my eye, I could see Adam staring at me with worry. I wished I could talk with him using the mind link, but we couldn't because we weren't shifted into our wolves. We couldn't communicate using the mind link in our human forms because we were not in our pack anymore; we were rogues now. Only pack members could communicate with the mind link in human and in wolf form.

Once we were outside, I closed my eyes, shielding them from the blinding light. It had been a while since I last enjoyed the sunlight.

They dragged us through halls and stairs, and eventually stopped in front of an old big metal door. My wolf was purring and constantly moving in my head, and there was only one explanation for that. Our mate was behind this door.

I breathed in and out, trying to calm myself and my wolf down. She still wanted to be with her mate even though it was pretty clear we might die today because of him. She kept telling me that Mason's wolf wasn't that bad and he actually wanted us, that it was just the human that's refusing and rejecting us.

I was caught off guard when the guards started opening the door. I looked at Adam, and he was staring back at me. His eyes were sending me a message, and I immediately knew what it was.

Don't worry. Everything will be okay.

I gave him a small smile and looked forward.

When the door was completely open, the three of us were dragged into the big dim room that screamed death. There wasn't anybody in the room, but I immediately smelled a wonderful smell and was soon greeted with a pair of dark eyes.

Alpha Mason was standing in front of us with an emotionless face. His manly eyes were hard, and they settled on me.

I wondered if he felt anything for me—whether it was anger, disgust, or something else—but I didn't really care.

I looked down but my head snapped up when I saw the thing that was in the middle of the room. It was a rope hanging from the ceiling with a loop at the end of it. Shock was definitely evident on my face, and I bet Kayla and Adam felt the same. The blood drained from my face, and my wolf was whimpering and whining in my head.

They are going to hang us! He's going to hang us!

"You all know the consequence for crossing my territory without my permission is death, yet you still crossed it," he said in a hard tone. I gulped when he looked at me with his cold eyes.

That's it, I'm dead.

"I don't care what the purpose was. You still did it, and I do not tolerate any rogues in my territory, no matter who you are."

I looked down and tried to prevent the tears from falling. If I was going to die like this, then I was not going to die like a coward.

When I looked back up, he nodded to the guard next to me and averted his eyes from mine. The guard grabbed my arm, and I immediately started to struggle.

"No! Let go of her!" Adam yelled. The guard was too strong and pulled me to the middle of the room.

"Please, kill me first!" Adam shouted desperately.

I looked at him through my blurry vision and saw his face was red. He was about to break down into tears. I gave him a small smile to lessen his worry, but it didn't do much.

Alpha Mason wasn't looking at me, and his hands were clenched. He looked furious. I didn't know for what reason, but it looked like he was about to burst.

The guard pulled me towards the rope, and my face started to sweat. He made me go on the hard stool and stand on it. I closed my eyes when I felt the rope go around my neck.

Well, I guess this was the end. I never would have thought my life would end this fast. I still wanted to do so many things in my life, but I guess that's never happening.

Adam growled hysterically, begging for them to let me go.

I opened my eyes and gave Adam a pleading look. I slowly glanced at the alpha, who wasn't looking my way. As if he knew I was staring at him, he did the same, his eyes pitch black. The guard was about to pull the stool away when we heard a loud growl.

"Stop!"

My eyes widened at the person who said that.

Alpha Mason.

The guard immediately stopped and looked at his alpha.

Alpha Mason closed his eyes and opened them back. His jaw was clenched, and it looked like he was fighting with himself.

"Let the girl go," he muttered really low. The guard looked shocked but obeyed and took the rope off my neck, releasing me.

My wolf barked in happiness, telling me he cared deep down inside. However, I wasn't in the mood to hear her blab, so I just shut her off.

Alpha Mason nodded again, and the guards pulled Adam towards the rope. My heart stopped, and my eyes widened.

"Wait! Please don't kill him!" I yelled.

"It's not your decision to make," he growled, looking at me.

"If you're going to kill the rest, then kill me with them. We came here together, so we should die or live together," I said.

Alpha Mason growled again and shook his head. He was angry, really angry. He remained silent for a while until he finally spoke, "Let them go."

The guards let Adam and Kayla go, and I sighed in relief.

"Don't think since I let you go, you're off the hook. You will all stay in this pack to work for us. My beta will choose what you'll do, and no matter how much you dislike it, you have no choice. It's either death or this."

We all nodded in agreement.

"If I hear that one of you did something wrong, I won't hesitate to kill you," he said while glaring at me.

I looked away from him and sighed. Well, it was nice that we didn't die.

The guards started to pull Adam and Kayla out the door. The guard that was holding me stopped. Alpha Mason slowly walked up to me with an emotionless face.

When he was closer to me, he looked at the guard holding me and nodded. The guard let go of me and walked away from us.

"Listen here. Don't think I let you go because I have feelings for you," he said.

I narrowed my eyes on him. I really wanted to say something back, but I held my tongue because I really didn't want to anger him more than he already was.

"I didn't do it for you. If it hadn't been for my wolf, you would have been dead by now."

I growled lowly when he turned his back on me and walked away. Oh, how much I wanted to just grab his neck and choke the living daylights out of him.

My wolf was happy even after what he said. All she got out of that was that his wolf cared. I mentally rolled my eyes at her, and the guard from earlier pulled and dragged me out the door.

We walked into a big room, where the beta was sitting on a chair and staring at us.

He got up and walked towards us.

"Since you three are staying here, then you're going to need to do something," he said.

"Both of you," he looked at Kayla and me, "will be helping around the pack house, whether it's cleaning or cooking or taking care of the children."

We nodded in agreement. That wasn't bad at all.

"And you," he said, looking at Adam and walking towards him. "What shall you do?" The beta smirked at him and nodded. "Let's see if you can fight."

With that, the beta shifted into his wolf form. Adam stood there shocked, then he also shifted. My eyes widened in worry.

What are they doing? Is he trying to kill Adam?

They moved in a circle and growled. The beta attacked Adam, but Adam was fast enough to move away. While this was happening, Kayla and I moved to the corner to not get hurt while they fought.

After jumping, biting, scratching, and all those violent moves, they finally shifted back. A guard came in and handed both of them shorts, which they immediately wore. The beta had a big smile on his face.

"And you," he said to Adam, "you will be a pack warrior. You will serve this pack and protect it. Is that understood?" he asked.

Adam smiled at that. He had always wanted to be a pack warrior, but our pack didn't let him because they always thought he wasn't fit to be one.

"Understood." He nodded. The beta looked at us and then at me.

"I don't know why the alpha agreed to let you guys stay in this pack, but if you do something that we don't like, you'll regret it," he said.

We all nodded, and he smiled a little.

Well, at least someone in this pack smiles.

"In a couple of days, we will hold a ceremony to officially make you guys members of this pack, but for now, my men will lead you to your rooms."

We followed the guards, and they dropped Kayla in a room. We walked further up the stairs, then stopped at another room. This one was for Adam, and mine was a couple rooms next to him, so that was the best thing. I went into the room and sighed.

It was a nice room, not too big nor small. It had a bathroom and a closet with clothes in it.

I couldn't believe that just a moment ago we were in the cells, and now we have nice rooms. I was thankful I didn't die nor did anybody else. It would have been horrible.

I sat on the bed and closed my eyes for a moment, thinking about those cold eyes that made a shiver run down my spine.

I lay down and got comfortable, welcoming sleep with open arms.

* * *

I slowly opened my eyes and yawned. I stretched my arms and looked out the window. It was sunny outside. I got up and headed towards the closet to pick out some clothes before hopping inside the shower.

Some time later, I decided to see Adam, so I silently walked towards his room, trying not to draw attention to myself.

On my way there, a door next to me opened, and a girl rushed out of the room. She bumped into me, making me fall to the ground in shock.

I looked up at her and saw that she was barely wearing any clothes. She had a tight short skirt on with a tight crop top. Don't get me wrong, I'm all about short skirts and freeing the knee. What made me frown was the way she was staring at me like I was a piece of trash that was in the middle of the road that needed to be thrown away.

She narrowed her eyes on me and placed her hands on her hips.

"Well, aren't you going to say sorry?" she asked.

I got up and raised a brow. "Sorry? You were the one who bumped into me," I told her.

She crossed her arms over her chest, and her face didn't hide the anger she felt. "Do you know who I am? Well, let me tell you. You don't want to mess with me," she hissed.

I just rolled my eyes at her. Did every pack need to have a show-off bitch who only cared about herself? Well, it looked like this pack did.

"Oh, really?" I asked sarcastically. "In case you can't tell, I don't care."

"You slut. You're lucky I'm busy, or I would have done something you wouldn't like. I'll let you off this time, but next time I won't hesitate to show you who you are dealing with," she hissed. "Watch where you're walking." With that, she left.

I growled lowly at her. Okay, it's clear I was not going to like her. I shook my head and continued to walk towards Adam's room. I knocked and entered it. Adam was standing by his closet, picking out clothes. When he saw me, he smiled and hugged me.

"I'm so happy you're okay," he said.

I hugged him back and smiled. "I'm happy you're okay too."

We pulled apart, and he frowned. "I was so scared yesterday when they were about to . . ." He didn't continue what he was about to say, but I just held his hand in mine.

"It's okay, Adam. I'm fine. We're fine."

He nodded, and his frown deepened. "But I'm still confused," he muttered.

I raised a brow and tilted my head. "What do you mean?"

He ran a hand through his hair and sighed. "I mean, I'm confused as to why the alpha let us go. We all know he doesn't do that. Why didn't he kill us?"

I looked down and bit my lip. I guess it's time to tell him why. He deserved to know. Besides, he is my best friend, but I was worried about what he would think of me after I told him. Would he still want to remain friends with me?

I guess there was only one way to find out.

"Because I'm his mate."

CHAPTER 6

"What?" Adam growled loudly.

I looked at him. His eyes had turned black, and his jaw was clenched. This was not a good sign at all.

"I'm his mate," I repeated, but this time, I was looking in his eyes. He growled again and closed his eyes for a moment before opening them and looking at me with a scowl on his face.

"You're his mate?" he said the last part, like it was poison in his mouth.

I sighed and nodded.

"Damn it," he yelled and punched the closet.

Shocked, I grabbed his hand and started rubbing it. "Adam, please," I whispered. "It's not like I chose to be his mate."

He sighed and calmed down but not completely, letting out some curse words from his mouth. "I can't believe it," he muttered with a hint of anger.

I sighed and made him sit on the bed before taking a seat next to him.

"All along, he knew you were his mate, yet he kept you in the dungeon," he growled out. He looked at me, and his eyes started to turn black again. "What kind of mate does that?"

"Adam, you need to calm down. I know it's complicated, but just like he doesn't want me, I don't want him," I told him. My wolf growled at me, telling me to take it back. She thought that he wanted us and that I wanted him too and that I was just in denial.

Right, like I could ever want him.

"He doesn't want you? You're his mate, for heaven's sake. Who doesn't want someone like you?" he asked in an angry tone.

"Well, he made it pretty clear when we met and when he was about to kill us yesterday," I told him.

Adam growled and ran his hands over his face. "And you don't want him?" he asked, but this time, he was calmer.

"You know I don't want that," I said softly, shaking my head. "Besides, even if I did want him, it wouldn't work out. He's cruel and evil, and that isn't someone I would want."

But deep down inside, I wished he wasn't like that. Maybe it would've made things less complicated.

"Yeah, I know. He doesn't deserve you, though. You deserve someone who won't hurt you," he said, looking away from me.

I furrowed my brows at him and frowned. "What do you mean?" I asked.

He looked at me and sighed. "I mean there is someone who deserves you. It just needs time."

I slowly nodded. So he's saying there was someone out there who deserved me? Someone who would be perfect for me? I wondered if that's true.

Adam looked away, and my frown deepened.

"Adam?"

"Yeah?" he responded without looking at me.

"Is there something wrong? Do you think differently of me now?" I asked, looking at him.

He snapped his head towards me and immediately shook his head. "No, Tiana, I would never." He grabbed my hands.

I sighed in relief. I really didn't need him ignoring me because he was the only one I got.

"Then why are you not looking at me?" I asked.

Adam seemed hesitant, like he didn't want to answer the question.

"Uh, it's nothing really. The news just caught me off guard," he muttered.

I raised a brow at him but slowly nodded. I didn't know what's bothering him, but I didn't want to push it further. The only thing that mattered right now was that his feelings towards me didn't change.

"Okay, so what do you think of this pack?" I asked, trying to change the subject. Talking about my mate with my best friend was just weird and uncomfortable.

"It's okay. I wish we could go back to our old pack, but that's impossible now. This pack will have to do, even with the scary rumors," he answered

I completely agreed with him. This was way better than being rogues, but I felt unsettled about the other pack members. Were they as cruel as everyone said? Would they accept us or reject us? I didn't have a slight clue on how we were going to survive in this pack.

"Do you think the rumors are true?" I asked him. He shrugged and furrowed his brows.

"I don't know. Maybe they are, but maybe they aren't. As far as I know, rumors are usually wrong, but that doesn't mean we should let our guards down," he answered.

I smiled at him and nodded. "Yes, you're completely right."

He smiled at me and placed an arm around my shoulder. "We have to stick together. We only have each other now," he said.

"Right again."

He chuckled and got up from the bed and went back to the closet. "Today is the first day of training, so I need to get ready," he told me.

I got up and walked towards the door. "Okay. Besides, I need to see if anyone needs my help. I'll see you later," I said.

He waved at me before looking back to the closet.

I walked down the hall and looked around the place, admiring the beauty of the pack house.

It was surely bigger than our old one. I always thought the house for this pack would be dirty and dusty, no lights and skeletons everywhere. Call me crazy, but that was what I thought. Turned out it was the complete opposite. It was fancy yet simple, and that was what made it beautiful.

My thoughts were interrupted when I bumped into someone, making me fall to the floor, again!

What is with everybody bumping into me?

I immediately thought it was the same girl that bumped into me a while ago but knew I was wrong when I felt my wolf move recklessly and smelt a familiar scent. I looked up and was greeted with dark eyes that stared at me like they could see my soul.

His face was emotionless, but I saw a hint of anger in his eyes. He looked at me up and down but didn't bother helping me get up from the floor.

Wow, what a great gentleman. Note the sarcasm.

When I was standing straight, I looked at him, and he growled deep down in his throat.

"Watch where you're going next time," he said in a low voice. I narrowed my eyes at him and furrowed my brows in anger.

Me? Watch where I was going? When he bumped into me!

"You're the one who made me fall," I said while looking into his eyes.

His eyes turned pitch-black, and he growled again.

Okay, this is not a good sign.

He slowly walked up to me, and I backed away. Every time he would take a step forward, I would take a step backward.

This went on until I was against the wall with no place to go.

Curse you, wall!

He came closer and placed his hands on my sides while looking at me with his angry eyes.

"Never ever talk to me like that, or I will have to show you your place," he said in a hard tone.

My wolf was really happy at how close we were, but all I could feel was anger.

"You can't tell me what to—" I was interrupted by his growl.

"I can because I'm your alpha, and you will listen to what I say without arguing," he hissed. I really just wanted to strangle him, but we all knew what would be the outcome.

"You are not my alpha," I hissed back. I guess he didn't like that because he smashed his fist on the wall next to me, which made me gasp.

"I will be in a matter of days, and I will not tolerate any behavior like this. Do you understand?" he asked.

I sighed angrily and looked away from him, but he grabbed my chin roughly, sending tingles erupting from his touch. That made me look at him.

"Do you understand?" he growled again.

My wolf was nagging at me the whole time to be obedient, but I disagreed with her. No way in hell was I going to submit to someone like him. But either way, I had to be respectful to my "future alpha."

"I understand," I muttered angrily.

"Good." He backed away and didn't take his eyes off me.

With that, he turned around and walked away, leaving me in my spot, wishing I could just punch his handsome face.

What . . . Tiana, what did you just say?

I huffed and walked back to my room but decided to try to find the kitchen to grab something to eat. I climbed down the stairs carefully, ignoring the stares I got from others and their whispering. It was pretty clear they had so many questions about me, like how I survived and how I was among the pack.

They could've at least tried to keep their voices down.

I kept walking around till I smelled food behind big doors, and opened it. I was then greeted by a huge kitchen, and I noticed there were some people eating. I was walking towards the fridge when a nice-looking lady came up to me and smiled.

"Hello, honey. Do you need anything?" she asked. I smiled at her and nodded.

"I'm actually quite hungry," I told her. Her smile even got bigger, which made my smile grow too.

"Of course, the rest of the pack members already ate breakfast, but there are leftover pancakes if you want," she said.

My stomach growled at the sound of pancakes—my favorite food for breakfast, lunch, or dinner. I could eat them any time of day!

"That would be great, thanks."

She grabbed a plate, placed three pancakes on top of each other, and put it in front of me. I got a knife and a fork and sat on the counter, pouring syrup on it and started to eat.

When I took my first bite, I moaned from the taste. It was delicious.

"It's delicious. Thank you!"

She chuckled and sat next to me. "So you're one of the new members who came into our pack?" she asked. I nodded at her and ate another bite of my pancake.

"How does everyone know about us if we only entered yesterday?" I asked.

"It's because our pack hasn't had any new pack members in years. It wasn't hard to miss. Although I am quite curious as to how you were able to enter this pack. It's none of my business, but I will let you know that there will be people who won't give up until they know," she stated.

I was thankful she didn't ask, but I also knew there would be people who wouldn't leave me alone just to get that piece of information out of me.

"Yeah, that's true."

"By the way, what's your name, sweetheart?" she asked.

"I'm Tiana. What about you?" I asked back.

"My name is Anastasia, but you can call me Anna."

"It's nice to meet you, Anna." I smiled at her and raised my hand.

"It's nice to meet you too."

We shook hands and smiled at each other. Well, at least I now knew not everyone here was bad.

After I was done eating, I placed my plate in the sink and turned towards Anna.

"Would you like some help with anything?" I asked. Her eyes perked up, and she smiled.

"If it isn't any trouble, I would like some help with cooking supper," she said.

"Of course." I nodded with a small smile.

"Thank you, dear."

"You're welcome, Anna. So where do I get started?" I asked.

She took out some stuff from the fridge and told me what I had to do. I helped with the salad and some other stuff, which was quite fun, might I say. After I was done, I excused myself and went to my room so I could clean up.

Once I made it to my room, I grabbed a summer dress because it was getting really hot. I took off the clothes I was wearing and wore the dress. When I was done, I sat on my bed and sighed. Somehow, no matter how much I tried to forget those dark eyes, I couldn't seem to do it.

God, how I hate him so much! Oh, and could I say that my wolf was so annoying? She kept bringing him up and purring in my mind. It was really annoying.

My head snapped up when I heard my door open. Adam walked in with a huge smile on his face and sat down on the bed next to me.

"Don't you have training?" I asked. He looked at me and nodded.

"I do. We're on break," he told me. I nodded in understanding and raised a brow.

"Well, don't you look happy?" I asked. His smile widened, and he nodded once again.

"Because I am," he said.

"And the reason is?" I asked.

"Well, the beta thinks I'm really good at fighting, and he said with practice, I might be in charge of the pack warriors," he stated happily.

"That's wonderful, Adam." I smiled at him and patted his back.

"I know. You know how long I have always wanted this," he replied.

"I know, and I'm happy for you. Did you make any friends?" I asked. Okay, now I just sounded like a mom asking her son's first day of school.

"I met a couple of people who were nice. I guess you could call them friends," he said, chuckling. He then looked at me and raised an eyebrow. "What about you? Did you make any friends?" he asked with a grin on his face.

I rolled my eyes at him and huffed while looking away. "I met this nice lady and helped her in the kitchen," I muttered.

He then started laughing. I snapped my head at him and scowled.

"Why are you laughing?" I hissed. He stopped and wiped a fake tear from his eye.

"Oh, Tiana, poor Tiana. Never able to make real friends other than me," he teased. I growled lowly and punched him in his arm.

"I am capable of making friends," I stated. He looked at me and shook his head.

"No, you can't. Just admit it." He continued to tease me. I growled at him, which made him laugh again.

"Shut up!"

"Or what?" he asked, raising a brow and grinning.

"Or this." I started to throw pillows at him, but he got up from my bed and ran towards the door.

"Is that all you got?" he asked.

I threw one more pillow at him, which made him run out of my room, closing the door behind him. I sighed and lay on my bed.

I jerked my body up when I heard my room door open once again and grabbed another pillow.

I threw it again, but this time, my eyes widened when I heard a feminine gasp.

Oops, that wasn't Adam.

I looked at the person who came into my room and was shocked when I saw it was a beautiful girl with an amused expression on her face.

"Oh my God! I am so sorry. I thought you were someone else," I apologized while getting up and walking towards her. She smiled at me, showing her perfect, straight teeth.

"It's no problem. I was just shocked. That's all," she said. I sighed in relief and smiled.

"Is there anything you need?" I asked, wondering why she was in my room.

She had a huge smile on her face and walked closer to me. "I just wanted to meet the new pack members everyone is talking about," she answered.

I chuckled and raised my hand towards her. "Well, I'm Tiana Sparks."

She looked at my hand but shook her head and pulled me into a hug. It caught me off guard, but I hugged her back. When we pulled away, she introduced herself, making my eyes widen and my mouth hung open.

"And I'm Lina. Lina Wood."

CHAPTER 7

"Lina Wood?" I asked, completely shocked.
"Yep, that's my name," she chuckled.
"You're Alpha Mason's sister?"
She smiled at me and nodded.
This is Mason's sister? The person who's supposed to be cruel and dark? The girl I had heard so many rumors about? This sweet girl is the sister of the feared alpha? Oh no. It's too hard to believe.

"But you're—" I was immediately cut off when she started talking.

"I know. I don't seem like the same person that all the rumors describe," she said. I slowly nodded in agreement and sat on my bed.

"No, not at all," I stated.

She chuckled again and sat next to me. "Rumors are rumors. Sometimes they're not true, and sometimes they are," she told me while nodding slightly.

I completely agreed with her on that one. It's wrong to judge someone based on what other people said, yet we made those mistakes a lot, and sometimes we didn't even notice.

"So all of them are wrong?" I asked.

She looked at me and shook her head. "Not all of them, but most of them are. Lots of people have something against our pack. That's why they make up fake rumors, like how we don't care about our pack members or how we live like wild beasts." She laughed a bit at the last part and shrugged. "But in reality, we live like normal people, and we care about our pack members. It's just . . ." She stopped at the end, leaving me confused.

"It's Alpha Mason?" I asked. That name made a shiver run down my spine, but I immediately shook it off. Lina smiled at me and nodded.

"Yeah, he's hard to deal with. It's just too complicated." She sighed while running her hand through her hair. She then stopped and furrowed her brows while looking at me. "Wait, why did you call him Alpha Mason?" she asked.

I frowned and wondered why she would ask that. "Why wouldn't I? He is an alpha," I stated. She raised a brow and shook her head.

"I know he's an alpha, but why are you calling him that when he's your mate?" she asked while putting a hand on her hip.

My eyes widened in shock. How did she know that? I didn't even mention anything to her.

"How did you know?" I questioned.

She giggled and scooted closer to me. "How could I not know? My brother killed every trespasser he ever had to deal with, yet he didn't kill you. It wasn't hard to find out, and hearing all the rumors going around the pack house, I guess lots of people know you're special."

I slowly nodded and sighed. "I guess you're right, but your brother hasn't really accepted me," I told her. It wasn't like I had accepted him either. He's too complicated. Boys are complicated in general.

"He went through some hard stuff. Just give it time," Lina whispered, holding my hand.

"I don't really care if he cares for me or not. I never really wanted a mate," I muttered, getting up from the bed.

She raised a brow at me while giving me a look that said she didn't believe me. It was true. Why would I lie about something like this?

58

My wolf was growling in my head like usual. I rolled my eyes at her and shut her off before looking at Lina again.

She also got up from my bed and moved to the door, opening it.

"How about we go see the warriors train? It's better than staying here all day," she said excitedly. I smiled at her and shook my head.

"I can't. I have some things to do," I said. She raised a brow at me and grabbed my hand.

"I'm sure it can wait." She started to pull me outside my room.

I sighed and started to walk with her. I did need some fresh air, and I could see Adam too even though I still wanted to punch him in the face for what happened a while ago. That's his normal self, teasing and making fun of me, but that's what I loved about him even though it could get annoying.

"What are you smiling about?" Lina asked. I snapped out of my thoughts and shook my head.

"It's nothing really," I stated.

She nodded and continued to walk. We went downstairs, and that's when I started to hear whispering again. I rolled my eyes and ignored them. Couldn't they keep their voices down?

Eventually, we made it to a big yard with lots of people training, but what made me want to turn around and head back was that Alpha Mason was in charge of them. Once I saw him, his head snapped over to my direction and his eyes darkened.

He didn't look so happy, but soon his gaze drifted to Lina, and he shook his head and looked away from us. I turned to Lina, and she was smiling at me. I raised a brow at her and shrugged while trying to find Adam. Unfortunately, I couldn't concentrate well enough because my wolf kept urging me to run into our mate's arms. I tried to ignore the familiar scent, but it just made the pressure my wolf was putting on me increase.

"Let's sit here and wait till their break so I can introduce you to a couple of friends," Lina said, successfully earning my attention. I nodded, and we sat on benches in comfortable silence. Every once in a while, I would glance at Alpha Mason but would immediately turn away.

Lina was talking about something when I felt someone staring at me. I looked up and saw Alpha Mason was looking right at me with no emotions on his face. That reminded me of what happened this morning, so I immediately kept my gaze away from him, ignoring his stares.

After a while, all of the warriors took a break and settled down. Lina got up from the bench and turned to me.

"Come on, let me show you my friends," she said.

Smiling, I got up and followed her, walking through the field. Like usual, I ignored the stares, but this time, I got them from males, which made my wolf uncomfortable. While I was walking, I glanced to my right and saw Alpha Mason standing not too far away from us with his arms crossed over his chest, staring right at me with cold eyes.

My wolf was yelping in joy, but I immediately turned around and concentrated on where Lina was taking me.

We eventually stopped in front a group of young handsome men, might I add, who were laughing and talking. Some of them noticed our presence and turned their attention toward us, smiles growing on their lips when they saw Lina.

"Hey, boys. How are you guys?" Lina asked. By now we had all their attention on us, and some looked at me inconfusion.

"We're good, just tired from all the training. How about you?" one of the men asked while glancing at me. Lina smiled and wrapped an arm around my shoulders.

"I'm good. I would like you to meet my new friend Tiana. She's one of the new pack members," she stated. They all smiled at me and started to introduce themselves. I smiled at each one and tried to memorize their names, but let me tell you this, I wasn't good with names.

"So, Tiana, what do you think of this pack?" one asked. I think his name was Tyler.

"It's nice," I answered. All of them nodded. One of them named Ryder stepped closer to us with a smirk.

"Did someone ever tell you that you're beautiful?" he asked.

My eyes widened and a small blush formed on my face. Yeah, I could tell he's a playboy

"Back off, Ryder. She isn't one to mess with," Lina said while smirking back at him. He raised a brow at her and crossed his arms over his chest.

"And why is that?" he asked while looking at me, then back at Lina. I was about to shut Lina up because I knew what she was going to say, but someone else interrupted her.

"Tiana!"

I turned my head and smiled when I saw Adam running towards us with a small smile on his face.

When he finally arrived, he engulfed me in a big hug then pulled away. "I was looking everywhere for you," he said while catching his breath.

"I was with Lina the whole time," I told him. He nodded and looked at Lina, but stared at her in confusion.

"Lina?" he asked. I nodded at him and looked at her, then back at Adam.

"Yes. Lina. Lina Wood."

His eyes widened, and he slowly nodded.

I turned to Lina and the group and smiled. "This is my best friend, Adam. He is also new," I introduced him. They all said hi to him, but I noticed Adam glaring at all the boys. I raised a brow at him but shook my head.

"So, Tiana, would you like to go on a date with me?" Ryder asked with a smug look.

I raised a brow at him and rolled my eyes. *Yes, definitely a playboy.*

I noticed Adam stiffened, and he was about to say something to him when we heard a loud growl, calling out to us.

"What do you guys think you're doing?" Alpha Mason growled while stalking towards us. When he was in front of us, he glared at the men. They all looked down to show respect.

"We were just talking, Alpha," one of them said.

"You weren't talking, you were fooling around. Head back to training, and if I see any of you slacking off, I will be mad," he ordered and then looked at me for a second with his dark eyes and turned away, stalking off.

I was there standing in shock, and so did everybody else.

"But we're still on break," Tyler muttered to himself.

All the men, including Adam, sighed and walked back to their positions. I looked at Lina, and she had a small smile on her lips, but I just decided to ignore her.

"Let's head back to the pack house," Lina said. I nodded at her, and we started walking towards the pack house. When we entered, we decided to sit on one of the couches and relax. I got comfortable and sighed.

"So how long have you known Adam?" Lina asked. I smiled at that and knew the answer immediately.

"We've known each other ever since diapers. His parents and mine were good friends," I told her but frowned at the last part. I really missed them, but I knew they were safe out there. I felt it, and that dream only made me sure about it.

"Is something wrong?" she asked. I looked back at her and shook my head.

"No, nothing's wrong," I assured her.

She smiled at me and nodded. "Well, you're one lucky girl." She giggled.

"Why am I a lucky girl?" I asked, raising a brow in confusion.

She continued to giggle but soon stopped. "Because you have one hot friend."

I rolled my eyes at her and shook my head. I would be lying if I said he wasn't good-looking, but he's just not my type. Besides, we'd been like siblings since birth, and that would just be weird.

"And I can tell you have lots of male friends," I told her while smiling. She grinned and removed her hair off of her shoulder.

"You can't blame me. They can't resist my looks," she said smugly.

I crossed my arms over my chest. "Oh, really?" I asked.

Nodding, she smiled. "Yes, really."

Then the mate topic crossed my mind, and I wondered if she had a mate. I was sure if she did, I would have seen him because mates usually stick together, but you never know.

"Did you ever find your mate?" I asked. Her eyes perked up, but she sighed and shook her head.

"Nope, not yet," she answered. I nodded at her and rested my head on the couch.

"Do you want one?" I asked while closing my eyes.

"I guess. I like the idea of one," she stated.

I nodded but tried to stop thinking about him. It was just mixing up my mind, especially with my wolf constantly whimpering to be with him.

I opened my eyes and lifted my head when I heard whispers from across the big room. I looked up to see a group of girls glancing at me with disgust. These girls were barely wearing any clothes, and their faces were caked up in makeup.

I looked at Lina, and she was glaring and growling at the girls.

"Who are they?" I whispered to her as she was staring at them with pure hate. I was sure I was not going to like them by the way they were acting and staring at me. People like those just ticked me off.

"Those are Chloe's minions, the pack slut who only cares about herself," she hissed. I nodded at her and ignored their stares.

"You guys have one too?" I chuckled.

She nodded at me then smiled.

"In my old pack, we had one, and let me tell you, I did not like her one bit," I told her.

"I bet Chloe is worse than her. She literally hooked up with most of the guys in this pack. She's so annoying, especially her minions," she said in disgust. She looked back at the girls and shook her head. "Let's go to my room because if I stay here any longer, I might slap one in the face," she said.

I laughed at that. We got up from the couch and headed towards the stairs. I didn't miss the glare Lina shot at them.

We walked until we stopped in front of a door. She opened it and led me inside. I smiled and admired her pretty yet normal room.

I sat on the chair that was next to her bed, while she sat on her bed. I was looking at the pictures on her desk, and one particular picture caught my attention. It was a picture of a small boy holding a girl. They were both smiling, and it looked like they were the happiest kids in the world.

"That photo was taken years ago." Lina's voice brought me back to reality. I looked back at her, and she had a sad smile plastered on her face.

"Who are these kids?" I asked. She closed her eyes for a bit, then opened them to look at me.

"That's Mason and me," she answered, leaving me shocked.

That's Mason? The boy who's happily smiling and looking like there wasn't one problem in his life? It was hard to believe. Yet, we couldn't judge someone from their outer appearance because they could be wearing an invisible mask that hid their true feelings.

"Things were different when we were small. It's just complicated." She sighed while shaking her head.

I really wanted to know more, but I knew not to. It looked like that was a sensitive subject, and I didn't want to upset her.

I looked at the time and gave her a small smile while getting up and facing her. "It's almost time for lunch. Let's go before it gets crowded," I told her.

She smiled at me, then nodded. "Let's go then."

We went downstairs and made it to the big dinner table. There were barely any people, so we took our seats and sat next to each other.

Anna came and placed some food on the table while smiling at us and walking away right after. Lina and I talked for a while until a scent made me stiffen. I looked up and saw Alpha Mason heading towards the dinner table and staring right at me, but he eventually moved his stare elsewhere.

Lina had a small smile on her lips, but I just ignored her and my nagging wolf who wouldn't shut up. I also drifted my attention elsewhere and avoided his stares. After a while, I heard Lina growl, and I looked up to see a familiar female.

"Chloe," Lina muttered.

Once she said her name, I immediately recognized her as the person who ran into me this morning. I furrowed my brows at her, remembering her rudeness. I was not surprised she's the Chloe that Lina was talking about.

Her minions were walking behind her while smirking at Lina and me, and all I wanted to do was strangle them.

I turned my attention back to Chloe, and she was walking towards Alpha Mason with a smirk on her face. I raised my brow in confusion but felt my wolf growl when she got closer to him.

What she said next made Lina and my wolf growl out in anger, and I would be lying if I said it didn't bother me one bit and I didn't want to punch her in her fake face.

"Mason, baby. I missed you so much."

CHAPTER 8

"What did she say?" I growled lowly. I glanced at Lina, and she was shooting daggers at Chloe.

```
Let me tell you if looks could kill,
Chloe would be ten feet underground.
```

"She's always like this," Lina growled in anger.

I looked back at the scene in front of me, and her hands were on Alpha Mason's shoulder. My wolf wanted to rip her hands off her body.

Alpha Mason huffed out in annoyance and got up from the seat, facing her with his arms crossed over his chest.

"Don't call me that," he roared, and his eyes turned darker.

Chloe pouted teasingly and placed her hands on his chest. Oh no, she did not do that. I felt my temper rise, and I wished I could just rip her throat out.

"But, baby—"

Chloe was caught off guard when Alpha Mason roared, and the few people who were in the dining room turned their heads in fear.

"I told you to not call me that, and if you annoy me one more time, I won't hesitate to kick you out of my pack because I do not tolerate any behavior like this," he growled out.

Lina and I had smirks on our faces, and they only grew when we saw Chloe's face. She was on the verge of tears, but she had an annoyed face on. She soon looked to the ground and nodded.

"Get out of my sight!"

She nodded again and ran off with her minions behind her, and right at that moment, I wanted to laugh so hard.

Once she was out of sight, Alpha Mason shook his head and turned in our direction. He and I made eye contact, and when that happened, his eyes turned back to normal for a moment, but he soon turned around and stalked out of the dining area. I kept my eyes on him until I couldn't see him and sighed.

I looked over to Lina.

"God, how much I hate her. She always tries to hook up with my brother to get the luna title. She can't get it in her head that he doesn't want her," she muttered out in annoyance.

At her words, my wolf calmed down, and I knew so did I. I didn't want to admit it, but I really wanted to snap her neck when she laid her hands on him. It was not like I wanted to feel that. It was all because of the mate bond.

I sighed and shook my head, trying to forget those thoughts.

"She's been trying to?" I asked. Lina looked at me and nodded.

"Yeah, like ever since she shifted into her wolf. She wants the luna title so badly, but luckily my brother is hard to get through. And we all know she will never be the luna," she said while giving me a small smirk. I rolled my eyes and ignored the last part.

"I can see you don't like her, and let me tell you, neither do I." I chuckled and she giggled.

"I hate her and her minions," she said, cringing.

I smiled a small smile and nodded at her in agreement. We continued to talk until everybody came down. When everybody sat down in their chairs, we all started to eat. I noticed Alpha Mason didn't come back and furrowed my brows in confusion.

Where is he? I immediately shook my head. *Stop thinking about him. It's none of your business where he goes.*

I looked at Lina, and she gave me a small smile before eating. I sighed and ate my food in silence, but what got on my nerves was the weird looks people were giving me. Not surprised.

After I was done, I got up from my chair and grabbed my plate.

"I'm going to put this in the kitchen, then go back to my room," I told Lina.

She nodded and continued to eat. I started walking towards the kitchen and out the dining room. When I entered the large kitchen, I noticed I was the only one there.

I shrugged and went to the sink to clean my plate. I was humming to a tune when a voice behind me caught me off guard.

"Hey there."

I yelled in shock and placed my plate on the counter before turning around with my hand above my heart.

"You scared me," I said while catching my breath. He raised a brow and smirked.

"Oh, did I?" he asked with a smug look. I rolled my eyes at him and started to walk away, but he grabbed my hand and pulled me back.

"What are you doing?" I asked, slightly annoyed. My wolf was whimpering in my head because she didn't like to be touched by another male.

He let go of my hand and put his hands in his pockets.

"So what do you say about the date?" Ryder asked.

I sighed and rolled my eyes once again. I looked at him, and all I wanted to do was wipe that smirk off of his face.

"No," I answered and turned around, starting to walk away.

"Why?" he asked while catching up with me.

"Because."

And with that, I walked off and up the stairs towards my room. I entered my room and laid on the bed before closing my eyes. A moment passed, and I was about to fall asleep when my bed bounced up, and I felt someone lie next to me. I snapped my eyes open and sighed in relief when I saw it was only Adam.

He turned to me and smiled, and I returned it.

"Finished training?" I asked and he sighed.

"Yes, finally."

I raised a brow. "Why are you here?" I asked. He made a fake gasp and pretended to be hurt.

"I can't just come to see my best friend?" he asked. I chuckled and tilted my head towards him.

"You could. It's just that I still haven't forgiven you for what you said this morning," I told him. He pouted his lip but soon smiled.

"Is Tiana still mad?" He cooed. I scrunched my nose at him while he laughed.

"Yes," I lied and scooted closer to him until he had no room left and fell to the ground.

"Ouch," he whined while looking up at me. I started laughing so hard while he had an annoyed face on.

"You always do this," he muttered while getting up from the ground.

I continued to laugh while he just stood there with a pout on his lips.

"Stop laughing!" He grabbed a pillow from my bed and started to hit me with it, but that only made my laughter intensify. "How does it feel to be attacked by a pillow now?" he said.

I stopped laughing and grabbed the pillow from his hands and threw it in his face.

"You deserved it," I said while catching my breath. He ran a hand through his hair and crossed his arms over his chest.

"It's not my fault you're sensitive," he muttered. I furrowed my brows at him and got up from my bed.

"What did you say?" I asked slowly. He stiffened and nervously smiled.

"Oh, would you look at the time. I have to go," he said while looking at his hand which, by the way, had no watch on, then rushing out my door.

I sighed and shook my head with a small smile, then sat back on my bed. I felt really tired, and all I wanted to do was fall into deep, deep sleep.

I laid down and stared at the ceiling thinking about life. I slowly closed my eyes, and soon enough, I welcomed sleep with open arms.

* * *

"Wake up, Tiana!" a voice said.

I slowly opened my eyes to be greeted with Lina's eyes. She smiled at me and pulled the covers off me.

"Come on, get up," she stated.

I raised an eyebrow in confusion and looked at the clock. It was still early. Why was she waking me up? So far, it had been a week since we stayed here, and I hadn't seen Alpha Mason after that scene at the dinner table. The whispering stopped a bit, but I still got the stares.

"Why?" I asked. She placed her hand on her hip and sighed.

"Tomorrow is the ceremony that's going to be held for you and the other new members. It's known that all new female members have to wear white dresses, so we're going shopping!" she said excitedly. I got up from the bed and looked at her.

"Is your brother even going to say yes?" I asked. She shrugged and smiled.

"He always says yes to me, so that's no problem."

I slowly nodded and went to the closet.

"Okay, just wait outside so I can clean up," I said while grabbing my clothes.

She nodded and exited my room. I walked into my bathroom and stripped out of my clothes and went in the shower. I closed my eyes for a moment, then opened them. These past few weeks, my wolf had been whimpering. She wanted to see her mate, and I didn't really know how to feel about that.

After getting ready, I walked outside of my room. Lina was there waiting for me, smiling.

"Let's go eat breakfast, then I'll go ask my brother," she said.

"What if he says no?" I asked. She looked at me and raised a brow.

"He won't say no."

I sighed and followed her until we made it to the kitchen. Anna was there making food, and when she saw us, she gave us a small smile.

"Hey, Anna. Mind making us something?" Lina asked. Anna shook her head.

"Of course not. I've made eggs and pancakes. Just sit down, and I'll give you some," she said. We nodded and did just what she told us to do.

Anna placed two plates in front of us, and we thanked her before eating. Once we were done, we got up and said goodbye to her and walked up the stairs.

"I'll go in, and you stay outside, okay?" Lina said.

I nodded, and we stopped in front of a door that Lina soon opened. I caught Alpha Mason's scent, and I was sure he caught mine too. My wolf was begging for me to open the door and jump in his arms, but I shut her off before she could do anything.

I couldn't exactly hear what was happening, but I started to guess things weren't going right when their voices got louder. I heard growls and complaints. Soon the door opened, and an angry

Lina walked out and slammed the door. I winced at the sound and raised a brow.

"What happened?" I asked.

"He said no!" she whined.

"I thought he always says yes to you?" I told her. She huffed and ran a hand through her hair.

"Because he does. I don't know why he didn't agree this time," she stated.

I nodded and she soon smiled, so I looked at her in confusion.

"Come with me." She grabbed my hand and pulled me down the stairs.

"Where are we going?" I asked.

"To the mall," she said in a *duh* tone. I furrowed my brows at her and stopped.

"But didn't your brother say no?" I asked.

Nodding, she whispered, "Yes, he did. That's why we're going in secret." My eyes widened, and I slowly smiled.

"Great idea."

She smiled back at me, and we went towards the front door. It's a good thing no one was here at the moment.

"We will shift into our wolves and exit the territory without us getting caught," she said.

I nodded. We opened the door and took off before anyone could see us. When we made it to the woods, we went behind trees, stripped, and shifted into our wolves.

We ran for a while until we were almost near the borders. Lina tilted her head, indicating we should shift back, so we went behind trees again and shifted and wore our clothes. I walked towards Lina, and she placed her finger on her mouth, then she came up to me and frowned.

"There are lots of guards in the area. How will we cross the borders now?" she asked with a sigh. I smiled at her and grabbed her hand.

"We will. Just don't make a sound." She looked at me in confusion but slowly nodded.

"How?" she asked.

"You'll see." I then concentrated on my powers. I opened my eyes and saw Lina looking at me in surprise and amazement. We were now invisible.

I placed my finger on my mouth, then we started to cross the borders and ran. After a while, my powers wore off, but luckily we were nowhere near the borders.

"H-How did you do that?" she asked, looking at me with wide eyes. I smiled at her and shrugged.

"It's in my genes," I answered.

"What do you mean?" she asked.

"I mean I'm a hybrid, half werewolf and half angel. It was passed down to me from my mom's side," I told her. Her eyes were still wide, her mouth hung open.

"You're a hybrid?" she asked.

"Yes."

"Why didn't you ever tell me?"

"Because it never came up," I said, shrugging. She slightly nodded but soon smiled.

"Tell me about that later. Let's go."

Soon enough, we made it to the city.

"Let's find you a dress fast before my brother finds out," she said.

We walked to a mall that was nearby and entered it. We checked many stores but didn't find anything. None of the dresses caught our attention.

A couple hours had passed, yet we still hadn't found anything. We decided to look at one more store, so we entered a shop and looked through their dresses.

"Oh my God! Tiana, try this on," Lina said excitedly.

I looked at the dress and smiled. It was beautiful. It was a short dress that was tight up to the waist but loose down the waist. I took it and entered the fitting room.

"You done?" Lina asked after a while.

"Yes," I said and then opened the door. Lina gasped.

"You're totally getting this one," she said. I agreed with her on that. It looked good on me. It looked great!

I closed the door and changed and got out of the fitting room with the dress in my hands.

"Let's pay for it so we can go home fast," Lina said. We went to the counter and paid for it.

We walked for a while until we reached the woods. We soon shifted and started running with our clothes and the bag in our mouths. After a while, we stopped and shifted back into our human forms and wore our clothes.

"Come on, before anyone notices that we're gone," Lina said while holding my hand.

"Oh, we noticed," said a familiar voice behind us.

Our eyes widened, and we turned around to find an angry Alpha Mason standing with guards by his side. I looked at Lina, who looked shocked, and all I could think of was one thing.

We're in big trouble.

CHAPTER 9

Alpha Mason slowly walked towards us. His face held anger, and his eyes were firmly set on mine.

"Mason," Lina whispered but loud enough for us to hear.

"Didn't I make myself clear that no one is allowed to cross our borders?" he asked roughly while turning to Lina and furrowing his brows. Lina looked down and played with her fingers but soon looked up and faced her brother.

"But tomorrow is the ceremony. We had to—" Lina was interrupted by Mason's loud growl, leaving us shocked.

"I don't care what the reason was. When I say no, it's a no. Do I make myself clear?" he asked and then turned his head towards me.

Breathing deeply, I nodded. He growled lowly and ran a hand through his hair, turning back to his sister.

"I don't want to see both of you outside of the pack house until the ceremony tomorrow. That will be your punishment for now," he stated and turned around.

"But Mason—" Lina started.

"Don't argue with me, Lina!" he yelled. Lina sighed in annoyance and nodded.

"Fine," she huffed.

He glanced at me one more time, then turned around and walked away as the guards took us back to the pack house. While we were walking, I kept on thinking about the ceremony tomorrow.

I was slightly nervous but didn't want to think much about it. I was kind of annoyed that he was making us stay in the pack house and forbidding us to leave it till the ceremony, but it could have been worse. He could have given us a punishment we wouldn't have liked even more.

Once we entered the pack house, I hurried to my room, ignoring the stares, and sat on my bed. I took the dress out of the bag and sighed. I got up and hung the dress in my closet but turned my head to the door when I heard it open.

Does it kill a person to knock?

Adam walked into my room and gave me a small smile. "Where were you?" he asked while sitting on my bed. I walked up to him and sat next to him, sighing once again.

"Lina and I went to the mall," I answered with a shrug. He looked at me and raised a brow.

"For what?" he questioned.

"We went to buy a dress for the ceremony tomorrow."

He nodded but furrowed his brows. "But why was the alpha angry?" he asked.

"Because he told us we weren't allowed to cross the borders, yet we did," I muttered.

Adam's eyes widened, and a grin grew on his lips. "That's my girl," he chuckled. I raised a brow at him and smiled.

"But now I can't get out of the pack house until tomorrow," I whined while pouting. He chuckled again and raised a brow at me.

"So? It's not like there's anywhere else to go." He shrugged.

"Actually, there are lots of places, and I also wanted to see you practice today," I stated.

"Don't worry, babe. This body isn't going anywhere," he cockily said. I scrunched my brows in disgust and elbowed him in the stomach.

"Eww, no. Besides, it's not like you have a nice body, anyways." I faked a gag, while he also faked a gasp and pouted at me.

"I do have a nice body. It's just that some people can't see that." He huffed while crossing his arms over his chest. "As a matter of fact, many women wish to be with someone like me."

I laughed out loud and wiped a fake tear from the corner of my eye, catching my breath before looking at an annoyed Adam.

"Okay, Mr. Big Ego, you have an okay body. Happy?" I asked while raising my eyebrow at him in amusement.

He huffed, and a small smile grew on his lips. "I'll take what I have."

Adam stayed in my room for hours. We eventually went and ate lunch but soon went back to my room and talked like good old times. Back in our old pack, we would spend most of our times together. We also shared many classes in high school so we would constantly see each other.

Lots of people thought we were mates because of how close we were with one another, but we would always clear things up and tell people we're just friends.

Adam was currently telling me about his training and how strict they were when a knock on the door interrupted him. I raised my brow in confusion and shrugged when Adam gave me a questioning look. He got up and walked towards the door.

"I'll get it," he said.

When he was in front of the door, he reached for the doorknob and turned it. I got up and walked towards him but stopped dead in my tracks when I saw who was outside of my room.

Alpha Mason furrowed his brows at Adam, and his eyes grew dark. I walked up to Adam, and his gaze turned to me. His already dark eyes grew darker.

He stood there for a couple of seconds staring at Adam and I before speaking in a harsh tone. "The ceremony is at 12 PM tomorrow. Don't be late." With that, he turned around and stalked off.

My eyes were wide as my wolf purred and whined to be with him. I looked at Adam, and his eyes were focused on the ground. His jaw was clenched, but as soon as I looked at him, he snapped his head up and shook his head.

"How I wish I could punch him," Adam muttered to himself, but it wasn't soft enough to miss. I rolled my eyes at him and placed my hand on his shoulder.

"You heard him. Don't be late," I told him.

He looked at me and sighed before nodding.

I didn't really know what would happen otherwise, but it was better not to find out.

* * *

I slowly opened my eyes and yawned when I felt someone poking my arm. I immediately thought it was Adam, but when I turned to the source, I was wrong.

"Lina?" I asked softly.

Lina was right above me with a big grin on her face. She stopped her poking and took the covers off me.

"Come on, sleepy head. It's almost 10 AM. We have to get ready," she said excitedly. I yawned again and sat up.

"Okay, let me just take a shower," I told her before getting up and walking to the closet to grab a towel and my underwear.

"You shower, and I'll be here waiting," she said while sitting down on a chair in the corner of my room. I looked at her in confusion and raised a brow.

"Why?" I asked.

She looked at me and placed her hand on her hip. "Because I'm doing your hair and makeup," she replied in a sarcastic tone.

I gave her a small smile as I started to walk to the bathroom. I placed the towel on the hanger and placed my underwear next to it. I took off my clothes and hopped in the shower.

While I was waiting for the water to heat up, I was thinking about the ceremony. I wondered how they welcomed new pack members. It was clear they hadn't had one for a long time, but that didn't mean it changed from when they used to have them, I think.

My old pack used to greet new pack members by having a ceremony like most packs, but sometimes what they did in ceremonies differ. Some packs had to chant words to be welcomed in the pack. In our pack, the new member had to say words of commitment to reassure their honesty to our pack.

Each pack differed, and I was quite curious and a bit nervous about how they did it here. I heard rumors, and they were not pleasant, but I guess there was only one way to find out.

I sighed when the water heated up and relaxed my tense muscles. I applied shampoo on my hair and cleaned it through. After cleaning my body and rinsing everything, I closed the water and grabbed the towel, wrapping it around my body.

I wore my underwear and walked outside the bathroom with the towel around my body. Lina turned her head towards me and smiled.

"I'll do your makeup and hair, then you'll change into the dress. Sounds good?" she asked while pulling the chair out for me.

"Yeah." I smiled at her and nodded.

"Okay, let's get started."

After a while, Lina was finished with my makeup and hair. My makeup wasn't too much; it was simple and nice. She also curled my hair, so my hair was down in soft, bouncy curls which I loved so much. She looked at me and smiled a big smile.

"You look perfect. Now change into the dress. I already picked the perfect shoes for you!" She squealed with excitement.

I laughed a little and got up from the chair, taking the dress from the closet and changing into it in front of Lina. I didn't feel weird because it's not like I had something she didn't. You know what I'm saying?

After I wore it, Lina came closer to me and stared up and down, inspecting the dress or me.

"You look beautiful." She squealed again. I laughed and smiled at her.

"Thanks, but what are you going to wear?" I asked, looking at her. She was still wearing her casual clothes. She looked at the clock and shrugged.

"I'm going to pick out some normal dress. We have more than half an hour until the ceremony starts, so I have time. I'll come and pick you up when it's time, but I'm going to go get dressed, okay?" she asked.

I nodded. She gave me a quick hug, then exited my room. I walked towards a mirror and smiled at myself. Don't want to brag, but I looked pretty good. I went to the windows and looked out of it to see lots of people strolling around and kids playing together. I smiled and decided to check up on Adam.

I slowly opened the door and saw no one was in the hall.

Why are the halls always empty?

I shrugged it off and walked towards Adam's room. While I was heading there, a clingy voice called out to me, making me stop. I turned around to see an angry Chloe rushing towards me.

When she was in front of me, she pointed her finger to me and furrowed her brows.

"Listen here, b*tch. Don't think that you're special just because Mason agreed to have you in our pack. I don't know why you're here, but if I see you anywhere near him, you're going to regret ever coming here," she sneered.

I raised a brow at her and crossed my arms over my chest, not bothering to hide my boredom. I really had no time to deal with someone like her. Who the hell did she think she was, telling me what to do? It was not like I wanted to be near him, anyway.

"Are you done? I'm quite busy," I told her while narrowing my eyes. Her eyes grew dark, and she growled lowly and stepped closer to me.

"You bitch," she growled out again and raised her hand towards me. I was about to grab her hand when someone else did. I looked up and smiled at an angry Adam.

Chloe looked up and took her hand away from his grasp and growled at him.

"Don't you dare try to lay a hand on her ever again," Adam growled at her.

She winced and stepped a couple of steps back. She huffed and shot daggers at me with her eyes, then turned around and walked away with her hands clenched.

Adam looked at me, and his dark eyes turned back to normal.

"You okay? " he asked. I smiled at him and nodded.

"I'm okay, but I could've handled her myself. Thanks, though," I told him while placing my hand on his shoulder. He sighed and smiled back at me.

"I know, but it feels good to be the hero once in a while." He chuckled and I laughed, then we walked back to my room.

We talked for a while until the door opened and Lina walked in wearing a black dress. I smiled at her, and she returned it.

"You guys ready?" she asked. We got up from the chairs and nodded. "Let's go," Lina said.

We got out of my room and out of the pack house. We walked until we made it to the same field where the pack warriors trained. The place was full of people who I didn't know. Some members looked familiar, but there were many who I had never seen before. I guess the whole pack was in there.

We walked through the crowded area, and I noticed the usual stares. But this time, I wasn't the only one they were staring at. They were also staring at Adam too.

I looked around and made eye contact with a person I hadn't seen in a week, Kayla.

She smiled at me and waved her hand. I returned that smile and waved back and was about to walk up to her when Lina grabbed my shoulder.

"Stay here. The ceremony is about to start," she said. I nodded and looked up to where the stage was placed.

Soon, Alpha Mason came up on the stage, and everyone in the crowd went silent.

I tried to keep my stare anywhere else but him. However, I eventually looked up at him, only to be greeted by his hard eyes staring back at me. My wolf purred in delight, but soon his eyes turned to the crowd.

"Last week three new members entered our territory, and today we will welcome them to our pack and make them one of us," he said in a loud, hard voice. Everyone's eyes were on their alpha, and not a single person spoke or said anything.

"If anyone is against them joining our pack, then speak now!" he announced. Not a single person spoke up.

He nodded and started to speak again. "We will now start with the ceremony. First member, come up."

Kayla walked towards the stage, and everybody's eyes were on her. She climbed up the stairs and stood in front of the crowd.

"State your name and previous pack," Alpha Mason said.

Kayla looked nervous but nodded and spoke softly, "Kayla Alex, and I used to be in the Red Star pack."

"Do you, Kayla Alex, pledge your loyalty and honesty to this pack?" he asked her.

"Yes, I do," she answered.

Alpha Mason nodded at someone, and the person walked up the stage and handed him a bowl and a small table. Alpha Mason placed the table between them and took something out of the bowl. Kayla's eyes widened, and when I saw what was in there, my eyes also widened.

In his hand was a small knife.

"Give me your hand," he ordered.

She gulped but did as he said and gave him her hand. He slid the knife over her palm, causing her to wince. Her palm had a scratch on it, which was dripping blood. He also slid the knife over his palm, and he placed his on hers. Kayla's eyes widened once more, and both of their blood dripped into the bowl.

He then took his hand off hers and looked towards the crowd.

"Next member," he said.

Adam nodded at me and walked towards the stage as Kayla went back to her seat. Adam said and did the same thing. I gulped when Adam was done and the alpha called for the last member, which was me.

As I walked towards the stage, everyone's eyes were on me, including Alpha Mason's. I stood in front of him while he stared at me intensely.

"State your name and previous pack," he ordered.

"Tiana Sparks, originally from the White Moon pack," I said.

"Do you, Tiana Sparks, pledge your loyalty and honesty to this pack?" he asked while staring directly at me.

"I do," I answered, meeting his stare.

He took the knife from the table and looked back at me.

"Give me your hand," he ordered again.

I placed my hand in front of him, and he grabbed it, sending tingling sparks from his touch. His face was hard and emotionless as he slid the knife into my palm. I winced slightly but held it in to not show the pain. He did the same with his hand and placed it over the bowl. I knew what I had to do next. I placed my palm over his, and when we touched, I felt the same sparks, but something else was also there, something different.

I felt all the bond I had with my new pack members and with my mate.

CHAPTER 10

I calmly sat on the grass and watched the children play and people walk by. It had been two weeks since the ceremony. Ever since then, I hadn't seen Alpha Mason much, and I was thankful for that. Whenever I saw him, things just got complicated. I sighed and placed my chin on my knee and closed my eyes.

This was relaxing: being outside of the pack house and sitting down on grass without being disturbed. If I stayed in this position, I would've fallen asleep. I slowly opened my eyes when I saw the children get closer to me. It looked like they were playing hide and seek. I smiled softly. That's my favorite game.

What? I'm still a kid at heart.

I furrowed my brows a bit when I saw a little girl with a frown on her face. The rest of the kids were in a circle, laughing, while she was standing outside, staring at them.

"Can I please play with you guys?" the girl asked.

All of the kids looked at her and laughed. I frowned at them and slowly got up.

"You want to play with us?" a boy asked. The girl nodded, and the children laughed again.

"We don't play with losers," a girl from the group said. The little girl looked like she was on the verge of tears.

"I'm not a loser," she told them. The same boy walked up to her, and that's when I started walking towards them.

"Yes, you are," he stated.

When I got near, they all looked towards me.

"Why can't she play with you guys?" I asked. The girl looked up at me but then turned her head down.

"Because we don't want her to," a girl said in an annoyed tone.

I furrowed my brows at them. Kids are the meanest creatures on earth. Trust me, I know. Besides, who would've wanted to be friends with them? Don't get me wrong, but they were just rude. I looked at the girl and back at the group.

"If you don't want to, then I'll just play with her," I told them. All the kids looked disgusted before one of the boys spoke.

"Go ahead, but we don't want to play with her. Come on, guys, let's go," he said, and they all turned around and started running off.

I stood there and slowly turned my head to the girl. She was looking down, and I sighed. I got on my knee, and she looked at me.

"Don't listen to them. You're not a loser. Besides, you don't want to be friends with mean people," I told her. She pouted her lip but nodded.

"Then who will I play with?" she asked. I smiled at her and grabbed her hand.

"Me," I told her. She looked at me and tilted her head.

"But you're too big to play," she said. I shook my head at her.

"You're never too big to play," I told her. Her eyes lit up, and she smiled a toothy grin.

"Does that mean when I grow up and become old and wrinkly, I can still play?" she asked. I raised a brow at her and slowly nodded. Her smile grew, and she laughed in excitement.

"What's your name?" I asked her.

Her smile fell, and she looked at me hesitantly, and that only made me furrow my brows slightly in curiosity.

"You want to know my name?" she asked.

"Why wouldn't I?" I asked her, slowly nodding. She shrugged at me and started to play with her fingers.

"Nobody ever wants to know my name," she answered. I frowned and didn't know what to say.

"Well, I do. So what's your name?" I asked her again. She smiled this time and raised her hand towards me.

"I'm Lily. What's your name?"

I took her hand in mine and smiled at her. "My name's Tiana."

"I like your name," she said.

"And I like yours too." My smile grew, and I let go of her hand. "So what were those kids playing?"

She frowned and pouted her lip again. The sight was so cute and sad at the same time. I mean, why would someone not want to play with a girl like her? She's cute and funny. Well, sucks for them.

"Hide and seek," she answered. I stood up as she looked up at me.

"Okay then, let's play that," I told her. She smiled and nodded eagerly.

For about an hour, we played and took turns. It was actually really fun, and it brought back so many memories when I was small. She was so happy and energetic. We soon decided it was enough for the time being and she had to go back to her parents. She ran back towards the pack house but stopped and turned around to wave at me. I smiled at her and waved back until she was out of sight.

I started walking towards the pack house but stopped when I felt someone staring at me. I knew it sounded stupid, but I really felt it. I scanned the area but couldn't find anyone until my eyes landed on the pack house and saw someone on the third floor looking at me from a window. I immediately knew who it was when my wolf started yelping.

Alpha Mason and I made eye contact, and he just stood there watching me. How long was he there? I didn't really know, but after a couple of seconds of just staring at each other, he finally stepped back and closed the curtains. A shiver ran down my spine, and I couldn't get his hard stare out of my mind.

Once I made it to the pack house, I looked at the clock and saw that it was 5 PM. By now, Adam should be done with training, so I decided to see where he was.

"Adam?" I said through the pack link.

After a while, he answered, "Yes? Is there something wrong?"

"No, nothing's wrong. Where are you?" I questioned.

"Why? You miss me already?" he teased. I groaned and rolled my eyes.

"No, I just want to come over so I could slap the living daylights out of you," I told him sarcastically.

"Oh, Tiana! I think that's the sweetest thing you ever said to me," he also said sarcastically. I shook my head and chuckled to myself.

"So?" I asked.

"I'm behind the pack house with a couple of friends," he stated.

"Okay, I'm coming," I told him and cut the connection between us. I walked towards the back door and opened it. There were a couple of people there but not much. I saw Adam with a group of guys and walked up to them. Once I was near them, Adam looked at me and smiled, making all the other guys look in my direction.

Some of them looked at me normally, but others had confusion written on their faces. I ignored them and gave Adam a hug.

"Hey," he said.

"Hi."

A guy from the group went over to Adam and poked his arm with his elbow, making him look at the guy with an eyebrow raised.

"Who's she?" the guy asked and stared at me. Adam put an arm around my shoulder and smiled.

"This is the one and only Tiana," he stated. All of them smiled at me, and I smiled back.

"You're Tiana? Well, no wonder Adam always talks about you," a boy said.

I raised a brow at him, and Adam stiffened next to me and scowled at the guy.

"Alex," he said sternly. Alex looked at Adam and grinned.

"What does he usually say about me?" I asked.

Alex looked over at me, and his grin grew, but he soon looked over at Adam and spoke, "Nothing much, just how you're a good friend."

I had a feeling he wasn't exactly telling the truth but decided not to push on it. "So you guys are pack warriors?" I asked. They smiled at me and nodded.

"Pack warriors in training," one guy said. I nodded, and Adam looked at me.

"Well, we're going to the city to get a few stuff. Would you like to come?" Adam asked. I shook my head at him.

"No, you guys go. I just wanted to say hi. Besides, I'm going to go see where Lina is," I told him. He smiled slightly and nodded.

"Okay, I'll see you later." He waved and walked away with the others.

I decided to go and relax in my room before finding Lina. As soon as I jumped on my bed, a yawn escaped my lips, and as usual, I ended up falling asleep.

* * *

I opened my eyes and groaned when I realized I had just fallen asleep. I looked at the clock and saw it was eight in the evening. I had slept for three hours. I groaned again when I felt my neck was sore. I sat up but my head snapped towards the door when someone opened it. I sighed when Lina came in with a smile.

"Would it kill you to knock?" I asked. She chuckled and shook her head.

"My friends and I decided to let our wolves run for a bit. I want you to come with us," she said.

My wolf started to jump in excitement at the thought of us running in the woods. I smiled slightly and nodded. "Sure, I'd love to come," I told her and got up.

I walked into the bathroom, fixing my hair and splashing water on my face before walking back to Lina. We walked out of my room, talking casually until we were outside. When we were there, I saw the same group I saw weeks ago when we first came here. Ryder saw me, and he gave me a flirtatious smirk. I just rolled my eyes at him.

"Hey, guys, remember Tiana?" Lina asked. All of them offered me a smile and nodded.

"Who could ever forget a pretty face like that?" Ryder questioned.

Lina rolled her eyes at him and punched his arm.

"Ow. What was that for?" he asked and glared at her.

"It's for being immature," she told him. He sighed, and Lina looked at the others. "Come on, guys. Let's go," she said.

We started walking towards the woods as Ryder kept complaining about how Lina was so violent. I silently chuckled and shook my head at him. Once we were deep in the woods, we went behind separate trees and took our clothes off and shifted into our wolves. I came out, and so did the rest. Compared to the rest, I was so small.

"Wow, your wolf is so small," Tyler told me through the pack link.

"I know, it's cute," Ryder said.

Tyler's wolf was brown, and Ryder's wolf was grey. I looked at Lina, and her wolf was silver. We walked further into the woods and started running.

At first, our pace was slow, but after some time, we went really fast. We then decided to split up and run in different directions. I ran through the branches and let the wind pass right through me. This felt so good. My wolf picked up her pace and started running very fast. If a human saw us, they would have just seen a light brown blur pass them.

I slowed my pace until I was in front of a beautiful lake. I didn't know the pack had a lake. I walked up to it and saw my reflection. I lowered my head, drank the water, and sat down next to it. I looked around the place and found it relaxing and quiet. I stayed there for a while, just listening to mother nature until I thought it was about time to go back before someone got worried about me.

I got up but stiffened when I heard a twig break. I snapped my head to the source of the sound but found no one there. I walked closer and stopped when I heard a low growl. I growled back, and whoever growled at me growled again. I sniffed the air to see if I might know this person, then growled again when I realized this wolf was a rogue.

What is a rogue doing in our territory?

I moved closer, and as soon as I did, a grey wolf with red eyes emerged from the trees. The rogue growled at me again but louder this time. I took a step back as soon as he took a step forward. I roared in warning, but that only seemed to set him off because he jumped towards me.

I immediately moved away and growled louder. I wasn't really afraid of him. I could easily use my powers and get out of here without him knowing, but I was caught off guard when he jumped at me again. I moved away and bit his leg. He let out a loud growl and shoved me aside.

I fell to the ground and hit my head on a big rock. I quickly shook my head and got up, but I wasn't quick enough because the wolf jumped on me and bit into my side. I whimpered in pain and was about to bite back when the rogue was thrown off me by another wolf.

I got up but stopped when I smelled a familiar scent. I turned my head towards a huge silver wolf biting into the neck of the rogue.

But this wolf wasn't just any wolf. This wolf was Alpha Mason.

CHAPTER 11

I watched with wide eyes as Alpha Mason bit down into the rogue's neck, violently ripping a huge piece of skin. The moving rogue was a lifeless one in a matter of seconds. My eyes ran over the dead wolf which shifted into its human form, motionless on the ground. I couldn't turn my attention away from the dead body, which was drowning in its own blood. This was the second time I witnessed someone being killed this month. Even though the rogue got what was coming for him, I felt a little sad for him.

I finally turned my attention elsewhere when Alpha Mason's wolf form slowly turned and met eyes with mine. His hard, angry eyes slowly shifted back to normal.

Since we both were in our wolf forms, our wolves took most of the control, and since they were mates, being close with each other was like instinct. I watched as my wolf stepped closer, and so did our mate. Alpha Mason growled lowly and moved in front of us, and his eyes ran over my fur.

He tilted his head slightly and rubbed the side of his head with mine. At the touch, I felt tingles on the side of my head. I tried to move away, but my wolf didn't allow it. I could tell from his eyes that his wolf was doing the same.

But after seconds of silence, his eyes finally went back to normal, and he stepped away immediately, and I knew his wolf wasn't in control anymore. He moved back and growled lowly, which made my wolf whimper.

"*Shift,*" he ordered through the mind link.

I stepped back and ran behind a huge tree to shift. No way in hell was I going to shift in front of him. Who knew what would happen if I did? I shook my head and shifted into my human form. I saw a man's shirt behind a couple of bushes and wore it since I left my clothes back where we started running. It was a usual thing to leave clothes splattered all over the woods because when one needed clothes, then they would find them around the woods.

The shirt fell down and covered what was important, leaving my legs on display. I sighed and walked back to where Alpha Mason was and saw he was in nothing but shorts. My eyes widened, and I couldn't help but run my eyes over his chest and abs. My wolf purred, and I had to shake my head to focus back on his face. His eyes were slightly darker and roamed over my legs for a split-second before looking at me with a hard glare.

Walking closer to me, he growled lowly, "What the hell did you think you're doing?" I furrowed my brows and glared at him.

"What did it look like I was doing? I was running," I told him in a sarcastic tone. His eyes turned darker, and he moved even closer to me.

"Don't you dare speak to me like that. You were running alone in the dark. You could have gotten yourself killed by being reckless," he stated.

I clenched my fist. In moments like these, I sure do wish looks could actually kill.

"I was not being reckless. I was with the others until we decided to split up. I could've taken care of myself and didn't need someone to come to my rescue," I told him. He growled lowly and clenched his jaw.

"I did not come to your rescue. I did what I usually do when there's a trespasser, so if I were you, I would shut that mouth of yours before you make me even angrier than I already am," he yelled.

"Don't tell me what to do. I don't get why you're so mad, but you need to chill and calm down before smoke comes out of your ears," I growled. I had a small smirk on my face, but it soon vanished when I was pushed roughly against a tree by the angry alpha.

> Okay, this might be exaggerated, but smoke was literally coming out of his ears.

"Did you forget who you are talking to? I am your alpha, and I will not tolerate someone speaking to me like that."

I furrowed my brows and clenched my fist. I didn't really care if he's the alpha. He could kiss my ass for all I care. "It's not my fault someone gets angry for every little thing," I muttered.

His eyes turned darker, and he slammed his fist right next to my head, which made my eyes widen in shock. He stepped back, and his glaring eyes never left mine as he muttered some curse words.

"God, you're impossible!" he growled out angrily and ran his hand through his hair roughly before his eyes turned back to normal. "If it weren't for my wolf, you would have been out of my pack in a matter of seconds, but if you talk to me like that one more time, then I will not hesitate to show you your place," he said and moved a step closer to me.

I was about to say something when we heard footsteps coming our way.

We moved away from each other and looked over to where the sounds were coming from. After a couple of seconds, we saw Lina and the others running over to us. Lina had a relieved expression on her face and came up to me, hugging me tightly. I sighed and hugged her back as guards took the dead body.

"Oh my gosh! I was so worried when we couldn't find you," Lina said after pulling away from the hug.

"I'm sorry. I kinda got distracted," I told her.

She gave me a small smile. "It's fine. What matters is that you're okay."

I smiled back at her and looked over to see that Alpha Mason was talking to a guard. Ryder and Tyler came up to me and smiled.

"I guess it was a bad idea to split up, after all," Tyler said and scratched the back of his neck. Ryder nodded and placed an arm around my shoulder.

"Well, I'm thankful you're okay. I don't know what I would have done if my future wife got injured," he said with a small smirk on his face. I rolled my eyes and was about to take his arm off of my shoulder when Alpha Mason growled, his eyes meeting mine.

"Everyone, head back to the pack house."

I looked away as we started walking towards the pack house. All I wanted to do was go back to my room, change out of my shirt, and hit the hay. We made it to the pack house, and thankfully, there weren't many people outside of their rooms to see the state I was in and give me weird glances.

I said goodbye to the others and walked up to my room and saw it was almost nine o'clock. I sighed and changed out of the shirt, threw it away, and wore my pajamas. I knew it was still early, but I was so tired, so I got under the covers and lay down.

I closed my eyes but opened them and groaned when the door opened. Lina came into sight with a pillow in her hand, and she had a huge smile on her lips.

I raised a brow as she walked up to me.

"Mind if I sleep here tonight?" she asked. I smiled and shook my head.

"No." I scooted over, and she laid down next to me.

"You and my brother aren't really getting along, right?" she asked. I sighed and turned my head towards her, shrugging.

After a moment of silence, she broke it.

"When I was small, Mason would do anything to make me happy," she started.

I raised a brow at her in confusion.

"We didn't really live a wonderful childhood, yet, he would do anything to make sure I had one. He went through so many things for me, and that's one of the reasons why I'm grateful for having him as my brother. To others, he's rude, cruel, and heartless, but to me, he's the strongest and bravest person I'll ever know," she said calmly. Lina turned her head towards me and sighed.

"He's not a bad person, Tiana," she whispered. "He's just a person who doesn't know how to express his feelings and needs time to recover from the pain of the past."

I sucked in a breath and didn't know what to say. Whatever happened in the past had scarred them both, and I didn't know if I wanted to know.

I nodded and gave her a small smile. She smiled back and closed her eyes as her breathing evened out, and she fell asleep. I, on the other hand, couldn't fall asleep from what Lina said. I didn't want to think of it much, but her words kept repeating in my mind.

I stared at the ceiling and remembered our conversation a while back. I sighed and ran a hand over my face. I guess I was being rude. Okay, I was rude. He saved me, and all I did was make it worse. I didn't know if I should apologize or not. I groaned and closed my eyes and tried to go to sleep.

After hours of trying, I finally sat up. I glanced at Lina, and she was sleeping with her mouth open and a drool was coming out of her mouth. I chuckled lightly and shook my head. I glanced at the clock and saw it was midnight. I couldn't go to sleep, but maybe a drink of milk would help.

I got up quietly, slowly opened the door, and exited my room.

I walked down the stairs and hoped no one was awake at this hour. I felt like I was doing something illegal, and if someone caught me, I would be in big trouble.

I eventually made my way towards the kitchen but stopped when I saw a tall figure standing next to the fridge. I gulped and thought it might be someone who was just hungry and needed a midnight snack.

I walked and saw that the figure turned his attention to me, and when I got closer, I knew who it was.

Alpha Mason looked at me with emotionless eyes and watched my every single move. I awkwardly walked towards the fridge as his eyes remained on me. Out of all people, it had to be him? I wanted to get a bottle of water, but he was in the way, watching me without saying a single thing.

"Uhh . . . Can you get out of the way?" I whispered.

He raised a brow at me. "Why?" he asked.

I calmed myself down before I could say something that I would regret later. "Because I need to grab something to drink," I answered.

He slowly moved away, and I grabbed a water bottle and closed the door. I moved back as his eyes were on me the entire time. I was about to walk off but decided to turn around.

He stood there with a hard look on his face, and I sighed and said something that I had been wanting to say.

"Thank you . . . for, um, you know, saving me and all that."

His hard look turned into a normal one, and he appeared a little taken aback from what I said. Before he could say anything else, I walked back to my room. I got back in bed, but Lina was occupying most of the space, and I could barely lay down.

I groaned and pushed her a bit, but that made her turn around and push me off the bed. I groaned again and got up from the floor. Well, at least I now knew Lina was a heavy sleeper. I pushed her again, and she said some muffled words about cupcakes and brownies and how good they would be as a couple. I raised a brow at her sleeping state and shook my head.

And I also found out today that she sleep talked and dreamt about food. Hey, I don't blame her.

I sat on my bed and grabbed the bottle of water and drank it. I placed it on the ground and laid down on my bed and closed my eyes. Before I fell asleep, I thought of one thing: someone's brown eyes.

* * *

I moved my head and scratched the bottom of my nose when I felt something tickle it. After a while, it stopped. I sighed and was about to fall back to peaceful sleep when that same feeling came back. I groaned and scratched my nose again. A small chuckle made me open one eye lazily and groan when I saw who it was.

Lina was next to me laughing with a feather in her hand. I rubbed my eyes and opened them, frowning at her.

"What are you doing?" I asked.

She smiled at me and replied, "Waking you up."

I raised a brow at her and sat up.

"You're waking me up with a feather?" I asked. Her smile grew, and she hid the feather behind her back as she made an innocent face.

"Feather? I don't know what you're talking about," she stated trying to hide the smile that had already formed on her face.

I gave her a knowing look, and she burst out in laughter.

"You should have seen your face," she said in between her laughs. I frowned and crossed my arms over my chest.

"What are you talking about?" I questioned.

She eventually stopped laughing and wiped a small tear that fell out of her eye. Her face by now was red, and her eyes were watery. I didn't really see what was so funny.

"You made this funny face when I tickled you with the feather. Oh, my God! I should've taken a picture," she said.

I shook my head and got up. I looked at the time and saw it was ten in the morning. I decided to shower and change. I was about to enter the bathroom when Lina called me.

"Later on today we're going out to the city to have some fun. Dress up nicely," she told me. I raised a brow at her and smiled.

"Will your brother agree this time?" I asked. She rolled her eyes and smiled at me.

"He will, and if he doesn't, then I'll make him agree," she answered.

I nodded and walked into the bathroom. I turned the water on and took my clothes off and hopped into the shower. I sighed when the hot water touched my skin. I closed my eyes and let my imagination take me elsewhere.

I didn't really know why, but I felt like whenever I showered, I thought of the stupidest or greatest things in the world. It's like outside, my brain wouldn't even work, but inside the shower, I was the smartest person in the world. Okay, maybe I exaggerated, but you get my point.

The shower was literally a place to think.

I sighed and washed before wrapping a towel around my body. I opened the door and was thankful when no one was in my room. I opened my closet and started picking out clothes to wear.

I snapped my head over to the direction of the door when I heard someone coming in my room. I didn't think much about it because I thought Lina came back but knew I was wrong when Adam came into view.

I held the towel tight in my hands and saw Adam standing there shocked. He soon blushed and looked away.

"Uh . . . Sorry, Tiana. I just wanted to check up on you," he stated. I nodded even though he couldn't see.

"It's okay," I told him. It wasn't really a big deal to me. If it had been someone else, then I would have turned red until I looked like a tomato, but Adam and I had known each other since we were kids, so we had seen each other naked before when we shifted.

"I'll be going," he said awkwardly as he moved towards the door.

"Okay."

He walked outside and shut the door behind him. I shrugged it off and brought my attention back to the closet. I eventually wore a summer dress and let my hair fall down and dried it. I slipped on some heels that weren't that tall and walked out of my room.

I met with Lina in her room, and we talked for a bit. We decided to go down to the dining room to grab some breakfast. On our way there, I noticed there were lots of people walking around the pack house. Once we made it to the dining room, we saw Tyler.

He smiled at us and waved. We waved back and walked up to him. He was telling us something about training when the doors opened, and you-know-who walked in. I tried to keep my eyes off him but couldn't help myself. He soon caught me looking at him, but I immediately turned away.

I heard the doors open again, and a group of teenage boys walked in with smug looks. I frowned at them and noticed I had never seen them before. The one that was in the front made eye contact with me and smirked. I turned around and looked at Lina and Tyler.

As they talked, I heard steps coming near us. I didn't really pay much attention to it, but soon that same guy I didn't know came closer to us. I didn't look at him and pretended I was engaged with whatever Lina and Tyler were saying until I heard him speak.

"Hey there," he said, placing his arm around my shoulder.

CHAPTER 12

I snapped my head towards him, surprised.
Who is he, and why is he touching me?
Tyler and Lina looked at the boy standing behind me, who seemed like he was my age or older. With the smug look on his face, he obviously found my state amusing.
Does this guy go to every girl and hit on them?
I glared at him, and thankfully, we didn't catch many people's attention.

I pulled away and was about to ask him who he was and why he was being this close with me when an angry alpha came stalking towards us with a dangerous glint in his eyes. He growled loud enough for people to hear, which made them exit the dining room as soon as possible. No one wanted to be in the same room with an angry alpha.

He walked up to us and grabbed him by his shirt, glaring at him with dark eyes. I kind of felt bad for the boy as his eyes widened in horror and he gulped in fear.

No, I take that back. He deserved it.

"Don't you dare touch someone you don't know without consent or I will do something you don't like," Alpha Mason said in a dangerous tone as he glanced at me.

I felt my cheeks redden.

"And I don't want to see you near her ever again. Do I make myself clear?" he asked. The boy immediately nodded, and

Alpha Mason roughly threw him to the ground and glared at him. His eyes were pitch-black, indicating that his wolf wanted control.

He stepped back and glanced at me one more time before walking out of the room.

I stood there trying to process what just happened. I looked at the boy as he got off the floor and sighed in relief when his alpha left.

I rolled my eyes in annoyance and stepped away from him.

Tyler stood closer to him, glaring. "You heard what the alpha said, Kyle," Tyler growled at him.

Kyle furrowed his eyebrows and returned his glare. "I don't really care what he said!"

Lina stepped forward and crossed her arms over her chest. "Oh, really? Because when he was here, it looked like you were about to piss your pants," she said with a smirk. Kyle growled again and stepped forward, but Tyler immediately got up to his face.

"Don't try to mess with Tiana again, Kyle, or with any of our friends. If you do, I won't hesitate to tell the alpha," Tyler threatened him.

Kyle smirked and turned his stare towards me. "Tiana? Nice name," he said as he backed away. "We'll be seeing each other more often." And with that, he walked off.

Tyler growled again, and Lina glared at the door. I looked at them and raised a brow. Judging from what happened, I could tell they didn't really like him. Neither did I.

"Who's he?" I asked.

Lina scowled and faked a gag. Tyler sighed and ran a hand over his face.

"His name is Kyle, and he's the male version of Chloe," Lina replied. I slowly nodded at that.

"In other words, he's a man whore," Tyler said. "He literally hooked up with most of the sluts in this pack, and it's kind of a goal for him to sleep with every girl."

I furrowed my eyebrows in disgust. Was I the only one who found these kinds of men unattractive? Because lots of girls think they were and they weren't.

"Be careful of him, Tiana. He's not good news," Lina said.

I nodded at her. No way was I going to go near him. He was everything I hated in one person. Okay, I exaggerated again but still ain't going near him.

They smiled at me, and we soon sat down at the table and ate breakfast. We talked for a while until Tyler got up to head to training. We washed up and left the dining room.

"Let's head towards the field so I can see the rest of my friends and ask Mason since he's the one training them today," she said.

I nodded and ignored my wolf purring at the sound of his name. We walked outside of the pack house and towards the field where everyone trained.

Some people looked our way but eventually focused on their training. I saw Alpha Mason from a distance, and he immediately turned his head towards us and made eye contact with me. I looked away and placed my attention anywhere else but him.

We walked towards the benches and stopped as Lina faced me.

"Okay, you sit here. I'll go talk to him. Let's just hope he's not in a grumpy mood or we'll have to sneak out again," she said with a smirk. I chuckled at her and shook my head.

"Let's hope," I said.

She smiled at me and walked towards him. I let my eyes roam the field and found Adam looking at me with a grin. He waved at me, and I waved back as he went back to training. I was watching him train when someone sat next to me on the bench.

I turned my head and found Ryder sitting next to me with a smirk on his face. I rolled my eyes at him.

"So, did you change your mind about the date?" he asked.

I shook my head at him and smiled. "No, I didn't," I answered.

He sighed but smiled a bit.

"Come on, you're the only girl who ever rejected me. Do you know how much that hurts my ego?" he asked. I chuckled at him and shook my head again.

"Well, someone has to show you your place," I told him. He crossed his arms over his chest and pouted teasingly with amusement in his eyes.

"Oh, really? Where's my place then?" he asked. I placed my finger under my chin and pretended to think.

"Under a rock," I joked. He faked a gasp and shook his head.

"You truly are something," he muttered but then looked at me with a smile. "And that's what I like."

I rolled my eyes at him and chuckled. I focused back on Lina and her brother as they were talking. Alpha Mason had a frown on his face as he glanced at me but turned his attention to his sister.

Lina had her hand on her hip and was poking her finger on his chest. It looked like she was giving him a lecture. I raised my brow at them in curiosity. It was an unusual sight to see an alpha getting lectured by someone else. At least that was what it looked like.

After a while of Ryder teasing and joking around, Lina finally came back with a smile on her face.

"We're going to the city," she said. I smiled at her and got up.

"That's great. Are we going now?" I asked.

She nodded and looked at Ryder as he got up.

"Can I come with you guys?" he asked. Lina shook her head no.

"No, unless you want to go shopping with us," she said. Ryder immediately shook his head and chuckled.

"No, I don't. Have fun you two," he said as he walked away.

We were heading back to the pack house to pick up a few stuff Lina needed when she stopped and smiled.

"This time, we're going in a car," she said. I tilted my head at her and nodded.

"Okay, but how come we didn't go in a car the other time?" I asked.

"Because the car belongs to Mason, and if he had noticed it was gone, he would have known we were gone too," she answered.

I smiled and nodded again. We walked outside, and there was a nice car in front of the pack house.

"Do you know how to drive?" I asked..

"Yes, I do," she replied.

We entered the car, and Lina drove off. After a couple minutes, I was holding onto my seatbelt for my dear life. Lina was one of the worst drivers I have ever seen. Who the hell gave her a driver's license?

"Lina, can you like, I don't know, slow down?" I asked.

She smirked at me and drove faster. I prayed that today wouldn't be the day I died because I still had lots of things to experience.

"If I die today, it's because of you," I told her. She chuckled and shook her head.

"Calm down, Tiana. I'm a perfect driver," she stated. I scoffed at her and shook my head.

"Yeah, so perfect you almost crashed into a freakin wall," I told her sarcastically. She rolled her eyes at me.

"Well, you're lucky that we made it." She parked in front of the mall. Well, that was fast. I sighed in relief and was literally going to fall to the ground and kiss the floor.

We got out of the car and walked into the mall.

"So, what are we going to do?" I asked. She turned to me and smiled.

"We'll walk around, buy some stuff, and eat lunch," she replied.

We walked through shops and before we were even there for five minutes, Lina stopped and smiled.

"Let's go in there. It looks like it has cute dresses," she said.

We checked out many clothes. Lina grabbed a couple of dresses and gave them to me. I raised a brow at her, and she pushed me towards the fitting room.

"Try some of these," she said.

"Why?" I asked her.

She didn't say anything and just rolled her eyes and pushed me into the fitting room. She closed the door, and I had three dresses in my hands. I sighed and took off my clothes and wore the first dress. I looked at the mirror and cringed at what I was wearing. I was wearing a red short dress that just made me look slutty.

"You dressed?" Lina asked from outside.

"Yeah, but I'd rather not show you," I told her.

"Just open the door," she demanded. I rolled my eyes and opened the door.

Lina cringed as well and shook her head.

I closed the door and dressed into another one. This dress wasn't as bad as the other dress, but it showed a lot of cleavage, and no way in hell was I going to wear that.

"So? How's the other dress?" she asked. I opened the door and let the dress do the talking. She shook her head again. I closed the door, then tried the last one. It was white and a little tight on the upper part of my body but hung loose below my hips. It landed right above my knees, and I smiled in approval.

I opened the door, and Lina's eyes widened, lips growing into a huge smile.

"Come on. Let's pay for that," she said. I raised my brow at her and grabbed my clothes.

"Wait, let me change first," I told her. She smiled and shook her head.

"No, you're staying in that," she stated. She pulled me out of the fitting room. We paid for the dress, then ripped the tag off. We got out of the store and placed my other clothes in a bag. I shrugged it off and continued to walk next to Lina.

We went from store to store, buying a couple of stuff. I didn't buy much, but Lina bought a lot, which I doubt would even fit in her closet.

After a couple of hours, I was tired. How could people do this all day? Lina and I decided it was time to eat lunch, so we ordered at the food section and sat down. We talked for a bit until Lina stood up and got our food. When it placed in front of me, I was literally drooling. I ate, and I bet from afar, I looked like a fat pig drowning itself in food. Yeah, I know. Sad.

After we were done, we just stayed there and talked. Half an hour later, Lina looked at me and smiled.

"I know an ice cream shop near here. You want to go?" she asked. I smiled but raised a brow.

"But we just ate," I told her.

"Fine, if you don't want to go then we won't," she stated, shrugging.

"I never said I didn't want to go, girl. Come on," I told her as I got up.

She chuckled, and we walked out of the mall. We got in the car, and thankfully, the ice cream shop wasn't far away or I would have passed out in the car from fear of Lina crashing us into a tree.

We entered the shop, and my eyes lit up. This place is a little kid's dreamland. My dreamland! It had everything you could call candy or sugar. The lady at the ice cream section was smiling at us.

"Hello, how may I help you?" she asked.

"We would like to get some ice cream. I want the strawberry one. What do you want?" Lina asked me.

"Chocolate," I told her.

The lady gave us our ice creams. We went and sat at a table and ate our food.

> Now, I know what you guys are thinking. How could we eat ice cream when we just ate lunch? Well, let me tell you, if I could eat this entire shop, then I would. Nobody could ever separate me from my food. Period.

Lina was saying some joke when she froze, and her mouth hung open. She was staring at the entrance with a shocked expression. I furrowed my brows in confusion and looked back to see a man walking into the shop. I looked at Lina, and she placed her finger over her mouth. She slowly got up and pulled my hand.

As the man went up to the counter, Lina and I walked towards the exit, so his back was facing us. I threw Lina a questioning look, but she gave me a look saying she would tell me later. We were about to leave when the same guy turned around, and his eyes widened.

"Lina?" he asked.

Lina's eyes widened, then she pulled me and walked fast to her car. I got on. The guy ran after us, but before he could catch up, Lina drove off. I stared at her in confusion, but she just sighed.

"Who was that?" I asked.

She didn't answer. After a while, she parked the car and got off, opening my door. I gave her a confused look, but she just asked me to get out of the car. I then noticed we were in front of a bar.

"What are we doing here?" I asked.

"We did say we're going to have fun," she said as she walked toward the door. We entered the bar, and there weren't many people in here since it was daytime. We sat on stools and Lina ordered drinks.

"Who was that guy?" I asked again.

She looked at me and shrugged.

"He was a guy I used to date," she said. "He was too possessive of me, so I ended it with him. I knew one day, I'd find my mate."

"You dated a human before?" I asked and she nodded.

"I really didn't want to face him again."

I nodded in understanding. She shook her head and sighed but soon smiled.

"Let's forget about that. We came to have some fun." She grabbed her drink. I smiled as I grabbed mine too.

We drank them and started talking about other stuff. Some guys tried to hit on us, but we didn't give them the satisfaction. We were laughing at a joke when Alpha Mason spoke through the mind link.

"Lina, Tiana, where are you guys?" he growled.

My eyes widened when he said my name. That was actually the first time he ever said that. Lina's eyes widened too.

"Why?" she asked.

"Tell me now!" he roared.

"We're at . . . a bar," she said hesitantly.

"Dammit, Lina! I told you to not go there!" he said, furious.

"What's wrong, Mason?"

He growled lowly and spoke, *"There are rogues around the city!"*

CHAPTER 13

Lina and I stood up, and we looked around for any signs of rogues. There weren't any, so we went straight out of the bar.

"Let's get out of here," Lina said as we ran toward the car.

We were so close when a man with red eyes jumped in front of us, causing a gasp to come out of my mouth. Our eyes widened as the rogue slowly walked up to us and growled loudly. We turned around but stopped when more men started surrounding us. I grabbed Lina's hand and gave it a squeeze. She looked at me, and I nodded.

I closed my eyes and concentrated on my powers. When I opened them, we were up in the air and invisible. Since I was combining my powers together, I knew it wouldn't last long, so I flew us as far away as possible before my powers faded away.

All this time, Lina had a huge smile on her face, but she didn't say anything. I slowly landed us on the ground, and my powers wore off. I heard growls from afar, but lucky for us, we weren't close. We were about to run into the woods when a car stopped right in front of us.

The front door opened to reveal the beta, whose name I still didn't know, with a serious expression on his face.

"Come in fast," he ordered.

Lina jumped in the car and sat next to him while I sat behind them. He pressed on the gas pedal and drove off as fast as he could. When we were out of the city, he slowed down a bit and sighed.

"What the hell were you thinking?" he asked Lina. She lowered her head and pouted her lips.

"We just wanted to have some fun," she claimed.

The beta furrowed his brows and glanced at her before placing his attention back on the road.

"The alpha specifically told you not to go to that part of the city," he growled lowly.

"I know. I'm sorry."

I frowned and patted her shoulders. "It's not only her fault. We went there together," I told him.

He glanced at me from the mirror and frowned but didn't say anything. We had been driving for a while. Then I noticed he kept glancing at me, so I raised a brow at him.

"I'm sorry," he said.

"Sorry for what?" I asked.

"I'm sorry for treating you badly. We didn't know you're the luna," he stated.

My eyes widened, and so did Lina's.

"What? I'm not your—"

"You're the alpha's mate, so that means you're our future luna. I shouldn't have treated you that way. I'm sorry," he cut me off.

I sighed and smiled softly. "It's okay, but how did you know?" I asked. He smirked and shook his head.

"Wasn't that hard to notice. Besides, I've known him since we were small, so I know how he reacts to the people he hates and loves."

I slowly nodded, wanting to change the subject. I didn't know which category I fit in, but I didn't really want to know.

"What's your name?" I asked.

He smiled at me and replied, "The name's Nick."

I smiled back at him as we entered our pack. "I would tell you my name too, but you already know it," I said.

He chuckled and nodded. He stopped the car when Alpha Mason and his guards showed up. Alpha Mason looked angry, really angry. He stalked towards us as we got off.

"Why did you disobey my orders?" he asked Lina.

Lina lowered her head and didn't answer. I frowned and walked up to him.

"It wasn't only her fault," I said.

He looked at me, and his eyes grew dark. He shook his head and stepped back.

"You two head back to the pack house and stay there while we deal with the rogues," he told us. We nodded and walked off but stopped when he called us.

"And don't do anything stupid," he said, but his attention was on me.

I scoffed and turned around, stalking off. Since when did I do something stupid? I shook my head, and we entered the pack house. We got lots of stares, but I shrugged it off and went up to my room. Once I opened the door, I was met with a worried-looking Adam. I raised my brow and was about to ask why he was here when he engulfed me in a huge hug.

"God, Tiana! Don't ever do that again," he said. I sighed and hugged him back.

"I'm sorry," I told him. He pulled away and gave me a small smile.

"It's okay. I was just worried about you," he told me. I smiled at him and sat on a chair.

"You know I can take care of myself," I said. He smirked but pinched my cheeks.

"I know, but that doesn't mean I can't worry about you," he cooed. I rolled my eyes at him and shook my head.

"Seriously, Adam?" I muttered. He chuckled and patted my head. I rolled my eyes again and punched him lightly in the arm.

"I'm not a dog," I said in amusement, and he raised a brow, placing his point finger under his chin.

"Really? Because all this time I thought you were one," he teased. I growled lightly, and he stepped back as I stood up.

"Easy there, pup," he said with a hint of amusement laced in his voice, and that was when I jumped on him, and he shrieked like a ten-year-old girl who was running for her life. He laughed and easily pushed me off, but I constantly slapped his chest that didn't affect him at all.

"I am not a pup," I said. He nodded but continued to laugh. I huffed and sat back down on the chair.

"You are one violent woman," he said. I rolled my eyes and ignored him as I looked out the window. He poked my arm, but I didn't say anything.

"Aww, is Tiana giving me the silent treatment?" he asked.

I didn't answer and continued looking at the distance like it was the most important thing ever. He poked my arm again, but I didn't react to him.

"You know I can't go a minute without you talking to me," he said. "Come on, I know you love me," he stated.

I looked at him and scrunched my nose, sticking my tongue at him. He chuckled and engulfed me in a hug as I rolled my eyes.

"I don't love you," I muttered. He faked a gasp and pretended to be hurt. "And all along I thought we had something," he said.

I chuckled lightly which only made him grin. He pulled away and looked at the time and smiled.

"Well, I need to head back to training. I just wanted to make sure you were okay. I'll see you later," he said as he walked out of my room.

I looked out the window again and saw Lily playing with a woman who I assumed is her mom. She caught my stare and smiled and waved at me. I smiled back and waved at her. She continued to play as I backed away from the window and decided to get out of my room.

I then saw Chloe and her minions approaching me. I ignored them and started walking away from them, but an arm stopped me dead in my tracks.

"You should have died and never came back," Chloe sneered. I yanked my arm out of her grasp and smiled at her.

"Aww, Chloe, I think that's the nicest thing you ever said to me," I said sarcastically. She growled and stepped closer.

"You stupid b*tch," she hissed and was about to hit me but stopped when Lina growled loudly and stepped in front of me.

"Do one more thing, and I'll report it to my brother," she said.

I smiled at her, and they backed away, looking clearly annoyed. Lina growled again, and they walked off with their imaginary tails between their legs.

Lina turned her head towards me and smiled.

"You okay?" she asked and I smiled back at her.

"Yeah, thanks."

"I want to apologize for what happened today," she said softly. I frowned and placed my hand on her shoulder.

"Lina, I'll say this again. It was not your fault. We went in there together, remember?" I asked.

"Yeah."

"Good," I said.

We walked downstairs and into the kitchen, and saw Anna doing the dishes.

"Hey there, young ladies," Anna greeted us, smiling.

"Hi," I told her. "Do you need any help with anything?" She nodded as she pulled out some vegetables.

"I actually need someone to make salad while I prepare some other stuff," she answered. I walked up to her and grabbed a knife.

"I'll make the salad. Lina, you help her out with something else," I said as I started to cut the vegetables.

We talked as we helped Anna out. I eventually finished the salad and told them I was going to the bathroom. As I walked out of the kitchen, I met Nick.

"Hey, what happened?" I asked. He sighed and gave me a small smile.

"We were able to catch all of them without humans seeing us. We killed most of them, but some are in the dungeon being tortured for answers," he replied.

I nodded and ran my hand through my hair. Well, that was good news.

"Where is—" I wasn't able to continue because he cut me off.

"Mason?" he asked with a smirk. "He's in the cellars interrogating them."

"Well, that's nice to hear. I need to go and wash up. I'll see you later."

He nodded his head and smiled at me. "Okay, take care."

With that, I walked off towards the bathroom feeling relieved.

* * *

I yawned and opened my eyes. I sat up and looked at the clock. It was eleven in the morning. It had been a day since the incident, and Lina told me to meet her today for some reason. I went towards the bathroom and washed my face and brushed my teeth.

I just felt lazy today, so I decided to wear a plain white shirt and shorts, and tied my hair in a bun. I walked out of the room and into Lina's. She looked at me and smiled.

"Perfect! How did you know we were training today?" she asked as she looked at my clothes. I raised a brow at her and tilted my head in confusion.

"Training?" I asked.

"Yeah, my brother wants us to train, so if something like that happens again, we are ready," she answered, grinning.

I nodded at her, and she walked towards the door.

"Come on, let's go. Today's training starts early."

We walked towards the field, earning stares and glares from the girls along the way, which was normal by now. There weren't many of them, but the ones who were there were big.

I saw Adam and he smiled at me, but he looked confused. I shrugged and brought my attention to Alpha Mason as he walked towards us. He glanced at me but looked away and started to speak.

"Today we're going to do something different, but first, I want all of you to run ten laps," he said as I tried to hold back my wolf who literally wanted to pounce at him.

We all walked towards the line, and when he counted to three, we started running. Ten laps wasn't much for a werewolf, so it was pretty easy. While I was running, I felt someone's eyes on me, but I immediately knew who it was. I didn't look back and continued to run.

I got a couple of wolf whistles from men. I assumed they were looking at my butt, but I rolled my eyes and ignored them. Once we were done, Alpha Mason came up and spoke.

"Everybody head towards the woods."

I furrowed my brows in confusion. *Why the woods?*

We walked until we were deep in the woods.

"You're going to team up with a partner today. You have to work together and make it out of the woods within twenty minutes. If something happens, howl and help will be on its way. However, the purpose of this is to work as a team and help each other in times like this," he said.

Everyone nodded and started picking their partners. Adam came up to me and placed an arm over my shoulder.

"Want to be my partner?" he asked.

I smiled and nodded, but we were caught off guard when we heard a loud growl. We turned our heads towards the source and found Alpha Mason walking towards us. Adam's grip on my shoulder tightened as he glared at him.

But what shocked me the most was what he said.

"She's not going to be your partner because she's my partner."

CHAPTER 14

"What?" Adam and I asked together.

Alpha Mason stepped closer and growled again.

"You heard me, pup," he said, emphasizing the word *pup*. Adam growled at him, which made him growl even louder this time.

"She's with me," Adam said.

I looked at him as Alpha Mason stepped closer. Did he have a death wish? I might think Adam was a pain in the butt and immature, but I didn't want him injured.

"Adam, it's okay. I'll just go with him." I gave him a knowing look, which meant if he disagreed, I would haunt his dreams and smack the living daylight out of him.

He huffed and furrowed his brows in anger but nodded. "Be careful," he said.

"Don't worry. I can take care of myself," I told him.

He chuckled but frowned when Alpha Mason told me to get ready.

To be honest, I didn't know why he wanted to partner up with me, but I shrugged it off and decided not to think about it. He glanced at me but immediately turned around and faced the others.

"Okay. On the count of three, we start," he said.

Everyone, including myself, nodded. He came up to me and stood by my side, and our hands brushed against each other, which made tingles erupt. I tried as much as possible to ignore my wolf begging me to kiss him. I shook my head and focused my attention towards the woods.

Once he said three, we started running. We went in a different direction as everyone else went another way. We soon stopped and faced each other.

"We'll shift, then continue," he said.

I nodded, went behind a tree, and took my clothes off. I shifted into my wolf and walked back to where we were. I was met with the same silver wolf I saw a couple of times. Once his eyes landed on me, they turned a darker shade, but he looked away and spoke through the mind link.

"*Let's start moving.*"

I held back my wolf and nodded. We started running, and a couple of times, his fur brushed against my fur, which made my wolf want to take control. I could tell his wolf was doing the same because of the constant change of colors in his eyes.

After a while, we decided to stop and drink water from a river. As he was drinking, I finally decided to ask why he picked me for a partner. I mean, it didn't look like he actually liked me or something. My wolf scoffed at that, and I shrugged at her. I didn't really care if he didn't. I shook my head and spoke.

"*Why did you partner up with me?*" I asked through the mind link. He lifted his head and stared at me but didn't say anything.

"*Because,*" he replied after a while. I mentally rolled my eyes at him.

"*Because why?*" I asked again. He growled lowly and stepped closer to me.

"*I don't really need to give you an explanation,*" he said. I huffed which made him step closer to me.

"*All I'm asking is one simple question. Is your ego that big for you not to answer a simple question?*" I asked. He was literally getting on my nerves.

He growled loudly. "*Don't forget who you're talking to.*"

I growled and stepped closer to him. Okay, I knew I shouldn't be fighting with him, but he had a brain that's harder than a rock.

"*You're going to pull that alpha card on me again?*" I asked.

"*You need to know your place,*" he growled out.

"*My place? Well, did you forget I'm your—*" I didn't get to finish when he growled again.

"*My what? My mate?*" he asked. "*Don't forget I don't want one, not now and never will.*"

My wolf whimpered, and I instantly felt something in me hurting, which I did not want to feel at all. I shook off that feeling and told myself I didn't want one too.

"*Why don't you reject me then?*" I asked as my wolf growled at me. His eyes widened and turned a shade darker. "*Since we both know we won't be good for each other,*" I stated.

He growled loudly but snapped his head over when we heard growls coming our way. He sniffed the air and growled. He turned to me and stepped closer.

"*Rogues.*"

My eyes widened. What's the deal with constantly being attacked by rogues? Did we have some sort of sign in front of the pack that says, "Welcome, Rogues"?

"*There's three of them,*" he growled as we started to run away from them.

"*I can take them on. You go,*" he said. I shook my head at him.

"*No, we can take them on together,*" I stated.

"*Will you not be stubborn for once and listen to what I say?*" he growled.

I slowly nodded as three wolves came at us from behind. He stopped running and fought the wolves. I had the urge to help but knew he could take care of himself.

I ran off but noticed one of the rogues behind me. I ran faster, and so did the rogue. I eventually stopped and faced it, growling at him. He growled back and walked up to me. He jumped at me, but I moved away and bit into his neck.

He growled again and pushed me off him. He bit into my leg, but I used my other leg to hit him in his face as hard as I could. I got up and bit into his neck again, but this time, I ripped a chunk of skin. He growled in pain, and I bit deeper. After a while of struggling, he finally became motionless.

I stepped away from the dead body and sighed in relief when I saw Alpha Mason running towards me. He stopped and looked at the rogue that was now in human form, drowning in its own blood. He brought his attention back to me and spoke through the mind link.

"*I took care of the other rogues,*" he stated. I nodded at him. "*I'm going to need more guards at the borders,*" he sent to everybody.

I went behind a tree and shifted. I grabbed a random long shirt and wore it. I walked out and saw Alpha Mason in shorts. He stared at me intensely. I pulled the shirt down so it would hide as much skin as possible and walked up to him.

Now, this was where my clumsy side kicked in because out of nowhere, I accidentally tripped. I was directly in front of Alpha Mason, so I fell on him.

I know, cliché.

He stumbled back a few steps but held my hips tightly. I slowly raised my head up and made eye contact with him, and let me tell you, our faces were so close. My eyes widened as his eyes turned darker.

His eyes flickered down to my lips, and I stood there speechless. Somehow, our heads got even closer, but we immediately pulled apart when we heard someone running towards us. Our heads snapped towards the source of the sound, and Nick and a couple of guards came into view.

"Alpha, Tiana, are you okay?" Nick asked. We nodded, and the guards took the bodies away.

"I want you to double the guards at the borders. I don't know why, but we keep having rogue attacks, and we don't want that," he said.

Nick nodded as he went and talked to the guards. Alpha Mason looked at me, and we stared at each other for a while, until he turned his back.

"Let's head back," he said. He then turned to Nick and told him, "You deal with the other pack warriors."

We returned in silence, and when we were in front of the pack house, he looked at me.

"Don't ever bring up the subject of rejection because that's never happening," he said and walked away.

I stood there with wide eyes and mouth hanging open. A fly could have just flown in it. Did I hear right? I didn't know what to feel. He told me he didn't want a mate, yet he didn't want to reject me?

I shook my head. He was indeed confusing, but I couldn't deny the feeling of relief that washed over me. I quickly shrugged it off and walked inside the pack house and into my room. Sighing, I laid on my bed and stared at the ceiling for a while. I just found it the most interesting thing at the moment.

Like how the white color was so bright or how the platform was smooth even though I couldn't really touch it. I knew I was having crazy talk, but it's what I did best.

I turned my head when the door slammed open and sat up as Lina and Adam came running towards me with relieved faces.

"What did I say about scaring me like that?" Adam asked and crossed his arms over his chest as Lina sat next to me. I smiled sheepishly at him as he looked down at me.

"I'm sorry. It wasn't like I was holding a huge magnet that pulled rogues towards me," I told him. He sighed and sat next to me.

"You're going to be the death of me," he muttered, which only made Lina and I chuckle.

We talked for a bit, and I had to listen to Adam talking about how he still couldn't get the hang of the showers here and how he's always struggling. I rolled my eyes at him and got up when I heard a knock at my door.

Wow, I thought this was the first time in a long time someone knocked on my door. I bet whoever was behind it was a gentleman, unlike some people.

But once I opened the door, I immediately took back what I just thought. There stood Ryder in all his glory. Once he saw me, he had a huge smile and engulfed me in a tight hug.

"Oh, thank goodness. I don't know what I would have done if my girlfriend got injured," he stated. I rolled my eyes and pulled away.

"Don't worry, I can take care of myself. And call me your girlfriend one more time, and you'll wake up with a tube down your throat," I told him as if I was asking him about the weather today. He chuckled but nodded.

He entered my room and sat on a chair. I noticed Adam was glaring at him. I raised a brow and sat next to him, giving him a questioning look.

"What is he doing here?" Adam whispered. I frowned at him and shrugged.

"The same reason why you and Lina are here," I told him.

He grumbled and continued to glare at him. I paid no attention to that and faced Lina. She was too busy talking to Ryder and discussing a dream she had last night. How interesting.

After a couple of hours, they left my room, and when my stomach growled, I decided to get something to eat. I walked out of my room and was about to head downstairs when I saw a maid coming my way, holding so many bed sheets. I walked up to her and smiled.

"Do you need any help?" I asked her and she smiled gratefully at me.

"Oh yes, please." She gave me a bed sheet. "Can you please take this to the alpha's room?" she asked. My eyes widened in hesitance, but her grateful smile made me nod.

"Sure, where is his room?" I asked. I just hoped I wouldn't bump into him.

"Go upstairs and walk till you're at the end of the hall. His room is to your left," she replied.

I smiled at her and nodded. I walked up the stairs and looked down the hall. This was the first time I had been here ever since we came last month.

I hesitantly walked down the hall until I was at the end. I looked to my left and saw a room. I then softly knocked. No answer. I sighed in relief and slowly opened the door. I was greeted by a plain white room with black curtains that were closed. I stepped inside but stopped in shock when I looked at the bed.

There on the bed was a sleeping man, and I knew who it was. Obviously, it was his room. Alpha Mason was sleeping on his back with his left arm over his eyes. I slowly walked further to place the bed sheet on the chair without waking him up.

This is what I get for being nice.

I placed the bed sheet on the chair and walked towards the door. I stopped and glanced back and scanned my eyes over his body. He was breathing evenly, and he looked so relaxed and so calm, never like when he's awake. I turned back and slowly walked up to him. I didn't know why, but I felt like something was pulling me towards him.

Once I was next to the bed, I could get a better look at his face. I examined it, and even though I didn't like the thought, I couldn't deny that he was handsome. I raised my hand, wanting to brush his hair. It looked so soft, and I just had to feel it.

I placed my fingers right above his hair and softly touched it, but as soon as I did that, his eyes snapped open and he grabbed my hand roughly. His eyes were dark but wide in shock, and the only thing I could think of was one thing.

Oh shit.

CHAPTER 15

I pulled my hand out from his grasp and backed away. His eyes turned a shade darker as he sat up.

"What are you doing here?" he asked roughly. I backed away some more and played with my fingers.

"I came here to give you the sheets for your bed," I replied. All I wanted to do at the moment was dig a deep hole in the ground and jump in it and never come out. His stare turned over to the sheets, then back at me. He got up and walked towards me, which only made me back away some more.

He stood in front of me, looking at me with hard eyes. Silence filled the room, and all that was happening was some kind of staring contest. That was what it looked like to me. He stepped forward as I stepped backward.

This is what happens when I'm nice. I get into trouble and don't know how to get out of it.

He continued to stare, and I didn't want to say something so he wouldn't get angry or ask why I was touching his hair because I didn't even know the answer myself. His eyes turned darker, and he turned his face to look somewhere else as he spoke.

"Get out."

I was taken aback and raised a brow.

"What?" I asked. He looked over at me and growled lowly.

"I said get out," he stated.

I nodded and walked towards the door. I grabbed the handle but looked back to find him watching me intensely. I snapped my head back to the door and opened it, walking out as fast as I could. I returned to my room and jumped on my bed.

I repeatedly hit my head on my pillow and screamed against it. I kept muttering how stupid I was because that somehow solved the problem.

I breathed in and sighed, slowly closing my eyes. My breathing evened out as I fell into a deep sleep.

* * *

I was placing my toys on the ground when I heard my mom call. I got up, opened my bedroom door, and ran down to the living room. I saw my mom and my dad sitting next to each other, with Adam beside them. I walked up and smiled at Adam.

"Yes, Mommy?" I asked. My mother smiled at me and kissed my cheek.

"Adam's parents are out on a vacation, so he will be sleeping in your room until they come back," my mom said.

I looked at Adam, and he was grinning at me. I nodded and looked at my mother.

"Good. Now you two go on and play," my mom said.

Adam and I ran up to my room and sat on the ground where the toys were at.

"Wow, you got new toys?" Adam asked with a huge smile on his face.

"Yeah. Mommy bought me new toys last week, and what I like the most is the toy truck she bought me," I said as I showed him the truck. His smile grew, and he scooted closer to me.

"You know why I like you? Because you're not like the other girls. You prefer cars and trucks and not Barbies." He gagged slightly when he said Barbies.

"I don't like Barbies," I said.

He nodded and looked at the truck I was holding.

"Give me that. I want to play with it," he said. I frowned and shook my head.

"No, I want to play with it. Play with something else," I told him.

"But I want to play with that." He pointed at the truck and I shook my head at him again. "Come on, Tiana. Share," he whined. I hugged the truck and shook my head for the third time.

"No, I don't want to share the truck." I pouted. He sighed and scooted closer to me.

"But you have to share with your mate," he said. I raised a brow at him in confusion.

"You mean a friend?" I asked. He smiled and shook his head.

"You don't know what a mate is?" he asked. I nodded at him.

"I do. It means friend," I replied. He shook his head again and smiled.

"No, a mate means someone you love and live together with for the rest of your life," he said. I thought about it, then nodded.

"You mean like a mommy and a daddy?" I asked. He smiled and nodded.

"How do you know this?" I asked.

"My mommy told me," he answered.

"So your mommy and daddy are mates?" I asked and he nodded.

"Do you want to be my mate? Because I want to be yours," Adam asked. I frowned and got up from the ground.

"Let me ask Mommy first," I said as I opened the door and ran downstairs with Adam behind me. I accidentally bumped into someone and looked up to see the alpha. He smiled at me and patted my head.

"Easy there," he said.

"Sorry, Alpha," I said with a smile.

"It's okay, kiddo. Just be careful where you run," he said.

I nodded and ran to where my mom was. I saw her in the kitchen, helping the cook with something. She looked down at me and smiled.

"Mommy?" I asked.

"Yes, sweetheart?" She kneeled down.

"*Adam asked me to be his mate. Could I be his mate?*" *I asked. My mom chuckled and pinched my cheek.*

"*Honey, you don't choose who your mate is. Fate decides who you get to spend the rest of your life with,*" *she replied. I thought about it and nodded.*

"*Are you and Daddy mates?*" *I asked.*

"*Yes, we are,*" *she answered.*

"*Will I have a mate?*" *I asked.*

"*Honey, everyone has a mate.*"

* * *

I opened my eyes and sat up. I looked over at the window and saw it was dark outside. I sighed and stood up and walked into the bathroom. That dream I had was a memory of when I was small. I didn't know why I had it. I shrugged it off and washed my face before fixing my hair and walking out of the room.

It wasn't that late at night, so some people were awake and walking around the pack house. I really needed to stop taking naps in the middle of the day because it was really messing up my sleeping schedule.

I walked down the stairs and into the living room, and saw Lina with Tyler, Ryder, and some other people whose names I forgot sitting on the couches, smiling, and talking. Lina raised her head up and waved at me, telling me to come over.

I smiled at her and walked up to them. They all looked at me and smiled, especially Ryder.

"Hey, guys," I said, waving my hand. They greeted me, and I looked at Lina.

"Sit down." Lina patted the seat next to her. I nodded and sat there.

"So, what are you guys talking about?" I asked and Lina shrugged.

"We're discussing the party we are planning next week for Lina's birthday," Ryder replied. I looked at Lina, and she shrugged again.

"It's your birthday next week?" I asked her.

"Yes," she answered, smiling slightly.

"That's awesome. I would like to help with the party," I told them. Lina frowned a bit and faced the others.

"Guys, I told you I don't really need a party," she stated. I raised a brow at her, and the others shook their heads.

"We are hosting you a party, whether you like it or not," Ryder exclaimed.

"Ryder is right. Why don't you want a birthday party, anyways? It's only once a year," I told her. Ryder smirked at me while Lina sighed.

"Because it's nothing really special. It's just the day I was born, not a big deal," she muttered. They shook their heads again, and Lina sighed once more.

"Lina, it's the day you were born. Of course it's a special day," I told her. She nodded at me and looked at the rest.

"Fine. We'll do a party, but I don't want one like last year where you guys took me out to a club and got me wasted to the point I was talking to a pole," she told us. Everyone laughed as she crossed her arms over her chest.

"Fine. How about we do it here in the pack house?" Tyler suggested.

"Yeah, that sounds good," Lina agreed, smiling.

"Great. We'll talk about this later on, but now I need to hit the hay," Ryder said as he got up and winked at me. I rolled my eyes at him, and all the others stood up as well.

"Yeah, I need to sleep. Tiana, are you coming?" Lina asked. I shook my head at her as I got up.

"No, I'm just going to stay awake for a while," I replied.

She nodded and waved at me before walking off. I looked out the window and decided to walk around outside for a bit to relax my mind. I opened the front door and closed my eyes as the cold breeze hit my face. I breathed in and walked out, observing the dark sky.

I continued to roam around the pack house. There were a couple of people who were outside too, so I wasn't alone. I gasped out in shock when I felt someone place their hand on my shoulder. I immediately turned around and sighed in relief when I saw it was only Adam. He looked at me with a smile, and I playfully punched him in the arm and smiled.

"Ow! What was that for?" he asked. I raised a brow as I continued to walk with him.

"That's for startling me," I said. He chuckled and shook his head.

"What are you doing out here?" he asked. I looked at him and shrugged.

"Just walking," I answered.

"Me too," he told me with a small smile.

We continued to walk and talk for a while. By now, there weren't many people outside. Adam kept making silly jokes that weren't even funny, but I kept laughing anyway because that's what made it funny.

"Can you ever tell a funny joke?" I asked. He looked at me and smiled.

"They are funny, Tiana," he said. I raised a brow at him and shook my head.

"No, they aren't. You come up with the weirdest jokes ever," I stated. He smiled and shrugged.

"Well, darling, these weird jokes make you laugh, so they are considered funny," he replied. I shook my head at him and patted his back.

"Fine, I'll let you think that if it helps you sleep at night," I told him. He pouted his lips, but they soon turned into a smile.

"But you still love them," he said.

I placed my finger under my chin and pretended to think about it. I looked at him and gave him a small smile as I nodded. "Okay, maybe I do like them a little."

"Good, because I don't think I'll ever find anyone who will ever like my jokes," he stated. I shrugged and patted his shoulder.

"You will, one day," I said.

He looked down at the ground but soon snapped his head up when we saw a car parking outside the pack house. Familiar teenage boys got out of the car, and it looked like they were drunk. They were laughing and walking like drunk people.

"Damn, that was a good party," one of the boys said, and they all nodded.

I immediately saw Kyle was among that group. I mentally gagged as he saw me and winked. The rest of the boys were talking about the party they were at as they walked into the pack house. Kyle was the only one that didn't enter and instead walked towards us.

I looked at Adam, and he gave me a confused look, but I shook my head at him and looked back to see Kyle trying to stay standing on his feet as he walked up to us.

"Hey, babe," he said. I cringed and stepped backward.

"Don't call me that." I crossed my arms over my chest. He smirked at me and stepped forward.

"Why? Does it bother you, babe?" he asked.

I growled lowly, and Adam stepped up, glaring at him.

"You heard her. Get out of here," Adam sneered. Kyle raised a brow and stepped closer to him.

"Get out of here? You don't tell me what to do. I can do whatever I want, and that includes talking to her," he said and looked at me.

"Well, I don't want you talking to me," I said.

"Babe, no one can resist me." He winked. Adam and I growled together. Then Adam grabbed him by his shirt, still glaring at him.

"I don't want to see you talking to her," he growled. Kyle furrowed his brows and took Adam's hands off of him.

"It's none of your damn business," Kyle growled. Adam pushed him slightly and growled again.

"It is my business when it comes to her," he said.

Kyle growled again and pushed him by the chest. I stepped up to prevent something bad happening, but Adam only pushed me softly aside.

"You're messing with the wrong guy," Kyle said. Adam raised a brow and scoffed.

"Oh, really? A guy who's immature and goes hitting on any random girl?" Adam asked.

Kyle's eyes turned dark as he stepped further and punched Adam right in the face. A gasp made its way out of my mouth as my eyes widened. Adam immediately got up and punched him in the face as well. I repeatedly told them to stop, but of course they wouldn't listen.

They continued to hit each other as I stood there, not knowing what to do. It was obviously a bad idea if I stepped in.

"Kyle, Adam! Stop!" I yelled but they continued with it.

Adam fell to the ground as Kyle punched him. I decided that standing there wasn't going to benefit anything, so I looked around to see if anyone could help but couldn't find anyone. I was about to shift into my wolf to stop them when I heard a loud, hard voice yelling at us to stop this instant.

Adam and Kyle stopped as they looked over to the source of the sound. I turned my head, and my eyes widened as I saw someone walking out the front door and looking at us with hard eyes. I immediately knew who it was from the familiar voice and scent.

We stood there shocked as Alpha Mason walked towards us with a dangerous glint in his eyes—and that wasn't something good.

CHAPTER 16

Kyle and Adam immediately got up from the ground and bowed their heads. Alpha Mason walked closer but kept his eyes on me which only made me gulp. This was bad, really bad. He stomped towards us as anger radiated from him. His hand was clenched at his side like he was ready to throw a punch. He turned his glare to Adam and Kyle as he growled out loudly.

"What the hell is going on?"

Adam looked at me. I breathed in and bit my lip. He looked at Alpha Mason as he clenched his jaw. "I was only giving him a warning," Adam said.

Alpha Mason's eyes narrowed on him as he took a step closer. "For what?" he growled lowly.

Kyle's eyes widened as he gulped and glared at Adam. "Nothing. He's lying," Kyle butted in.

Adam growled which only made Alpha Mason growl as well. I glared at Kyle but kept my mouth shut, knowing Adam could handle it.

"For what?" Alpha Mason growled again but loudly this time. Kyle placed his head down, and I snickered softly but brought my gaze back to Adam.

"For bothering Tiana. He wouldn't leave her alone," Adam muttered.

Alpha Mason's gaze turned to me as his eyes darkened but soon glared at Kyle and stepped towards him. "Is that true?" he growled.

Kyle flinched as I crossed my arms over my chest.

Okay, maybe this isn't too bad, I thought to myself.

Kyle remained silent and didn't say a word, but that only made Alpha Mason angrier.

"I asked if that was true!" he roared out in anger.

Kyle looked up and sighed. "Yes, it's true," he muttered lowly.

I raised a brow and widened my eyes when he stepped closer and threw a punch directly at Kyle's face, sending him crashing to the ground. Kyle looked back up with fear evident in his eyes. I tried not to feel guilty because he did this to himself.

Alpha Mason punched him again, which made him wince in pain. Adam backed away and placed his hand on my shoulder, trying to tell me everything was okay. I sighed and nodded, looking away from the scene in front of us.

Alpha Mason eventually stopped and backed away as guards came running towards us. He looked at me, and his eyes immediately turned back to normal. I didn't miss the growl that came out from his mouth. The guards picked Kyle up from the ground, as Alpha Mason glared back at him.

"I gave you an order, but you defied me. I am your alpha, and you will obey my orders without any arguments. You will stay in the dungeons for two weeks as punishment, and if you disobey me once again, I will not hesitate to kick you out of my pack and make you a rogue. Do I make myself clear?" he asked.

Kyle huffed, which only made Alpha Mason growl again.

"Do I need to repeat myself?" he sneered. Kyle gulped and shook his head.

"No, Alpha. I understand," he replied.

Alpha Mason looked at the guards. "Take him away," he told them.

They nodded before saying, "Yes, Alpha," and walking away with Kyle in their grip.

Alpha Mason turned his attention to us and clenched his jaw. He was looking at Adam's hand on my shoulder but immediately looked away and turned around.

"Go back to your rooms. I don't want to see any of you out at this time," he ordered.

We nodded and walked back into the pack house with him behind us. I looked back and saw Alpha Mason looking at me with his hands in his pockets. His stare was emotionless. I turned away and walked up the stairs and into my room.

I sighed and lay on my bed, thinking about what had happened today. I groaned and rubbed my face before closing my eyes. Before I fell asleep, I thought about one thing: *Why is this mate thing so frustrating?*

*   *   *

I groaned when I felt light shining right at me. I wasn't one of those girls who woke up happy and beautiful as if they didn't even sleep at all. No. I was one of those girls who woke up with eye boogers and drool at the side of the mouth. There was nothing to be embarrassed about. It's natural. I opened my eyes and sighed as I got off my bed and checked the time.

It was still early, so I decided to take a shower and change. It had been a week since that incident with Kyle, and today was Lina's birthday. I wasn't able to buy her a present because of all the stuff that's been going on. One of my main reasons was my laziness. Today, however, I had decided to go to the city and buy something for her.

I had Nick's permission, so I didn't need to ask you-know-who. I just needed to take a guard and a friend with me. I went to my closet to pick out a red summer dress and some underwear. I walked into the bathroom and stripped out of my clothes before jumping into the shower.

I sighed when the water hit my skin. *Now, this is what I call relaxation.* After I was done showering, I wrapped a towel around my body and dried my hair first. Then I wore my clothes, tied my hair into a ponytail, and brushed my teeth before walking out of the bathroom.

I was met with the cold breeze and shivered slightly. I wore heels and walked towards Kayla's room. It's been a while since I last saw her, so I decided to take her with me. Well, if she agreed. I stopped in front of her door and knocked on it.

After a while, the door opened, and I was met with a smiling Kayla.

"Tiana, it's been so long! How are you?" she asked. I smiled as she pulled me into a hug.

"I'm good," I said as she pulled away. "How are you?" Her smile grew as she let me in her room.

"I'm fantastic," she replied but soon tilted her head. "Is there something you need?" she asked.

"I'm going to the city today and was wondering if you could accompany me," I told her. She thought about it but finally nodded with a smile on her face.

"Of course, that seems fun. Besides, I haven't gotten out of the pack house in a long time," she said.

When I first meet her, she seemed like a shy and insecure person, but now she was a little different. I guess with time, a person changes with time.

"You wait here while I go change into something presentable," she said.

I looked at her pajamas and chuckled softly. She walked into her bathroom with some clothes, while I sat down on a chair and waited.

Her room was like mine and everyone else's. There's a bed, closet, bathroom, and some other stuff. I looked around the plain room and turned my attention back towards the bathroom door when it opened. Kayla walked out in a summer dress. She was really pretty, and I wouldn't doubt that the guys would fall head over heels for her. I was nowhere like her.

"You ready?" I asked as I got up from the chair.

"Yes, let's go," she answered, smiling. We left the pack house and met the guard who was standing next to a car.

"Are you Tiana?" he asked.

"Yes, I am," I replied.

He nodded and opened the car door for us. We smiled gratefully at him before we sat inside. The driver was already waiting in front and the guard before sat next to him.

The driver started the car and drove off. I looked at the guard and saw his emotionless face, causing me to roll my eyes.

Why can't the guards ever loosen up?

It was not like something would attack any moment now. Well, I couldn't really complain. It was their job. I glanced at Kayla, and she was staring out the window. She turned to me and smiled slightly.

"So, I'm guessing the reason we're out today is because of Lina's birthday?" she told me.

"Yes, it is. How did you know?" I asked, smiling. She shrugged.

"I heard some pack members mentioning it. Lots of rumors go by really quick," she answered, "especially the one about you and the alpha."

I sighed and placed my head against the window. Of course the rumors wouldn't stop too soon.

"You heard about them too?" I sighed again. She nodded at me.

"So? Is it true?" she asked. I looked at her and raised a brow.

"Depends. What are these rumors?" I asked.

"Some say you're related to the alpha, and that's why he let us stay. However, I know that's not right because if you were, you wouldn't be in the dungeons when I first came here. Others say you're his mate," she said. I slowly nodded, urging her to continue. "And some others say you're sleeping with him."

My eyes widened, and I looked at the driver and the guard in embarrassment, but they weren't paying attention to us, I think. They didn't even have a reaction, and for that, I was thankful. I looked back at Kayla, and she was staring at me with wide eyes.

"Oh, Tiana," she groaned. "Please don't tell me—"

"No, I'm not," I immediately cut her off. She sighed in relief and nodded.

"So they are all wrong?" she asked.

Sighing, I muttered quietly, "No, the second one was right. I'm his mate."

"It all makes sense now. No wonder he didn't kill us," she stated, nodding slowly. I ran my hand through my hair and shook my head.

"Can we like, not talk about this?" I asked softly.

"Yes, sorry," she answered.

I smiled gratefully at her as we talked about the party tonight. After a while, we made it to the city, and the driver parked us in the city center, telling us that he would remain here until we came back. Kayla, the guard, and I got out of the car and started walking.

"So, what are you planning to buy?" she asked. I thought about it and shrugged.

"I don't really know. Maybe a dress and a necklace. Something like that," I replied.

One thing you should know about me is that I'm horrible at buying presents.

"Well, while we are at it, I want to buy a dress for tonight. I don't really have anything nice to wear."

I nodded as we continued to walk.

We had gone to several shops, but I still couldn't find anything that was Lina's type. We entered another shop, hoping I could find something there. I looked at a couple of dresses till I saw a black one. The dress was beautiful, and I could imagine how it would look on Lina. I checked the size and smiled gratefully when I saw it was her size.

I grabbed the dress and smiled at Kayla.

"I think this will work. I just need to find a necklace or a bracelet," I told her. She nodded as she scanned the dresses in her hand.

"I'm going to see if any of these look good on me," she said, walking into the fitting room.

I looked around the shop and saw a jewelry section, where several necklaces were on display. I checked each of them until I saw one that caught my eye. It wasn't much and wasn't too little. It was cute yet simple. I bet Lina would like it, so I decided to buy it.

I was grabbing the necklace when I heard familiar voices coming from another part of the store. My eyes widened when I realized who they were, and I mentally groaned.

Please, not them again. Of all people, why does it have to be them?

"This dress is perfect for you, Chloe. Just wait until Mason sees this on you. He'll totally fall to your feet."

I backed away and saw Chloe and her minions appear.

"I know. He can't play hard to get for too long," Chloe said.

I growled lowly but stopped before they could hear me.

"Yeah, you're right. I mean, who would not be attracted to you?" another girl said. I mentally gagged and cringed.

Well, if I were a boy, I wouldn't be attracted to her.

I backed away with the necklace in my hand and returned to the fitting room. Smiling, Kayla opened the door.

"Did you find the perfect dress?" I asked. When she nodded, I quickly grabbed her hand, wanting to escape the place. "Good. Now let's get out of here," I told her.

We paid for our stuff and walked out. I sighed in relief that they didn't see us. I didn't really want to face her or her minions. While we were returning to the car, we grew silent and things just kind of turned awkward.

I looked over Kayla and decided to ask her a question. "So, have you found your mate yet?"

She stopped and looked at me, hurt evident in her eyes.

I realized what I had asked was a sensitive subject, so I immediately apologized. "I'm sorry. I didn't mean to—"

"It's okay," she cut me off and started walking again. "It's just hard for me to talk about that."

I nodded and gave her a smile, which she returned. When we got inside the car, I glanced at Kayla one more time with a hint of confusion before looking out the window and leaning my head against the glass.

CHAPTER 17

I slowly opened my eyes and was greeted by the blue sky. I slightly furrowed my brows in confusion when I felt a pair of strong arms wrap around me and carry me princess style. I averted my eyes and saw Adam looking straight ahead. I must have fallen asleep in the car. I was too tired, so I was not surprised. I was about to let Adam know that I was awake so he could set me down on the ground when I smelled a familiar scent.

I immediately closed my eyes so I could avoid any contact with him. His scent grew stronger and stronger as Adam walked closer to the pack house. I tried to even out my breath to make it look like I was fast asleep. All of a sudden, Adam stopped dead in his tracks and growled really low that I bet no one heard except me.

"Alpha," Adam said in greeting. There was a silent, awkward pause before he spoke.

"Hand her over."

Adam growled lowly once again as I felt my wolf purr in delight. "I can take care of her, Alpha," Adam said. Alpha Mason's scent grew stronger as he stepped closer.

"Hand her over," he growled.

Adam sighed in frustration, and I felt my body being lifted into the air, held by another set of arms. I didn't want to admit it, but it was really comfortable. Alpha Mason turned around and started walking into the pack house. My wolf was yelping with joy while I was trying to make it look like I was in a deep sleep, but it was really hard when he was the one who was carrying me.

He walked up the stairs while holding me in a tight but careful grip. He eventually stopped and opened a door with his one hand and entered a room which I was guessing was mine. I really wanted to open my eyes to see what his face looked like but held it back so I wouldn't be in an awkward state.

He gently placed me on my bed, and I knew he was still next to me because of his scent. He stood there for a minute or two and then moved a piece of my hair away from my face with his hand. I felt my cheeks heat up and started to move my head so it would look like I was starting to wake up.

His scent got weaker and weaker by the second as I heard my bedroom door open then close. I slowly opened my eyes to be greeted by nothing, only a hint of his scent that still remained in my room. I bit my lip and shook my head.

What just happened? I sighed in frustration and sat up as I ran my hands through my hair. *Why on earth did he offer to carry me?*

I shook my head and tried to get rid of those thoughts, but my wolf wasn't really helping. I ignored her and shut off the connection between her and I as I looked at the time.

It was almost three o'clock. The party would start at seven, so I had plenty of time to get ready. I got up and walked towards the door but stopped when it opened. Adam gave me a small smile when he saw me. He stepped into my room, but I caught his hesitation.

"Hey," I greeted him.

"Hey, Tiana," he said, handing me the bag where I placed Lina's present. "I found this in the car."

I gave him a grateful smile and took the bag from his grasp.

"Thank you, Adam." I placed the bag next to my bed. He scratched the back of his neck, smiling.

"You're welcome. Well, I guess I'll be going." He turned around, making his way to the door. I raised a brow at his weird behavior and called out to him.

"Adam."

He stopped and looked back at me. "Yes?"

"Is there something wrong? You're acting a little strange," I told him.

He sighed and shook his head. "No, everything's fine. I'm just a little tired."

I nodded, not fully convinced, but I let it slide as he gave me a small smile and walked out my room.

I shrugged and decided to walk outside before I got ready. I noticed Adam's scent was still lingering in the air, so I followed it out the backyard. There were a couple of people walking around with friends or mates; most of them had huge smiles on their faces. I decided to let my wolf run for a bit.

I walked towards the woods and behind a tree, then I took my clothes off and shifted into my small wolf. I started running as fast as I could, letting the cool air pass through my fur. My wolf was purring in happiness as she stretched her legs and ran through the woods. After a while of me having full control, I decided to let her have all of it so she could run as much as her heart desired.

* * *

I immediately ran into my room and started cursing at my wolf. I couldn't believe she ran for three hours and a half. This was the last time I was giving her full control because I couldn't trust her in anything. Now I only had half an hour to get ready, and that was all because of my wolf.

Sighing in frustration, I stripped out of my clothes and wore the black dress that I chose. I looked in the mirror and inhaled deeply.

It's okay, I psyched myself.

I usually got ready in less than ten minutes, so I could do this. All I needed to do was apply a little makeup and fix my hair, and that's it. I opened my drawer where I placed all my makeup in, and my eyes widened when I saw it was empty.

Shit. Shit. Shit. Shit. Where's all my makeup?

I looked through all the drawers but found nothing. It was not like a makeup ghost came walking in and stole it, right? Then where did they go? I snapped my head over to the door when someone knocked. I opened the door and saw Kayla outside my room.

"Hey, here's all your makeup." She handed me a bag. I raised a brow at her, and she gave me a sheepish smile.

"I came here an hour ago to ask if I could borrow your makeup since I didn't have any, but you weren't here, so I just took them myself. I hope you don't mind," she said. I shook my head at her and gave her a small smile.

"No, not at all. If you'll excuse me, I need to get ready," I told her.

She nodded and walked away. I closed the door and headed towards the bathroom so I could start. I applied foundation on my face and a hint of blush on my cheeks. I then put a layer of mascara on my eyelashes and placed lip gloss on my lips. I decided that was enough and grabbed a brush and started to fix my hair.

By the time I was done with my hair, there were ten minutes left till the party started. I relaxed and walked out of the bathroom. I grabbed some heels and wore them, then looked in the mirror. I got to say, I looked quite good.

I turned and grabbed the bag that had Lina's present and walked out of my room. I headed towards Lina's room and knocked on her door, and soon enough, she opened it and greeted me with a smile.

"Wow, girl! You look beautiful," she said, looking me up and down, then engulfing me in a hug. I chuckled as I hugged her back, then pulled away.

"I look beautiful? You should go see yourself." I stepped into her room. She was wearing a red dress, and her hair was down in curls. She really was beautiful.

She laughed, and I handed her the bag.

"Happy birthday, Lina," I greeted her. With a huge smile on her face, she opened the bag.

"Aww, Tiana! You didn't have to," she told me. I scoffed at her and shrugged.

"Yes, you're right. I didn't have to. But I knew if I hadn't, you would have murdered me and hid my body in your closet," I said. She gave me a smirk and nodded.

"Oh, I wonder how you knew," she said. I chuckled again and shrugged.

"It's a sixth sense," I told her, giving her a smile as she laughed.

"Oh, I also have another present for you."

She raised a brow and tilted her head. "Really? What is it?" she asked.

I gave her an evil smirk and walked closer to her. "A happy birthday song," I replied.

Her face fell, and then I started singing her the happy birthday song as loud as I could. Her face scrunched up as she placed the bag down on the ground.

"Tiana, stop," she said, but I didn't stop. "Tiana, your voice is horrible!" she yelled. "For God's sake, Tiana. Have mercy on my ears." She grabbed a pillow from her bed and threw it straight to my face.

I stopped the singing and frowned at her.

"You could have ruined my makeup," I muttered.

She smirked and shrugged. "And you could have ruined my ears. Has anyone ever told you that you have a horrible voice?" she asked.

I smirked and placed the pillow back on her bed. "Has anyone ever told you that you're a horrible driver?" I asked.

"Yes, you." She pointed at me.

I nodded and smiled at her. "Yeah, and you have too."

She shook her head as she opened her bedroom door. "Whatever, let's get going," she told me.

I nodded, and we walked downstairs together. As we made it to the party area, we got stares from everyone and we heard a lot of whispering, but I didn't pay much attention to them because I was too busy looking around.

The place was dim, but the colorful lights livened up the mood. There were drinks and food on the sides and music blasting in the air. Lots of people were drinking and dancing to the music. Lots of people also came up to Lina and wished her a happy birthday, giving her hugs.

"Hey, girls!" Tyler and Ryder shouted through the loud music.

"Hey," we said, greeting them.

"This is great. Thank you for all of this," Lina said.

"Anything for the birthday girl," Tyler told her. She smiled at him, then looked at me.

"Come on, let's all dance." She grabbed my hand. I smiled back at her and nodded.

The four of us walked to the middle of the room where everyone was dancing and rubbing their bodies against each other. We grooved to the music and laughed like we were drunk. After ten minutes, I told Lina I needed a break and headed to where the drinks were being served.

I took one drink and gulped it down my throat, then turned my head to the side when I heard someone speak.

"Easy there. You don't want to choke." Ryder smirked.

I rolled my eyes at him and drank another shot. "What do you want?" I placed the drink on the table.

He raised a brow and crossed his arms over his chest. "Don't you already know?"

I nodded and rolled my eyes again. "Yes, you're right," I said. "It's a no."

He pouted but then chuckled. "Why not?"

"Because I said so. Besides, if you knew who my mate was, you wouldn't be hitting on me."

"Mate? You mean the alpha?" he asked, smirking.

My eyes widened, and I slowly nodded. "Yes, how did you know?"

"Ain't hard to notice," he replied.

I raised my brow in confusion. "Wait, if you know, then why the hell are you still hitting on me?"

"Because I could still have a chance seeing that you guys aren't all lovey-dovey . . . and because it's fun."

"Fun?"

"Yeah, getting on his nerves," he said with a smirk.

I patted his back. "I think I like you a little more now," I chuckled.

He laughed as well. "And I think that's the nicest thing you've ever said to me," he gushed.

I rolled my eyes at him. "And the last time." I looked around and saw that the backyard was empty. "The loud music is giving me a headache. I'm going outside for a bit."

He nodded and smiled. "Want me to come with you?"

I gave him a small smile but shook my head. "No, thanks. I want to be alone."

He nodded again, and I then stepped outside the pack house. The loud music got quieter as I walked farther. I sighed and inhaled the fresh air as I closed my eyes. I stood like that for a minute until I felt another presence coming near me. I opened my eyes and turned my head and saw Alpha Mason walking towards me with his hands in his pocket and with an emotionless face on.

I stood there hesitantly, not knowing if I should just walk away or stay put. He walked closer until he was right next to me, staring forward and not looking at me. He stood there silently, not saying a single word.

"What are you doing out here? Why aren't you inside?" he finally spoke and glanced at me.

"Getting a bit of fresh air," I told him softly. "Also the music was giving me a headache."

He nodded and kept his attention anywhere else but me. There was an awkward silence, and I didn't know whether I should get up and walk away or say something.

"Uh . . . What are you doing out here?" I asked.

He glanced at me but soon looked away. "The same reason why you're out here," he said.

I rolled my eyes and scoffed. He looked at me and raised a brow.

"Did you just scoff at me?" he asked with hard eyes, but I could tell there was a hint of amusement in there somewhere.

"Oh, my apologies, Alpha," I said sarcastically. "I forgot who I was standing next to."

He frowned and averted his eyes away from me. "Don't call me that," he said quietly.

I looked at him and raised a brow. "Don't call you what? Alpha?"

He growled lowly and looked at me. "That. Just call me Mason. It feels weird coming out of your mouth," he said roughly.

My eyes widened in shock. He told me not to call him alpha when a couple weeks ago, he kind of told me otherwise. It was not like it bothered me; it just felt different now.

"Okay, Mason," I said slowly, nodding.

His eyes darkened when I said his name, and it occurred to me that was the first time I ever said his name without saying alpha. I just never felt comfortable saying his name by itself. It was kind of hard to explain.

He stepped closer to me and growled lowly. I didn't want to admit it, but I also moved closer. My wolf was yelping in my head, telling me to jump him.

"I like it," he said in a low voice. I gulped as his eyes grew darker.

"You like what?" I whispered.

His eyes glanced down at my lips, then back to my eyes.

"I like my name coming out of your mouth," he said, which made a shiver run down my spine.

At that moment, it felt like there was a magnetic force pulling us together, and it was too hard to pull away. His head lowered as he stepped closer to me.

Our bodies were so close, and our lips were inches away from each other. As his head lowered even more and his eyes grew darker, I bit my lips.

And as soon as I did that, his lips were on mine.

CHAPTER 18

He pulled me closer to him as he deepened the kiss and held my face in his hands. I stood there shocked, but eventually my surprise vanished and I kissed him back. I held onto his shirt and squeezed it before he pulled away, leaving me standing and looking up at him in confusion.

What the hell did we just do? Did I really just kiss him?

He looked down at me with pitch-black eyes that held desire, but he soon closed them shut as I tried to regain my thoughts. He eventually opened them once again, and his eyes were back to normal. He took a step back as I tried to find the words to say, but it was like I became mute.

He breathed deeply and took another step back as he ran his hand roughly through his hair.

"That was a mistake," he muttered.

I gulped and felt a hint of sadness even though I didn't want to feel it. My wolf turned from yelping in joy to whimpering in sorrow.

"My wolf took control. That was never meant to happen," he growled, and before I could say anything, he turned away and walked back into the pack house.

I took a deep breath and closed my eyes. Why did I enjoy that kiss? I didn't want to, but I did, and there was no denying that. But also, why was I bothered that he left me? I mean, if he didn't leave me, then I sure would, so why did I feel angry? I shook my head and ran my hands through my hair. I shouldn't really care. I decided to just go back inside and have some fun and act like that never happened.

The music got louder as I walked closer and into the pack house. I cringed when I saw two people making out like their lives depended on it. I rolled my eyes and squeezed past them and continued to walk.

My eyes widened when I saw a couple of people passed out on the floor and people drinking like there was no tomorrow. I turned my head and saw Lina dancing like crazy. She caught my stare and waved her hand at me.

"Tiana! Where were you? Come join the fun," she yelled as loud as she could through the blasting music. Smiling, I walked towards her.

Maybe this will set my mind at ease.

Lina grabbed my hands and we danced like reckless teenagers. Everyone around us did as well. I loved it.

Ryder came up to us and handed us drinks. We took them and gulped them down in one go, then told him to get us more. The music got louder and everyone got looser, rubbing their bodies and shoving their tongues down each other's throat.

I giggled as Ryder and Tyler joined us. After a while, we went to drink some more. Since we were werewolves, alcohol didn't really affect us as much as it did with humans, so we were still sober. However, that didn't mean we couldn't get drunk if we consume a lot.

I gulped down one drink and another. I knew I looked stupid, but it was the only way I could get him out of my mind. Besides, it was going to take a lot more than this to get me drunk. After the music got a little low, I decided to do something I would never have done if it hadn't been for Lina's birthday—I stood on top of the table.

I shouted for everyone's attention, and they all stopped and looked at me. Some gave me weird glances, and others laughed.

"I would like to have everyone's attention!"

Almost everyone looked at me, and I smiled in satisfaction.

"Good," I muttered to myself. "I would like to offer a toast to my best friend." I looked at her, and she had a huge smile on her face. "I hope today has been a great day, and I'm happy to have a friend like you."

I heard a couple of *awws* as everyone grabbed a drink.

"Oh, enough of all the sweet talk. Cheers!" I yelled as everyone else raised their drinks in the air, then gulped them down their throats.

I got down from the table as everyone else started dancing and doing the stuff they did before I interrupted them. Lina gave me a hug and Ryder patted me on the back, then we all started dancing again. Yup, too many dancing tonight.

After a couple of hours, the party came to an end, and everyone went back to their rooms. Lina gave me a hug, then pulled away with a huge smile on her face.

"Thanks for everything," she said. I rolled my eyes at her.

"It's not like I'm the one that planned the party," I told her. She chuckled and shook her head.

"Yeah, you're right. You didn't even do anything." She crossed her arms over her chest.

"I did, actually. I came to the party, and I also bought you a gift." I smirked.

"Yeah, whatever." She shrugged, rolling her eyes and stepping back. "I'm going back to my room. I'll see you tomorrow." She waved her hand, then walked up the stairs and out of my sight.

Looking around, I felt sorry for whoever was going to clean the mess up. I sighed and walked up the stairs and back to my room.

I changed into my pajamas and lay on my bed. I looked at the clock and saw it was almost midnight, so I closed my eyes and thought of the kiss. I tried to forget it throughout the whole party, but it was always on the back of my mind, and I hated it. I grabbed a pillow, placed it on top of my face, and screamed into it.

This was how I got all my frustration out.

After hours and hours of staring at the ceiling, I decided to get water. I did try sleeping, but every time I closed my eyes, I thought of you-know-who. It was so frustrating. I got up and slowly opened my bedroom door and walked carefully downstairs to not wake anybody.

As I was doing so, I noticed the living room lights were on. I shrugged it off and assumed it was someone cleaning all the mess. As I made it at the end of the stairs, my breath got caught in my throat.

There was Mason, passed out on the floor with drinks all around him. My guess was he drank himself to sleep. I slowly walked to the kitchen so I wouldn't wake him up.

I was heading back when I heard him groan. He looked like he was in an uncomfortable position. I didn't know if I should just ignore him or help him back to his room, but thanks to my wolf, she made me feel slightly guilty for thinking of just leaving him there.

I slowly walked up to him and stood there for a while, staring at him.

What do I do now?

I kneeled and poked his arm.

"Mason," I whispered. He didn't move. I sighed and poked him a little harder. "Mason, wake up."

He stirred a bit and eventually opened his eyes, looking lost. He must have drank a lot to get drunk to the point of passing out, but why would he do that?

"Tiana?" he groaned, looking at me.

"Yes, it's me. Get up so I can help you get back to your room," I told him, ignoring his stare.

He raised his hand. I looked at him, confused, and stiffened when he cupped my cheek.

"Tiana," he whispered. I gulped but shook his hand off.
"Come on, Mason. Get up."

He tried to get up but failed. I grabbed his arm and pulled him with as much strength as my body allowed. He was eventually on his feet, but I still had to hold him so he wouldn't fall. I could tell he wasn't himself. Of course, he wasn't. He was drunk. He kept staring at me as I helped him to his room.

It was hard because of his weight, but we eventually made it to his room. I opened his door and walked him towards his bed. He lay on it and closed his eyes. I sighed and took his shoes off so he could be more comfortable.

I didn't know why I was doing this, but I felt like I needed to. I was about to turn around and walk away when he grabbed my hand. I looked at him, and his eyes were open once again.

"Come here," he whispered. I shook my head at him.

"I can't. I need to get to my room." I tried to release myself from his grip.

He ignored me and pulled me towards him, which had me falling on top of him. He stared at me for a while before speaking, "You're beautiful."

My eyes widened, and I didn't know what to do.

He raised his hand and let his finger roam my cheek. "You were beautiful today," he whispered.

If it hadn't been for my werewolf hearing, I wouldn't have heard it. I gulped and turned my head away. "I need to go," I told him softly.

He didn't say anything but held my face with both hands, pulling my face closer to his. My breath was caught in my throat when his lips landed on mine for the second time today. My eyes were wide with shock as his lips moved against mine.

Gripping his shirt, I eventually closed my eyes and responded to the kiss, which was slow and soft. I pulled away when I needed to catch my breath. I looked at him as his eyes closed and his breathing started to even out. His hands let go of my face, and his head tilted to the side.

Did he just fall asleep on me? I shook my head and bit my lip. I guess it was for the better. He would probably think that what happened was a dream. I pulled away and looked at him. I had the urge to sleep and cuddle with him but shook my head once again.

I couldn't believe we kissed again. Maybe it was just because he was drunk. He didn't mean the words he said, but my wolf told me otherwise. I shut her off and slowly walked out of his room.

Well, there goes my sleep.

CHAPTER 19

I groaned in frustration when I felt someone was constantly poking my cheek in the middle of my peaceful sleep which, might I add, was something I hadn't had in a long time. I growled and hoped that whoever it was would stop and leave before I strangle their throat without feeling a single remorse.

But, of course, this stupid person continued and chuckled instead. I groaned loudly as soon as I smelt a familiar scent. This wasn't the first time this person tried to disturb my slumber. I moved my head.

"Adam, I swear if you touch my face one more time, you will regret being born!" I threatened.

He chuckled again, and when I didn't feel his finger on my cheek, I relaxed, trying to fall back to sleep. But the second I let my guard down, he did it again rather roughly.

I snapped my eyes open and growled, glaring at Adam, who was holding his laughter.

"You bastard!" I quickly launched myself at him.

He burst into laughter as I hit him as hard as I could in the chest, which only led to me being held upside down and thrown on my bed.

"How many times do I have to tell you to never wake me up?" I hissed as I sat up and glared at him. He smirked and shrugged.

"You can't blame me that you're so obsessed with your beauty sleep," he told me. I raised a brow at him and elbowed him in the stomach.

"Beauty sleep? I haven't got this 'beauty sleep' for a while now," I said as I continued to glare at him.

"And why is that?"

I averted my eyes away from him and thought about last week. A week had passed since Lina's birthday, but I hadn't seen Mason much. It was like he was giving me the silent treatment. Not like I cared, though. But ever since then, whenever I saw him, he would turn away and walk off. Lina had said he didn't get out of his office and socialize much lately.

I had been thinking about him and that kiss this whole time. No matter what I did, I couldn't stop and that caused me to lose some sleep, which got me so frustrated. I didn't want to think about it, but it was so damn hard. I didn't know if him staying away from me was for the better or worse.

I looked back at Adam, who was raising a brow.

"It's nothing, really. Just some stuff that has been bothering me," I replied.

He slowly nodded and soon smiled.

"Why did you bother waking me up?" I lay back on my bed.

"Come on, Tiana. We haven't seen each other for a while now because of my training. Don't you want to spend time with your favorite man?" he asked, pouting.

I smiled and lightly smacked him in the face to wipe his pout. It was kind of true. Adam and I didn't spend much time with each other because of his training. He was in better shape than the last time I had seen him. He sometimes seemed a bit off, though, and I didn't know the reason why. Maybe it was because of his training. But I was thankful he was his normal self right now.

"Favorite man? Please, you're my least favorite man," I teased. He rubbed his check and pouted again.

"Ouch, you hurt me physically and emotionally," he told me. I rolled my eyes as I sat up once again.

"What do you want to do?" I got up and walked towards my closet.

"We can go to a park and walk around. Relax for a bit," he suggested.

I smiled and nodded. That sounded like a good idea. Maybe that could take my mind off things.

"That sounds great. You wait outside as I get ready."

After a few preparations, I opened my bedroom door and caught a scent that threw me over the edge. Looking to my right, I saw Mason and Adam standing directly in front of each other, glaring. They turned their heads towards me, but before long, Mason looked back at Adam and narrowed his eyes on him.

"I don't want to repeat myself." And with that, he immediately turned away and walked off before I could say anything.

Adam glared at Mason's back as he walked off. Adam then averted his eyes as I looked at him in confusion.

"What happened?" I asked.

He took a deep breath and shook his head. "Nothing."

I raised my brow at him and crossed my arms over my chest. "Well, it didn't look like it."

"Please let it go. It wasn't anything important," he told me.

Sighing, I said, "Okay, let's go get some breakfast first."

Adam followed me, and as he did so, I couldn't help but look at him and wonder what all that was about. But for now, I shrugged it off. We soon made it to the dining table, just in time as food started to be served. We sat down and started to eat. After we were done, we walked to the living room.

"Tiana!"

I looked back when I heard my name being called. Lina excitedly ran up to me. I gave her a questioning look as she was catching her breath.

"I got awesome news," she exclaimed.

"What is it?" I asked.

"Mason and I own a mansion on an island, which we haven't visited since we were kids because of certain circumstances. I've just decided that we should go there to have a little vacation. Doesn't that sound fun?" she asked with excitement in her eyes.

I smiled and looked at Adam, who was smiling as well.

"That sounds great. Where is this island?" I asked.

"It's a small island not too far from the borders. It's called Woodsgreen Island. It only takes an hour or two by plane. My parents owned it, but it soon became ours. There is a small city on the island that we can explore too," she answered.

"When do we go?" I asked.

Her smile grew as she spoke, "Now!"

My eyes widened. "Don't we need to book a flight first?" I asked.

Shaking her head, she gave me a pointed look. "No, we'll go using our private jet."

I rolled my eyes. *Of course, they have a private jet.* However, I found this really interesting. Maybe it would take my mind off Mason.

"Who's coming?" I questioned.

"I'm bringing Tyler and Ryder. You can bring Adam, if you want," she replied.

Before I could say anything, Adam spoke, "Oh, I'm coming alright. Right, Tiana?"

I chuckled and shook my head. "Nope. I don't want him to come," I said in a teasing tone. Lina smirked as she played along and Adam gasped.

"What? Why?" he asked.

"Because you're annoying." I smirked at him. "And because you woke me up."

"Very well. Adam won't come," Lina spoke.

Adam's eyes widened, and he looked at me with pouty lips. "Oh, come on. I swear I won't do it again," he begged.

"You promise?" I asked, looking at him.

"Yes, I promise."

I smiled and looked at Lina. "Yes, he's coming. Do you need to ask permission first?" I asked.

She nodded and was about to speak when someone else did.

"Permission for what?" Mason asked as he entered the living room. All heads turned to him.

Smiling, Lina walked to him and said, "Oh, brother, my lovely brother."

Mason narrowed his eyes on her and crossed his arms over his chest. "What is it now?" he asked.

Lina then told him about the trip.

Mason stood quietly before looking at me. "No," he spoke.

Lina rolled her eyes and grabbed his ear, pulling him towards the corner and whispering in his ear. I found that sight rather funny.

He growled lowly and ran a hand through his hair. "Fine, but I'm coming."

My eyes widened. I didn't want him to come. I knew it sounded rude, but one of the reasons why I wanted to go was to stay away from him.

Lina shook her head and whispered some other stuff in his ear.

He gave her a look of defeat and sighed. "Very well," he whispered. "How long are you going to stay?"

"As long as we want," she replied.

He sighed in frustration but nodded as he looked towards me. "I'll make the arrangements for the private jet," he muttered and walked off but not before glancing at me.

Lina had a satisfied smile on her face.

"How did you do that?" I raised a brow at her.

"I threatened him," she replied.

I nodded with a smile on my face. "I'm going to go pack," I said.

"Yeah, me too," Adam told us.

After an hour of packing, I was ready to go. I sat on my bed and thought of Mason. I was relieved that he wasn't coming, but somehow I felt a little disappointed. I sighed, grabbed my bag, and walked out of my room.

I shouldn't feel this way.

This vacation was a perfect opportunity for me to stop thinking about this mate thing. It made me so confused.

Downstairs, I saw Tyler and Ryder talking. I placed my bag next to theirs and greeted them.

"Hey, guys!"

They greeted me back with hugs and then we talked about how much fun we were going to have and how it was going to be amazing. After a while, Lina and Adam came down with their bags too.

"Come on, guys. Someone is taking us to the private jet," Lina said.

We nodded as Lina and the rest of us walked out the pack house. We placed our bags in the back and got inside the car.

After an hour or so, we made it to a small place that looked like an airport. There was a jet not too far away from us. Lina smiled and pointed at it.

"That's our jet. Let's go," she said excitedly.

We got out of the car and walked towards it. This was my first time going on a jet, and I was really excited. We took the stairs that led us inside the aircraft. I looked around and was amazed by its beauty. This was awesome.

We then took our seats. Adam sat next to me as I sat by the window. Lina, Tyler, and Ryder sat directly in front of us. I looked out the window as the jet started to set off the ground, and I couldn't help but think of one certain person.

And that person was Mason.

CHAPTER 20

I turned to Adam when I heard him whisper while looking out the window.

"Wow, it's beautiful."

I smiled slightly as I also looked out. "Yeah, it is."

Aside from the empty blue sky, the beautiful huge ocean was what caught my attention. I was one of those people who were afraid of the vast water.

> Just imagine being stranded in the middle of it, not knowing what the hell is under you.

I was terrified of sharks, and we also couldn't tell what else could be swimming in these waters. Only time would tell.

That's why I was more of a pool person, not the beach type. And even if I did go to the beach, I wouldn't get into the water.

I looked back at Adam and raised my brow when I found his eyes on me and he had a smile on his face.

"What?" I asked.

"Nothing." He shook his head and faced away from me.

After twenty minutes in the air, a flight attendant came and asked us if we wanted something. Adam and Ryder asked for food while the rest of us asked for drinks. With a smile on her face, Lina kept telling me how much fun we were going to have.

I was excited as well, and I hoped this vacation would be as good as I was hoping for it to be.

I was looking out the window when Adam spoke again. "I'm glad."

I turned to him in confusion. "You're glad about what?"

His eyes turned a shade darker, and it took him a while to reply.

"I'm glad he didn't come."

I was caught off guard. I knew exactly who he was talking about. "Why?"

"Because he would have made things difficult and awkward. Besides, I still don't like him," he answered.

Even though Adam didn't give me a solid reason, it wasn't hard to guess that he wasn't fond of Mason. I mean, many people didn't like Mason, so I didn't really expect Adam to like him. As for Mason, he didn't look like the type of person who was fond of anybody, more like everybody.

I nodded slowly. I didn't really know what to say. I did agree that he could have made things difficult and awkward, but I couldn't agree about the last part. Yes, I wasn't fond of him, but I didn't loathe him at the same time. It was not like I had a choice.

I pushed those thoughts away and looked back at Adam, wanting to change the subject.

"So, how is your training coming along? Is Nick too hard on you?"

"It's okay. Nick is a little harsh, but it's only for the best, especially with the rogue attacks we've been getting lately."

I nodded. "What's up with all the rogue attacks this pack has been getting?"

He shrugged as he ran a hand through his hair. "I don't really know, but this is the strongest pack we're talking about. I won't be surprised that they have enemies. And you know rogues. They will do anything to take down an alpha. It's what they do," he replied.

"I guess that makes sense," I muttered.

With a smile on her face, the flight attendant came back with our drinks and food. Adam started chugging his drink down his throat like a hungry pig. If I were a human, I would question how he was still fit when he ate too much, but since I was a werewolf, I already knew the answer.

Our metabolism was fast. We burned fat a lot faster than humans, so it was easier for us to remain fit. Another explanation was related to our wolves. We had to let our wolves run so they wouldn't lose their sanity. If they didn't, they would go a little nuts. They had to have control at times, and because of that, we ran and exercised a lot.

If it hadn't been for those two reasons, I would have been as round as a watermelon. What could I do? I loved food.

After staring out the window in silence for a while, I heard a low snore next to me. I turned towards Adam and smiled when I found him asleep. I shook my head and chuckled slightly. Lina laughed, too, when she saw Adam. I smiled at her and scooted to the front a bit to talk to her.

"How much more time till we land?" I asked.

"I think we have half an hour left or less," she replied.

"Lina?"

"Yes?"

"How exactly did you threaten Mason?"

She smirked and shrugged. "I know him. I know his weak spots."

I furrowed my brows at her. Well, I didn't really think a guy like Mason had a weak spot, but I guess everyone had one.

"What did you tell him?" I asked.

Her smirk grew. "Well, now that I think about it, I threatened and bribed him at the same time, but I'll tell you later," she stated.

I raised a brow at her in confusion. "No, tell me now."

She shook her head and gave me a smile. "Oh, would you look at that! Ryder came out of the bathroom. I need to go do my business." She immediately got up and walked towards the bathroom.

I glared at her back. I had a feeling that whatever she told Mason wasn't in my liking. I groaned and rested my head.

Ryder came back and sat in his seat. He looked at me and winked. I rolled my eyes and kicked the back of his seat.

"Hey, easy on the chair," he said in a voice laced with amusement.

"Don't worry. You sitting on the chair will damage it enough," I told him.

He laughed, then shook his head. "It's not like I'm fat," he exclaimed. "Besides, you love my body."

I rolled my eyes again. "Yeah, I love it to the point that I would die for it," I said sarcastically.

"I always knew you couldn't resist me," he said with a smirk on his face.

"Whatever helps you sleep at night," I muttered as he winked at me again.

"Do you really want to know what helps me sleep at night?" he asked.

I mentally gagged and shook my head. "Please spare me from your dirty mind," I said and looked away.

I heard him chuckle as I stared out the window and stayed like that until the jet landed.

We exited the jet and were met by a beautiful huge mansion surrounded by trees. Words couldn't describe the feeling I had when I laid eyes on the gorgeous nature around us.

We carried our bags as we slowly walked toward the mansion. I couldn't believe that Lina and Mason owned a large part of this island, but it's not that surprising when you actually thought about it. Mason was the alpha, after all.

"Okay, everyone, go pick a room and unpack your bags. Then we'll decide on what to do later," Lina stated.

We all nodded and started walking around. I picked a room upstairs, placed my bags on the ground, and started hanging my clothes in the closet. I didn't know how long we would stay here, but I got enough clothes to last me a week or two.

After I was done, I decided to look around. The room wasn't big, but I liked it. It had a bathroom and a balcony, and the bed could fit two people. Lina had mentioned earlier that all the rooms in this mansion had this kind of bed. Opening the door to the balcony, I stepped outside and heard my companions' voices.

I looked down and saw everyone below. Adam looked up at me and smiled.

"Tiana, come down here. We're going to shift and run for a bit," he stated. Smiling, I ran outside and was greeted by the others.

"Don't go beyond the borders because a couple of miles from here is a small city. We don't want to frighten them," Lina said, looking at us.

Right at that moment, I decided to do something else.

"You guys run. I'm going to let my wings spread for a while and fly," I said.

It had been a long time since I last flew. Just like how my wolf needed to have control at times, I also needed my wings to spread out, even though I couldn't fly for a long period as I was only a half angel. If I were a full angel, I would have to fly a lot just like how my wolf needed to run regularly.

"Fly? What are you? A bird?" Ryder joked.

I then remembered that Tyler and Ryder still didn't know about me being a hybrid.

"No, she's a hybrid," Adam answered his question.

Ryder and Tyler's eyes widened.

"What? Really?" Tyler asked.

"Yes, I even saw her wings before. They're small and so cute," Lina gushed.

"So you're saying you're half angel?" Ryder asked.
I smiled and nodded. "Yes."

"That's so cool! I've never met an angel in real life. They are really rare, especially a hybrid one," Tyler said, astonished.

"Yeah, we are. I guess it was luck that it was passed down to me from my mother's side," I said.

"What can you do? I heard every angel has their own powers," Ryder asked.

"I can do three things, but since I'm a hybrid, everything has its limits. I can fly, obviously. I can also heal injuries and turn invisible along with another person," I stated.

Ryder and Tyler started telling me how cool I was, making me roll my eyes. We then started walking towards the trees.

"Well, we are going to shift now. We will be running underneath you," Lina said.

I let my wings grow while they were shifting. Soon they saw my wings and stared at them in awe. I smiled, lifting my feet off the ground and flying.

They ran behind me as I looked around the island. I was able to see the ocean, and it was beautiful. From a distance, I saw some lights, and I guessed that was the city Lina had talked about. I lowered myself so no one would see me and continued to fly.

After half an hour, my wings gave out, and I landed on the ground. Ryder, Tyler, Adam, and Lina shifted back to their human forms and walked up to me.

"I'm tired. Let's head back to the mansion," Lina said. We all agreed with her and returned.

"So, what else are we going to do today?" Adam asked.

Lina smiled as she looked at the time. "I was thinking of strolling around the city tonight. I heard the lights are really pretty at sundown. We could go to a club or something too," she replied.

"That sounds great," I told her.

"Yeah, it does. When will we go?" Tyler asked.

"After a couple of hours, I need to rest from all the running," she answered.

Tyler nodded as I excused myself to my room.

* * *

I applied a coat of mascara and lipstick before I backed away, looking at myself in the mirror. I had worn a simple dress and matched it with some heels, while letting my hair fall down loosely. I ran my hand through my hair before I opened the door and walked downstairs.

Adam smiled when he made eye contact with me and gave me a hug. "Beautiful as always," he told me.

I smiled at him as a thank you. "Where's Lina?" I asked.

"She's in the car with Ryder and Tyler," he replied.

Adam and I walked towards the car and got in the back.

"You ready, guys?" Lina asked as she started the engine.

We all answered yes, then we drove off. I stared out the window as the car moved. This was one small island, but the city did not disappoint me at all. Lina was right, the lights were really pretty. There weren't many buildings, but there were lots of cars and lights everywhere.

After a while, Lina finally stopped the car and looked back at us.

"We're here!" she exclaimed.

"Where are we?" Adam asked, looking around.

"We're in front of a club. I thought it would be nice to stop here and have some fun," she answered. We all smiled and agreed.

People were coming in and out of the club. I didn't really expect a club on an island like this, but I guess I was wrong.

As we entered, loud music hit my ears and the smell of alcohol violated my nostrils. I cringed and looked away when I saw a person who was literally on top of another. Adam placed his hand behind my back. We earned lots of stares as we walked further in.

"You guys stay here while I go get some drinks," Adam yelled through the loud music.

We nodded and sat down at an empty table. It didn't take long for Tyler and Ryder to attract women, who eventually pulled them to the dance floor. Lina sat next to me and we talked about random things through the banging music.

"I have to go to the bathroom. I'll be right back," she told me after a while and I nodded.

When she walked away, I started looking around for Adam. I didn't want to be left alone as I felt lots of stares burning right through my back. I stiffened when I felt someone place his hand on my waist. I turned around, only to be greeted by a man who was staring at me like I was his lunch.

I quickly removed his hand from my waist.

"Hey, beautiful," he said.

"Don't hey me," I responded, clearly annoyed. I mean, how come every time a girl went to a bar or a club, a guy would hit on her? I mean, it's expected. "Shoo, leave me alone," I said and turned around.

The guy placed his hand on my waist again and pulled me closer to him this time.

I huffed out in annoyance and was about to use my werewolf strength to push him away when I heard a deep, familiar voice that had me whipping my head and my eyes widening in shock.

"Step away from her or I will bury you alive."

CHAPTER 21

I stood there in shock, my mouth hanging open as rage started to build within me.

How come I can't get away from him?

Mason was standing in front of me with pitch-black eyes and his fist clenched. The man holding me tightened his grip and smirked. Mason's eyes averted to where his hands were and immediately threw a punch to the man's face. The man fell down to the ground, gripping his jaw and groaning.

My eyes widened and I stepped back as I looked at the angry man on the floor.

He got up and faced Mason with a look that clearly said he wasn't giving up. Mason's jaw clenched, and he stepped closer to the man.

"Get out of my face before I make you regret ever being born," he snarled.

The man's eyes held a hint of fear in them before it immediately went away. I knew that at this moment, I had to stop them before Mason did something he would regret or most likely get us in trouble. I stepped towards Mason and placed my hand on his arm. He snapped his head to me and growled.

"Mason," I said calmly. "It's okay. Let it go."

"You heard the pretty lady. You can go now," the man said, smirking.

I narrowed my eyes on him and tightened my grip on Mason's arm. This man was signing his own death warrant, and I certainly didn't want to be a part of that.

Mason growled but not loud enough for the man to hear, and threw a punch once again, making him fall to the floor for the second time.

"I don't want to repeat myself. Get out of my sight before I change my mind and do something worse," Mason told him in a deep voice.

By now, his eyes were darker than ever, and once the man saw this, his eyes widened in fear and he immediately got up and ran away from us. Mason kept his eyes on him until he was out of sight. There was a crowd of people who were looking at us, but they immediately turned away when Mason glared at them.

"What the hell are you doing here?" I asked, furrowing my brows at him.

He snapped his head to me and frowned. "What do you mean? You don't want me here?"

I huffed out in frustration and shook my head. "You said you weren't coming."

He shrugged, his face devoid of any emotion. "Well, I changed my mind."

I was about to ask what had caused it when Adam and Lina appeared at the same time. Adam was holding our drinks but stopped dead in his tracks when he saw Mason. His face immediately fell, and he glared at him.

"What is he doing here?" he asked, looking at Lina.

I looked at her too, and she gave me a sheepish smile.

"Well, I told him to come. He does need a break from all the alpha work, and Nick is taking care of the pack while he's gone. Besides, I knew that if I told you he was coming, you wouldn't come with us," she said the last part to me.

I sighed and ran my hand through my hair. "Yeah, you're right, but I can't really do anything." I frowned. It was not like I could kick him out or something.

"Let's go back to what we were supposed to do," she said and grabbed a drink.

We also grabbed ours and sat down. I felt Mason's stare burn through my back, but I knew if I wanted to get out of here with no drama, then I better avoid him as much as possible. My wolf wasn't really helping at all, though.

We drank while Tyler and Ryder kept dancing. Adam and Mason, on the other hand, had a glare competition every once in a while. I ignored Mason and tried to keep my gaze anywhere but him. I looked at Lina and raised a brow.

"Tell me, what did you tell Mason to keep him from not coming from the start?" I asked.

She gave me a weak smile but shook her head. "I'll tell you when we head back," she answered.

"Why can't you tell me now?" I asked.

She shrugged and I shook my head, deciding to forget about it and think about something else. After a while, I couldn't help but sneak a peek at Mason. Unfortunately, I accidentally caught his stare. I looked away and saw Lina smirking at me. I shook my head at her and looked down to the ground.

A couple of girls approached us, their eyes firmly locked on Mason. He kept his eyes on me but soon turned to the girls that were surrounding him.

"You want to dance?" one girl asked.

He scoffed and shook his head.

"Come on, just one dance," the girl said.

Mason looked really annoyed, but before he could say anything, I spoke.

"Can't you see you're annoying him? He doesn't want to dance with you," I told them. They all glared at me.

"Let him speak for himself," one of the girls said while crossing her arms over her chest.

"His attitude is already speaking for him. Get out of my sight before I grab a fork and pop those fake boobs of yours," I said, clearly annoyed.

They all gasped and Mason glared at them before they all hurriedly walked away from us. I sighed in frustration and looked over at Mason to see him smirking at me. I raised a brow at him in confusion but was left embarrassed when I realized what I had done.

I just acted like a jealous girlfriend, and that wasn't a good thing. Lina also smirked at me while Adam looked pissed. I felt my cheeks redden and immediately looked down.

What have I done? Why did I react like that?

I literally wanted to disappear at that moment due to embarrassment.

Great going, Tiana.

"Tiana, Lina, come dance with us," Ryder yelled. Lina smiled and nodded.

Shaking my head, I said, "No, you go. I think I'm just going to stay here."

"Please, Tiana. Come dance with me. I don't want to dance alone," she begged.

"No, she's staying here," Mason spoke.

I looked at him and raised a brow.

"Don't listen to him, Tiana. Please." She gave me a pouty face.

I looked at them both and nodded. "Fine," I said.

Line smiled while Mason frowned. I got up and was about to walk away from the table when Mason's voice stopped me.

"Tiana, stay here."

I looked at him and frowned. *Why does he want me to stay?*

"Don't listen to him, Tiana," Lina said. "He's just jealous that you'll be dancing in front of every male in this club." She wiggled her brows.

I rolled my eyes and shook my head at Mason. "I'm going to accompany Lina," I told him.

His frown deepened, but before he could say anything else, Lina grabbed my hand and pulled me to the middle.

We started dancing with Tyler and Ryder. Every once in a while, we would grab a shot and gulp it down all while laughing and dancing. I soon felt loose and started to move freely. I looked back at Mason, catching his eye and looking away. He was obviously not liking this.

Ten minutes in, I looked at Mason again. He huffed, got up from his seat, and walked towards us. I furrowed my brows in confusion, then my eyes widened when he grabbed my waist. I looked at him, but he wasn't looking at me.

"Oh, so my brother finally decides to join," Lina spoke.

My eyes were fixed on his grip on my waist. *What is he doing?*

"Say another word, Lina, and you'll regret it," Mason threatened.

Lina chuckled, and Mason let go of my waist but stayed close to me. Lina continued to dance while I just stood there all stiff. Were they expecting me to dance when he's this close?

Lina grabbed my hand, and I took that as a yes. Amusement was written all over her eyes, so I started to dance again but in a much stiffer manner. What could I do? I couldn't dance my heart out when he's this close.

Mason didn't really dance. All he did was stand behind and watch us—more like me. You get the point. It was awkward at first, but I soon decided to let go and enjoy.

After a while, we decided to leave. It was getting late, and we were tired. We exited the club and walked towards the car.

Mason was really close to me, and every once in a while, Lina would give me a smirk, making me roll my eyes.

We soon made it back to the mansion. I excused myself so I could get ready for bed. I looked at Mason, then turned away and walked towards my room. I closed the door behind me before changing into pajama shorts and a t-shirt. I then laid on the bed, but before I could even close my eyes, someone knocked on the door.

I opened it and saw Lina smiling at me.

"Yes, Lina? Do you need anything?"

She looked hesitant as she played with her fingers. "I'm sure you're not going to like this, but I did it because I knew you'd thank me later," she said.

I raised a brow at her and shook my head. "Oh no, what did you do?" I groaned.

"Well, remember I 'threatened' Mason to not come?" she asked and I nodded at her.

"Well, I know it was a lame threat, but it actually worked. I also know he isn't fond of Adam, so I said if he came with us in the morning, I was going to make Adam and you share a room."

My eyes widened at her words. "That's your threat? Really?" I asked and placed my hand on my hip.

She nodded and looked down. "There's more . . . Since I knew you wouldn't come with us if he came along, I told him to come later on, and if he did that, you and him would share a room," she said the last part quietly.

My eyes widened even more. "You said what?" I yelled.

She gave me a small smile and stepped back. "You are mates, Tiana," she told me. "You can thank me later."

And with that, she ran off before I could say anything else. I stood there with my mouth hanging wide open. *Why the hell did she do that?* I ran my hands through my hair. I was pretty sure there were enough rooms in this huge mansion, so Mason didn't need to stay in my room.

I huffed out in annoyance and was about to close the door when Mason appeared in front of me. I looked at him as he stared at me.

"You don't really think I'm going to let you sleep in the same room as me, do you?" I questioned.

He gave me a small smirk and stepped inside. "This is my room," he spoke.

"Then I'll sleep in another room," I said and turned away.

"There are no other rooms," he told me.

I looked at him and placed my hand on my hip.

"You can't be serious! I'm sure there are plenty of rooms in this mansion!" I exclaimed.

He stayed silent and just looked at me. I then huffed out in annoyance and turned away but stopped when he grabbed my hand.

He walked closer to me, and his eyes turned a shade darker. "Just stay here. Maybe then, my wolf will stop all the nagging," he whispered.

I gulped and looked down.

"Please," he said in a low voice.

I sighed and looked at him, and at that moment, it was like my mouth spoke on its own.

"Okay."

CHAPTER 22

I ran my hands through my hair.
Yeah, I'm regretting this already.
His stare remained on me as I looked down and walked towards the bed. *What did I get myself into?* Huffing, I grabbed some pillows and a blanket, and neatly placed them on the floor. I turned around to see a confused Mason.

"What are you doing?" he asked.

I sighed and crossed my arms over my chest. "I agreed to stay here, but I didn't agree to sleep on the same bed with you."

He stepped closer to me and shook his head. "No, you won't be sleeping on the floor," he said.

I rolled my eyes at him. "Yes, I will."

"If you want, I'll sleep on the floor," he told me.

I shook my head and frowned. "No, you sleep on the bed while I sleep here," I argued.

"Can you not be impossible for once?" He sighed.

"Sure, says the guy who demanded for me to stay," I said to myself. However, he heard and sighed again.

"Fine, do whatever you want," he grumbled in frustration and lay on the bed, closing his eyes.

I looked towards the door and thought of getting out but knew that would be too mean. He did say please. I lay down and wrapped myself with the blanket, closing my eyes.

I am staying, but no way in hell am I sleeping in the same bed with him, even though my wolf is dying to.

Inhaling deeply, I pushed those thoughts away and tried not to think about the person who was right next to me and fell asleep on the hard floor.

*   *   *

My eyes snapped open when I felt a hard grip on my waist. I slowly turned my head to find Mason's sleeping figure right next to me. My eyes widened when I found his arm wrapped around my waist in a possessive manner. I was also on the bed! Didn't I sleep on the floor?

I groaned and swatted his arm away from me. He transferred me to the bed while I was asleep! Mason started to stir and slowly opened his eyes. As he made eye contact with me, his eyes soon turned a shade darker. I sat up and gave him a glare.

"Why am I sleeping here?" I asked, running my hand through my hair.

He sat up as well and looked away from me. "You really think I'm going to let you sleep on the hard floor?"

I frowned and looked down. Well, if he's stating it like that, then I can't really be mad at him. I looked up and met his stare.

"Uh . . . It would've been okay, but whatever." I stood up and walked to the closet, grabbing some clothes. I turned and found Mason standing right behind me.

"Did you sleep well?" he asked.

I nodded and stepped back. "Yeah, I did."

He scratched the back of his head and muttered, "Well, I guess I should go see Lina."

"Yeah, you go do that," I said awkwardly.

He turned away and walked towards the door but stopped when I called out to him.

"Mason."

He turned around and looked at me.

"Thank you. I wouldn't have enjoyed sleeping on the floor," I told him.

His eyes widened and then he gave me a weak smile. Even though it didn't reach his eyes, it caught me off guard. This was one of the first times I actually saw him genuinely smiling.

"You're welcome," he whispered.

I returned the smile before he exited my room. I sighed and shook my head. I was warming up to him, and I didn't know if that's a good thing. I pushed the thought aside and prepared myself for the day.

When I walked out, I saw Adam approaching me. He gave me a smile and hugged me.

"Good morning," I greeted him, hugging him back.

"Good morning, Tiana. Did you sleep well?" he asked.

"Yes, I did. Did you sleep well too?"

He nodded and gave me a small smile. "Come on, Lina made breakfast, and she told me to come and get you."

Once we made it to the dining room, Lina greeted me with a hug. I smiled at her and hugged her back.

"So, how was the night?" she asked while wiggling her brows.

My eyes widened, and I punched her arm lightly. "Lina! Seriously?" I asked.

She laughed and nodded. "What happened? You got to tell me everything."

I raised a brow at her and shook my head. "Nothing happened, Lina. Besides, I'm still pissed at you," I told her.

She smirked at me and tilted her head. "Sure you are. I bet you're thanking me in your head."

I rolled my eyes and crossed my arms over my chest. "Whatever," I muttered. "I'm hungry, let's get something to eat." I tried to change the subject and walked towards the table. I looked around and found everyone, except Mason. I sighed and sat down on a chair and started eating what was on the plate. Lina came and sat next to me and started to eat as well.

"So, what are we going to do today?" I asked.

She smiled and looked at me. "I was thinking about swimming," she answered.

I raised a brow at her. "At the beach?"

She gave me an amused look and nodded. "No, in the toilet," she replied.

I gave her a glare and shook my head. "I'm not going with you," I told her.

"What? Why? I have picked out a perfect bikini for you!" she stated, confused.

I shook my head again. "Nope, I don't like swimming at the beach."

"Why? Who doesn't like swimming at the beach?" she asked.

I shrugged and frowned. "I just don't like it," I answered.

"Fine. You won't swim, but you're still coming. Please!" she begged.

"Okay," I muttered.

"Great!" she exclaimed and then we went back to eating our food.

* * *

I looked at myself in the mirror, then walked towards the door when I heard a knock. I opened it and was greeted with an excited Lina.

"You ready?" she asked.

I nodded and looked at the bag that was in her hand. "What's in there?" I asked as I pointed at it.

"Oh, you know, a dead body!" she exclaimed sarcastically and I rolled my eyes at her.

"What else would be in here? Lotion, sunblock, sunglasses, bikinis, and some other stuff," she explained.

I crossed my arms over my chest. "Please tell me I won't regret letting you choose my bikini," I told her.

"Oh, you won't be the only one who will love it," she muttered to herself.

I raised a brow at her and gave her a confused look. "What?" I questioned.

She shook her head and smiled at me. "Nothing, come on. Let's go. The rest are waiting for us in the car."

We exited the house and walked towards the car. Lina sat in the driver's seat while I sat behind. I looked to my right to see Adam and Mason sitting next to me. They both looked stiff, probably hating the fact that they were too close to each other.

Well, don't they look happy?

I gave a small smile to Adam, and he returned it. Mason frowned and looked out the window, away from my direction. I looked down on my lap as Lina started the car and drove off. It didn't take long for us to arrive. Lina parked the car, and we exited the car with the bags.

I looked at the ocean and smiled. It was indeed beautiful.

"Isn't the view beautiful?" Lina asked.

I smiled at her and nodded. "Yes, it is," I stated.

"Come on, guys. Let's go!" Lina said.

We all started walking towards the sand. I took my shoes off, placed them in the bag, and looked at Lina.

"Where will we change?" I asked.

She looked around and pointed to a small room that I assumed was a bathroom. "Over there," she answered.

I nodded, and we started walking towards it. Once we were inside, I grabbed the bag and looked at Lina.

"What bikini should I wear?" I asked.

She smiled and took out something that made my mouth hang open.

"Do you really think I would agree to wear something like that?" I asked.

"Come on, Tiana. Now is not the time to be stubborn," she said.

I shook my head and frowned. "Lina, that is not a bikini! That is something a stripper would wear! It's barely going to cover up anything."

She sighed in frustration and shoved the bikini into my hands. "Tiana, you're going to wear this. Besides, I didn't pack anything else for you," she said.

I furrowed my brows at her. I didn't want to wear this. I'd rather stay in my clothes, but it looked like Lina wouldn't take no for an answer.

"Fine, I'll wear it," I groaned.

She smiled a big smile and hugged me. "Great!" she exclaimed excitedly.

"Just pass me a towel," I told her.

She pulled out a towel from the bag and gave it to me. I wouldn't wear whatever this thing was unless I covered myself. No way was I embarrassing myself in front of everybody.

Lina entered a stall while I entered the one next to her. I took my clothes off and wore the bikini. I cringed when I looked at my body. If only I had grabbed something for me when we were back at the mansion. I wrapped myself with the towel and sighed. *Much better.*

I opened the door to see Lina standing in front of me. She was wearing a bikini similar to the one I was wearing. I rolled my eyes at her and walked out.

"Why are you covering yourself?" she asked.

I shook my head.

"Well, at least let me see how you look," Lina said.

I sighed and opened the towel. Her eyes widened, and a smirk grew on her lips.

"Damn girl, I never knew you had a body like that," she exclaimed.

I raised a brow at her in amusement and returned the towel to its position. "Seriously, Lina?" I placed my hand on my hip.

"If I were a guy, I'd totally do you," she stated with a smirk.

I rolled my eyes at her and softly punched her on the arm. "That's nice to know," I said sarcastically.

She chuckled and grabbed the bag that was on the ground. "Mason's nose is going to bleed once he sees you without the towel," Lina said in amusement.

I looked at her and shook my head. "That won't happen because I'm not taking the towel off," I told her.

She smirked at me and shrugged before looking forward. "We'll see."

We started walking to where the guys were. Ryder looked toward our direction and smirked at us. I rolled my eyes at him and looked away. My eyes widened when I laid eyes on Mason. He was in nothing but swimming shorts. Everything else was visible to the human eye, more precisely his chest—his attractive chest.

I looked away and mentally slapped myself upon realizing what I was thinking. I glanced back at Mason to see him staring at me. I awkwardly looked away and saw Lina smirking at me.

Can I go a day without seeing her smirk?

We continued to walk until we were in front of everybody. Ryder came up to me and wrapped an arm around my shoulder.

"So, are you going to show me what's under that towel?" he asked with a smirk on his face and started to wiggle his brows.

I swatted his arm off of me and rolled my eyes at him. "No," I stated and he pouted.

Adam walked to us and glared at Ryder before looking at me. "Want to swim, Tiana?" he asked.

I shook my head at him. "No, you know I don't like to get wet."

"Yeah, I know. You're like a cat," he said, smiling.

"I think I'll take that as a compliment," I told him.

He chuckled and nodded. "Well, I'm going to go swim."

I gave him one last smile before he walked away.

I looked to my right and saw Mason staring intensely at me. I immediately looked away and grabbed the bag that Lina was holding and opened it. Might as well work on my tan. After applying some sunblock on my skin, I grabbed another towel and placed it on the sand. I lay on it and closed my eyes, letting the sun do its thing.

> Now, I know what you guys are thinking. How will I get a tan when I have a towel wrapped around me? Well, I don't really care. I'm never taking it off.

After a while, I got up to see where Lina was. I saw her swimming and splashing water at Tyler and Ryder in the distance. I smiled at that and then snapped my head to the right when I felt Mason's presence. He looked down at me with a face devoid of emotions.

"Do you need anything, Mason?" I asked, getting up.

"No." He shook his head.

I gave him a confused look and saw Lina walking towards our direction. I brought my attention back to Mason and tilted my head slightly.

"Then why are you standing here?" I asked, not trying to sound rude. I mean, he walked up to me and stood really close. He must have wanted something.

He shrugged and looked away from me. "I can't stand here?" he asked.

"That's not what I meant—" I started but immediately stopped when Lina passed by me and pulled my towel, leaving me standing there, embarrassed. I looked up to see a shocked Mason and a smirking Lina.

"Oops, my bad!" Lina exclaimed.
My eyes widened but soon turned into a glare.
Oh, she's dead!

CHAPTER 23

Mason's eyes roamed over my body, and his eyes immediately turned dark. After a couple of seconds of just standing there, he snapped out of it and kneeled, grabbing the towel and wrapping it around my body in a possessive manner, leaving me stiff. He looked back, and thankfully, no one was staring at us.

Lina's smirk didn't disappear, and neither did my glare. She stepped closer to us as Mason looked at me with dark eyes. I didn't know if that was a bad thing or not. He soon looked down at the sand and stepped back.

"Don't take the towel off," he ordered and then looked at Lina. I frowned in confusion and stared at him.

"Why? Don't be a party pooper, Mason!" Lina whined.

"Because I said so." He looked at me, his face emotionless.

"Do as I say, Tiana," he told me.

I gulped and nodded. I wasn't going to take it off even if he didn't order me. He took another step back and immediately turned around, walking off. I couldn't miss the way he tightened his fist, like he was holding himself back from doing something. I shook my head and brought my stare to Lina, who was smiling sheepishly.

"B*tch, you are so dead," I yelled and ran towards her.

Her eyes immediately widened in amusement and she started running too, all while laughing her butt off.

"Come on, Tiana! Don't be mad! Did you see how my brother looked at you?" she asked but didn't stop running.

"I don't give a shit at how he looked at me! You did it on purpose when you knew I didn't want anyone seeing me like that," I said, successfully grabbing her arm.

"And why is that? You have one sexy body, and you should be proud! Besides, I know Mason's wolf begged him to take you right then and there," she said, laughing.

I punched her shoulder lightly and shook my head. "No, don't say that! I don't need to imagine that!"

I really don't. Just thinking about it was making my wolf crazy. Besides, our situation wasn't the appropriate time for doing something like that. He barely tolerated my presence when I was around, so that would never happen.

"Well, he was. I saw it in his eyes," Lina spoke.

I shook my head again and let go of her arm. "I hate you," I grumbled. "You embarrassed me. It's a good thing that nobody was looking, or I don't know what I would have done."

"Aww, I love you too," Lina gushed. "And I'm sorry, but I'm glad I did it. Now Mason won't stop thinking about you, and maybe he'll decide to confess his undeniable love towards you," she said the last part in a joking manner.

I rolled my eyes at her and shook my head. *Yeah, in her wildest dreams.*

"I was quite surprised when he covered you, but at the same time, I know why," Lina spoke.

I huffed and shook my head. "I know what you're going to say."

She smiled and nodded. "Because he didn't want anyone else seeing what's his," she squealed.

I rolled my eyes. "Sure, I'll go along with that if you just shut up," I told her while crossing my arms over my chest.

She rolled her eyes at me and smirked. "You know I'm right. You just don't want to admit it," she said.

I ignored her and started walking away.

Sure, like I would believe that. He barely even looked at me with any emotion on his face, but it's not like I cared. I guess it was for the best.

I pushed those thoughts aside and sat on the sand. I watched the rest play in the water while I enjoyed the view. Fortunately, Mason wasn't anywhere in sight. I didn't know where he wandered off to, but I was thankful he wasn't here to make things awkward.

I stayed like that for a while until Tyler and Ryder came walking towards me with smiles on their faces. I raised a brow at them in confusion as they stood in front of me.

"Tiana, come play in the water with us," Tyler spoke.

I smiled at them and shook my head. "No, I'm fine staying here."

"We won't take no for an answer. We came here to have some fun, and sitting on your ass all day isn't fun," Ryder said and nodded at Tyler. They gave me a smirk, and before I could say anything, they carried me as they ran towards the water.

My eyes widened, and I repeatedly shook my head, demanding them to let me go.

However, they did not listen and threw me into the water like some dying fish on shore. I pushed my head above the water and gasped for air. By now, Ryder and Tyler were laughing their heads off, perhaps because of how I looked.

I glared at them, but my glare soon disappeared when I saw a towel floating at a distance and realized that it was mine. I immediately sunk my body into the water to cover myself as much as possible. But judging from the smirk on their faces, they already saw everything and they didn't really mind.

I rolled my eyes and glared once again. If looks could kill, they wouldn't only be six feet under. No. They would be ten feet under.

"This is not funny," I growled.

The laughter calmed down a bit, and they looked at me with amusement in their eyes.

"It actually is. You got to see the look on your face when we dropped you. It was hilarious," Ryder said and Tyler nodded in agreement.

I growled and launched at them in an aggressive manner, starting to act like a kid that was throwing a tantrum. This only made them laugh even more, throwing me in the water again.

I gasped for air and started splashing them. "You bastards! You got me all wet," I growled, grabbing Ryder and pushing him into the water. I let go when he raised his head up to gasp for air.

"You're crazy!" Ryder said with amusement laced in his voice. "You could've killed me."

I rolled my eyes at him and punched his arm. "I wish I did," I muttered with a smirk on my face.

Tyler started laughing, and Ryder pouted. "Ouch, that hurt me right here," he said, pointing at his chest.

I rolled my eyes again but glared at Tyler when he splashed water on me.

Soon, Lina joined us and we stayed like that for a while, splashing and laughing together. My opinion about the beach changed at that moment, and I actually liked the water now. It was really refreshing and nice.

I was about to jump on Lina when I saw Mason walking towards us with a blank look. I stared at him, and he caught my eye. His eyes were hard as he looked at us.

Lina looked at me and smirked. "Mason! Come join the fun!" she yelled.

He shook his head and stood there watching us. It felt weird, and I couldn't bring my attention elsewhere when he was just standing there and looking at us like that. I ignored his presence and continued to have fun with Lina.

I gasped when Adam came from behind me and carried me, throwing me into the water. I ran up to him and jumped on his back, trying countless times to push his head in the water, but he only laughed and threw me off of his body, which had me falling into the water again.

I growled playfully and pushed with all my might to get him to fall, but that only led to Adam carrying me again and holding my body up in the air. Before he actually had the chance to throw me, Mason's voice stopped him.

"That's enough. Let's head back."

Adam put me down, and Lina looked at her brother with a frown.

"What? Why?" she asked as we walked out the water and towards Mason.

"Because I said so. Besides, I have some stuff I have to deal with back at the mansion," he said.

I looked up and made eye contact with him.

"You go deal with your stuff, Mason, but we are staying here," Lina argued.

Mason's eyes turned to Lina, and he growled deeply. "Lina, don't defy me. It's an order."

Lina rolled her eyes and sighed in frustration. "Fine, whatever," she groaned. "Party pooper," Lina muttered under her breath.

We all grabbed our stuff and I wrapped myself with a new towel. When everyone was ready, we walked back to the car and soon drove off.

Sitting in the car with a tense Mason was really awkward. No one said a word because it was really obvious that he wasn't in a happy mood, and if someone spoke, we would see his bad side. I didn't know what happened for him to be like this, but it was better to not ask. We soon made it back, exited the car, and carried our stuff back to the mansion.

"I'll make lunch, so be here at three, then I'll tell you guys what else I have planned for today," Lina said with a smile on her face.

We smiled at her and headed back to our rooms. I hurried into my room before Mason could even look at me or say something, and shut the door. I placed my stuff back to where they were supposed to be and sat on the bed. I recalled everything that happened today and smiled.

It was a nice day, and I was happy we had fun. I was just curious what else Lina had in store for us.

* * *

I walked out of the room and towards the stairs. When I looked down at my wrist to check the time, I bumped into someone and stumbled back. Two arms were instantly wrapped around my waist tightly. My wolf started yelping, and Mason's scent hit my nostrils. I slowly looked up to meet his worried eyes.

"Are you okay?" he asked in a deep voice.

I immediately pulled out of his grip when I realized how close we were. "Yeah, didn't see you there," I muttered.

He placed his hand in his pockets. "Lina told me to tell you that lunch is ready."

Taking a step back, I said, "I was actually going there."

I headed towards the dining room with Mason awkwardly walking next to me. The tension between us was too high. I glanced at him to see him looking at me. I immediately turned away and wondered what I could do to lessen this tension.

"So, when are you heading back to the pack?" I asked.

His eyes turned a shade darker and his jaw was clenched. "Why? Do you not want me here?" he asked.

My eyes widened, and I stopped walking. "That's not what I meant. I'm sure you have lots of stuff to do, and the pack may need their alpha," I told him.

"Nick is taking care of that. It's really none of your business. I'll head back when I want to," he said with a hard tone and walked off angrily.

I stood there confused. What did I do to get him to act like that? My wolf started nagging at me, telling me that I made him feel like he was unwanted. I didn't know that would get him angry. If I had known, I would have never asked.

My wolf didn't stop, so I eventually blocked her out before she made me feel even guiltier than I already was.

I sighed in frustration and entered the dining room. I looked around but didn't see Mason. Of course, he always disappeared at moments like these. I didn't know if I should talk to him or just let things go. I sighed again and approached Lina.

"You hungry?" Lina asked.

I gave her a weak smile and nodded. "When am I not?" I questioned.

She chuckled and shrugged. "You got a point."

"So what are you making?" I asked.

Grinning, she took out some plates and cups. "Your favorite, macaroni and cheese!" she exclaimed.

"Yes! Thank you! I've been craving that for a while now," I told her as I took out a bottle of soda from the fridge.

"You're welcome. Also, come help me set the table. Tyler, Ryder, and Adam have been complaining that they want to eat for hours now. They're literally pigs on foot." Lina chuckled.

I laughed and helped her. "Yeah, you're right," I said.

When we were done, they came walking in and sat on their chairs. Lina looked around, and a confused expression crossed her features.

"Where's Mason?" she asked me.

I looked down at my plate. "Don't ask me. How should I know?"

She shrugged and sat down next to me. "I don't know. I was guessing that you would have known," she replied.

I shook my head and started eating. Lina stayed silent and ate as well. The rest chatted as I only focused on my food. After a while, the door opened and Mason walked in.

Lina looked at him and frowned. "Where have you been, Mason? You're late."

"I had some business to deal with," he said while looking at me.

I frowned and looked down at my plate.

"Well, okay. Just eat so we can get going," Lina said.

The rest looked at Lina in confusion.

"Where are we going?" Adam asked.

Lina smiled at him and stood up from her chair. "We're going hiking! So get ready and wear something suitable. We are going to have so much fun," she answered and said the last part to herself.

Everyone smiled, but I raised a brow at her.

Hiking? Don't humans do that?

I mean, we're werewolves so we usually just shifted and ran in the woods, but not hike. It sounded weird to us, but I guess doing something different might be nice.

Lina excused herself. I decided to change into something else, so I got up and glanced at Mason one more time to see him eating his food silently. I then turned around and walked off. Once I entered my room, I picked out my clothes and shoes, changed into them, and tied my hair into a ponytail. When I reached the living room, everyone was already there.

"Is everyone ready?" Lina asked as she climbed down the stairs.

We all nodded and walked towards the car. This whole time, I ignored Mason's presence and focused on something else. I just felt like whenever we were close to each other, things would get awkward and tense. Well, there were a couple of times that things went just fine, but today wasn't one of those times.

Moreover, this mate bond didn't help at all as it confused me even more. And him always having an emotionless face made things harder. Oh, let's also not forget about him being bipolar.

One day he was all comfortable and calm, then the next he was as stubborn as a rock.

I sighed in frustration and pushed those thoughts aside. Now was not the time to be thinking about this. I shouldn't really care if he's like that, and it was not my business to ask about his mood.

We soon drove towards the woods. This time, it wasn't silent. Everyone's mouth, except Mason's and mine, were busy. Lina sang random songs while Adam, Ryder, and Tyler chatted about something that wasn't important. After twenty minutes, Lina parked the car on the roadside, and we got out. I looked around and found it nice.

The trees were close to each other, and the air was refreshing. It looked like a perfect place to hike. We got into the woods with a bag of water, food, and emergency supplies, not like anything was going to happen. We were werewolves, so we could take care of ourselves.

"So what is the purpose of this again?" Mason asked.

Lina looked at him and placed her hand on her hip. "To have some fun and act like humans for once. We will split up into teams and hike our way out of the woods without shifting, and whoever makes it out first wins," she explained.

"Does that sound good?" Lina asked and we all nodded.

"Good. Now I'll team you up. Mason and Tiana, you're together," she said with a smile on her face.

Shocked, I looked at Mason, whose eyes were already on mine.

Okay, now I know her real purpose.

I was about to protest when Mason grabbed my hand and started walking further into the woods, leaving the rest behind. I stared at our hands, and when we were out of sight, I said, "You can let go now."

Stopping, he looked at our hands then at me before letting go. From time to time, we talked about stuff but nothing serious.

We were climbing a steep hill that was filled with rocks and sticks when I noticed that it was getting dark.

Once we were at the top, I decided to confront him about what happened today.

"Mason," I whispered.

He stopped in his tracks and looked down at me. "Yes?"

"I'm sorry about today. I didn't want you to get the wrong idea. It's not like I don't enjoy your company. Well, it's not like I enjoy your company either, but you get what I mean," I told him but then placed my hand on my lips when I realized what I just said.

I slowly looked up to meet Mason's eyes but was caught off guard when I saw him smiling at me. *Mason actually smiles?* I thought, dropping my hand back to my side.

"You're something else," he muttered, stepping towards me.

"Uhh . . . I am?"

He chuckled slightly, and by now, we were so close to each other.

"Yeah, and I like it," he whispered.

I gulped and tilted my head down, but he raised my chin up and looked at me.

"You do?" I asked stupidly.

"Yeah," he whispered again.

His stare moved to my lips, and I knew where this was going. I thought about pulling away, but I was too caught up in the moment. Holding my face gently, he looked into my eyes and softly placed his lips on mine.

I closed my eyes and placed my hand on his chest, while he continued to kiss my lips passionately. We stayed like that until we heard Lina's voice.

"Mason? Tiana? What are you guys doing up there?"

I immediately pushed Mason away and stepped back, but that only led me to stumble on a rock. Unfortunately, gravity did its thing and I fell down the steep, steep hill.

And the last thing I saw before I blacked out was Mason's worried face.

CHAPTER 24

I slowly stirred when I heard a loud voice laced with anger and worry boom in the air. I couldn't exactly tell who it belonged to as I was still half asleep, but it was somehow familiar. After a while, I opened my eyes but immediately shut them due to the bright light and winced in pain.

I was fully awake now, conscious of the voices around me. I soon realized that everyone was in some kind of argument. I didn't open my eyes again to avoid confronting them, more so that my head was still in pain and spinning, and I was too tired to move. Instead, I listened to them, curious as to why they were having an argument.

"Mason, calm down," Lina spoke. "She's going to be fine. She just needs to rest."

"How do you know that, Lina? You're not a pack doctor," he growled. "Look at her. She's unconscious and she's not healing as fast as she's supposed to. This isn't good."

"She hit her head when she fell, Mason. Of course, she's unconscious. But she will heal soon, so give it a little time. And going back to the pack isn't worth it," she told him.

Mason growled, and I could hear his frustration. "She's supposed to be healed by now. It's been a goddamn hour, and she hasn't woken up yet. Something is wrong," he exclaimed in a rough voice, making Lina sigh.

"There is a reason for that, and I'm sure Tiana would be happy to tell you herself," she said.

"Yeah, Lina is right. Tiana's wolf heals slower than ours. I don't think going all the way back to the pack house is worth it," Adam cut in.

"And why is that?" Mason asked.

I slowly opened my eyes to see everyone in front of me. I figured right now was the perfect time to make my appearance and explain to him what I really was.

"Because I'm a hybrid."

They all turned to me, their shoulders sagging in relief.

Lina smiled and placed her hand on mine. "Oh, thank goodness you're awake," she said.

I slowly got up and winced when my head throbbed in pain.

Lina helped me sit up and pointed at Mason. "This guy over here acted as if you're dying and wanted to take you to the pack doctor."

"No, it isn't worth it." I shook my head. "The hit to my head just made me black out, but other than that, I'm completely fine." I looked at Mason, who was in shock.

"You're a hybrid?" he asked lowly.

I slowly nodded at him. "Yes, I'm half werewolf and half angel. That's why it takes me a little longer to heal compared to you guys."

He nodded and placed his hands in his pockets. "That explains it," he muttered.

"Yeah, if she was a full werewolf, the hit to her head shouldn't have affected her," Adam spoke and smiled.

I returned it and nodded in agreement.

"Are you okay? Does your head still hurt?" Tyler asked.

"I'm fine. It hurts a little, but I should be completely healed soon."

Tyler nodded and smiled at me as well.

Mason looked intensely at me. He then turned his stare to the others and spoke, "Tomorrow, we are leaving. We have stayed here long enough. So pack your bags and be ready."

Lina was about to argue, but Mason gave her a warning glare.

"Fine," she grumbled lowly and sighed in frustration.

Mason turned to me one more time before stalking out of the room. I then brought my attention to the rest of the group and gave them a weak smile as they stepped closer to me.

"You gave us a fright back there," Ryder spoke with a hint of amusement in his voice.

I pouted at him, but my pout soon turned into a smile when he pouted as well. "Sorry, it wasn't really my intention," I told him.

By now, Adam and Lina were sitting by me on the bed while Ryder and Tyler were on the chairs in front of me.

"Yeah, I know. It wasn't like you purposely fell off that steep hill and blacked out just to frighten us . . . Ha! More like Mason," Ryder joked.

I rolled my eyes at him as Lina and Tyler chuckled. I looked at Adam to see him staring intensely at me. I raised my brow at him, but he shook his head and gave me a small smile.

"Anyway, what caused you to fall?" Tyler asked.

My eyes widened for a split second when I remembered what exactly had happened, and I immediately wanted to forget about it. My wolf started purring in delight at that memory while I wanted to shove my head into the ground and not come out due to embarrassment. Like, how did I go from kissing him one second and then falling down the hill in another?

Stupid, Tiana.

I brought my attention back to Tyler and shrugged. "I don't really know. I guess I tripped."

He slowly nodded, not looking too convinced, but shook it off. "Oh, well, it's good that nothing worse happened."

I nodded at that and smiled. "Thankfully, nothing did." I looked at Lina when she got off my bed.

"Well, since my thick-headed brother wants us to leave tomorrow morning, we'll have to wake up early. With that, I might as well sleep now," Lina grumbled.

Ryder crossed his arms over his chest. "Why does your brother always have to rain on our parade?" he asked.

Lina pouted and shrugged. "I don't know, but I hate it," she whined.

Tyler shook his head in amusement and placed his hand on her shoulder. "Yeah, we can tell," he said. "Now let's go and leave Tiana so she can rest. I'm sure she needs it."

Lina waved goodbye and then walked out of the room with the rest. Adam was the last one to leave, giving me a small smile. As he did so, I didn't miss the look on his face. It was as if he wanted to tell me something. I shook off that thought and stood up to change into my pajamas.

I wouldn't sleep any time soon, especially after what had happened, so I just laid on my bed, staring at the ceiling and thinking about everything. I thought about how my life had changed in an instant.

I thought about Mom and Dad. I knew they were okay. I knew that dream I had in the dungeons wasn't just a dream. It was some sort of message to let me know that they were okay. I didn't know how they did it, but I knew it was their doing. I missed them deeply. No one knew when I would see them again. With all that's going on, I usually forgot about what had happened not too long ago, but it was always on the back of my mind.

A tear slipped out of my eye, but I quickly wiped it away.

I needed to be strong for them. They wouldn't want me worrying about them like this. I sighed as I thought about Mason. He was so weird. I didn't know if that's supposed to be a bad or a good thing, but it's like he had different personalities. He changed in the blink of an eye, like what had happened today. He went from chuckling to growling in anger in a split second. He was so hard to understand, and I didn't really know if I wanted to.

Kissing each other didn't help at all. At those moments, I couldn't back out, like something was pulling me towards him. Just thinking about it made my wolf purr. Ugh, she wasn't helping either. I wish things weren't so difficult.

My mind continued to think endlessly. I didn't know how long I had been staring at the white ceiling, but after some time, I heard a soft knock on my door. I raised my brow in confusion and sat up.

Who would need me at this time?

Before I could stand, the person opened the door and slowly walked into my room. Adam came into sight and gave me a small smile. "I had a feeling you're awake," he spoke softly and sat next to me.

"What are you doing here?" I asked, confused.

He shrugged and said, "I couldn't really sleep and figured you weren't asleep either."

"And why is that?" I questioned.

"Oh, I don't know. I guess I know you well enough to know you usually stay up late at night," he answered.

I smiled and nodded. He was silent for a while, and after observing his face carefully, I knew something was wrong.

"Adam . . ."

"Yeah?"

"What's wrong? I know there's something going on in that head of yours," I whispered.

He stared at his hands for a couple of seconds, sighing, and looked at me. "Nothing, but I do have a question that I've been meaning to ask you."

I nodded and gave him a small smile. "Go for it."

Sighing, he asked, "Are you and Mason a thing now?"

My smile immediately dropped, and I looked at him in confusion. "What? Why are you asking that?"

He sighed again and shrugged. "I don't know. It's just that I've been noticing you guys are really close to each other."

I shook my head at him. "No, we're not close to each other," I whispered and he nodded. "Besides, you know I can't repeat that ever again," A tear wanted to slip out of my eye due to the memory, but I held myself back.

Adam looked at me intensely, immediately knowing what I was thinking about, and placed his hand on mine.

"Tiana," he whispered. "It's been about two years."

I nodded at him. "I know," my voice cracked, "but it still hurts. No matter how long it's been, I can't forget the pain."

Adam pulled me into a hug. I buried my face on his chest, tears falling from my eyes.

"It's okay, Tiana. Trust me, things will get better. You can't let memories like those bring you down again," he whispered.

I pulled away. "Yeah, you're right. I hope so."

Adam gave me a weak smile as he softly wiped the tears on my cheeks. I placed my head on his shoulder as we talked about our memories back in our old pack. We stayed like that for a while until he stood up.

"Well, I got to go. It's getting really late. If you need anything, make sure to tell me, okay? Know that I'm always here," he told me.

"Okay, thank you, Adam," I whispered.

"You're welcome, Tiana." He placed a gentle kiss on my forehead and walked out of my room, softly closing the door behind him.

I sighed and placed my head on the soft pillow. I closed my eyes and forced those bad memories away. I didn't want to think about them ever again. They just made me weak, and I didn't like that at all. Soon, my body relaxed and my mind calmed down. After a while, my body started drifting off into the abyss.

I was so close to falling into a deep sleep when I heard my bedroom door gently open. I was too tired to open my eyes and see who it was, but I figured it was Adam. He must have forgotten something and came back.

However, my mind was immediately awakened when Mason's scent hit my nostrils. I forced my breathing to remain even, and I acted as if I was asleep to see what he was going to do.

Why is he in my room at a time like this?

The room went silent, but I knew he was still there because his scent roamed the air, hitting me strongly as I inhaled.

His scent soon became stronger, and I assumed he was slowly walking closer. I was so confused, but I kept my act. After a minute or two, he caressed my cheek, which made tingling sparks erupt from our skin contact. He continued all the way to my hair, letting his fingers softly grasp its ends, and sighed.

I then felt my bed lean to the side when he sat on the edge.

Millions of questions ran through my head as he stayed there in silence. I could feel his stare burning through my eyelids, and it took me all I got to not open them.

His scent soon became stronger, and the next thing I knew, his lips were softly pressed against mine. It didn't last long as he soon pulled away. I didn't know why he did that, but it left me shocked. He gently cupped my cheek for a moment.

"Dammit," he cursed under his breath and got off the bed.

His scent soon weakened and then disappeared into thin air, as if it was never there. Shocked, I immediately opened my eyes and placed a finger on my lips as my mind registered what he just did.

Right then and there, I knew I wasn't getting any sleep tonight.

CHAPTER 25

I hopped into the shower and immediately sighed in relief when the warm water hit my tensed muscles. I tilted my head back in satisfaction and closed my eyes for a moment.
This is heaven.
After I was done, I stood in front of the mirror and frowned when I saw the bags under my eyes.
It had been a whole week since we left the island, and let me tell you, it had been hectic and boring. After what had happened that night, I avoided Mason at all cost. Whenever I saw him, I immediately turned away and walked off. I barely made eye contact with him, and when I accidentally did, I averted my eyes immediately. I didn't want to confront nor talk to him. It was too hard to explain why, but I didn't want to get caught in these feelings. It's better this way.
I didn't know if Mason had caught on, but it was like he had been trying to talk to me. I, of course, always found a way to escape before he could actually do anything. Besides, I didn't think he really cared.
He was mostly outside of the territory doing some business this week. He would return for a while and then leave. I guess it's an alpha thing, but I saw this as an advantage. Maybe with him gone for a while, I could get my thoughts together and brush these unwanted feelings off. Hopefully. I shook my head and pushed these thoughts aside.

Lately, Lina and I had been helping around the pack house, so I thought of asking her if she wanted a day out because I definitely needed one and we both deserved it.

I knocked on her door and it soon opened, revealing a happy Lina.

"Hey!" she greeted me and pulled me into a hug.

"Hi, how's your morning?" I asked, breaking the hug.

"It's fabulous since you're here," she gushed.

I chuckled and sat on her bed. "Do you have any plans today?"

She shook her head and sat next to me. "No, not really. Why? Do you want to go somewhere?"

"Yeah, kinda. I was thinking of going outside or something," I stated, smiling.

"That sounds good. Also, Mason isn't here to stop us," she said with a huge grin plastered on her face.

I awkwardly nodded in agreement. "Okay, let's head out. But before that, I need to let my wolf out for a run and grab some breakfast."

Walking towards her closet, she said, "Sure. I'll get ready, and let's meet in the dining room for breakfast."

"Okay, bye," I said as I got up and walked towards the door.

I greeted some pack members before walking out the pack house. My wolf had been nagging to be let out and to run in the woods for a while now. I figured she wasn't going to stop until I let her. Couldn't blame her, though. She needed to have control every now and then.

I was walking towards the woods when I smelled a familiar scent that immediately caused me to stiffen and stop dead in my tracks. I snapped my head towards the direction of the scent, making eye contact with Kyle. His smirk seemed like it wasn't going away any time soon.

He wasn't too far away from me but not too close either. He raised his hand and gave me a small wave, sending shivers down my spine.

I hadn't seen him since the incident that had caused him to be locked up in the dungeons for two weeks. He must have been released last week, but I didn't see him roam around the pack's territory.

I furrowed my brows at him and then continued walking towards the woods, ignoring his presence. I felt his stare burn holes through the back of my neck. This guy was weird, and I didn't want anything to do with him, especially after that troublesome thing.

I finally made it into the woods and stopped to observe the beautiful nature around me. The chirping of the birds floated in the air as the quiet wind softly caressed my face. I closed my eyes and took a deep breath. When I opened them, I started taking my clothes off and immediately shifted into my wolf.

My wolf ran as fast as she could, her brown fur dancing in the wind. She passed numerous trees, lakes, rocks, animals, and anything one would find in the vast woods. When she noticed that she was getting closer to the borders, she turned around and ran in the other direction.

My wolf was in a pleasant mood at this moment. Her tongue was out as the wind hit her face, and she yelped in joy. After a while, she headed back to where the clothes were and shifted back.

That was enough running for today. Once shifted, I grabbed my clothes and immediately put them on before anyone roaming the woods could see me.

I was about to head back to the pack house when a voice stopped me.

"What are you doing out here?"

I snapped my head towards the direction of the voice and was met with an emotionless Mason. I frowned at him and wondered why he was here. I wasn't expecting him to return to the pack this soon. He continued to stare at me and took a couple of steps closer.

"I was out for a run," I answered him.

He took another step closer. "You shouldn't have run too deep into the woods. Don't do it again without my permission."

My frown deepened. "And why is that?"

His eyes turned dark. "Because I said so," he said in a hard tone.

I scoffed and shook my head. Of course, he was going to say that. I decided I didn't want to get into a childish argument with him. I didn't want to be in his presence from the beginning, so it would be better if I just walked off.

"Whatever," I muttered and turned around.

Before I could take two steps, Mason grabbed my hand. I looked at him with a frown plastered on my face. "What?" I tried to loosen his grip which, by the way, was sending tingling sensation throughout my body.

"Explain," he ordered.

I furrowed my brows at him in confusion. "Explain what?" I asked, annoyed.

He growled lowly and pulled me closer to him. "Don't act as if you don't know what I'm talking about. Explain to me why you keep running off when I appear," he said.

My eyes widened, and I stared at him for a moment. "What are you talking about?" I asked, trying to sound stupid.

"You know exactly what I'm talking about, Tiana," he growled.

I looked down to my feet before looking up to him seriously. "No, I don't."

He growled and tightened his grip. "Tiana, answer me. That is an order."

I huffed in annoyance and anger for using the alpha card on me. "Maybe I just don't want to be around you. Just leave me alone and forget whatever has happened between us because I want nothing to do with you," I stated in a harsh tone.

He was caught off guard. A sullen look crossed his feature for a split second, and then his emotionless face took over again. I quickly regretted saying those words, realizing I had said it in a really rude way.

Shit.

He let go of my hand and roughly pushed me against a tree in an aggressive manner, his eyes turning pitch-black. I gasped in shock, and he growled lowly.

"Listen here. Just because we've had a couple of nice moments, you now mean something to me. In all those times, my wolf was in control and I let him for his sake. It was never me, so don't get any ideas. You are nothing to me. I am your alpha, and you will respect me and you will not raise your voice at me. Do you hear me?"

I remained shocked, and when I didn't answer, he growled loudly. "Do I make myself clear?"

I knew what I had said wasn't necessary and it was really rude of me, but his words lit a fire in me that all I wanted to do was punch him in the face. His words affected me a little, I couldn't deny that.

My wolf whined in pain and begged me to apologize. However, if his words were true, then I wanted nothing to do with him. It was better this way. Maybe this would make it easier for me to forget what had happened between us.

Call me selfish, but this was for the best.

"Yes," I growled.

He pulled away from me and clinched his fist. "Good. Now head back to the pack house," he ordered.

I growled in frustration one more time before running off. I kept telling myself that this was for the better and that I would thank myself in the future. However, my wolf filled me with guilt and it didn't make me feel any better.

I ran into Lina's room to find her fixing her hair. She turned over to me and smiled. "You ready?" she asked.

"One problem though," I said.

She furrowed her brows and tilted her head to the side in confusion. "What is it?"

"Your brother is here."

Her eyes widened, and she frowned. "Really? Dammit! Now we won't be able to go anywhere," she whined.

I shrugged. "Maybe he'll leave again later today."

"Hopefully. Let's just get some breakfast, and we'll see what happens there," she said, sighing.

We arrived at the dining room and saw there were already a couple of pack members eating.

We grabbed some food on the table and sat down. While eating, I tried to push away the memories of what had happened not too long ago. I looked at Lina when I saw her place her fork down and zoned out, looking like she was communicating with someone through the mind link. I furrowed my brows in confusion and wondered who she was talking to.

After a couple of seconds, she snapped out of it and turned to me.

"Who was that?" I asked.

"Mason. He informed me that there is a pack meeting after an hour and he wants everyone to attend. He says it's important," Lina answered.

I frowned when his name came out of her mouth. I tried not to think too much about it but couldn't help wondering why Mason would want to have a pack meeting. "Oh, I hope it's nothing bad," I said.

"Me too," she muttered and went back to eating.

I just stared at my plate and sighed. I needed to get these thoughts out of my head.

After eating, I told Lina I would see Adam and meet up with her at the meeting. I walked up to Adam's room and knocked on his door. He soon opened it, looking tired as hell, and then went back to his bed without saying anything.

I frowned at the sight and sat on the edge of his bed. "What's wrong with you?"

He groaned and turned his head towards me. "I'm really tired," he grunted.

"Why? Did you not sleep well?"

He shook his head and groaned again. "No, not at all." He raised his head from the pillow and pouted. "Nick was really hard on us yesterday. Training, training, and more training. I barely slept a wink. Why am I a pack warrior again?" he whined like a baby.

I raised my brow at him in amusement and patted his head. "Aww, poor Adam," I said as if he were a child.

"I'm serious, Tiana," he whined and pouted.

I chuckled and nodded. "Yeah, I know. You just have to hang in there. Being a pack warrior has always been your dream, remember?"

"Yes, I remember, but thinking about it was always easy," Adam said, sighing.

I shook my head and slapped his arm. "Stop being a baby," I joked.

He looked at me and pouted even more. "Ouch. That hit me right here," he said and pointed at his chest.

I rolled my eyes at him. "Did you hear about the pack meeting we're having today?"

He sat up and nodded. "Yeah, Nick brought it up yesterday." He sighed and ran his hand through his hair.

"Do you know why?" I asked.

He shook his head. "Nope, not a single clue."

I nodded and got up. "Well, you get ready so we can head out together," I ordered in a playful manner.

He narrowed his eyes on me and stood up. "Are you ordering me around?" he asked.

I smirked and shrugged. "Maybe. If I didn't, then you would be lost in life." I chuckled.

He growled playfully and grabbed me, carrying me on his shoulders.

I squealed in shock as he opened his bedroom door and gently yet playfully dropped me on my bum.

"You wait out here. I have to get dressed," he ordered with a smirk on his face.

I rolled my eyes and got up when he closed the door. *Did he really just do that?* While I was standing there in silence, I smelled Mason's scent. I immediately stiffened and snapped my head towards the direction of the scent.

I saw Mason walking towards my direction.

He stopped dead in his tracks and looked at me, his face blank. I didn't move nor look anywhere else. After a couple of seconds, he looked away and walked past me, as if I wasn't there. I kept staring at him until he was out of sight. I sighed and placed my head back on the wall and took a deep breath. His scent lingered in the air, causing my wolf to whine. I huffed out in annoyance.

Adam finally opened the door, smiling.

"What took you so long?" I asked jokingly, trying to lighten up the mood as my wolf kept spreading negative vibes. "Had to take time on your makeup and hair?"

His eyes lightened up in amusement, and a chuckle escaped his lips. "Yes, as a matter of fact I did. I ran out of foundation, so it took me a while to find a new one in my drawer and open it. It was a hassle," he said sarcastically.

I burst into laughter at his words, and he started to laugh as well. I pretended to wipe an invisible tear as we started walking.

"What on earth am I ever going to do with you?" I asked.

He rolled his eyes and smiled. "It should be me who's asking that question," he stated and I chuckled.

As soon as we arrived at the living room, we greeted a couple of pack members and a few of Adam's friends in the training. We sat on the couches for a while, just chatting. I used that opportunity to not think about anything that had to do with Mason because, in a while, I had to face him whether I liked it or not.

And let me tell you, I was not excited, but my wolf thought otherwise.

After half an hour or so, it was time for the pack meeting. It would take place at the back of the pack house, so Adam and I got up and walked towards the back door, together with the others. There were many pack members standing and waiting for the meeting to begin. I saw Lina and started walking towards her direction, with Adam following suit. When she saw me, she smiled and waved.

"Hey," Adam greeted.

"Hi, Adam. How is your training going?" Lina asked and I smirked at him.

Adam sighed and answered, "It's going good."

Lina nodded and turned her face to me. "Tiana, come here for a second," she said and stepped away.

I furrowed my brows in confusion and shrugged at Adam before walking closer to Lina. "What is it?" I asked.

She sighed and ran her hand through her hair. "Did anything happen between you and Mason?"

My eyes widened, and I slowly yet hesitantly shook my head. "No, why? Did something happen?"

She shrugged then crossed her arms over her chest.

"Not really. It's just that I'm noticing that something's off with him. He's in an angry mood," she explained.

I sighed but shook my head again. "I don't know. Maybe it's something else."

She nodded slowly. "Maybe," she muttered and looked in the direction where everyone else was looking.

I saw Mason, Nick, and the third-in-command, whom I never really met nor talked to, come into sight. They walked to the stage as everyone else remained silent and kept all their focus on them.

"The meeting's starting," Adam said as he stood next to me.

I nodded and looked up at the stage to see Mason looking straight at me. I immediately averted my eyes and turned to Nick, who was talking to someone. After a moment, I glanced back at Mason, and he was now looking elsewhere. I sighed and waited for one of them to speak up.

"I know I have gathered you guys here today in a short notice, but I have received some warnings that can't wait. This past week, I was with several packs to discuss this issue. Thankfully, we are not under any threat, but I have received some warnings that cannot be taken lightly and we must keep our guards up," Mason spoke.

Once he stopped, everyone burst into questions and had confusion written all over their faces.

"Recently, other packs have seen creatures right outside of their borders. We still have yet to confirm what these creatures are. All that has been said is that they are seen at night and the only thing they can make out of them are their red eyes, so these may be rogues for all we know. They have been spotted in other packs, so we don't know if they'll try to come into our territory. This is just a warning. I don't want anyone to go outside of the pack house at night without my permission from now on. Is that clear?" Mason asked the crowd.

Everyone nodded and said yes.

I frowned at that thought. That was just weird and creepy. What could they be?

I mean, if they were rogues, then it was not a surprise. Rogues were known to roam around the borders and try to injure anybody in their path, but if they're not rogues, then what were they? I looked to Lina and Adam to see them both looking confused as well.

"Do you think they are rogues?" I asked them.

Lina and Adam shrugged.

"Maybe. Rogues have red eyes, so it may be them," Lina explained.

Adam nodded in agreement.

"Maybe," I muttered. I looked back to the stage when Mason spoke.

"Good. Now make sure you inform Nick or me if you see anything."

Everyone nodded.

Mason sighed and ran a hand through his hair. "You may be excused."

And with that, everyone started going back to the pack house while Mason, Nick, and the third-in-command walked down the stage. Mason stopped and turned his head to me for a split second before walking off.

I sighed and turned to Lina. "I'll be in my room if you need me." I said goodbye to her and Adam before walking off.

* * *

It has been two hours since the meeting, and all I did was lay on my bed and stare at the ceiling. I sighed and couldn't help but think that this was going to be a boring day. My mind kept repeating the scenario with Mason this morning and at the meeting. I couldn't push those thoughts aside no matter how much I wanted to.

I sat up when Lina opened my bedroom door and walked in with a smile on her face. I raised a brow at her as she sat on the edge of my bed.

"Why do you look so happy?"

"Because . . . Mason has to visit another pack, so that means we can go outside," she stated happily.

I frowned and ran my hand through my hair. "But didn't he say we shouldn't get out of the pack today?"

Lina shook her head. "No, he said we shouldn't be out at night. We won't. We'll go to the city and have some fun. Then before it gets dark, we come back," she explained.

I hesitantly nodded and thought about that. He did say not to be out at night, and he didn't say not to be out at all. Besides, I thought I needed this girls' day out. It might take my mind off of things.

"I guess you're right," I said as a smile crept onto my face.

She clapped her hands and squealed. "Great because I heard there is this carnival in the city today! I was thinking of going there. It's been ages since I last went to one," Lina exclaimed, gushing in excitement.

I laughed. "Yeah, me too. But we'll have to come back before sunset. I really don't feel like getting into trouble today."

"Don't worry, we won't."

After that, I fixed myself up as Lina waited for me. Once I was done, I walked up to her.

"Don't we need to get some kind of permission?" I asked her and she nodded.

"I already did. Since Mason or Nick isn't here, I asked Brandon and he said we can go as long as we have guards with us and return before sunset," Lina explained.

I raised a brow at her. "Who's Brandon?"

"He's the third-in-command," Lina answered.

I nodded in understanding.

"Come on, let's go before my brother magically appears and stops us from going."

Once we got out of the pack house, we hopped in Lina's car.

"Please drive slowly this time. I really don't feel like dying today," I said, teasing her.

She rolled her eyes and nodded. "Don't worry. If you had to die, it wouldn't be in a car crash. It would be in my own hands," she sarcastically said with a smirk on her face.

I rolled my eyes at her.

Two guards soon got into the car and sat at the back. They didn't say anything and just sat there in silence. Lina started the car and drove off.

I looked out of the window as we got closer to the city. Thankfully, the city wasn't too far away. Once we were there, a crowd of humans came into sight. They were everywhere.

```
It's very important to know that
when you're with humans, you try to
act as human as possible to not
expose yourself to them. It isn't
hard at all.You just try to keep
your wolf hidden and control your
strength. That's it.
```

After a couple of minutes, we all exited the car. The guards walked behind us as we strolled around the city.

We ate lunch, bought ice cream, and looked around a couple of shops. After all those, Lina decided to go to the carnival for a while before heading back. The carnival wasn't too far away, so we walked there with the guards behind us.

When we arrived, Lina smiled and pulled me towards the entrance. At that moment, I felt like I was a kid all over again. I hadn't been in one since I was small, and I couldn't help but think that it was so nice. Lina, being the fat girl she was, bought cotton candy even after all the stuff we had eaten. But hey, I couldn't blame her.

We went on a couple of rides and played childish games, all while having the time of our lives. After an hour or so, I noticed it was almost dark outside. I looked at Lina and tapped her shoulder.

"Let's head back before it gets dark," I told her. She looked at the sky and nodded.

I wasn't that worried because we had guards with us. The only thing I was worried about was getting into trouble with Mason.

Lina soon started driving towards the pack house. When we were finally out of the city, the sun started to set and that got me worried. I told Lina to drive a little faster before Mason came back and saw we weren't there. And that's what Lina did.

Soon, it eventually grew dark. We were driving on a narrow path that was full of trees when Lina pressed on the brake aggressively, causing me to jolt out of my seat. If I hadn't worn the seatbelt, I would have crashed my head into the glass.

I immediately looked at Lina in horror, her expression shocked and scared as she stared at something in front. I slowly looked in that same direction and gasped in shock at what I saw—a red-eyed creature with fangs as pointy as knives.

A bloodsucker.

CHAPTER 26

My eyes widened even more as the guards leaped out of the car and immediately shifted.

The red-eyed creature that was white as snow stared at me for a good five seconds. It was the creature that could suck every inch of blood and have no feelings of remorse. A vampire.

For a mere human, this creature had just come out of a horror story, but vampires weren't fictional characters in our world, at all. Of course, if werewolves and angels existed, so did vampires and other fictional characters, including witches and wizards. It's just that vampires were rare in a werewolf community. Like how we had packs, they had kingdoms. We chose not to mess with them and they chose not to mess with us due to conflicts we had in the past. Unfortunately, there were times we crossed paths, and when that happened, it would get ugly.

Let's just say that we had bad blood.

Vampires were common, like werewolves, while angels and witches were rare. Unfortunately, the two species that had to be common were werewolves and vampires, which wasn't a perfect match.

The vampire that was right in front us hissed at the two guards that leaped on him, and dodged them. The guards viciously growled at the bloodsucker. I looked at Lina and saw the worry in her eyes. I gulped and looked back in front of us to see that the vampire made a run for it as the two large werewolves chased it. I choked when the vampire stopped for a split second and made eye contact with me, a smirk crawling on his pale lips, showing off his fangs.

This sent shivers down my spine, and immediately after that, the bloodsucker disappeared into the night, like it was never there. All I could think of was the two cold eyes that looked like it could stare right through me.

Lina was blabbing some stuff I couldn't understand as she got out of the car to talk to the two guards that were now in their human forms and completely nude. I shook my head and immediately wanted to get back to the pack house.

I still couldn't believe that I saw a vampire.

I never even wanted to come across one in my entire life, but I did and it's not good at all. I was confused as to why it was so close to the pack borders and why it fled like that immediately without pulling a fight. It's known that if they were seen, they would do anything to get a taste of blood. I guess we were lucky that one wasn't willing to put up a fight.

I shook my head again.

We were in big trouble. No doubt, Mason was already coming right at that instant. I got out of the car.

Lina came up to me and placed her hand on my shoulder. "Are you okay?" she asked, worry laced in her voice.

I slowly and hesitantly nodded. "Yeah, I am. I'm just shocked."

"Yeah, me too. Why would a vampire be this close to our pack?" she asked in a low, confused voice.

I shook my head and tried to rub off the chills that ran down my arms. "I don't know, but you and I both know that we're in big trouble."

She sighed in frustration and nodded. "Yes, I know. As a matter of fact, Mason and some pack warriors will be here in a couple of minutes. As soon as I saw that nightwalker, I immediately mind-linked him. And let me tell you, he's not happy at all. He made it to the pack house a long time ago," Lina explained.

My frown deepened at her words. *Great.*

I looked at the guards that were on the lookout but immediately turned my head when I remembered they were completely nude. Just after that, I heard sounds coming towards us. I snapped my head and Lina stiffened. I knew it was Mason who was going to make an appearance any second now.

And boy was I right.

Mason came into sight looking angry as hell, the pack warriors following suit. He gave both Lina and I deadly stares, which made my wolf whine. He immediately walked up to the guards who explained what had happened while Lina and I stood silent.

"Go patrol the area. I want that bloodsucker, dead or alive," Mason growled.

The pack warriors nodded and immediately ran into the woods.

Mason turned to our direction, and a growl erupted from his chest. I looked at Lina to see a worried expression on her face. I snapped my head back to Mason when his scent got stronger, and saw him walking up to us.

As soon as he was in front of us, another growl erupted from him and he spoke in a very low voice, "Head back to the pack house. I will deal with you both later."

Without a second thought, we did as he told, along with a couple of guards behind us. Since we were already close, we just walked and didn't use the car. Besides, I didn't think Mason would trust us to use the car anymore.

When we made it to the pack house, some people gave us weird glances, especially because of the fact that the guards walked in right after us. I excused myself, not wanting to deal with anyone right now, especially an angry Mason.

While I was walking to my room, I couldn't help but wonder why a vampire was near our borders, if what happened was a big deal, and if it was just a normal vampire who merely crossed our path by accident. I mean, it could happen. What if he meant no harm? I immediately shook my head at that, disagreeing with myself.

Just earlier today, Mason had called a meeting to discuss this issue. No doubt the creatures he was talking about were vampires. Were there more of them? And if there were, why did they wander by the borders? Wandering there wasn't just something one could do as it was considered a threat, especially if you're a rogue or a vampire.

All I knew was no one would ever be allowed to leave the territory anymore, especially at night. And I was sure Mason would make sure that everyone stuck to that.

Letting out a huge sigh, I walked into the silent room and sat on my bed, waiting for Mason to barge in any minute now to give me a long lecture that might never end.

* * *

I had been staring at the blank white ceiling for a while now, thinking about what had happened today. A lot of questions ran through my mind, but I couldn't find a good answer to them. I bet I was not the only one confused. I bet Lina didn't exactly know what to think at this moment as well.

I was so caught up in my thoughts. I couldn't seem to get that bloodsucker out of my mind. It was the very first time I had ever laid eyes on one, and it was not a good first impression. Of course, it wasn't. He was a vampire, for God's sake. His kind screamed death. I just hoped whoever that vampire was, he wasn't a threat and everything would go back to normal.

I was pulled away from my thoughts when my bedroom door slammed open and a worried Adam ran inside. I sat up and frowned at him while he sighed in relief when he saw me.

"Dammit, Tiana. Don't scare me like that ever again," he said in a low voice and pulled me into a hug.

My frown deepened, but I hugged him back anyway. "What's wrong?" I asked him even though I knew the answer.

He soon pulled away and ran his hand through his hair. "I was so worried that something might have happened to you. Before you came back, we received a message from the alpha that they saw a creature near our borders and that they were coming back immediately. And when we found out that you and Lina weren't here, let's just say the alpha didn't take it so easily."

"Oh," I muttered, not liking that Mason was angry. "What did he say about the creatures?"

"He said that while he was in another pack, someone reported that something was lurking outside our borders. He didn't specifically say what it was, but he told us, the guards and the pack warriors, to keep a lookout. We didn't know if it's a threat of some sort, but he said that nobody was allowed to exit at night," Adam explained and frowned. "Not really sure why only at night and not some other time."

I sighed, knowing exactly the reason. "Because it was a vampire he was talking about. They only make an appearance at night."

His eyes widened, and a low growl erupted from his throat. "A what?" he asked, completely shocked.

"A vampire," I repeated. "We saw it when we were coming back, but surprisingly, it didn't attack us and just ran away into the woods," I explained.

Adam's eyes held worry and confusion as he processed my words.

"How can that be? Vampires and Werewolves haven't crossed paths in centuries. We both know that our kind shouldn't be near them or chaos may erupt," Adam questioned and I shrugged in confusion.

"I don't know, Adam. Maybe it was by accident. All I know for now is that Mason is trying to catch that bloodsucker," I said.

Adam and I stiffened when we heard footsteps heading to my room.

"Speaking of the alpha," Adam said in annoyance as Mason's scent hit my nostrils.

My bedroom door was slammed open for the second time today. An angry Mason came stalking into my room but immediately stopped dead in his tracks when he laid eyes on us sitting on the bed together. His eyes turned a shade darker. A very low growl came out of his mouth, so low that I barely heard it.

"Out," he shouted at Adam without a second thought.

Adam furrowed his brows in confusion and glanced at me before looking back to Mason. "Why?" he asked.

I looked at Adam with wide eyes. I surely didn't want him to anger Mason even more.

"I said, out! Don't make me repeat myself for the third time," Mason growled once again as he stepped closer to us.

I narrowed my eyes at Mason and then looked at Adam and nodded. He sighed in frustration and whispered, "I'll be back soon." This only made Mason growl again, and I couldn't help but glare at him.

I still didn't forget what had happened this morning. I didn't really want to talk to him even though I knew it was my fault.

Adam glared at Mason before getting up and walking out of my room. I slowly looked at Mason and knew what he was here for. I knew I deserved whatever lecture I was supposed to get for disobeying his orders, but this stubborn mouth of mine had a mind of its own and couldn't help but be stupid at times like these.

"What do you want?" I asked in an annoyed tone and I immediately regretted it. *Dammit.*

"What do I want?" Mason growled, and my eyes widened at his rough tone. "Did you forget what happened just moments ago?"

I sighed and shook my head. "I didn't. I know why you're here. I get it, I disobeyed your orders and you want to give me a long ass lecture. I'm sorry, okay? We just thought that we'd be here before the sun sets," I said, trying to explain.

"Well, you didn't! What would have happened if you didn't have two guards with you?" he shouted and my frown deepened. "You wouldn't be here by now. Do you get that, Tiana? And that's all because you're stubborn as hell to actually listen for once!"

I furrowed my brows at him and growled back. I couldn't help but get defensive. I knew I wasn't in the right place, but it was just how I was.

"I'm stubborn? Really, Mason? Go look in the mirror and see how you act. Yes, we disobeyed your orders, and I'm sorry for that, but I'm not the only one who has issues," I growled harshly.

His eyes turned completely black, and he stepped closer to me. "Watch your mouth," he warned. "Remember who you're talking to," he sneered.

I scoffed and crossed my arms over my chest. "Don't pull that alpha shit on me," I shot back. "See what I'm talking about? I can't speak my mind without you pulling that shit on me."

He shook his head. "We are going off topic, Tiana," he said in a raised voice. "You are too impossible to deal with! Why can't you just sit down quietly for once?"

I furrowed my brows. "What, Mason? You expect me to agree and obey your every word like everyone else does?" I growled.

"Yes, because I am your alpha—" he started.

"There we go again. You are not my alpha," I yelled at him, and he pushed me against the wall, glaring at me with his cold eyes.

"I am. As long as you are in my pack, I am your alpha, Tiana," he hissed.

I closed my eyes to calm myself down, knowing I got out of hand. I thought of what I had said. I guess I was rude. I opened my eyes and sighed. "Just get out of my room," I said, not wanting to argue any longer.

He shook his head. "No, you will listen to what I have to say," he said stubbornly as he looked into my eyes.

I pushed him away. "Just get out. You're right. I'm stubborn and my mouth gets the best of me. I don't really feel like arguing with you right now." I turned away and heard him huff out in annoyance.

"You're so hard to deal with," he muttered, taking a step away from me.

I snapped my head, ready to tell him that he was the same, and saw that he was gone, his scent remained to linger in my room.

I frowned and sat on my bed, thinking about what just happened. I shook my head and shut off the connection with my wolf when she lectured me for having an argument with my mate.

Great! I guess that's two fights in one day, I thought to myself What a nice day it was. Note the sarcasm.

But now that I thought about it, he didn't give me a punishment. I sighed and was thankful for that, but all I could think of was those words he kept telling me, which I knew were right in some way.

Am I really hard to deal with?

CHAPTER 27

Two weeks. It had been two damn long weeks since that day, since the day I fought with Mason and we encountered the vampire.

So far, the vampire was nowhere to be seen. Unfortunately, neither Mason nor the pack warriors were able to catch him. No one saw him ever again, and everything slowly got back to normal. These two weeks, Mason wasn't in the pack house often. He was in other packs discussing the issue. I was not sure what he was planning on doing, but I was happy that I didn't bump into him as much.

Our pack was still on the lookout just in case, but I couldn't help but think that maybe that was just a coincidence. I mean, if the vampire meant us harm, why didn't he attack us that day? What if our guards were up for no reason? Either way, people were able to get out more often even at sundown as long as they had guards with them.

My wolf had been whining since then, and it was so annoying to the point that I wanted to pull my hair out. She didn't like how I had acted that day; I didn't like how I had acted either. But what had happened, already happened. Besides, I wasn't the only one that was being stubborn and rude. I guess I did start it when we had disobeyed his orders, but I couldn't keep my mouth shut.

I would be lying if I said I was happy where we left off. I couldn't help but feel guilty. I knew that if I wanted to be on good terms with him, I should face him and talk about what happened. This wasn't healthy. And no matter how much I didn't want to see him, I knew I should. Maybe then my wolf would calm down.

I looked at the TV that was in front of me and sighed when I found nothing interesting after switching from channel to channel. Some pack members passed by the living room, where I was, but most of them just ignored me. I didn't really socialize with the pack that much. I barely knew people, but I didn't really care. I was happy with the people I already got along with.

I furrowed my brows in disgust when a familiar scent hit my nostrils. It wasn't a natural one, though, just too much perfume. I looked to my right, and someone that I wasn't too fond of came walking into the living room.

Chloe looked at me, and a disgusted expression crossed her face. I rolled my eyes and looked away. From the corner of my eyes, I could see her and her minions approaching. I tried my best to ignore her, but I couldn't help but look at her when she was so close to me.

When I laid eyes on her caked face, I raised a brow at her.

"Get off," she ordered.

I frowned and tilted my head. "Excuse me?" I glared at her. *How rude. Who does she think she is? The luna?* I scoffed at that one.

"I said, get off. You're sitting on my spot," she ordered as her minions nodded in agreement.

I raised a brow and looked down at the couch before looking back at her. "Oh, I'm sorry, but I don't see your name on it," I said innocently, a small smirk crawling on my lips.

Her eyes turned a shade darker, and a growl came out of her mouth. "Someone needs to teach you your place."

I crossed my arms over my chest and stood up facing her. "I know my place very well, but can you enlighten me where your place is?" I asked her as she growled one more time.

"Bitch, you don't know who you're talking to, do you?" she hissed, and I raised my brow at her.

"No, I don't really know. But let me enlighten you, I don't really care," I spat at her.

She gasped, and her eyes darkened with anger. "Bitch," she repeated.

My eyes widened when she raised her hand in the air, ready to slap me, then someone caught her hand. I looked at my savior and saw the last person I expected.

```
         Take  a  guess,  a  wild  guess.  If  you
         guessed Mason, then you're right.
```

Since when did he come back? I thought to myself. I was then shocked when he growled and glared at Chloe, whose eyes were filled with fear.

"Chloe! What did I tell you the other time?" he asked.

"You didn't tell me anything," she whined as his grip tightened on her hand.

"I did," he growled.

I frowned at that and wondered what he told her. Was it something about me?

"Why are you defending her?" she asked out of anger.

He growled again, but before he could say anything, she continued.

"Why did you tell me not to go near her and bother her? You don't treat anyone like that, not even me!"

I was taken aback at her words. Mason growled again, but this time even louder. I looked around, and luckily there wasn't anyone near us at the moment.

"Enough," he yelled, causing Chloe to whimper and flinch. "When I tell you something, you listen. Do I make myself clear?"

She turned to me and gave me a deadly glare, then looked back at Mason. "This isn't you," she whined. "This girl," she pointed at me, "changed you. It's all her fault."

My thoughts ran wild when she said that. Did I really change him? How so? Besides, why was she acting as if she's his ex-girlfriend or something? My wolf growled at the thought, and even though I shouldn't really care, I couldn't help but dislike it. Just a little.

"Chloe," he said in a dangerous tone. "That's enough. Get out of my sight."

She huffed out in annoyance and soon walked out of the room with her hands clenched in anger. As soon as she was out of sight, I looked at Mason and didn't really know what to say.

He soon looked at me, and we silently stared at each other for a couple of seconds before he took a step back. I was debating with my inner self whether to thank him or ask him what she had meant. But before I could even open my mouth, he was out of the room in an instant. I stared down at the floor and sighed.

With each passing day, things got more confusing and it just made everything harder for me. I sighed and ran my hand through my hair in frustration.

The next thing I knew, I was being pulled to a hard chest and someone's arms wrapped me. I looked up to see a smiling Adam staring down at me. I smiled back and hugged him as well.

Maybe talking to Adam will get my mind off things for now.

"I missed you so much," he said, teasingly. I rolled my eyes and pulled away.

"The last time you saw me was like four days ago," I told him.

He chuckled and shook his head. "No, it was five days ago," he corrected.

I shrugged. "Same thing."

"Still. Didn't you miss me?" he asked with puppy dog eyes and a pouty lip.

I crossed my arms over my chest. "Ha! Me? Miss you? Never in a lifetime," I spoke jokingly. His pout grew even more, and I couldn't help but laugh.

"Of course you do. Do I have to remind you that I'm your only best friend?" he questioned.

I furrowed my brows at him and gave his shoulder a soft punch. "You're not my only best friend. I have Lina, remember?"

He shrugged. "Well, I've known you longer," he muttered.

I rolled my eyes at him. "So, how was that training thing with Nick?"

He sighed. "It was okay but tiring too. I barely got any sleep."

Since Adam was a pack warrior in training, he had to go to this place that I didn't know where exactly and practice. It was kind of like a camp.

"Poor you!" I said sarcastically.

He rolled his eyes but then smiled. "I have training practice any moment now. Are you going to come and watch?"

I shrugged but soon nodded. "Yeah, I really don't have anything to do right now."

"Great! Meet me in the yard," he said before walking out the back door.

Since I hadn't had lunch yet, I decided to head to the kitchen to grab something to eat. I opened the fridge and saw some leftover pizza. I took three pieces out because, being the pig that I was, less than three wouldn't satisfy me. I placed them in the microwave and waited for them to be ready. I was looking at my nails in silence when I heard someone enter the kitchen. I looked up and then glared when I saw Kyle.

A smirk crawled onto his lips, and he strolled towards me.

I tried my best to ignore him because, trust me when I say this, Chloe was already enough for today. I didn't need anyone else raining on my parade. I turned around and grabbed a plate, placing my pizza on it. The next thing I knew, one of my slices was gone and it was in someone else's hand.

I glared at Kyle.

Oh, hell to the no! Not my pizza!

"Give it back." I growled at him.

"You have two. Isn't that enough?" he asked, smirking.

I growled again. Right then and there, I plotted his death. No one lays a hand on my food. "No! Hand it to me right now before I make you regret it," I threatened him.

His eyes lit up in amusement, and he leaned towards me. "What are you going to do? Call your sweet alpha to come to your rescue?" he questioned. "Well, guess what? He's not here."

I stepped closer to him. This was what he's getting for laying his nasty fingers on what's mine. "No, I won't. But do you know what I can do?"

He raised his brow, looking bored.

"This." I raised my knee and hit him right where the sun didn't shine.

He groaned in pain and fell to the floor with my pizza still in his hands.

Right at this moment, his eyes lit up with fury and I couldn't help but feel satisfied. I took a step back with the plate in my hand and smirked at him.

"Oh, you can keep the pizza. I don't want it anymore since you've touched it." And with that, I walked out of the kitchen as fast as I could before he could catch up.

I was at the yard with a satisfied smirk on my face. I knew he wasn't going to come after me since there were people around. Besides, I wasn't afraid of him. I saw Adam with the other pack members and waved at him. He gave me a smile and then continued training. I sat on the bench and started eating in delight.

I continued watching Adam do whatever he did in boredom as I had nothing better to do and it went on for about an hour. I soon decided to head back inside to do something else, maybe see Lina or something. I said goodbye to Adam and walked towards the pack house. My thoughts went to Chloe and Mason, and I couldn't help but wonder where he was at the moment.

*   *   *

I had been staring at the ceiling for who knows how long. I noticed I had been doing it more often these days. I guess it became a habit. Thoughts about what had happened today and two weeks ago kept running in my head. It hurt already. I still hadn't decided whether I should apologize to him for being such a brat or thank him for at least sticking up to me.

Maybe I should do both.

I sighed and sat up. If I didn't do this now, then I would think about it for a long, long time, especially with my wolf involved. I ran my hands through my hair and stood up.

Let's get this over with.

I exited my room and hesitantly walked towards Mason's office, all while thinking of what I should say. Once I was there, I knocked on the door.

Nothing.

I knocked again, but nobody responded. I tried to open the door, but it was locked. Maybe he wasn't here. I looked around the hallway and wondered where he could be. I decided to start walking to see if I could bump into him because that's what we were best at, bumping into each other when we least expected it.

I soon caught a glimpse of Nick and walked up to him. Maybe he knew where he was.

"Hi, Nick," I greeted him.

He smiled at me. "Hello, Tiana. Is there something I can help you with?"

I smiled awkwardly and hesitantly spoke, "Uhh . . . yeah, there is."

He nodded for me to continue.

"Do you know where Mason is?"

His smile grew. "Yes, as a matter of fact, I do. But why?" he questioned.

I didn't know what to say, but before a word could come out of my mouth, he spoke.

"I'm just teasing you. He's in his room, taking a break from all the work he has to do."

I smiled at him. "Thanks," I said before walking away.

Well, that wasn't awkward at all.

I slowly went up to the floor where his room was and turned a corner but immediately backed away when I saw someone in his front door. I poked my head, and my eyes widened when the said someone entered without even knocking. Although, that wasn't the reason why I was shocked. No. It was because that person was the last person I wanted to see today.

Chloe.

She walked into his room like she owned the place.

I frowned and took another look to see her closing the door behind her. Right then and there, I felt a sting in my heart and never did I hate her so much before.

And the only thing that was running in my mind was, *"Why on earth is she in Mason's room?"*

CHAPTER 28

I stared at the closed door for a while, debating whether I should mind my own business or be the nosy person that I was and eavesdrop. My wolf told me to do the latter, but that would make me feel uncomfortable. Whatever they did wasn't really my business, but I knew I wouldn't be able to stop thinking about it until I knew exactly what was going on.

Of course, my wolf had already jumped into conclusions, heartbroken that her mate was with another female in one room. But I knew better than to do just that. I ain't that stupid.

Yes, I was confused why she was in Mason's room. But you never know, maybe he wasn't there at all.

After a long discussion with my wolf, I sighed in frustration, feeling the urge to place my ear on the door. And so I did.

Even with my wolf hearing, I heard nothing.

I furrowed my brows in confusion. The only thing I could hear was the silent breaths of a person. I had stayed like that for a while now, but not a single sound was made. Nothing. My wolf was confused as well, telling me to open the door and see what was going on, but I mentally shook my head. I wasn't going to do that.

I finally decided to give up and turn around because I didn't want to stick my nose in someone else's business. Nick might have told me that he was in there, but maybe Mason wasn't really.

But if he was, why was Chloe in there? That question had roamed my head for the millionth time.

My wolf started whining, telling me that maybe they were a thing. I rolled my eyes. Of course, my wolf would say something like that. But maybe she was right. I didn't know why, but I found myself hoping they weren't. It would make things even more difficult.

I started thinking about the possibility of them being an item. Maybe she hated me because Mason used to date her. I didn't think she knew I was his mate. Even though I had told myself I shouldn't care because it was not my business, I couldn't help but feel disappointed.

I took a step forward but stopped dead in my tracks when I finally heard Mason's angry voice.

"What are you doing?" he bellowed.

I slowly turned my head towards the door and listened.

"Chloe!" he growled. "What are you doing in my room?"

I heard Chloe stutter, and by this time, I knew I was too caught up in the moment to leave.

"I was just checking up on you. You looked stressed, so I thought of giving you a massage," she said in a low voice, which made me gag.

I heard Mason growl once more. "I was asleep, and you dared to enter my room without my knowledge?"

Chloe whined, "I was only trying to help."

"I don't need your help. Get out of my room and don't even think of entering again without my permission," Mason ordered.

"Why are you like this, Mason? Is it because of that new werewolf?" she questioned.

I frowned and furrowed my brows in confusion.

"Chloe . . ." he warned.

"No. I see how you look at her. You don't look at someone like that, for God's sake. Why her? What's so special about her? What does she have that I don't?" she asked in anger.

My frown deepened, and I wondered whether they were talking about me or someone else.

"Chloe, stop! That's enough," he roared.

"No, tell me, Mason. What does she have that I don't? Why on earth do you act so differently around her?" she asked, a growl coming out of her mouth.

My eyes widened a bit at that.

"Chloe, I don't need to justify my actions to you. You don't need to know!"

"Why is it so hard to tell me?" she asked, anger and frustration laced her voice.

"Dammit, Chloe! She's my mate! Do you understand now? She's my damn mate," he yelled at her.

I stepped away from the door with a surprised expression plastered on my face.

"What?" she asked, completely surprised.

"Get out now," Mason growled lowly at her.

I knew that enough was enough and that I shouldn't stick around any longer. I left so I wouldn't get caught.

* * *

I was running away from something. I didn't know what it was, but all I knew was that I should run and not look back. I was already out of breath and really tired, but I didn't dare stop. I ran like my life depended on it, and maybe it did.

I wanted to shift into my wolf so I could run even faster, but I couldn't as my panic prevented me from feeling her.

I continuously tried contacting her, but she wasn't there. This brought tears to my eyes. Where was she?

I also tried to let my wings out, but they wouldn't budge. What the hell was happening? I didn't know who I was running from and where I really was. Trees were everywhere, and by the way they prevented the sunlight from entering, the place was really dark, frightening me.

I looked for a single living creature in the forest but found nothing. This place screamed death—a place I would never want to stay in. I stopped for a split second to catch my breath but then immediately started running when I heard footsteps behind me.

I ran and ran for who knows how long. It was never ending.

I soon accidentally tripped on a rock and came falling down to the ground. I winced as I felt tingles of pain on the right side of my ankle. Groaning, I tried to stand up but then fell back to the ground. My face became pale as the footsteps became louder and louder by the minute. I gulped when a wicked laugh echoed in the air. I knew very well that if I wanted to get out of this alive, then I needed to get back up.

As I finally stood on my feet, I took a step forward and hissed in pain. I breathed deeply, but my breath got stuck in my throat when three werewolves appeared from the trees, looking at me.

I stared at them with wide eyes. It was their eyes that frightened me. They were red, meaning they were rogues. And by the way they were looking and growling at me, I knew they were not good at all. When I stepped back, one of them growled. Then they all started approaching and I backed away in horror, but I unfortunately wasn't going anywhere.

Who are they? What's happening? Where am I?

All these questions ran in my head. I had to close my eyes for a split second to calm myself down only to see the rogues stalking towards me when I snapped them open. I looked at my surroundings and planned on running, but where was I supposed to go?

I soon decided to head back.

I made a run for it and the three rogues chased. But before I could get too far away from them, I bumped into a hard chest, making me fall really hard to the ground for the second time. Wincing in pain, I slowly trailed my eyes upwards to see who it was.

It was wearing a pair of black shoes. I didn't know why I was being slow, but I knew whoever it was, it was going to frighten me. The vibes that surrounded this person were dark, I could feel it. My eyes widened when I saw its face, and I gasped out in shock.

Its red eyes stared down at me, like they could see right through my soul. Its fangs were as pointy as knives and the smirk crawling on its pale lips made a shiver run down my spine.

A vampire.

* * *

I jolted, sweat covering my face like a second skin. I breathed in and out deeply, and ran my hands through my hair. I looked around and sighed in relief when I saw that I was in my room, safe and sound.

I shook my head and bit my lip when I recalled the dream.

What a nightmare!

That was one of the weirdest and creepiest things I had ever dreamt of. It felt so real but unreal at the same time. What creeped me out was the fact that the same vampire I saw two weeks ago was in it. I guessed since I kept thinking about it, it was bound to invade my dreams.

It still gave me the chills, though. I knew that nightmare wasn't going to leave my mind anytime soon.

I looked at the clock to see that it was two in the morning. It was pitch-black outside and quiet too. I got up and looked out of the window, just admiring the dark sky that had sparkly stars brightening it. I inhaled and closed my eyes, which made me feel a little better.

I turned and walked towards the door, needing to get myself a glass of water before I fainted from dehydration. Not wanting to wake anyone up, I slowly walked down the stairs.

As I made it to the kitchen, I turned the lights on and smiled when I saw the fridge.

Maybe I should get myself something to eat, I thought.

I poured some water in a cup and gulped it down. I glanced out the window and coughed in horror when I saw someone staring right at me.

My hands were shaking when I placed the cup on the counter, and in the next second, I screamed like my life depended on it.

I couldn't clearly make out who it was because of the blurry glass, but I could see its eyes and the shape of its face. I ran outside the kitchen, ready to alarm anyone in the pack that there was an intruder, when someone covered my mouth, preventing me from screaming one more time, pulling me outside the pack house and into the backyard.

I was ready to freak out, but the familiar sparks made me shut up and furrow my brows in confusion instead. The hands that were covering my mouth loosened a bit as my back rested on a hard chest that I now knew who belonged to.

"Calm down. It's just me," Mason whispered in my ear, making a shiver run down my spine.

He took his hands off my mouth. I immediately turned and saw him looking intensely at me, but I could point out a hint of amusement in his eyes.

"Wha—" I started but stopped to catch my breath. I closed my eyes and then opened them. "What are you doing out here?" I asked with a frown on my face. "Do you know how much you frightened me? You scared the living daylights out of me! I was literally about to inform the whole pack that there was some kind of psycho outside. I mean, who on earth just looks through a window like that, especially at two in the morning! It's creepy. I thought you were a—"

Mason laughed lightly, the sound of it immediately cutting off my blabbering.

My eyes widened at his amused face. He barely smiled, and now he was laughing. Was that even possible? He had always been so serious. His laugh made him look much younger and more good-looking.

"Why are you laughing?" I asked.

"You should've seen yourself," he told me, chuckling. "It's okay. It was only me. No psycho over here."

Surprisingly, I laughed as well. I then saw him staring intensely at me again, so I looked back down.

"So, what are you doing out here?" I asked for the second time.

He sighed and looked ahead. "I couldn't sleep, so I came here to get some fresh air. Then I saw the kitchen lights turn on. I looked through the window to see who it was, and that's when you started screaming. I had to pull you out here so you wouldn't wake anybody up," Mason explained.

I nodded and couldn't help but smile at him.

"What were you doing out of bed?" he asked.

I frowned when I remembered the dream. "Couldn't sleep, so I decided to get myself a cup of water. That's when you showed up."

I stared at his face as a small smile appeared on his lips. I didn't want to admit it, but I liked that he was smiling, that he wasn't frowning and serious. It wasn't every day that I get to see a smiling Mason.

I knew this image of his wouldn't get out of my head any time soon.

"Well, you should head back," he spoke calmly. "Go get some rest."

Slowly backing away, I said, "Head back as well. You need rest too."

He nodded and placed his hands in his pockets. I then remembered why I wanted to see him today, so I turned to him again.

"Oh, also I want to say thank you for sticking up for me today. I really appreciated it," I told him.

"Anytime," he said, smiling.

And with that, I walked into my room with a soft smile on my face.

CHAPTER 29

"Are you crazy, Lina?" I placed my hand on my hip. "Stefan is the hotter one. He's not only hot, but he's so sweet and kind, unlike Damon." I shook my head, completely disagreeing with her opinion.

"I'm the crazy one?" she asked. "Are you hearing yourself right now, Tiana? You're picking Stefan over Damon. That's just absurd. Are you blind, my friend?" She waved her hand in front of my eye.

"I'm perfectly fine. It's just that I prefer Stefan over Damon. He's the perfect man, unlike Damon who is so mean and evil," I said the last part to tick her off.

"Oh, hell to the no! You did not just diss my man," she shrieked playfully and leaped on me.

I squealed in shock as both of us fell from the couch and onto the hard floor, laughing our butts off. I pushed her off me.

"You're one of a kind, girl! Everyone loves Damon, and you're the first person I know that picks Stefan over my future husband," she told me as she thought of the man that she would never have.

"It's because I like nice guys. Not everyone is into bad boys. Besides, he isn't your future husband. He's a vampire, remember? Mortal enemies!" I reminded her.

She released a dreamy sigh and looked at me, a wide smile crawling to her lips. "But he's a hot vampire! I would ditch this place for him anytime, anywhere," she cooed.

I rolled my eyes at her and shook my head.

We were having *The Vampire Diaries* marathon in Lina's room at the moment. I didn't know how many episodes we had already seen, but we had been watching it to the point where we looked like cavemen whose food was splattered on the ground. The curtains were closed shut, like we were some vampires hiding from the light. Our hair was in all directions because of our constant mini fights, due to the fact that we did not agree on the same guy. Our faces were also filled with every emotion one could possibly think of because the series was literally a roller coaster of emotions.

Earlier today, I couldn't decline when Lina proposed this marathon. This was one of my favorite series even though the characters were vampires, the ones we disliked the most.

"You're saying you would date a vampire?" I asked her with a brow raised.

"If he's like Damon, then yes, I would," she said dreamily.

I rolled my eyes at her. "Well, good luck with finding one."

"Thanks, I'm going to need it," she said, jokingly.

We brought our attention back to the episode and watched it with a little bickering here and there. She would defend Damon while I would defend Stefan. We eventually got into another fight.

"Take it back!" With a scowl on my face, I pushed her off the couch again.

"No," she shrieked and laughed as she hit the floor.

"Take it back, Lina, or I will do something you won't like," I threatened her.

She smirked as she got off the ground. "Oh, really? Like what?" She crossed her arms over her chest.

"I'll eat this." I grabbed the last slice of pizza from her plate, which she was saving for a particular moment in the episode.

The smirk on her face fell, her eyes a deadly glare. "You wouldn't," she growled.

"Oh, I would," I teased.

As soon as that left my mouth, she took a step closer to me while I hung the pizza towards my now open mouth.

"Ah ah ah, I wouldn't take a step closer if I were you," I threatened.

She gave out a sigh, and her shoulders fell in defeat. "Fine, fine. I take that back. Stefan does not look like a donkey," she said as she eyed her pizza carefully.

I looked at the pizza and then back at her. "Great," I said happily. And with that, I took a bite.

Lina gasped and her eyes widened in horror. "You traitor!" She jumped on me for the hundredth time today.

I laughed hysterically as she attempted to hurt me in any way possible, and we fell to the floor.

"I can't believe you. I thought we were friends," she spoke dramatically.

I rolled my eyes, then snapped my head when I heard someone speak from the door.

"You both are drama queens," Adam said with a smile on his face, staring at us with disbelief.

We scowled and stood up, wiping off the dust from our clothes.

"We're not drama queens," Lina defended.

Adam rolled his eyes. "Yes, you guys are. Anyone in their right mind would think that. Your voices could be heard from the end of the hall."

"Um, no, we're not. Anyone in their right mind would do the same. It's Damon we're talking about here," Lina argued.

"Sure, I'll go along with that," he said sarcastically, unconvinced.

"Whatever," Lina muttered. "What are you doing here? You're interrupting our marathon."

Adam looked at the tv and raised a brow. "Seriously? You do know that vampires are our mortal enemies, right?" He said exactly what I had said a while ago.

Lina and I looked at each other and shrugged.

"We don't care. They're hot," Lina said.

I smiled and nodded. "She's got a point."

Adam furrowed his brow and glared at the tv, which had Stefan and Damon on it.

"Hot? No, they're ugly, especially the brown-haired dude."

My eyes widened at what he said about Stefan, and a growl escaped my lips. Lina laughed her butt off while Adam looked at me in horror when he realized what he just said.

"Oh, shit," he muttered. "I'm sorry, Tiana. I didn't realize—"

I cut him off by jumping on his back and repeatedly hitting him. He started screaming like a teenage girl.

"How." *Hit.* "Dare." *Hit.* "You." *Hit.* "Say." *Hit.* "That." *Hit.* "About." *Hit.* "My." *Hit.* "Favorite." *Hit.* "Man?" I squealed as he threw me to the ground.

"Favorite man?" Adam scoffed. "I'm your favorite man!" he said with no room left for discussion.

I growled and got up, but before I could disagree with him, a familiar scent entering the room hit my nose.

All of us turned to Mason, who was standing by the door with a straight face.

The last time I saw him was a couple of days ago.

And ever since last week, the day he had frightened me through the window, we actually started talking. I had seen him here and there without arguing. We had small conversations, then that was it. Nothing much, but who knew Mason could act like a normal person.

"Is there something wrong, Mason?" Lina asked him.

His eyes went from Lina to the TV, the room, and me. He then looked at Adam and turned his attention back to Lina.

"No, I just need help with some papers. I want you to come with me to my office," Mason answered.

"Okay then. Bye, guys! Let's continue this later on." She waved goodbye and left with Mason.

Adam looked at me and shrugged. "I guess it's only you and me now."

He sat on the chair and turned on the volume while I sat next to him and grabbed the bowl of popcorn. Then we continued to watch the episode.

* * *

I was walking down the hall when I noticed I was close to Mason's office. I slowed my pace when I was almost next to his door and then stopped when I heard a growl coming from inside, which undoubtedly belonged to Mason. I frowned in confusion.

"Dammit! How the hell am I going to finish this on time?"

I wasn't sure whether he was talking to himself or someone else. My wolf told me to check up on him and see if I could help with anything, while my logical brain told me to mind my own business. I sighed in defeat and knocked.

"Come in," Mason growled in annoyance.

I hesitantly opened the door and peeked into the room to see him sitting alone. *Wasn't Lina with him or something?*

Mason looked up to meet my eyes and then frowned. "Tiana?" he asked, a little surprised. "Is there something wrong?" His face turned serious.

I entered and saw that the office was a mess. Papers were everywhere, as if a mini hurricane had taken place not too long ago. Stress radiated off Mason while I was flabbergasted.

"What happened here?" I asked him, not answering his question.

His eyes widened when he looked around, like he hadn't noticed the mess until I pointed it out. A huff of frustration escaped his lips, and he ran both of his hands through his hair.

"Dammit," he cursed again. "I don't have time for this." He looked at the papers that were scattered around.

I couldn't help but feel bad for him. He must be under a lot of pressure.

"What's wrong?" I asked him, wanting to know the reason why he was under this much stress. He looked at me, and his eyes softened. I stepped closer to his desk as another sigh of exhaustion made its way out of his mouth.

"I have lots of paperwork to deal with. They are all from the other packs, due to that vampire incident. We're trying to look for a solution, and I have to handle some stuff. They're expecting all of these to be done by tomorrow, but I can't seem to finish. And this mess—" he looked around "—isn't helping at all."

I nodded in understanding. "Wasn't Lina with you? Can't she help?"

He shook his head and ran his hand through his hair one more time. before looking at me. "She was, but Nick called her for something that had to do with the pack warriors."

"I can help you," I said but then my eyes widened when I realized what I just said. "I mean, if that's okay with you."

He stared at me in disbelief. He then snapped out of it, giving me a small smile. "I'd appreciate it."

I gave him a small smile as well and took another step towards him. "Okay, what can I do?"

"First, I'd like you to clean this mess. I can't work in a dirty environment. Then once you're done, I want you to organize these files." He pointed to a bunch of files on his desk. "And then when you're done with that, I want you to look through the papers here and let me know if you see anything important," Mason instructed.

I nodded in understanding and started doing my job.

Mason immediately got back to work. After twenty minutes or so, I was completely done tidying his office. I glanced at him, but he didn't look at me. He was too caught up in the work he was in. I grabbed the files that were on his desk and started organizing them on the shelf.

When I was halfway through them, I felt someone staring at my back. I turned around to see Mason looking at me. I raised a brow. "Is there something wrong?"

He shook his head and immediately went back to what he was doing.

When I was done organizing, I sat on one of the chairs in front of his desk and grabbed the stack of papers, skimming through them.

They were mostly peace declaration letters from other packs. I assumed they didn't want to be on our pack's bad side. Friendly wasn't Black Shadow's reputation as it was known as the deadliest pack of all. Of course, the rumors were mostly exaggerated, but some details were actually true. I showed them to Mason one by one, and he told me to keep them on the side.

Some of the papers were boring stuff that I understood nothing about. The others were letters from other alphas, asking for a meeting of some sort.

I looked through the rest and didn't find them important. As I made it to the last one, I realized that it was another letter.

What's with all the letters? Have these people heard about technology or what?

I opened and skimmed through it. My eyes widened. This letter discussed the vampire issue. An alpha wanted to meet up with Mason to propose a solution. At least, that's what it said. I immediately showed it to Mason, and when he read it, he nodded.

"Okay. Thank you, Tiana." He placed the letter on top of his desk.

I realized that I had finished everything, so I slowly got up. "Well, I guess I'm done here," I told him.

"I appreciate it, Tiana. Thank you," he said. He was grateful, if his voice was any indication.

I smiled at him and shook my head. "There's no need to thank me. Do something else in exchange, and we're tied," I said with a smirk on my face, completely kidding.

He raised a brow in amusement. "So everything you just did wasn't from the goodness of your heart?" he asked.

"Good? In me? Ha!" I laughed out loud.

He chuckled. "Well, what can I do for you then?"

Thinking that he's playing along, I turned around and opened the door. "Take me out to dinner, and we're tied," I said jokingly and walked out of his office.

* * *

"Shit," Adam cursed for the hundredth time. "How are you so good?" he asked as I won again.

I smirked and shrugged. "Oh, I don't know. Maybe because I'm awesome?"

After playing for about an hour now, Adam had a look of defeat as he stared at the chessboard, which he had found in his room, inside a small closet. We guessed that it belonged to his room's previous owner. He took it and came over to me, challenging me for a match. Little did he know that I was a chess master.

When he lost the first time, he declared another match, then another, then another. He kept saying he was going easy on me, not wanting to admit defeat, but I kept winning and winning, slowly waiting for him to give up.

"Dammit," he muttered under his breath. "I can't believe I lost to a girl," he whined.

"Let me rephrase that. You lost about twenty times to a girl." I laughed, and my laughter got even louder when Adam pouted.

He whined like a baby and shook his head. "Ugh . . . You need to teach me your ways."

I shrugged, and a smirk crawled onto my lips. "Oh, I don't know. It doesn't look like you'll be learning any time soon," I said, teasing him.

His eyes furrowed, and a scowl appeared on his face. "Tiana." He tried to growl, but it came out as a whine.

"I'm kidding. I'm kidding," I said between laughter.

He sighed and stared at the chess board, like he'd learn something just by doing that. I rolled my eyes and got up to head to the bathroom to do my business. I'd been holding it in for a while because Adam wouldn't let me off the hook until he won, but he never did. Before I could enter, I heard a knock on my door. I frowned and looked at Adam.

Who could it be? Lina?

"I'll get it." Adam got up and opened the door wide.

Mason's scent immediately made its way to my nose, and my eyes widened upon realizing that he was right in front of my room.

What is he doing here?

Mason's eyes turned black as he looked at Adam, whose eyes held curiosity in them. I bet he was wondering why he was in front of my room just like me.

Mason turned to me and then back at Adam.

"Can I help you, Alpha?" Adam asked.

I frowned at his tone. He didn't sound too happy at his appearance.

"No, I didn't come here for you," he said.

Obviously, he did come to my room.

Mason looked at me, and his dark eyes faded back to their natural color. "I came to speak to Tiana," he said.

Adam looked at both of us and sighed. I gave him a small smile, telling him it was okay if he left. It wasn't like Mason would hurt me.

Adam's frown deepened, and he walked out of the room without a word, causing my smile to drop. I mentally shook my head at him. I needed to talk to him later.

I brought my attention back to Mason. A straight expression appeared on his face as he took a step closer to me.

"Get ready by seven. I'm taking you out to dinner."

And with that, he was out of my room, faster than light.

My eyes widened and my mouth hung open. A fly could have flown in.

It took me a moment to comprehend his words, and when it did, my wolf started freaking out. I, on the other hand, was shocked. Did he really take my words seriously? I was only kidding.

But it looked like it didn't matter because he was taking me out to dinner, and that kept roaming in my mind. My wolf was more than happy that, for once, she and her mate could connect in some way while I was still too shocked to think of anything.

When I first came here, I had never thought that Mason and I would have a decent conversation, but now he's taking me out to dinner, and that surprised me to an extent.

I knew no matter how much I wanted to stay away from this mate bond, deep down inside me, I was sort of happy.

CHAPTER 30

"He what?" Lina shrieked. "He asked you on a date?" she screamed, flabbergasted.

My eyes widened, and I shook my head. "He did not ask me on a date. He just thought that I was serious when I told him we would be tied if he took me out to dinner." I explained to her.

Immediately after he told me to be ready by seven, I went and told Lina, not exactly sure what to do. She then freaked out and jumped to conclusions, saying Mason finally dared to ask me out and would soon reveal his undying love to me. I know, stupid. I couldn't help rolling my eyes at that. I explained to her that he's just trying to thank me for helping him, but she said I was being naïve and dumb.

"That doesn't matter now because you guys are going on a date," she squealed happily.

I frowned at her. "For the hundredth time, it's not a date," I exclaimed.

She looked at me, then crossed her arms over her chest, giving me a look that said I was delusional. "Okay, okay. I'll go along with that, if it helps you sleep at night," Lina told me.

I nodded even though I knew she wasn't taking this seriously. "Thanks," I breathed out. "Now, can you help me pick something to wear?" I looked at my closet, then back at her.

Her eyes perked up in excitement, and she nodded eagerly. I didn't know what to wear. I didn't know whether I should wear something casual or fancy, but then I thought about it. It was only dinner. I was not going to some party.

Lina pulled out a lot of clothes that I never knew I had. She pulled out dresses, skirts, and tops. I looked at her with wide eyes as she threw random clothes on my bed that was turning into a huge mountain of clothes.

"How about this?" Lina showed me a really tight dress that I once wore but never again because of how much skin it showed.

"No, I don't want a slutty outfit. I want something normal." I explained to her.

She pouted, a defeated look plastered on her face, like she wanted me to wear it so badly. She then chose something else. "What about this?" she asked with a huge smile on her face.

I looked at the dress and shook my head. I didn't like it. It looked like it should be worn for luxurious parties. "No, Lina. I'm going out to dinner, not to a high-class party. For all I know, he's taking me out to McDonald's."

She chuckled at my statement. "Well, don't be sad if he does. McDonald's is delicious."

I rolled my eyes but nodded.

She started looking for something else while I wondered who was going to clean this mountain of a mess on my bed. I silently scoffed. Of course I am.

"I swear, if you say no to this one, I'm going to slap you," she threatened.

I saw her holding a skirt that had the right length and a cute top that had a design on it. I liked how the two would go well, which was exactly what I wanted.

"That's nice," I told her, smiling.

She sighed in relief. "That's good because I was serious when I said I would slap you if you didn't like it."

I rolled my eyes at her, which brought a chuckle to her lips.

"Wow, you're so nice," I said sarcastically.

"That's what friends are for." She handed me the skirt and the top.

I had half an hour before seven, so I had to get ready fast. I went to the bathroom and changed into the clothes Lina handed over to me. I looked in the mirror and smiled. I wasn't one to brag, but I looked good.

While I was brushing my hair, my thoughts went straight to everything that had happened today. I was still surprised that Mason and I were going out to dinner. Some might call it a date, but I saw it as a thank you dinner. Nothing more, nothing less. However, my wolf thought otherwise. She kept yelping in joy as she repeatedly said that we were going on a date with our mate.

I told her it wasn't, but just like Lina, she disagreed. I sometimes felt bad for my wolf. It was not her fault that she couldn't be with her mate. It's just that, our circumstances were preventing her. Even though I didn't want to accept Mason, I couldn't deny the fact that his wolf and mine have a connection.

Every werewolf had its connection with their mate, even though the human side of us might not want to be with them.

Yes, Mason was hard to deal with and was the type of person I'd like to stay away from, but my wolf kept telling me that he wasn't bad, that he just needed time, that he already felt something for me. I didn't know whether I should listen to her words or not, but I knew not to get too attached.

I knew Mason wasn't that bad. The rumors about him weren't exactly true, and I knew better than to trust a rumor. He's actually not that bad when he's not moody or angry. The image of him smiling came in my head, and I couldn't help but smile. I wished he was like that all the time. Maybe then and there, these feelings we had because of the mate bond might change and maybe our relationship too.

All I knew for now was to keep everything on the low. I didn't want to put myself in pain, so I reminded myself to be careful even though I knew the mate bond was getting harder and harder to resist.

I sighed and started to apply some makeup. I didn't put on a lot because I wasn't really a makeup person. I just applied mascara and lipstick before looking in the mirror one more time and walked out. Lina was sitting on my bed in silence, looking dazed off. Her head snapped to my direction, and she smiled when she laid her eyes on me.

"Oh my God! You look beautiful." She came closer to me.

I smiled at her as her eyes ran over my body in excitement. "Thank you." I couldn't help but think that she was happier than me. I snickered to myself. Of course, she is.

"Wow, how will my brother hold back?" A smirk crawled on her lips.

My eyes widened, and a scowl was plastered on my face. "Lina," I warned.

She smiled at me and raised her hands as a sign of defeat. "Okay, okay. Sorry," she muttered and then looked at the clock.

I turned my attention to where her eyes were and saw that I had about ten minutes to go.

She started walking towards the door. "Come on. I bet Mason is waiting," she said.

I nodded and wore my bracelet before walking up to her.

"Will Nick look over the pack while Mason is gone?" I asked, wanting to make sure the pack wouldn't be in danger if the alpha left.

Lina rolled her eyes. "Yes, don't worry. Nick has everything under control. He always does when Mason is in other packs. I don't blame you, though. It's a luna instinct." She said the last part with a smirk on her face.

I gave her a warning glare, and she chuckled. I opened the door, but before I could step foot outside, Lina placed her hand on my shoulder, a sad expression on her face.

"Have fun, Tiana. And remember, let loose. You guys are mates, after all," she said with that same sad smile.

I didn't know why she looked sad. Something then clicked in my head. She wanted a mate, that's it. I smiled at her and started walking towards the stairs. I exhaled deeply and shook my head.

Unlike me, Lina wanted one. I felt so bad for her. The only thing I could do right now was hope that hers would come along sooner.

As I was halfway down the stairs, I caught Mason's scent, making me nervous. I then saw him talking on the phone. He was wearing a pair of jeans and a shirt. His eyes roamed over me before meeting my eyes.

"I'll call you tomorrow so we can decide on a day for the meeting," he said and remained silent as he listened to the person on the other end. "Okay. Thank you, Alpha Alex." He hung up and turned his attention to me.

"Hey," I said, quietly looking at his face. He had a straight face, clear of any emotions.

"Hi," he greeted. "You ready?"

I nodded, not trying to make the situation more awkward than it already was. "Yeah," I answered.

He put his phone in his pocket, and I gave myself a silent reminder that I had to buy one. I never bought one because I didn't think they were necessary, especially since we have mind links. But I had thought about it and decided I might need one to talk to someone from outside the pack.

After walking out of the pack house, we silently entered the car and then Mason drove off. He didn't say a single thing and only focused on the road. I didn't want to say anything that might make him pissed, so I decided to stay quiet.

We eventually made our way to the city. I wondered where he was taking me, but I didn't ask. I instead looked out the window and leaned my head against the glass, admiring the city lights. I glanced at Mason to see him looking straight ahead with an emotionless face on.

Did something happen?

I didn't think about it much because knowing Mason, he always had an emotionless face on. He must have felt my stare because he turned to me for a second before looking back ahead.

"Is there something wrong?" he asked.

I shifted in my seat and glanced at him once again. "No," I replied.

He raised a brow. "Is there something on my face?"

I rolled my eyes, and I couldn't miss the tiny smirk that crept into his lips. "No," I repeated.

"Then why were you looking at me like that?" he questioned.

I looked down at my hands, not knowing how to reply. "Is it bad if I just look at you?" I asked him.

His smirk grew. "No, but there must be a reason," he said.

"I was wondering why you always wear a mask," I told him quietly, in all honesty.

This made him look at me in surprise, and his eyes turned a shade darker. I didn't know if I should have said that or not. He looked back at the road and didn't say a single word. The tension in the air was so thick that if I had a knife, I would cut right through it.

Silence hung in the air, only the sound of the car could be heard.

"Sometimes, wearing a mask keeps someone from getting hurt or hurting someone else," he said so softly, I barely heard it.

I looked at him with wide eyes as he kept his on the road. His words registered in my mind, and as I was thinking about it, he stopped the car in front of a place. Before I could say anything, he spoke.

"We made it."

I looked at the place and then nodded, deciding not to ask him about what he just said. I didn't want to send him into a bad mood. It's better to leave it be, if he didn't want to talk about it.

We silently approached the place that had "James Diner" in big letters. Mason held the door open for me.

I smiled at him. "What a gentleman," I said with a hint of sarcasm in it.

He smirked. "Why, thank you. It took you long enough to notice," he said jokingly.

I rolled my eyes and entered the diner with him following me. The man behind the counter gave us a polite smile.

"Table for two?" he asked, looking at us both.

We nodded, and he told us to follow him. He led us to a table and handed us the menus.

"We will be back after a moment to take your orders," he said before giving us another smile and walking off.

The place is nice. I never expected Mason to come to a place like this. *Was this his first time coming here?*

As if he had read my mind, he spoke, "I come here often. The food is good, and it's calm over here. They don't get many customers, so it's always quiet."

I nodded even though his eyes were on the menu. "This seems like a nice diner," I said.

"Yeah, it is."

"So, I'm guessing you like silence," I said.

He looked at me and asked, "Yes, I do. What about you?"

I shrugged, not really sure. "It depends, actually. There are times when quiet is boring and there are times when I wish I had some peace and quiet," I stated.

He gave me a small smile which surprised me a bit. "Boring? What do you see as fun?" he asked.

"Hmm. Well, talking is fun, playing is fun, beating Adam in a game of chess is fun, and doing a marathon of *The Vampire Diaries* is fun," I said with a smile on my face.

He laughed, and I watched him in amazement.

"Vampires?" he questioned. "That's fun? Watching them is fun?" He looked at me with amusement written all over his face.

"Yes, it is. You should try it sometimes. It will take you on a roller coaster of emotions," I said.

And when those words left my mouth, he laughed again. I couldn't break my stare from his laughing state. I couldn't deny the fact that he was beautiful when he laughed, when he let loose, not when he wore a mask.

"You want me to watch a girl series?" he asked.

I furrowed my brows and shook my head. "It's not a girl series. Lots of men watch it," I told him.

He rolled his eyes and shook his head. "Even though," he said.

I smirked at him. "One of these days, I'm going to force you to watch one episode, and when you do, you'll want more."

He raised a brow at me in amusement. "We'll see about that," he said with a small smile on his face.

I smiled back and looked down at the menu.

Who knew Mason and I would be sitting at a diner, looking like decent people, not bickering with each other and talking about a series that I adored. Yes, this was surprising, but I liked it. It was a change, and sometimes change is good.

Not long after that, a waiter came up to us and asked for our orders. We gave him our order, and he walked away. Mason and I had small talks here and there. He looked more loose than when we first came here, and I was thankful for that. I didn't want to have dinner with a stiff Mason.

I then remembered the phone call he had before we drove off. Who was Alpha Alex? I debated whether I should ask him or not. But of course, my stupid mouth had a mind of its own.

"If you don't mind me asking, who's Alpha Alex?" I asked.

"He's the alpha who requested a meeting to discuss the vampire problem. We had that call to arrange the meeting," Mason explained.

"Do you think we are in some kind of threat?" I asked him.

He frowned and shook his head. "I don't really know, but it's better to be safe than sorry."

"True, we should be ready for anything."

After a while, our food came and I didn't hesitate to dig in, not caring if I looked like a pig in front of Mason's eyes. He was right, their food is good. I heard a quiet chuckle, and I looked up to see the amusement in Mason's eyes.

"What?" I asked.

"Usually, girls like to eat politely in front of a man," he stated.

I rolled my eyes at him. "Oh, well, sorry to break it down to you, but I'm not like all the other girls," I told him.

His face brightened, and he gave me a small smile. "I know, and I like it," he said before handing me a napkin and pointing to the side of his lips.

I felt my face heat up, and I immediately took the napkin from him and wiped my lips. He looked down at his food and ate. I stared at him for a moment before I continued my feast.

Once we were done, Mason looked at me.

"Ready to go?" he asked.

I nodded. "Yes."

Mason left the money on the table before we got up. Then we walked side by side towards the exit. The man at the counter gave us a smile, and I returned it politely. I smiled a bit more when Mason held the door open for me for the second time today.

"A gentleman, you are," I said, amusement dripping in my voice.

His eyes lit up, and he smiled. "Well, it's nice to know that you're noticing it." He played along and I laughed.

We eventually entered the car in comfortable silence and started making our way back to the pack house. I glanced at Mason to see him looking good, better than how he was earlier. I looked away before he caught me staring at him.

My wolf was happy, more than happy to enjoy a moment like this with her mate. She kept yelping in joy, and I couldn't stop the smile from crawling onto my face. I was happy as well because of the dinner and because of my wolf's joy. I couldn't disagree that this was a nice night.

"Why are you smiling?" he asked, glancing at me for a split second.

"I'm smiling because my wolf is happy," I told him in all honesty.

He had a surprised expression on his face, but it soon disappeared and turned into a small smile.

"My wolf is happy too," he said softly.

My heart started to beat faster than it should. We were now out of the city. Trees surrounded us as the air blew softly, singing a soft melody.

My eyes widened when Mason stopped the car on the side of the road and brought his attention towards me.

"But my wolf isn't the only one that's happy." He stared at me with dark eyes. I gulped nervously. "I'm happy too. I may not be showing it, but I am," he told me as his eyes started changing colors.

I tried to get some words out of my mouth, but my body wouldn't let me. I was too engulfed in shock to speak.

We were now in the middle of nowhere, staring at each other. I opened my mouth to say something, anything. But before I could do that, Mason cupped my cheeks and pulled me towards him, smashing his lips into mine.

My eye went wide, but they eventually closed as if they had a mind of their own.

I kissed him back as he tried to pull me impossibly closer, but the kiss didn't last long when we heard a low growl emerging from the trees.

My head snapped to the direction of the sound and heard Mason growl out loud. My eyes widened when I saw a black wolf emerge from the trees.

And this wolf wasn't just any wolf, no, it was a rogue.

CHAPTER 31

I watched in shock as the rumbling rogue came stalking towards us, causing a vicious growl to erupt from Mason's chest. I looked at Mason to see him carefully eyeing the rogue with a dangerous glint in his eyes. He was ready to pounce out of the car any minute now. I looked back at the rogue and mentally shook my head. He came growling at the wrong person.

Before I could even blink, Mason was already in his wolf form, running towards the rogue.

My breath got caught in my throat when Mason didn't waste any time, digging his teeth into its neck. The rogue growled out in pain as blood started flowing down his body. Mason obviously didn't need any help. He could take the rogue down in a single second, but that didn't stop my wolf from worrying. She kept growling at me to help him even though Mason had told me not to get out before he jumped out of the car.

Besides, I wasn't that dumb. If I get out, Mason might get distracted and that might give the rogue a chance to attack him.

I watched as Mason bit into the rogue once again, causing the latter to howl in pain. I then snapped my head towards the trees when I saw familiar wolves running towards the scene. Nick and our pack warriors came into sight, but by now, the bloody rogue was already unconscious. I knew he wasn't dead because his chest kept rising and falling. Nick and Mason then transformed back to their human forms. When they were fully dressed, I walked up to them.

"What happened?" Mason growled out in anger. "Who is he?"

"We found him right in front of the borders. We were chasing after him," Nick said.

Mason looked at the rogue that was lying on the ground, then back at Nick.

"Take him to the dungeons. Let's see if we can get something out of his mouth," Mason sneered.

Some pack warriors nodded and grabbed the rogue in a tight grip, then walked off into the woods and out of sight.

"Do you think you'll get something out of his filthy mouth?" Nick asked.

Mason growled which caused me to frown. "I'll make him . . . even if it means death," he said lowly.

Once they noticed me, Nick's emotionless eyes softened and Mason's angry face relaxed a bit.

"Tiana," Nick greeted. "I'm sorry for what happened. Are you okay?"

I couldn't help but think that he wasn't just asking about the incident that just happened, he was also asking about our dinner. I nodded and turned to Mason to see him talking to the pack warriors. I then looked at Nick and gave him a small smile. "Yes, everything is okay," I replied.

Nick returned the smile and then went to talk to a pack warrior.

I turned towards Mason's direction when his scent got stronger and saw him walking towards me. His face was devoid of any emotions, his emotions hidden from anyone who would lay eyes on him. I frowned at his appearance but couldn't blame him. What just happened wasn't something pleasant, especially after the nice dinner we just had.

"Head back to the pack house with Nick," he said softly with a frown on his face. I stared at him and then back at Nick, who was waiting for me.

"What about you? Are you coming?" I asked and he shook his head.

"No, I need to deal with that rogue," he answered.

I slowly nodded in understanding and backed away. Before I could reach Nick, I saw Mason staring at me and I sighed.

"How was your night?" Nick asked as a small smile crawled onto his lips and I returned it.

"Surprisingly, it was nice," I told him as we started walking towards the pack house with a few warriors behind us.

"That's good. Mason needed something like that," he stated softly and I nodded.

"It was going well until . . . you know." I sighed.

"Let's see if we can get something out of him. Maybe he knows why we've been getting rogue attacks lately," Nick said.

"Do you think he has something to do with them?" I asked.

Nick shrugged, and his eyes darkened. "I really don't know, Tiana."

When we arrived at the pack house, Nick said goodnight and told me to go to my room. I didn't have to hear him twice and rushed.

Once I stepped foot into my silent room, a sigh escaped my lips. I turned the lights on and immediately changed out of the clothes I was wearing. By now, I was exhausted, so I didn't waste any time and jumped on my bed. As soon as I closed my eyes, there was a loud knock on my door. I groaned and sat up.

"Come in," I shouted.

My bedroom door opened, and an excited Lina entered. As soon as I saw her, I already knew exactly why she was here. I rolled my eyes and laid back down on my bed.

"Tell me everything," she squealed. I looked at her and rolled my eyes again at her excitement. "Where did you guys go? What did you guys do? Was he nice to you? Did you guys kiss?" she asked as she sat on my bed. I sat up, and her excited face turned into confusion. "Wait, how come Mason isn't in the pack house? Please don't tell me you ditched him! Oh my God—"

"Lina, I didn't ditch him." I cut off Lina's blabbering before she could say anything stupid.

Her confused face relaxed. "Then where is he?" she asked.

I sighed and ran a hand through my hair. "You see . . . while we were on our way back here . . ." I said but paused to look at her.

She furrowed her brows, and confusion was written on her face once again. "What happened, Tiana?" she asked worriedly.

"We encountered a rogue," I answered.

Her eyes widened, and a gasp came out from her lips. "A rogue? Oh my God! You can't be serious! I can't believe that of all days, it had to appear tonight!" she said, standing up.

"Calm down, Lina. Everything's okay. We were on our way home anyway, and Mason dealt with him. He's now in the dungeons," I explained.

Her face relaxed, and she sighed in relief. "Well, that's good. At least no one got hurt," she spoke.

"Thankfully, no one," I reassured her.

Lina nodded and then smiled once again. "You didn't tell me. How was the date?" she asked excitedly. Her worried state completely vanished like it was never there.

I rolled my eyes and stood up. "Lina," I groaned. "How many times do I have to tell you that it was not a date?" I crossed my arms over my chests and raised a brow at her.

She rolled her eyes. "Okay, okay. Just how did it go?" Lina asked.

I smiled as I began to recall what happened, which led her to smile as well. "It was actually nice. We went to this diner and ate some good food, then we were out. Nothing special, but nothing bad either," I told her.

She started squealing, and I couldn't help rolling my eyes again.

"Oh my God! You loved it, didn't you?" Lina gushed.

A chuckle escaped my lips, finding it funny that she was happier than me. "I would be lying if I said I didn't like it." I turned around and sat on my bed.

Lina started squealing some more, like a fat pig excited for food.

I chuckled again and shook my head at her. "Calm down there, Ms. Piggy," I joked.

She laughed and sat next to me. "I'm like so happy. You and my brother are finally getting along."

I smiled at her reaction and shrugged. I didn't know if those were the right words, but I couldn't deny the fact that something was changing. I didn't know what to feel. I was still confused. But my wolf was a hundred percent happy, and I was glad for her.

Lina stood up, and a sigh of relief came out of her mouth. She gave me a smile and ran a hand through her hair. "I'm happy that things went well," she told me and I smiled at her. She then checked the time before looking back at me. "I should go now. Goodnight, Tiana."

"Night, Lina," I said back.

And with that, she was out of my room. I sighed in exhaustion as I fell on my bed that felt like fluffy clouds. After my long day, all I wanted to do was sleep without anyone interrupting my slumber. I closed my eyes and a yawn escaped my lips. I felt like I would fall into the deep, deep abyss any minute now, the place where I couldn't think about my worries or my problems and just relax for a short period of time.

Unfortunately, I couldn't just have that because someone knocked on my door, making my eyes jolt open and my body jerk off the bed.

I sighed in annoyance as my sleepy state vanished. *Can I ever get a good night's sleep without anyone interfering?* Groaning, I stood up and glared at the closed door. *Did Lina come back?* I wondered.

I soon frowned when I picked up a scent, confused as to why he was here. I opened the door and faced a silent Mason.

I stared at him as he looked into my eyes. Like usual, Mason held no emotions but his rough expression relaxed a bit as he placed his hand in his pocket.

"Is there something wrong, Mason?" I asked. "Did something happen to the rogue?"

He shook his head and stepped closer to me. "No, the rogue is still unconscious, so we're waiting for him to wake up," Mason explained.

"Oh, okay. So why are you here?" I asked him, still confused about his presence at a time like this.

His eyes widened and a cough escaped his lips as he looked down. I furrowed my brows in confusion when he pulled something out of his pocket. "You dropped this in my car," he spoke, showing me the bracelet that I was wearing earlier.

I looked down at my wrists in shock to find nothing around it. It must have fallen without me noticing. I looked back at Mason and gave him a small smile.

"Thank you," I whispered. I grabbed my bracelet from his hand, and Mason's serious eyes relaxed, showing a glint in them.

"You're welcome, Tiana," he whispered back. It was so soft that if I weren't a werewolf, I would never hear it.

I cleared my throat and looked into his dark eyes, ones I could get lost in forever.

"I want to apologize," he spoke. I frowned at his statement. "The rogue ruined the night for you."

I immediately shook my head, disagreeing. "It wasn't your fault. In fact, I had a nice time." With a smile on my face, I assured him that it was indeed a night I would like to repeat and that he was not at fault for what happened.

"You had a nice time?" he asked as his smile turned into a smirk, making my breathing hitch.

I scoffed and rolled my eyes. "Don't make me repeat myself," I told him.

A chuckle escaped his lips, and his eyes lit up in amusement. "I'm glad you liked it." He placed both his hands in his pockets. "Maybe, one day, we could do that again," he spoke softly.

"Maybe," I whispered.

And with that, he turned around and walked off.

I couldn't break my gaze away from him until he was out of sight. A sigh escaped my lips, and I ran my hand through my hair. I smiled as my wolf purred out in delight. I closed the door and placed the bracelet on the bedside table.

"Maybe," I repeated to myself.

I lay on my bed and fell into the deep slumber that had been calling out to me since I got here.

CHAPTER 32

A yawn escaped my lips as I opened my sleepy eyes to a bright morning. I groaned in annoyance when I realized that a knock at my door had woken me up. I sat up and rubbed my eyes. Then I stalked towards the door, not really caring that I looked like a caveman who hadn't showered in years. Whoever was behind this door had disturbed my slumber when all I wanted to do was stay in bed longer.

I turned the doorknob and opened the door to see a frowning Adam. I rubbed my eyes once again and looked at him with confusion written all over my face.

"Didn't I ever tell you never to wake me up?" I asked, tilting my head as his frown deepened.

"Sorry, but if I didn't come, then Lina would," he spoke.

I raised a brow and stepped back, letting him enter my room. "What do you mean?" I asked.

He raised the bag that was in his hands. "Lina had to do something, so she told me to give this to you. She said thanks," he explained and handed it to me.

I opened it and saw a couple of my clothes that Lina had borrowed a couple days ago. "Thank you," I said and placed the bag on the floor.

Adam nodded and didn't say anything.

I frowned when I noticed the frown on his face, which wouldn't seem to disappear. I stepped closer and placed a hand on his arm. "Are you okay, Adam? You don't seem very well."

He looked at me, and a sigh escaped his lips. "Yes, I'm okay. Training is just tiring me out."

"Okay, hang in there," I told him.

He nodded and placed his hands in his pockets, stepping back. "So, I heard you went out yesterday."

My eyes widened as I recalled last night, the night I had dinner with Mason and we encountered a rogue. I couldn't help but think of when Mason came to my room and handed me my bracelet.

I brought my attention back to Adam when I heard him cough. I shook my head, snapping out of my thoughts. "Yes, I did," I answered.

His frown deepened as he spoke, "And I heard you went out with the alpha."

I slowly nodded, not so sure where he heard it from.

"Yes, that's true," I spoke, "but how did you know?"

As soon as I confirmed it, a low growl erupted out of his chest. "Dammit, Tiana," he cursed and ran a hand through his hair.

I frowned and looked at him in confusion. "What's wrong, Adam? How did you know?" I repeated my question.

He growled again and clenched his jaw. "The whole pack knows. Apparently, someone saw you and Mason in the same car, driving off last night, so rumors erupted. Some say you guys are a thing, and others say you are seducing him to be the luna of this pack. There are a lot of rumors, Tiana. Tell me, why did you go out with him?" he asked me in a hard tone.

I stepped back, trying to register his words in my head. People actually thought I was trying to get along with the alpha to be the luna? I mean, the pack didn't know I was his mate so, of course, they would think that, but I still saw that as unacceptable. What if I hadn't gone to have dinner with him? What if I had some business with him and they saw? Would they still spread those rumors?

I shook my head in disbelief. This wasn't good. I just hoped it wasn't such a big thing.

"Tiana!" Adam growled, snapping me out of my thoughts. "Tell me, why were you with him?" he asked again.

I sighed and took another step back. "Adam, we went out to dinner. I helped him, so it was kind of like a thank you dinner. Nothing more. Let's just hope the rumors will go away soon," I explained.

His frown deepened and he didn't say a word.

"Besides, the pack doesn't know I'm his mate. So it's not that surprising that a person would spread a rumor once they saw a new pack member together with the alpha."

Adam growled lowly, and I shook my head.

"Tiana, was that all? Just a thank you dinner or something else?" he asked.

I furrowed my brows and crossed my arms over my chest. "Yes, Adam. Why?"

He signed and ran a hand through his hair. He didn't answer my question but asked me another one instead. "Tiana, do you feel something towards him?"

I frowned and took a step back, not liking where this was going. "Adam," I spoke, "what are you trying to say?"

He took a step closer to me. "Just answer me. Do you feel anything towards him?" he asked.

I looked down and clenched my fist. "Adam, you and I both know that I don't want to." I shook my head.

"Does that mean—" Adam wasn't able to continue as I cut him off.

"Don't worry. I don't feel anything towards him," I told him. He sighed and gave me a small smile.

I wasn't able to wipe the frown off my face because my wolf and I knew that no matter how hard I tried to ignore this mate bond, my feelings for him were too strong and I didn't want to admit it.

"Tiana, I don't want you to get hurt again . . . especially since he is your mate," Adam spoke softly.

I shook my head and faced him. "Don't worry about me, Adam. I know what I'm doing."

He nodded and pulled me in for a hug. I sighed and hugged him back, knowing he's just worried about me. We soon pulled away, and the smile on his face dropped.

"What are you going to do about the rumors? I'm afraid people will start to pick on you. Do you think it's a good idea to talk with the alpha about this?" Adam asked.

I shook my head. "No, I don't think it's worth it. If it gets out of hand, then I'll talk with him, but I don't think they'll try to approach me."

He nodded and placed his hands back in his pockets. "Okay, just be careful," Adam said.

I gave him a smile. "Don't worry."

"Okay. I have to go. I have training today. If you have nothing to do, come over and watch. I'll see you later."

As soon as he was gone, I sat on my bed with a frown on my face.

Great. Now I'm going to have to deal with whatever the pack members think about me.

I sighed and shook my head. *I shouldn't really care about their opinion.* I walked towards the bathroom with clothes in my hand as a yawn escaped my lips. I cleaned up and did my business. After I was fully dressed, I looked in the mirror and sighed. My stomach then growled, so I decided to go to the kitchen to get something to eat before I faint out of hunger.

As I walked through the halls, I noticed lots of eyes staring at me. Of course, their eyes would be on me with all the rumors around. I tried my best to ignore the stares and the whispers that they weren't trying to hide.

Geez, how rude.

I kept hearing some stuff here and there, about how I was seducing the alpha and trying to be the luna of the pack. I scoffed at that one. If only they knew.

I entered the kitchen to see lots of pack members eating breakfast. As soon as they noticed, their eyes turned to me and the whispers began to float in the air. I didn't pay much attention to it and walked towards the fridge. Since I wasn't that hungry and mainly because I didn't know how to cook other things, I grabbed two eggs for my breakfast.

As I started making some scrambled eggs, I noticed that their whispers got louder. Again, they weren't trying to hide any of it. I rolled my eyes in annoyance. I heard lots of words that made me want to head up to whoever was speaking and slap them in the face, but I held my ground, not wanting to show that I cared.

"Slut."

"Bitch."

"What a whore."

"No wonder why Alpha didn't kill her. She has been seducing him this whole time."

"She's not even pretty."

"All she wants is the luna title."

"That bitch stole my mate."

I growled quietly at all their remarks but then snapped my head back when I heard the last part, knowing exactly who it was from—the one and only Chloe.

I narrowed my eyes on her angry, caked-up face. She started approaching me slowly as her minions walked behind her. Everyone's eyes were on us. Some had shocked expressions on their faces while others had anger and hate.

Great, now everyone thinks I'm a mate stealer.

I brought my eyes back to Chloe, her fist clenched and eyes twinkling with hatred. I stepped back, not wanting to cause any sort of drama that would just end up hurting my head.

"Did she say mate?" Someone gasped.

"Yes, she did!" someone else replied.

"Does that mean that girl—" they pointed at me "—is trying to steal her mate? How awful!"

My eyes widened at that, and I growled lowly. I looked at Chloe, who was now standing in front of me with a smirk on her face.

"You see what you brought to yourself? This is what happens when you touch something that's not yours," Chloe sneered.

I calmed myself down. I didn't really have any time for this, and all I wanted to do was walk away, but that would make me look weak. I crossed my arms over my chest, looking into her eyes.

"Last time I checked, he wasn't yours either," I told her.

Her eyes widened in anger, and a growl came out of her throat. "Back off. He's mine," she growled.

I shook my head. "You and I both know that's not true," I whispered in her ear and gave her a smirk. Anger flamed up in her eyes. "He's not your mate."

"How dare you say that, you mate stealer," she snarled loudly. Before I could say anything else, a fist flew right towards me and landed on my cheek, making me fall to the hard floor.

My eyes widened as I felt my lip throb in pain. I looked at Chloe to see a satisfied smirk on her lips, and everyone else smirked too. I furrowed my brows, but before I could get up and land a punch on her face, a loud growl erupted in the air, making everyone's stares shift towards the source of the sound.

My eyes widened when I saw an angry Mason walking towards us, making the smirk on Chloe's face vanish. Everyone in the kitchen stood, staring at us with wide eyes.

"Chloe," Mason's stern voice echoed through the kitchen.

"Babe, I can explain. She attacked me fir—" Chloe started but was cut off by his growl.

Mason glared at her and his eyes turned black, indicating he wasn't happy. Nope. He was mad. I immediately got off the floor and his eyes went down to my lips, then back at Chloe. He stepped closer to her, and his glare intensified. Another low growl was heard in the thick air.

"You made a wrong move, Chloe. I'll deal with you later," he sneered.

With that, he grabbed my hand and pulled me out of the kitchen, causing everyone to stare at us in shock. I was surprised as well, but I remained silent as we made our way to the empty clinic.

"Sit," he ordered as he searched for something.

I sat down and stared at him as he grabbed a small cotton ball and something that looked like medicine. I didn't know what to say. I mean, what could I say after he had seen all that? It was quite embarrassing to know that he had witnessed someone punch me that easily. If only he didn't intervene that early, I would've shown Chloe she was messing with the wrong person.

"It's okay," I told him, knowing he was going to help me with my bruised lip. "It will heal fast."

Mason didn't say anything and walked towards me. His eyes went down to my lip, then at my eyes. "We don't want these lips of yours to be infected now, do we?"

I shook my head and remained silent. I looked at Mason putting all his attention on my busted lip. I tried not to wince as my lips stung when he placed the cotton on it. His eyes went up to mine, and he pulled the cotton away.

"I'll deal with her. She won't bother you from now on," Mason spoke.

"It's okay. You don't have to," I said softly.

He shook his head. "No, she needs to learn her place."

I slowly nodded and didn't say anything else. He started rubbing the cotton on my lip again. I thought about Chloe's behavior ever since I came into this pack and decided to ask him the question that was always in my mind.

"Chloe hates me, and I'm guessing it isn't for no reason. Were you and her a—" I started but stopped when Mason growled. I looked at him to see his eyes darkening.

Mason backed away and shook his head, looking into my eyes. "No, we never were. She's just trying too hard and can't get that I don't want her," he spoke. "I've never even been in a relationship."

A cough escaped my lips, which was immediately followed by laughter. I laughed like that was the funniest joke in the world. As soon as my giggles died down, I looked at Mason to see him staring at me seriously.

"What's so funny?" he asked.

"The joke—" I started but stopped when I saw that his face held no amusement to it. "Wait, you weren't kidding?"

Mason frowned and shook his head. "Does it look like I'm joking?" he asked.

I stared at him in utter shock. *He wasn't joking!* I couldn't believe that Mason had never dated before. Even though I couldn't believe it, my wolf was happy that her mate had never dated another girl. I stayed silent and watched as he went back to cleaning my lip. The whole time he was doing that, I thought of what he had said.

After a while, he backed away and inspected my lip. Contentment then crawled onto his face while confusion crept on mine.

"All done," he said. "But there's one more thing I got to do for it to be completely healed."

I raised a brow at him. "And what's that?"

As he leaned closer, amusement sparked in his eyes and his smirk grew. "This." He placed his lips on mine, causing my eyes to widen in shock.

CHAPTER 33

Mason slowly pulled away, and I let out the huge breath that I was holding in. He had a smirk on his face, his eyes going down to my lips then up to my eyes.

"There," he whispered. "All better." I couldn't help myself from smiling as he backed away.

"Thanks, but you didn't have to," I told him with amusement laced in my voice.

A chuckle came out of his mouth, and he placed his hands in his pockets. "Oh, trust me. I wanted to," he said.

I felt my cheeks redden, and I looked down. I heard another chuckle from him, which caused me to look up. "What's so funny?" I asked.

He stepped closer to me and raised his hand, softly touching my cheek. My eyes widened again, realizing how close our bodies were.

"You're blushing," he said. "I don't get to see that often."

"Take a picture. You won't see it for a long time," I joked.

Smiling, he stepped back and grabbed his phone from his pocket. "Oh, that's exactly what I was going to do." He immediately snapped a picture.

I stared at him in disbelief. "Hey! I was kidding! Delete that picture now," I told him and crossed my arms over my chest.

Mason smirked and shook his head. "I'm afraid I don't have time to do that." He looked down to his wrist which, might I add, was bare. "I have to go. I'll be sure to stare at your picture whenever I have time." He smirked.

"Oh no, you won't," I warned, glaring and taking a step closer. He chuckled and was out of the room before I could do anything. I sighed and shook my head, a smile crawling on my lips at what he had said.

"Idiot," I muttered to myself.

I started walking towards my room to place a small band-aid on my lip, wanting to cover the bruise until it completely healed. I thought about Mason again, and a chuckle escaped my lips at the memory of him taking my picture. How embarrassing. I'd have to find a way to delete it.

I entered my room and embraced the silence, letting a sigh escape my lips. I went inside my bathroom and snickered at my reflection.

What a lame throw. She could have done better.

Chloe might have caused a bruise, but I couldn't help myself from thinking that if I were in her place, I would have thrown a stronger one.

Doesn't sound too bad. I might as well arrange that.

I went down on my knees to reach the cabinet under the sink and opened it, looking for a band-aid. "I'm pretty sure I had some in here," I muttered to myself.

After a while, I groaned in frustration when I couldn't find any. I brought myself closer to the cabinet, not wanting to give up. Then out of desperation, I entered the tip of my head inside and dug for whatever I could find. I knew I might look weird, but what could I do? The cabinet was pretty big. Although I was pretty sure I looked like a dog digging his grave.

I smiled when I saw the small box of band-aids resting deep under the pile of rubbish.

"Ah, there you are." I sighed and grabbed the box, but as soon as I did that, someone spoke behind me, causing a gasp to escape my mouth and my head too hit the roof of the cabinet.

"What the hell are you doing?" the voice asked.

I groaned in pain and pulled my head out, seeing an amused Lina. "I was looking for the box of band-aids, but can you not do that next time?"

A laugh erupted out of her while I groaned again and rubbed my head.

"That freaking hurt," I whined.

Her laughter died down, and she crossed her arms over her chest. "Why do you need that for?" she asked.

I rolled my eyes and stood up, facing her. I pointed at my lip and raised a brow. "Are you blind, Lina? Can you not see this?"

Frowning, she looked at my lip and soon gasped. "Oh my God, Tiana! How did that happen? Oh my gosh!" She pulled me into a hug and started to fake cry. "Please don't leave me. Don't die on me, my friend."

I rolled my eyes and pushed her, seeing a smile crawling onto her lips. "Ha-ha, very funny," I grumbled.

She broke out into laughter and wiped a fake tear from her cheeks. "I'm sorry, I couldn't help doing that. But seriously, what happened?"

I rolled my eyes and crossed my arms over my chest. "Chloe happened."

Her happy expression vanished and was replaced with an angry one. "What do you mean? You're saying Chloe was the one who did this?" she asked.

I nodded. "Yes, that is exactly what I'm saying."

A growl escaped her lips, and she shook her head. "I'm going to show that bitch her place. Who does she think she is?" Lina exclaimed, agitated.

I placed the box on the counter, facing the mirror. "Apparently the luna," I muttered and Lina rolled her eyes. "The rumors gave her the ability to play Ms. Victim."

Lina's frown deepened, and she stepped closer to me. "Yeah, I heard a couple of people talking about it. But don't worry,

I taught them a lesson they would never forget." She said the last part with a smirk.

I rolled my eyes, and she only chuckled.

"Besides, these will soon fade away. It's only a phase. And as long as Mason is on your side, you have nothing to worry about," she added.

I glanced at her and gave her a smile. Thinking about Mason made me feel a little better. I shouldn't have cared what anyone else thought of me. It's what I thought of myself that truly mattered. I looked back in the mirror and sighed.

"Hopefully," I whispered and opened the box. I grabbed a band-aid, placing it on the bruise. "Anyways," I said as we walked out the bathroom, "what are you planning on doing today?"

She shrugged. "I don't know, really. What about you?"

I shrugged as well and turned to her. "I don't know either, but I'm going out to the yard to watch Adam train. He told me to stop by."

Lina nodded and walked towards my bedroom door. She turned to me and gave me a smile. "Well, I'm going to go check up on Nick, see if he needs any help. If you need me, call me through the mind link."

I nodded and returned the smile. "Okay, bye," I said.

"Bye." And with that, she was out of my room.

I ran my hand through my hair and exited my room a little later. As I was heading to the yard, I ignored the stares I was getting from the pack members, as well as the whispers that didn't surprise me at all.

I let out a sigh as soon as I stepped foot outside the pack house. When I reached the yard, I saw the warriors in training running on the track and spotted Adam. I smiled at him, and he returned it. He then turned his attention to someone else and continued running. I walked towards a bench and sat on it, observing the pack warriors working out. I couldn't lie, those men were damn good looking.

I snickered at myself and rolled my eyes when my wolf started nagging at me, lecturing me to not look at any other male other than our mate.

I mentally shook my head and blocked my wolf out. I looked back at the warriors and saw Adam looking at me. He waved and smiled, and I waved back. Then he turned around and went back to training. I didn't mind sitting out here and watching Adam train. It's actually quite relaxing.

Adam is my best friend, and I knew that all his life he always wanted to be a pack warrior. I didn't know why, but it's his dream. And since he's my best friend, I needed to be the good friend that I am and support him and watch his training every now and then. Besides, I would rather sit out here than inside the pack house.

The air around me was quiet and refreshing. I closed my eyes and inhaled deeply, breathing in the clean air. The wind blew in a soft melody, which caused my muscles to relax. I slowly opened my eyes and sighed. I was the type of person who appreciated nature. I preferred to stay outdoors than indoors. I liked to sit on the soft grass every now and then and close my eyes to listen to the birds chirping and the wind blowing. This not only calmed me down but my wolf too. She had been nagging me these days and hurting my head. The two solutions I knew was to block her out or calm her down which, might I add, was really hard to do.

I was brought out of my thoughts when Mason's scent hit my nostrils. I snapped my head in the direction of his scent to see him walking towards the pack warriors.

He stopped and turned his attention to me. His eyes lit up, and a smirk crawled onto his lips, causing me to roll my eyes. He looked away and talked to the warriors, who all nodded their heads and then resumed running. I watched in silence as Mason started training them.

A little later, I snapped my head to my back when I heard someone gasp for air. I frowned when I saw a shaken Ryder running towards me with a pleading look on his face. I raised a brow at him when he stood in front of me, his hands on his knees. As soon as he caught his breath, he sat next to me and placed his hands on mine.

"Tiana, my best friend," he said with a fake smile on his face. "How are you doing? Hope good! You know you're my favorite person in the whole wide world, right?" he said.

I crossed my arms over my chest and sighed. "What do you want, Ryder?"

He let out a nervous laugh and placed his hand on my shoulder. "What?" he asked. "I can't hang out with my best friend?"

I rolled my eyes and gave him a pointed look. "Ryder, what do you want?" I asked and then shook my head. "No. The question is, what did you do?"

He groaned and ran his hand through his hair. He then looked around and sighed in relief.

What on earth happened to him?

"Listen, Tiana. I got myself into deep shit, and I mean deep shit. I need your help to get me out of it," he said.

I frowned at his words. "What the hell did you do?" I asked.

He let out a shaky breath and scooted closer to me. "Let's just say that a possessive male mate is after me."

My eyes widened, and I shook my head. "And why is that?" I questioned, even though I knew exactly what he had done.

"How was I supposed to know that she was mated? I flirted with this girl and her mate heard me inviting her to eat lunch together. So he went all caveman on me. I thank the Lord I was able to get away from him, but he's still chasing me," Ryder explained.

I whacked him on his head. "You idiot! You deserve it. You don't flirt with a girl who has a mate," I lectured him.

Frowning, he shook his head and rubbed the spot where I hit him. "As I said, I didn't know she had a mate," he groaned. His eyes then widened after looking behind us.

I turned around and saw a tall, buff man running towards us.

Shit! What did he get himself into, especially with a guy that huge? I mentally shook my head at his stupidity. *You will be missed, Ryder.*

"Shit shit shit," Ryder muttered under his breath. He looked at me with a pleading look and wrapped his arm around my shoulder. "Please get me out of this, Tiana! I'm dead. I'm too young to die," he begged.

I frowned at him. "How on earth can I get you out of this mess? Besides, I have nothing to do with this," I told him.

Ryder wasn't able to say anything else because the buff guy was already in front of us, boiling in anger. Ryder and I both gulped as we stared at the guy that was shooting death glares at Ryder.

"Listen, buddy," Ryder started. "You got this all wrong. I wasn't flirting with your mate."

The guy let out a growl and grabbed Ryder by his shirt while I stood up from my seat. "Do I look stupid to you?" he asked. "I know what I heard. You invited my mate to a date!" he growled.

I stared at them with wide eyes, not knowing if I should interfere or not.

Ryder shook his head and gave the guy a pleading smile. "No, no, buddy! I wasn't asking her on a date. You see this girl over here?" Ryder pointed at me. "She is your mate's friend, and she told me to tell your mate that she wants to have lunch with her today. That's all. Don't kill the messenger," Ryder explained.

My eyes widened at his lie and the buff guy stared at me, inspecting me. His angry face relaxed a bit, and he dropped Ryder to the ground. I gave Ryder a death glare as he threw me a look that begged me to play along.

Oh goodness, what had he gotten me into?

The tall guy walked towards me with a rough expression plastered on his face. "You're my mate's friend? I have never seen you around her before."

I glanced at Ryder and sighed. He owed me big time. I brought my attention back to the big guy and nodded. "Yes, we're friends. We met recently and I told Ryder, the guy you're trying to kill, to tell her that I'm inviting her to lunch today," I explained to him, trying to sound convincing.

The guy gave me a look, telling me that he didn't believe me. He crossed his arms over his chest and asked me the one question that I dreaded. "Well, since you're her friend, tell me her name," he said.

I gulped and glanced at Ryder, planning his death ceremony in my head. That's if I don't die today. He smiled at me and told me to relax. I glared even harder at him and looked back at the guy who was waiting for an answer.

"Her name is Crystal," Ryder told me through the mind link.

I let out a sigh of relief. Of course, Ryder would know her name. He knew every single girl in this pack. I guess I could postpone his death ceremony.

"Her name is Crystal," I told the guy.

The guy slowly nodded and stepped back, glaring at Ryder then at me. "I expect to see you both eating lunch today," he said. He then took another step back and turned around, walking off.

My eyes widened, and I snapped my head over to Ryder. What did he expect me to do now? Ask the girl to eat lunch with me?

Ryder scratched the back of his head and let out a nervous laugh.

"What the hell am I supposed to do now?" I growled at him. "What did you get me into?"

Ryder frowned and stepped closer to me. "Listen, Tiana. I'm sorry, but please help me. Just talk to the girl and ask her to eat lunch with you. That's it," he begged.

I sighed and crossed my arms over my chest. "I don't even know the girl."

"I'll show her to you, and all you got to do is meet her and become friends. It's not that hard," he said.

I shook my head. "It's not that easy either," I told him.

He gave me a pout and looked down at the ground.

I rolled my eyes and shook my head again. *Ugh! The things I do will soon lead to my death.* "Fine, I'll do it, but you owe me," I said.

Ryder looked at me, and a smile grew on his face. He pulled me into a hug and squeezed me to the point where I couldn't breathe. "Thank you, thank you, thank you," he said happily and pulled away. "You're the best."

"Yeah, yeah, whatever," I muttered.

I averted my eyes towards Mason's direction and saw him walking towards us, not looking too happy. I completely forgot he was here.

Ryder stepped away from me and gave me one more smile before walking off, not wanting to deal with another angry male.

Mason glanced at Ryder, who wasn't too far away from us, and then at me. "What was he doing here?" he asked.

I raised a brow at his question. "Nothing, really. Just stopping by," I told him. I didn't want to tell him the truth because I thought it would be better if no one else knew.

Mason nodded and placed his hands in his pockets. "Okay," he muttered, not sounding too happy. "What about the guy who was here a while ago?"

My eyes widened slightly. I dropped my head down before looking back at him. Moments like these make me wish that someone would come and interrupt us.

"Ugh . . . well," I started and scratched the back of my head. "He's one of Ryder's friends," I lied. They're definitely not friends.

Mason slowly backed away. "Okay then. I need to get back. Just want to make sure everything is okay," he said.

"Everything's okay. Don't worry," I assured him.

He turned around and walked off. I let out a breath of relief and shook my head.

Ryder would be the death of me.

*   *   *

"You're coming with me!" I demanded.

Ryder shook his head and groaned. "No, I'm not. The guy was going to kill me, for God's sake. I'm not risking it," he argued.

I crossed my arms over my chest and growled at him. "You got me into this mess, Ryder! So you're coming with me to confront the girl!"

He groaned again and stood up from the couch, staring at me with a face that said he wasn't going to budge. "No, I'm not, Tiana! Please don't make me! I'll show you the girl, and you do the rest. I'm not going to risk the chance of her possessive mate seeing me."

I groaned this time and stood up. "Fine, but I'm not letting you off the hook." He would suffer my sweet revenge sooner or later.

Ryder smiled and nodded, soon pulling me into a hug. "Thank you, thank you, thank you!" he squealed.

I rolled my eyes and pushed him away. "Let's just get over it," I grumbled. "Come with me and show me the girl."

He nodded and placed his arm around my shoulder, grinning from ear to ear. "On to our mission," he said.

I whacked his arm off my shoulder, and he chuckled.

We walked out of my room and down the stairs. I looked at Ryder to see him looking for the girl. I didn't know what the girl looked like, so it was up to him to find her. As soon as we made it to the living room, he smiled and nudged my arm. I looked at him, then he brought his head closer to mine, whispering into my ear.

"I found her."

I looked around, then back at him. "Where?"

"She's over there. You see those girls over there? She's in the middle," he answered.

I looked in the direction he was looking at to see a group of girls at the end of the room. I breathed in and nodded.

Well, here goes nothing.

CHAPTER 34

Ryder gave me a nod and a soft smile, assuring me that things would go fine.

I breathed deeply and took a step forward, ready to confront the girl who would either decline my offer or save Ryder's ass from her protective mate. I slowly walked towards them, hoping and praying they wouldn't judge me based on the rumors that had spread like wildfire and accept my request to just have lunch together, just this once.

I stopped and looked back at Ryder, glaring at him because of what he was making me do today. He gave me a cheeky smile and waved his hands, gesturing for me to go on and not chicken out, which caused me to huff. Once I was in front of the girls, I gave them a friendly smile and brought my attention to the girl that was in the middle.

"Hi, Crystal! I'm Tiana!" I spoke and reached my hand out towards her.

The girl frowned in confusion and looked towards her right.

"Shit, Tiana. That's not Crystal. She's the girl to your left," Ryder said through the mind link.

My eyes widened, and I mentally smacked my head and whacked Ryder's head as well.

"Great job at describing her to me, Ryder."

"Ugh . . . I'm Crystal," the girl next to the person I had spoken to said in a soft voice.

I gave her an apologetic smile and stepped backward. "Oh, I'm so sorry." I reached out my hand for the second time, facing her this time. "I'm Tiana. I was wondering if I could talk to you."

The confused girl shyly shook my hand, then looked at her friends who had similar expressions written on their faces.

"You're one of the new pack members, right?" a girl from the group asked.

I looked at her and nodded. "Yes, I am."

The girl smiled and reached her hand towards me. "It's nice to finally meet you. We never get new members and having one is quite refreshing. The name is Stella," she told me.

I smiled at her kindness and shook her hand. "It's nice to meet you too. My name is— Wait, I already introduced myself . . ."

The girls started laughing and then introduced themselves one by one, and I couldn't help myself from sighing in relief. They seemed nice, so I had nothing to worry about.

"So, what can Crystal help you with?" Stella asked. She then placed her arms around her shoulder and Crystal squirmed in her place. "As you can see, our Crystal is a little shy."

I nodded and saw her blushing, looking at the ground in embarrassment.

I debated whether I should talk with her alone or in front of her friends. She did seem very shy, so it looked like talking with her alone would be quite hard. I also wondered if I should tell them about what had happened or just play along and ask if we could eat lunch together.

"I'm not shy," Crystal whispered, and her friends rolled their eyes. She looked at me and played with the hem of her shirt. "Don't listen to them." She pouted. "I'm not shy," she repeated. "I'm Crystal." She reached her hand out towards me, and we shook hands for the second time.

Talk about awkward.

Stella shook her head. "Crystal, she already knew that."

Crystal's eyes widened, and she slowly nodded. "Oh. How did you know my name?"

"Well . . . it's a long story, actually," I muttered, deciding not to lie. They seemed cool, so I wasn't worried. Besides, I wasn't about to follow Ryder's plan; he screwed up every time. I stepped closer to them and glanced behind me to see Ryder looking at me confused. I gave him a small smile, and he raised a brow.

"How're things going?" he asked in the mind link.

"They're nice, so I'm not lying to them," I answered.

His eyes widened and he stepped closer to us, but I gave him a warning look, telling him to stay away. *"What if she goes and tells her mate? I'm dead the second he finds out,"* he asked worriedly.

I rolled my eyes. *"Whether or not she does, it's your problem, not mine. I don't think she will, though."*

I looked back at the girls. "You see that dumbass over there?" I pointed at Ryder.

Ryder gulped and gave the girls a nervous smile, slowly backing away and turning his attention elsewhere.

Crystal nodded, recognizing him. "Yes, he talked to me today. Who is he?" she asked.

"Well, he got me into his shit . . ." I started.

I explained to her how he had told her mate that I was her friend and that he didn't ask her on a date but just told her what I had supposedly asked him to. I also revealed how her mate was expecting to see me eating lunch with her today or else Ryder's funeral would be planned out.

By the time I was finished, the girls started laughing. Crystal looked a little confused but nodded. "I don't mind hanging out with you," she said.

I smiled at her, and a sigh of relief escaped my lips.

"And I won't tell my mate, not because of your friend but because you're friendly." She smiled while the other girls nodded.

I thanked the Lord that they were friendly and not stuck-up bitches. "Thank you so much," I told her. "You're a lifesaver."

Her smile widened, and she looked down, blushing. "You're welcome," she whispered.

"You're going to have to get used to that. She's always blushing, and she's so shy," one of the girls spoke.

Crystal stuck her tongue out. "I'm not shy," she defended herself and crossed her arms over her chest, annoyed.

"Yeah, yeah, if that helps you sleep at night." The girl smirked.

Crystal rolled her eyes and looked at me. "When do you want to meet up?" she asked.

"How about after an hour? Let's meet here," I suggested.

She nodded in approval and smiled. "Okay, that sounds good. I need to go see John and tell him I'm meeting a friend for lunch," she said and gave me a wink.

I laughed and nodded. "Okay. Also, thanks for understanding."

"Oh, it's no big deal. And maybe if you want, we can become real friends?" she asked nervously.

I gave her a heartwarming smile. "That sounds nice. I do need to make more friends around here," I told them.

"That's great!" Stella squealed. "You seem really cool to be friends with."

"Thanks," I said, surprised at how friendly they were. Ryder was lucky they were nice, or I would have begun digging his grave.

"Well, I'll see you guys later," Crystal spoke.

"Goodbye!" I waved at her, and she smiled at us.

And with that, she turned around and walked away.

I looked at the rest and took a step backward. "I need to go. It was nice meeting you guys," I said.

"It was nice meeting you too. We should have talked to you sooner," a girl from the group said.

"You're right. We should hang out and get to know each other better," I suggested and they nodded.

I looked back to see Ryder waiting impatiently, so I waved the girls goodbye. "I'll see you guys around."

Ryder's eyes widened when he saw me approaching him, and walked quickly towards me. I smiled at him, and his face immediately relaxed.

"How did it go?" he asked.

"It actually went pretty well. Be thankful that they understood our situation because if they didn't, I wouldn't continue what you had gotten me into," I replied and placed my hand on my hip.

His lips broke out into a smile, and he engulfed me in a bear hug, suffocating me with his tight grip. "Thank you, Tiana. You saved my ass! I don't know what I can do to repay you."

I pulled away. "We'll talk about that later. You owe me big time." I crossed my arms over my chest and gave him a stern look.

He let out a nervous laugh and scratched the back of his neck. "I'm starting to believe that you're planning my death ceremony," he said in a soft tone.

I smirked at him and nodded. "Oh, trust me, I am."

* * *

I strolled the hall, making my way towards the living room to meet up with Crystal. I was slightly nervous about what her mate would do, but I tried not to think about it too much. Overthinking wasn't healthy for my state of mind. When I did, I would get overwhelmed with stupid scenarios that might lead me to lose my sanity if I didn't stop.

On my way there, Mason's scent hit me and I saw him walking towards me. As soon as he was in front of me, I gave him a soft smile.

"Hey," I whispered.

He returned the smile, but it didn't really reach his eyes. "Tiana, where are you going?" he asked.

"I'm going to meet up with someone. We're eating lunch together," I replied.

Mason frowned as he stepped closer to me, his face held confusion. "Who?" he asked, his eyes turning a shade darker.

A smirk crawled onto my lips, and I tilted my head. "Why do you want to know?" I questioned.

"Because I want to. Is there a problem?" he questioned, frowning even more.

I crossed my arms over my chest, shaking my head. "No, not at all. But what would you say if the person I'm eating lunch with is a boy?" I raised a brow.

A low growl emerged from his chest, and his eyes turned pitch-black. "I would say cancel it because that idea doesn't please my wolf, and he's this close to grabbing you and throwing you over my shoulder so you won't accompany your friend," he answered.

My smirk fell, and I looked at him with wide eyes. I felt my cheeks burn and my heartbeat slightly pick up its pace. His response took me off guard, but I wondered if what he said was truly only his wolf's intentions.

I mentally shook my head and brought my attention back to him. "Your wolf, huh? You sure it's not you who doesn't approve of the idea?" I asked.

He seemed taken back. "I . . ." He cleared his throat and looked away for a split second. "Yeah, I'm sure." His face went serious.

I slowly nodded, a little disappointed. I mentally scoffed at myself, not liking the way I feel. "Okay. Well, I have to go. Don't want to be late," I said and turned away, wanting to get away from him.

These past few days felt different. It seemed like the tension between Mason and I was slowly fading. I didn't know if that was a good or a bad thing, but all I knew was that I was starting to feel something towards him. I couldn't deny it anymore, no matter how much I disliked the idea.

Before I could take another step forward, he grabbed my hand and pulled me towards him. I looked at him, then down to his grip.

"You didn't answer my question," he whispered.

I gulped at how close our faces were, his breath fanning my face.

"Question?"

"Yeah . . . Who are you accompanying?" he asked again.

"Oh, I'm having lunch with a new friend. Her name is Crystal."

He nodded, and a smirk started growing on his lips. Moving his face closer to mine, he gently rubbed his nose against my cheek. I closed my eyes as he then softly dug his nose into my hair, inhaling my scent.

I didn't know what was happening to us as I was too caught up at the moment. I felt like something was pulling me towards him, preventing me from escaping. I inhaled deeply when his breath fanned my ear, causing a shiver to run down my spine.

"Have fun, Tiana," he whispered in my ear and pulled away.

I opened my eyes, looking at him. "Thanks." I pulled away and immediately turned around, walking off.

I was in a state of shock, not knowing what exactly had happened back there. My wolf, however, wasn't. She was yelping in pleasure because of that little moment. I shook my head and forced my thoughts aside. I needed to focus right now. I'd think about them later.

I entered the living room, which was occupied by a number of our pack members. Some glanced at me, and others didn't. I breathed out and looked around, trying to find Crystal.

"Tiana!"

I snapped my head towards the source of the voice. I smiled when I saw Crystal walking towards me. After giving each other a quick hug, my smile dropped when I saw Mr. Buff Guy approaching us with a frown plastered on his face. He carefully looked at us, his stare lingering on me. I dropped my head down, kind of nervous of his presence.

"So this is your friend, Crystal?" he asked, wrapping an arm around her waist.

Crystal looked at me and smiled. "Yes, she is, John," she answered.

Mr. Buff Guy, or should I say John, slowly nodded and gave me an intimidating look. "How did you meet her?"

I raised a brow at him, not liking his tone when he said *her*. It was like it burned his tongue. "Umm . . . Excuse me, but I have a name. It's Tiana," I said and crossed my arms.

He glared at me. "Your name isn't important." He looked back at Crystal, waiting for her to answer his question.

Crystal gave me an apologetic smile. "We met . . . ugh . . . yesterday. She invited me to have lunch together so we could get to know each other more," she replied.

Her mate didn't say anything but gave me a warning look. I raised a brow at him, not liking his attitude towards me.

It seemed like Mr. Buff Guy and I would become great, great friends. Note the sarcasm.

It was obvious he wasn't fond of me. His glare never left, and it was like he wanted to take his mate away. I looked back at Crystal and smiled.

"Well, if you don't mind, John. I'm stealing your mate for a while." I gave him a slight smirk, grabbing Crystal's hand and pulling her towards me.

"I'll see you later," Crystal said to her mate and waved at him.

Mr. Buff Guy didn't look so happy that I was taking his mate away from him. He glared at me like I was a man trying to flirt with his girl.

I smirked at him. "Oh, stop looking at me like that. I'm not going to hit on her. We're friends, remember?" I said in a matter-of-fact tone.

Crystal let out a laugh while Mr. Buff Guy's frown deepened.

"I'm sorry," she whispered to me. "He's always so stiff. You're going to have to get used to that."

I nodded at her. "I could tell."

She smiled at her mate and bid farewell. Then John kissed her on the cheek.

And take a guess what he threw at me, a wild guess. A glare. He gave me a glare. Surprising, right?

I smiled sweetly at him and placed my hand on Crystal's shoulder. "Bye."

We turned around and walked away.

*   *   *

"Your mate looked at me like I was about to kidnap you any minute and run off," I told Crystal, shaking my head.

She gave me a soft smile and shrugged. "He's been like that ever since I met him. He doesn't really socialize that much," she said and then ate her fries.

"How did you meet him?" I asked, taking a bite of my macaroni and cheese.

At the moment, Crystal and I were outside the pack house, sitting on the grass. We decided to eat here because inside was quite boring and there were lots of people.

"I met him when I turned eighteen. He's one of the pack warriors. One day, while I was walking, I caught his scent and that's when we met," she explained.

No wonder he was so buff and tall. He was a pack warrior.

"What about you? Do you have a mate?" she asked hesitantly and I raised a brow at her. "I've heard a couple of rumors here and there, but I know better than to believe them."

I nodded, knowing exactly what she meant. "Well, it depends on what kind of rumors you've heard. Some are right, and others are wrong. If it's about me going out with Mason yesterday, then it's right. But if it's about me trying to seduce him, then it's wrong," I explained.

"Wait, so you actually went out with him yesterday? And why are you calling him by his first name?" she asked.

"Ugh . . . well, it's because he's my mate," I hesitantly told her.

I didn't really know if it was wise of me to tell her that. It wasn't like I was trying to keep it a secret. Moreover, Mason and I weren't all lovey-dovey. And if the whole pack found out, then they would start treating me differently and expect me to be a luna.

Her eyes widened, and she coughed on her fries. I gave her back a pat and handed her water. She gulped it down, inhaled deeply, and looked at me, shocked.

"You're our luna?" she asked. "How come the pack doesn't know? The rumors floating around are making you look so bad. If they knew, they would give you more respect!"

I nodded, understanding what she meant. "It's just that, Mason and I, we don't have a strong relationship. We met over two months ago, and we barely get along. It's too confusing." I sighed.

"And why aren't you guys getting along? You're mates, for goodness sake. Soul mates!" she asked, shocked.

I rubbed my face and shook my head. "I-I don't know. It's because I have this secret. And also when I first met him, he didn't approve of me and I didn't approve of him either. I had my reasons, but I won't deny that I do have feelings for him. These past few days, we've been getting closer to each other and it's making me so confused." I ran a hand through my hair.

"Secret? What kind of secret do you have that prevents you from being happy with your mate?" She looked at me with determination in her eyes, wanting to know what was keeping me away from him.

"Promise me you won't tell anyone? No one in this pack knows, except for my best friend Adam," I told her. This was a huge load on my shoulders and maybe, just maybe, if I told her, I would feel a little better.

She gave me a soft smile and placed her hand on mine. "I promise, Tiana. I won't tell a soul. You can trust me."

Breathing in, I looked at her and told her my secret.

CHAPTER 35

I walked towards my room and sighed. I felt like a huge weight was lifted off my shoulders after telling everything to Crystal. I had let my heart out to her today. I had told her my worries and my fears and the thing that had caused a huge gap in my heart, something I hadn't told anybody since I came here.

I had told her my secret.

I didn't want anyone to know because it was too complicated. It might have made me who I was today, but I knew keeping it hidden was for the best, not just for me but for Mason too. I didn't know if I made the right choice in telling Crystal since I barely knew her, but I felt completely better after I did. And she was understanding.

Sometimes, telling a stranger your worries or secrets was better than telling your best friend because the former didn't know you. They had nothing against you, and they wouldn't judge you. And that's what I did today. I felt guilty that I hadn't told Lina because she was my best friend, but I preferred to keep it low. Maybe when the time was right, I would tell her.

I walked into my room and embraced the silence that surrounded me. It was getting dark, but my wolf was pushing me to run. I decided to let her for a bit because it had been a while since she was out. Maybe it would stop her from being nagging. I walked towards the closet to change into something comfortable.

I planned on running just around the pack house because I didn't want to come across a rogue or a bloodsucker. What happened yesterday made me cautious, and so everyone else. It could have been a coincidence, but I was choosing to be on the safe side. Also, I didn't want to get on Mason's bad side, knowing that if he saw me in the woods, it would anger him like the last time.

I walked downstairs and towards the pack house entrance. I opened the door and bumped into a hard chest. My eyes widened when strong arms wrapped themselves around my waist, keeping me from falling to the hard ground. I looked up to meet a pair of dark eyes that could seem to look right into my soul.

Mason looked down at me and gave me a questioning look. "Where are you going at a time like this?" he asked.

I raised a brow at him. "At a time like this? It's not even seven," I stated.

"That doesn't matter. It's dark outside. I need you safe," he whispered.

I slowly nodded. "I'm only going out for a run. My wolf needs to be let out."

He shook his head and his hold around my waist tightened, sending tiny sparks around my body. "No, not even that," he said stubbornly.

I sighed and frowned. "Please, Mason. I won't go far away. I'll be near the pack house. My wolf won't shut up until I let her out," I begged him with a pleading look. I had to run for a bit before my wolf would make me lose my sanity.

Mason stared at me and let out a long sigh. "God, you're impossible to deal with," he muttered under his breath and I frowned at him. "Fine, but only if I come with you. I'm not risking you getting into trouble," he told me.

I broke into a smile and immediately nodded. "Okay," I said happily.

I looked around to see a couple of people staring at us. We were by the door, and his hands were still wrapped around my waist possessively. I immediately pulled away from him, not wanting them to get the wrong idea. I didn't want the rumors to get worse.

Mason let out a cough, and I snapped my head towards him.

"Come on. Let's go," he said, grabbing my hand, causing my eyes to widen.

We then walked towards the woods. After I was fully shifted, I emerged from behind the tree and was greeted by Mason's silver wolf. The first thing he did was walk towards me and licked my face. His wolf had most of the control now.

My wolf snuggled closer to him and let out a purr. Mason let out a growl and rubbed the side of his face against mine. I slowly pulled away from him. He looked at me like I was his prey, his eyes pitch-black, inspecting my every move. This made my wolf very excited and she growled playfully.

I slowly backed away as he stepped further, and in less than a second, I turned around and made a run for it. I ran as fast as I could, with Mason right behind me. He was catching up, so this made me run faster. I heard a playful growl erupt from his chest, which made my wolf yelp.

The next thing I knew, Mason was on top of me as I crashed to the hard ground. I growled at him as he looked down at me playfully. I yelped in shock as he bit my ear, but not hard enough to hurt. I growled again, and he bit my other ear in response.

"Trying to run away from me, huh?" Mason spoke through the mind link.

I whined when he bit a little harder.

He pulled away, realizing his bite was a bit too much. He whimpered and started licking my ear and my face. My wolf purred again. He pulled away and looked at me. I pushed him off and jumped on him.

"Run? No, you chased me," I told him, looking down at him.

He let out a growl. *"I was chasing after my prey,"* he said.

I mentally raised a brow at him. *"Prey? Oh, so I'm now your prey, huh?"* I asked.

"Yes, you're my prey. And when my prey runs away from me, I chase it," he replied in a low voice.

Shocked, I slowly got off him, then I started running for the second time, making him chase after me once again. He growled, and my wolf growled back.

We stayed like that for a while. I couldn't help the goofy smile that kept appearing on my face as he chased me. I felt like a kid once again. It felt nice, and I liked this playful side of him.

After a while, I noticed Mason wasn't behind me anymore. I frowned in confusion and looked back to see him standing there, zoned out. It looked like he was talking with someone through the mind link. I slowly walked up to him. His eyes were pitch-black, and a low, dangerous growl emerged from his chest. I looked at him carefully, then took a step closer to him.

"Mason, what's wrong?" I asked him through the mind link.

His head snapped to me, his eyes darkening into the shade of black that screamed danger. Another growl came out of his chest, and he looked angry, really angry.

"I have to head back to the pack house. Something came up."

"What happened?" I asked.

"I don't have time to explain. I have to go. Be sure to follow me back to the pack house. I don't want you out here for long," he said and immediately turned around and ran off.

I stared at the spot he was standing on not too long ago in confusion. *What happened?* I hoped it was nothing bad because he looked very mad, and that wasn't good.

I decided to head back to check up on him, making sure everything was fine and there weren't any problems. I ran towards the place where I left my clothes at and shifted. I emerged from behind the tree, and a gasp of shock escaped my lips when I saw John right in front of me.

I placed my hand on my heart, trying to slow my heartbeat. *Goodness, where did this guy come from?* I looked at him and frowned. "What are you doing here? You almost gave me a heart attack," I asked.

His emotionless face didn't change, and he just shrugged. "I was going out for a run until I saw you," he said, not looking too happy.

I raised a brow at him and stepped closer, giving him a polite smile only to receive his glare. *Geez, what up with him and his glares?*

"Can I ask you a question?" I asked.

He frowned and shook his head. "No."

My eyes widened at his rudeness, so I stood in front of him and crossed my arms over my chest. "Hey, hey, hey, buddy. What crawled up your ass this morning?"

He snapped his head at me and growled. "Watch your mouth!"

"Watch your attitude," I shot back, smirking. "What's up with you? You're so rude. All I did was ask you a question!"

His eyes widened. Calming himself down, he closed his eyes and breathed in. He then opened them and stared down at me. "What's your question?"

"Why do you hate me?"

He raised a brow at me. "Hate?" he asked.

I nodded. "Yeah, I mean, I barely know you and I haven't done anything to you, so how come you're always glaring at me like I've stolen your mate?" I asked.

He rolled his eyes and started walking away.

"Hey, where are you going?" I walked up to him. *How rude. I just asked him a question!*

"I don't have time to answer meaningless questions," he replied.

I rolled my eyes at him. "Fine. Can I ask you another one then?"

He shook his head. "No."

How surprising.

I started walking behind him, but he stopped and turned to me, glaring.

"Why are you following me?" he questioned.

I scoffed at him. "Don't get ahead of yourself, buddy. I'm not following you. I'm going back to the pack house, exactly where you're going," I replied.

He gave me another glare before turning around and walking off. I was behind him until we reached the pack house.

I went to Mason's office to check on him, and as soon as I was in front of the door, I stopped dead in my tracks after hearing his angry voice boom in the air. I sucked in a breath as he continued to growl loudly and something fell on the floor, making a crashing noise.

"What do you mean he's dead?" he yelled.

My eyes widened at what he said. *Dead? Who died?* I stepped closer towards the door. I started getting worried, hoping it wasn't someone I knew or loved.

"Alpha, the rogue had silver in his system, slowly killing him. He woke up for only a short period of time before blacking out. Judging from the tests, it had been in his system since last night. He had a perfect amount of silver for him to die slowly," someone explained.

Mason growled and smashed something, making me flinch. What are you trying to say?" he growled.

There was a moment of silence.

"I'm saying the rogue was meant to die. His death was planned out, and whoever injected the silver in him wanted him to die today."

CHAPTER 36

My eyes widened at what I heard. I stood behind the door, surprised and confused.

The rogue that we encountered yesterday was dead? And that was because he had silver in his system? But why and how? Who would do that? It was all too confusing, and I felt worried.

"Dammit!" Mason growled from inside the office, and the next thing I heard was a loud crashing sound. "He was supposed to give me answers, but now he's dead!" he yelled in anger.

I flinched hearing his voice. I remembered Mason telling the guards to take the rogue to the dungeons for questioning, but now he was dead. The questions we had about the constant rogue attacks wouldn't be answered.

"Alpha, please calm down. We don't want the members of this pack to be alerted of something that may not be important," the man spoke.

Mason growled and murmured some other words. After a moment of silence, he spoke again, "You can go now. I have an important call to make."

"What should we do with the body?" the person asked.

I heard a growl, then another moment of silence.

"Dispose it. I don't care where, but get rid of it," Mason replied.

"Yes, Alpha."

And with that, I opened the door and stood there, looking at an angry Mason and at a man who I recognized as the pack doctor. The pack doctor stared at me in confusion while Mason looked at me with wide eyes, knowing that I heard their conversation.

I stepped back, letting the pack doctor pass. I then looked at Mason to see him staring intensely at me. I closed the door and stepped closer to him.

"Did you hear?" he questioned.

I nodded. "Yes. I didn't mean to, but I heard everything. I came over to check up on you," I answered.

His hard stare relaxed a little at what I said, and he let out a huge sigh.

"What are you going to do?" I asked.

He sat on his couch and ran a hand through his hair, looking frustrated. I sat across from him.

"I don't know," he muttered, shaking his head.

"What if that rogue had nothing to do with the attacks? What if it was just a coincidence?" I questioned.

His head snapped to me, and his eyes turned serious. "Whether you're right or wrong, I still need to take action for the safety of the pack. Just in case there's a threat," he told me.

I slowly nodded, understanding where he's coming from. He wanted to make sure his pack was safe from whatever threat there might be. These past two months, we had been having rogue attacks, and we didn't know if we're safe or not, even though this was one of the strongest packs there was.

"What are you planning?" I asked.

He sighed and grabbed his phone from his desk. "I need to make a phone call to an alpha to arrange a meeting tomorrow. Hopefully, we can find a solution," he grumbled.

I nodded and stood up, walking towards him and then sitting next to him on the couch. He stared at me, and that's when I noticed the bags under his eyes.

He looked very tired and sleepy. It seemed all his energy had been drained, and I felt bad for him. I placed my hand on his shoulder, feeling the sparks erupt from the contact.

"You look tired. Have you been sleeping well?" I asked.

"I'm perfectly fine, Tiana," he whispered.

I shook my head, not believing his words. "No, you're not. It's written all over your face. You're exhausted," I told him. "When was the last time you slept?"

Mason looked down at his hands, then back at me. He shrugged, making me frown. "I don't know. It doesn't really matter," he muttered.

I raised a brow at him. "It does matter. Did you forget that you're the alpha?"

"And since I'm the alpha, I have many things to do and don't have time for sleep," he told me.

I shook my head, disagreeing with him. "Wrong," I said. "Since you're the alpha, you're responsible for your pack and you can't lead a pack when you're very tired."

He looked at me, amusement written on his face. "Still, I don't have time for sleep," he argued and started dialing a number on his phone. "I have an important call to make."

I rolled my eyes and snatched the phone from his hands.

He gave me a pointed look. "Tiana," he said carefully. "I'm not in the mood to deal with your stubbornness. Hand me the phone."

I shook my head and gave him a small smile. "No can do, Alpha. Right now, you're going to rest and you'll make this important phone call in the morning," I ordered, causing a long sigh to escape his mouth.

"Tiana," he groaned.

"Oh, stop whining." I grabbed his neck, pulling him down to me. He shot me a confused look, and I gave him a soft smile.

"What are you doing?" he asked.

I placed his head on my lap and started playing with his hair. "I'm putting you to sleep since, you know, you're not listening to me," I answered.

A soft, playful growl came out of his chest. "I'm not a child. I can sleep if I want to, and I don't need to be put to sleep," he argued.

I rolled my eyes and tugged harder on his hair, causing a groan to escape his lips.

"What was that for?" he asked, rubbing his head softly.

I smacked his hand, and he placed it back to his side. I then started rubbing on the spot I tugged on. "For arguing with me. Just listen to me for once and sleep."

He let out a sigh and started to get comfortable on the couch. I started running my hand through his hair, and he let out a satisfied growl. I stopped for a second, but he grabbed my hand and placed it back on his head.

"Don't stop," he murmured, sounding tired.

A smile crept onto my lips, and I continued playing with his hair as his head lay on my lap. After a while, his breathing evened out and his chest rose and fell. I then knew he fell asleep—on my lap. I couldn't control the goofy smile that appeared on my face.

It felt nice, and I couldn't deny it.

I slowly closed my eyes and placed my head against the wall, falling into a deep, deep sleep beside Mason.

* * *

A satisfied sigh came out of my lips as I snuggled deeper into the warmth that surrounded me. I relaxed as I felt strong arms around my body, holding me close. I felt the person carrying me open a door and enter a room that had Mason's scent all around.

Mason. He was the one carrying me. His scent engulfed my senses, and I felt sparks erupt at the touch of our bodies. A little yawn escaped my lips, and I felt myself slowly being placed on a soft, comfortable bed that was filled with his scent.

I stirred a bit, slowly waking up, but I was too tired to open my eyes.

I felt Mason brush a strand of hair out of my face and softly brush his finger along my cheek. I slowly opened my eyes to meet his beautiful orbs. I looked around to see that it was dark and started wondering how long we had slept.

"Shh," he whispered. "Go back to sleep. It's late."

I looked back at him to see him staring intensely at me. I smiled. "Did you at least sleep well?" I asked.

He gave me a small smile, then stroked my hair. "I did, but now it's your turn to sleep. You were in an uncomfortable position. You could have gotten a sore neck," he said. "Go to sleep."

"You too." I grabbed his hand, pulling him towards me. "Sleep."

He let out a deep chuckle and moved closer to me. "If I sleep, will you sleep?" he asked.

I smiled, nodding my head. "Yes."

He lay down right next to me, facing me. We stared at each other for a moment, then he raised his hand and pushed a strand of hair behind my ear.

"Goodnight, Tiana."

A yawn escaped my lips, and I slowly felt myself falling back to sleep.

I felt safe and warm. Being here with Mason made me feel different and weird, but I liked it. I liked it when I see this side of him, and it made me happy knowing that he was showing it to me. When my eyes started feeling heavy, I looked at Mason one more time before completely closing my eyes.

I thought of us, leaving me confused and curious.

What were we? Friends? Strangers? Alpha and a pack member . . . or mates? We had never talked about this subject, knowing it wasn't what we wanted . . . but was it? Was this what we truly wanted?

"Mason?" I whispered softly.

"Hmm?" He continued to play with my hair.

"What are we?" I asked.

"What do you mean?"

"What am I to you?"

I felt him go stiff but slowly relax after a moment. I was too tired to care and realize what I had just asked him.

"Tiana," he whispered, "go back to sleep."

I yawned again and got comfortable, welcoming the darkness with open arms. I was too sleepy to ask him again and wait for an answer. I didn't know why I asked him that, but I did. It didn't look like he wanted to answer, but I was too exhausted to think too much of it.

Before I fell asleep, I heard him say something, but my brain wasn't functioning properly for me to register it completely. He said something I knew I would forget in the morning and not pay much attention to.

It sounded like, "You're important . . ."

CHAPTER 37

"I swear on my dead hamster's soul, if you don't give that back, I will murder you, dig a big grave, and bury you without anyone knowing. Then I'll tell everyone that you moved away to Canada because you don't want Trump as your president!" I hissed.

Ryder looked at me with wide eyes, amusement present in them with a hint of fear. He slowly backed away and gave me a sheepish smile. "Ouch, babe. You'd do that because of this?" he asked, showing me the last piece of bacon that he stole from my plate.

I growled at him and stood up from my chair, facing him. "I'd do more. That's nothing compared to what I want to do with you now. Give it back!"

He slowly shook his head. "No can do. This man over here," he pointed at himself, "needs all the energy he can get. So if you don't mind, let me enjoy this bacon."

I growled as he raised the piece of bacon to his mouth, ready to eat it.

"Man? Oh, I'm sorry, but I don't see a man in front of me. I see a pussy," I shot at him.

His widened eyes snapped to me, looking at me in shock. "Did . . . did you just call me a—" he started but soon growled.

"You heard me loud and clear, you pu—"

"Stop!" he yelled. "I am not a pussy."

"Yes, you are."

He shook his head and gave me a pointed look. "No, I'm not," Ryder hissed.

"Yes, you are," I said angrily. "Now give me back my food!"

Thankfully, there weren't many people in the kitchen to witness our bickering. This was all Ryder's fault because he was the one who started it. I was just minding my own business, eating my breakfast, when all of a sudden, the mutt snatched the last piece of bacon from my plate, making me very angry. No one, and I mean not a single soul, must steal my food!

"No, this is what you get for calling me a pussy," Ryder growled and then shoved the bacon into his mouth like a hungry pig.

Fuming, I let out a low growl from within my chest.

RIP bacon. You will be missed.

"You bastard!" I yelled and then attacked my prey.

His eyes widened and he stepped back, turning around for the door. Before he had the chance to move an inch, I jumped onto his back and tackled him. He let out a feminine scream and begged me to get off.

Pussy all right!

"You ate my bacon!" I shrieked and hit his back.

"Get off me!" Ryder screamed like a girl.

"No! You deserve to die, you bastard! Why him? He was innocent!" I hissed and punched his arm.

```
Now I know what you are thinking!
Overdramatic much? Nope, my food is
worth everything.
```

"I'm sorry! I'm sorry, okay? I won't do it again! Now get off me!" Ryder shrieked as I continued to hit his back.

"I'll make sure you won't do it again!" I growled and pulled his ear.

"Tiana, it's just bacon! You're overreacting!"

Another low growl came out of my chest, and I pulled on his hair, making him yelp in pain. "I'm not overreacting!" I said loudly.

"You are!"

"No, I'm not!"

"Yes, you are!"

"No! I'm not!"

"Yes—"

"No," I shot back, "I'm not!"

Ryder opened his mouth to argue back but stopped when a low voice echoed from behind us. "What the hell are you two doing?"

We snapped our heads towards the source of the sound. Mason stood there, staring at us in confusion and a hint of anger. I looked around to see no one but us. My eyes widened when I realized the position I was in.

I was on Ryder's back and he was holding my legs that were wrapped around his waist. Ryder immediately let go of me, and I got off him and stood on my feet. I looked at Mason to see him walking towards us. It had been a week since I last saw him, the night I slept in his room. From what I heard, he was busy with all the meetings he had with the other packs. I didn't know exactly what he was doing, but it had something to do with rogues.

"She started it!" Ryder spoke as he pointed at me, which totally surprised me. "She attacked me, and I was only defending myself!"

Mason looked at us as I glared at Ryder.

"He's lying!" I hissed. "He started it!" I told Mason as I pointed at Ryder.

"Did not!" Ryder argued.

"Did too!"

"Did not!"

"Did too!"

"You started it!" Ryder yelled.

"No, you did!" I hissed.

We started bickering again until Mason's loud voice cut us off. "Enough!" Our heads snapped towards him and we shut our mouths. Mason didn't look too happy. He glared at us and stepped closer.

"What's going on between you two?" he questioned.

Pouting, I looked at him and pointed at Ryder. "He stole my bacon and ate it!" I whined, dropping my head down. I was trying to act all innocent. Well . . . technically, I was, but you get my point.

"Liar!" Ryder hissed.

I snapped my head at Ryder and glared. I then looked at Mason and pouted even more. "I'm telling the truth, Mason. He ate my bacon, and I'm still hungry!"

Mason glared at Ryder and walked closer to me, giving me a slight smile. "It's okay. I'll make you some more," he told me.

My eyes widened at what he said, and Ryder's mouth hung open.

"You will?" I asked and he nodded.

"You said you're hungry, right? I'm going to make myself breakfast, so I'll make you some too."

I slowly nodded and smiled at him. We stared into each other's eyes until Ryder let out an awkward cough. Mason snapped his head to him, and his relaxed face turned serious.

"You can go now," he ordered him, his voice deep.

Ryder nodded in fear and turned away. Before he walked out of the kitchen doors, I could've sworn I heard him say something that sounded like, "The alpha smiling? Now that's a sight I'll never see again."

Mason turned to me, and his eyes lit up. "Come," he whispered and walked further into the kitchen.

I followed him as he opened the fridge. "You know how to cook?" I asked him, a little surprised.

He glanced at me and nodded. "Yes, I do. Didn't expect it?"

"Honestly, no," I told him.

A smirk crawled onto his lips. "Well, I know how to cook lots of things. You'll be surprised if you see what I can do," Mason chuckled.

I raised a brow at him and crossed my arms over my chest. "Oh, really? Then I'd like to see what you can do someday." I then sat on a chair.

"Okay. Then one of these days, I'll invite you to have lunch with me." Mason smiled.

"Okay, sounds cool."

He took out some eggs and other stuff before he started cooking. I rested my chin on my palms and stared at him. I couldn't stop the smile that crawled onto my lips. Who knew Mason Wood, one of the strongest alphas, can cook? This was surprising.

"How did you learn to cook?" I asked him.

He went stiff, causing me to look at him in confusion. He slowly turned around, his eyes dark. A moment of silence had passed, so I already understood that he wasn't going to answer my question. Soon, he placed the eggs and bacon on two plates and served them on the big table.

"Here, eat," he said softly.

I nodded and smiled gratefully at him. He sat in front of me and started eating quietly. I looked at my plate, then at him to see him staring intensely at me. "I didn't mean to ask you something that would bother you," I whispered.

His eyes widened, and he placed his fork on the table. "No, you didn't do anything. It's just that . . . there are some stuff I cannot answer," Mason explained.

"I understand."

He smiled softly and looked down at my plate. "Come on, eat."

I smiled at him and nodded, eating breakfast for the second time today.

* * *

I was sitting on my bed when Lina came walking in like she owned the place. I raised a brow at her, and she gave me a sly smile.

"What are you doing here?" I asked.

"Well, hello to you too," she greeted, and I rolled my eyes at her. "Can't I just come here to see my best friend?"

"No, you can. I just thought you came here to tell me something." I shrugged.

"Actually, I did," Lina said with excitement in her tone.

"Okay. What do you want to tell me?" I asked.

"Well, Ryder's birthday is coming up in a week, and I want to plan a surprise party for him," Lina squealed.

I nodded, smiling at her. "Oh, okay, but why are you the one planning it?"

"Because he played a big part in my birthday party, so I want to repay him. Besides, he's my friend," Lina explained.

"And a bacon thief . . ." I muttered.

She raised a brow and shot me a confused expression. "Huh?"

I smiled at her and shook my head. "Oh, I was just saying what a nice person he is," I said sarcastically.

```
Now, don't get me wrong. I don't
hate him, he's one of my closest
friends. It's just that he stole my
food, and that was unacceptable! So
I need my revenge after the bacon
incident and getting me into that
mess with Crystal and her possessive
mate.
```

Speaking of Crystal. Crystal and I met here and there, and talked a lot. We also sometimes hang out with her friends, who were all really nice. She was the total opposite of her mate, who was as stiff as a rock. I had bumped into him a couple of times, and he would growl and glare at me. If I said something, he'd cuss at me. He really got on my nerves. I tried being nice and mature, but he wouldn't budge. It was like something was up his butt hole that wouldn't come out.

I looked back at Lina to see her nodding, not looking convinced.

"Okay, I don't know what he did to you, but do you want to take part in planning the party?" she asked.

I placed my finger on my lips and thought about it. *Would I really want to help organize a party for that bacon stealer? Hmm . . .*

"Sure, sounds fun," I told her.

She smiled and clapped in excitement. "Great!"

"What's great?" Adam suddenly appeared standing by my door with a smile plastered on his face.

"That's none of your business!" Lina scowled at him.

Adam frowned and rolled his eyes. He walked towards us and looked at me. "Anyway, Alpha Mason gave us a break from training, so we decided to play a game we haven't played for a long time. I came to ask if you would like to play with us."

Lina broke into a huge smile and nodded eagerly. "Yes! We'll come!"

Adam looked at her and rolled his eyes. "I wasn't asking you. I'm asking Tiana."

Lina frowned and stuck her tongue out. "Still. I'm coming whether you like it or not!" she grumbled.

"Whatever," he muttered and turned his attention to me.

"So, what do you say? We haven't played this since high school," Adam asked.

I nodded, smiling. "Sure, but what's the game?" I asked. He smirked down at me, and my smile dropped.

Uh-oh, that smirk is bad news.
"Dodgeball," Adam answered.
I immediately started shaking my head. "Nope. No way am I playing that ever again. Go with Lina. I'm not playing!" I said, memories flooding my mind. Let's just say dodgeball and I were never a great match.
"What? Why?" Lina whined.
"It's because she always got hit back in high school—on her head, her back, her waist, and her butt. She was like the main target," Adam explained, chuckling.
Lina's eyes widened in amusement, and I continued to shake my head.
"I'm not playing!" I said stubbornly. "I freaking hate that game. It's like I'm signing my death warrant!"
"Oh, come one, Tiana! Getting hit with a ball doesn't kill you," Lina pointed out.
"Well, it may kill me!" I hissed and crossed my arms over my chest. "What if it hits my head, huh? I could get a concussion!" I might be overreacting, but I truly despised that game. And no way in hell was I ever going to play it ever again.
"So, I take it you're not coming?" Adam asked.
I shook my head. "Nope. I'm not."
Adam and Lina looked at each other, then a smirk slowly broke on their faces. I looked at them in confusion as they walked closer to me. My eyes widened when I realized what they were going to do.
"Oh, hell no—" I couldn't continue because as soon as those words left my mouth, they already grabbed me by my arms and pulled me onto my feet and out the door.

CHAPTER 38

"I swear, if you two don't put me down, I will make you regret the day you were born!" I yelled and tried to release myself from their strong grip.

Adam and Lina laughed and continued to pull me towards the backyard. They couldn't get it into their thick heads that I didn't want to play, forcing me on this.

I knew I might be exaggerating, but dodgeball and I spelled disaster. We were like fire and water. Worst enemies. I had horrible memories with it. In fact, I always ended up in the medical office, holding a bag of ice to my lips, nose, head, jaw, or cheek. Even though it wasn't allowed to throw the ball at someone's face, it would eventually strike me in the head.

`Don't ask why. I don't know either.`

"Will you stop struggling?" Lina asked, tightening her grip on me.

My head snapped at her. "Will you let me go?" I pleaded.

She gave me a sly grin. "Nope," she replied, popping the *p*.

I let out a sigh of frustration, and that only made Adam chuckle.

"Do you find this funny? Dragging me to my own death?" I snapped at him.

He let out another chuckle. "Come on, Tiana. You have to face your fear!"

"Fear? I'm not afraid! I'm just trying to avoid being attacked by balls! They freaking hurt, and they're hard and big!" I growled at him.

"That's what she said . . ." Adam muttered.

"Huh?"

He shook his head, and a smirk crawled onto his face. "Nothing. And don't worry, you won't get hit by one . . . Trust me."

I furrowed my brows at him, knowing so well he's not to be trusted. "Fine, fine. I'll come with you. Just let me go," I said.

Lina released me as soon as Adam lost his grip. "Yay! We're going to have so much fun!" she said happily.

I shook my head and scowled, "I know I won't."

As soon as we reached the backyard, I caught sight of the pack warriors, laughing in joy, as they didn't have to train for once. I also caught a glimpse of Mason seriously talking to some people.

Somehow feeling my gaze, he turned and looked at me. His tense face relaxed, giving me a small smile that I barely noticed. I then dropped my head down when the people he was with looked at me too. They brought their attention back to Mason, when he continued speaking.

Adam seemed tense when I looked at him while Lina smiled happily as she glanced between Mason and me. I raised a brow at her.

"What's with that goofy smile?" I asked.

She looked at me with eyes twinkling in excitement. "My ship is sailing," she whispered.

I furrowed my brows at her in confusion. "Huh? Did you say ship?"

Her smile widened, and she looked over at Adam, ignoring my question. "Come on. Let's go!"

Fine . . . Ignore me like I'm not here.

I felt Mason's eyes on me while we were walking. I met his stare to see the hint of confusion in his face. I supposed he was wondering what I was doing here.

"*Adam forced me to play with them,*" I told him through the mind link and he slowly nodded.

I could've sworn I saw him glare at Adam for a couple of seconds before staring at the others. I looked at Adam to see him glaring at Mason too. I rolled my eyes and nudged him in the stomach with my elbow. He snapped his head to me and raised a brow.

"If I were you, I would stop with all the glaring before your eyes pop out," I told him. He scowled and looked away.

Geez. What crawled up his ass?

"Okay, guys! Split into two teams. Let's get this game started!" a pack warrior spoke with a grin on his face.

Instantly, we split up. Adam was on my team while Lina was on the other. Everyone seemed excited. Well, except for me as my frown never left my face. I wasn't looking forward to this game, and that was why I was using Adam as my shield. Since he was tall and good at this game, he would keep me safe . . . Well, I hoped so.

Okay . . . Maybe he wouldn't.

When we played this game in high school, I would always hide behind him, not like it did me any good. He would always forget that I was behind him and move, causing all those dodgeballs to hit me instead. It was a pain in the ass.

I saw Mason sitting on a bench, watching us. He stared into my eyes and gave me a small nod. I smiled crookedly at him, then brought my attention back to the game.

"So, are you going to hide behind me?" Adam asked.

I nudged him. "As long as I'm still in the game, I'm using you as my shield," I muttered.

Adam didn't seem to mind. In fact, he had a smile on his face. "Okay then, if that keeps you happy." He brought his attention back to the group, while I scanned the warriors and instantly gulped.

There were a couple of females but most of them were males, and all of them were tall and buffy. Not a good thing. It would be a miracle if I was not the first one to be out.

I heard a whistle, and that's when the game started. I held onto Adam's shirt as balls started flying around. I squealed in shock as he moved towards my right, leaving me visible to the enemies. I immediately went to him and scowled as he let out a chuckle.

I had my guards up, carefully inspecting my surroundings. I immediately moved as I saw a ball thrown from behind me. I let out a breath of relief as it missed me. I kept looking back and forth, trying not to be hit.

One by one, people from my team and the other group were out.

My eyes widened when I noticed there were barely five people left in my group, including Adam and I. I was surprised I lasted this long. Most likely because of Adam, knowing he was a champion at this game.

Also, I stayed this long because I was determined not to lose. I was determined to not get hit.

I squealed in shock as I saw a ball heading directly towards my head. I instantly ducked, avoiding it. I sighed in relief but soon frowned when Adam was hit.

There goes my life. I'm a goner.

"Dammit!" Adam cursed as he stepped away from me. He looked back and smiled when he saw my worried face.

"I'm going to die," I told him in a dramatic tone.

"No, you're not. You're doing great," he chuckled.

And with that, he walked away. I gulped when I saw that only a few people remained in the game. This was a miracle. For once, my prayers were heard. Thank you, Lord!

After constantly trying to avoid being hit, I was the last one left from my group. I gulped in fear as I saw the look of determination in the opposing team's eyes. They were very much ready to take me out. I was their lone target, and knowing myself . . . I was screwed.

Mason stared at me with an amused glint in his eyes. I could tell he was surprised. I was too, especially that I was as stiff as a rock, my movements so ungraceful. Every time a ball was headed towards me, I would just take one or two steps away.

I then yelped when one of the buff guys threw the ball at me, which I successfully avoided. This was so not fair—little me against many buff males whose looks were fixated on me, like I was their food. It's not my fault my team was a bunch of pussies.

> Yeah . . . I know, I know. I'm a bigger pussy than all of them. But hey, look at me now. I'm the only one in.

"Come on! Take her out! She's just a girl," one of them yelled.

I furrowed my brows in anger. *Just a girl? This girl could dig your grave and bury you alive!*

"Oh, you're just mad that a girl is better at this game than you guys! Afraid your ego will be smashed?" Lina yelled, who was already taken out a while ago.

I smiled at her and was about to shoot back at them when I felt something hit my nose hard, making me fall to the ground, wincing in pain.

I heard gasps around me. I closed my eyes when my head started to pound. Then I felt something drip out of my nose and immediately knew it was blood.

Dammit.

This was what I meant when I said dodgeball and I had never been a good match.

I snapped my eyes when I heard a loud growl erupt in the air. I looked up to see a furious Mason stalking towards a warrior, whose eyes widened in fear and guilt.

I was taken aback when Mason grabbed his shirt and threw a punch right at him, making him fall to the ground. Lina immediately went up to him and pulled him off the guy. Mason looked angry, really angry.

Adam ran towards me, helping me stand on my feet. "Shit, Tiana, you're bleeding! Are you okay?" he asked.

I looked up at him and winced when the pounding in my head grew stronger, making me feel dizzy. I slowly nodded and kept the palm of my hand over my nose, trying to stop the bleeding.

Adam took out a tissue from his pocket and handed it over. I silently thanked him and covered my nostrils. Mason then came closer and snapped Adam's hand off my shoulder, pulling me towards him. My eyes widened as he did that, and everybody's eyes were on us.

"Shit," Mason cursed as he saw my bleeding nose, his eyes filled with anger. He grabbed my hand and turned to the group. "I'll be sending Nick to watch over you guys." He then glared at the guy who threw the ball at me. "I'll deal with you later."

The guy looked down in shame as he held his jaw.

I felt sorry for him. It wasn't really his fault. It was just a game. Besides, I always ended up like this whenever I played that stupid dodgeball.

Mason pulled me towards the pack house, and I followed him like a lost puppy. I looked down at his grip on my hand, then back at him.

"Where are we going?" I asked.

He looked at me, and his serious eyes softened. "To the pack doctor," he answered.

Of course, where else would he be taking me? To his room? Oh, shut up, Tiana!

Mason glanced at our intertwined hands, then slowly let go. I gulped as his eyes darkened. He looked away and nodded, motioning for me to continue following him. We entered the pack house, and because of the state I was in, I attracted a couple of stares.

As soon as we made it to the medical room, Mason opened the door and we were greeted by a man who looked like he was in his late twenties. He looked at us, and his eyes widened.

"Alpha," he greeted and then he saw me. "Her nose is bleeding."

"Yes, she was hit by a dodgeball," he replied.

The man, who I now realized was a pack doctor, nodded and gave me a soft smile. "Sit here," he said as he pointed at the bed. I nodded and sat down while he wore some gloves before walking up to me.

"Please remove the tissue so I could see it." He then wiped the blood I had on my nose. "It's not broken," he assured me. "I'll go get some ice so you can place it on your nose until the bleeding stops."

I looked at Mason to see him staring at me. He came closer and sighed. "Does it hurt?" he asked.

I shook my head. "Not really. You could say I'm used to it," I told him.

He furrowed his brows in confusion. "What do you mean?"

"I'm horrible at dodgeball. Every time I play that game, I end up with this," I explained with a smile on my face, trying to calm him down.

He frowned. "But you were great just a while ago."

I shrugged. "I'm shocked myself. I guess I was lucky this time."

He slowly nodded.

"I'm sure the guy didn't mean to hurt me, so there's no need to punish him." I was a little worried for the poor guy. Knowing Mason, he'd be announcing his death ceremony.

His frown deepened. "He hurt you," he claimed.

"It's a game. He didn't mean it. Just let it go," I told him.

He looked at me and huffed in frustration, not saying anything else.

Soon, the pack doctor came with an ice pack. He smiled at me and removed the tissue from my nose, replacing it with the ice pack. "You're not bleeding too much. The bleeding should stop soon," he said.

I gave him a smile. "Okay. Thank you, Doctor . . ." I stopped when I realized I didn't know his name.

"Sam."

"Thanks, Doctor Sam."

"No worries. Why don't you relax for a bit until the bleeding stops?" Doctor Sam suggested.

I nodded and got comfortable on the bed. Mason looked at me and sat on a chair. I raised a brow at him when I realized he was going to stay.

"You're staying?" I asked him.

He crossed his arms over his chest. "I have nothing better to do, so might as well stay," he said and I slowly nodded.

"When the bleeding stops, you can leave. I'll be in my office doing some paperwork. If you need me, just call." Doctor Sam then looked at Mason, nodding his head. "Alpha."

I looked at Doctor Sam's back as he walked away and couldn't help but think he was cute. He was pretty young and good-looking, which was rare in packs.

"Since when did he start working here?" I asked him.

"Not too long ago . . . Why?" he asked suspiciously.

I shrugged. "No reason. He just looks really young."

Mason frowned, his eyes narrowed on me, looking not too happy.

"And good looking . . ." I said the last part to myself, but I knew he heard.

It's not like I was going to hit on him or something. I was just stating facts, and I couldn't help wondering what Mason's reaction would be.

My question was soon answered when the shade of his eyes darkened, sending shivers down my spine. He got up from the chair and slowly moved closer. He was clearly pissed.

Mason leaned towards my ear and growled lightly. "Tsk, tsk. You shouldn't have said that." He paused before he continued, "My wolf doesn't like the idea of you calling another man good-looking."

I gulped as I stared into his eyes. *Great going, Tiana.*

"And he sure doesn't like you looking at someone else other than me," he growled softly.

I opened my mouth to say something but was left with no words. I was flabbergasted. He was too close. My wolf, however, was her usual self, yelping and purring in joy.

A soft gasp escaped my lips, and I removed the ice pack from my nose when I felt his lips softly touch the crook of my neck, leaving me stiff. But what he said next made my heart skip a beat.

"And I'd be lying if I say I don't agree."

CHAPTER 39

I took the red, knee-length dress out of my closet and placed it on my bed. It was beautiful, one of the best dresses I had ever bought. Smiling, I thought of today, which was the bacon stealer's birthday. Yes, I still held a grudge against Ryder. However, I was pushing it aside for now and being a mature person.

On the previous days, I helped Lina plan out the party. It was hectic, but in the end, it turned out awesome. The party would take place in the pack house since Mason didn't approve of going out to the city to celebrate. He said the rules nowadays were really strict and we need to watch our back.

But whether it's here or outside, it would still be awesome.

I sighed and sat on my bed at the thought of Mason. I looked at the dress and smiled.

I wonder if he will like this dress on me, I thought. My eyes then widened, and I ran a hand through my hair. *Dammit. It's getting harder and harder to deny it.*

I bit my lip at the memory of us in the medical room. Ever since then, I couldn't get him out of my head. Was there something wrong with me? Every time I saw him, it would flash in my head and a blush would color my cheeks.

It felt weird, but I wouldn't deny that it felt nice too.

Every time he smiled at me, not only did my wolf purr out in joy but I also had to grip onto something before my knees gave out. Things had changed between us, and I guessed it was for the better. I remembered at the beginning, when I first came here, I kept denying this mate bond. Now, it was different. I was not denying it anymore, and I didn't want to.

I wonder what Mason thinks of the mate bond. Is he feeling what I'm feeling?

Another sigh escaped my mouth, and I looked at the clock to see that there was one more hour before the party. I got up so I could change when I heard a knock on my door.

"Tiana, open up," Lina yelled from the other side.

I opened the door, looking at her all dressed up. Her eyes ran up and down my body before a scowl crossed her features.

"You're still not dressed?" she asked.

"I was just about to change," I replied.

She gave me a pointed look and shook her head. "Now? The party is about to start."

I looked back at the clock to make sure my eyes weren't lying to me. Once I saw that indeed there was still an hour left, I turned back to Lina and raised a brow. "We still have an hour left."

She rolled her eyes. "I guess it was a good thing I didn't let Mason come to see you," she muttered under her breath, eyeing my pajamas.

My eyes widened at her words, and I stepped closer to her. "Huh? What about Mason?" I asked. A sneaky smirk crawled onto her lips, and her eyes lit up.

"Mason asked about you, so I told him you were in your room. He was about to come here, but I suggested I'd check up on you. It's good he didn't see you like this. Now go and change. I'll wait here," she ordered.

Once I had the dress on, I couldn't help the smile that graced my lips as I looked into the mirror. The dress fitted me like a glove. It was indeed beautiful. I did a little twirl and felt satisfied.

I let my hair down and combed it until it was soft and tangled free. Then I applied my makeup and checked myself in the mirror once again before opening my door.

Lina's eyes widened as she looked at me up and down, a huge smile making its way to her lips.

"Oh my God, Tiana! That's a beautiful dress!" she squealed happily.

I smiled and nodded in agreement. "I know it is. I got it a long time ago but never had the chance to wear it."

"Once Mason sees you, he won't hesitate to tap that ass." Lina gushed as she looked at my body.

I gulped at her words and looked at her with wide eyes. "Do you hear yourself right now?" I asked.

"Yes, I do. All I'm saying is he won't be able to control himself tonight." She smiled.

I shook my head. "No, I'm saying you don't care if your brother gets laid. What kind of sister wants that?" I questioned.

Her eyes lit up in amusement, and she took a step closer to me, placing her hands on my arms.

"Tiana, it's not about him getting laid. It's about him being with his mate. He cares about you, and I can see it in his eyes. You do too, so don't try to deny it. You both are so stubborn, that's why you aren't still together yet. If one of you just accepts what you feel, it will be easier. But believe me when I say this, you have changed him, whether he or you notice it or not. Even if the entire pack can't see that, I see it," Lina explained.

I looked at her with wide eyes as I tried to swallow the lump that had formed in my throat. It was like a slap of reality, and it kept ringing in my head.

Does he really care for me?

That very thought made my head turn and my heart flip. I brought my attention back to Lina and only nodded, lost for words as nothing could escape my mouth at the moment. Lina backed away with a contagious smile on her face.

"Do you really think so?" I whispered.

"I know so."

I bit my lip and brought my head down. After a moment, I looked back at her and smiled. "Come on, let's go get a head start."

Whenever a party was held in the pack house, it usually took place in this empty room, which was big enough for dancing, food displays, and so much more. Most importantly, the room was away from the TV and other furniture, preventing people from destroying them.

From where we were, we could hear the loud music blasting in the air. I guessed they started the party earlier than it was supposed to be. I looked at Lina and asked a question. "Will Mason be here?"

Her eyes lit up, and she nodded. "Yes, he will. He told me he needed a break from all the work. You can say I was surprised, but I secretly know the reason behind," she answered.

I slowly nodded but didn't ask what the reason was. I secretly knew too.

We walked into the room to see it full. Lina smiled and glanced at me. "Come on, Tiana. Let's have some fun tonight," she screamed through the loud music. I grinned at her and nodded.

We went further into the room to see many people dancing, eating, drinking, and chatting. We soon spotted Ryder, so we walked towards him, pushing through the dancing bodies. He soon saw us, and in less than a second, he engulfed us in a tight bear hug. We squirmed until he let go.

"Thank you so much. This is awesome!" Ryder yelled through the loud music. We smiled, and Lina patted his back.

"Anything for my man," she said. "Wait until you see what else I got for you." Ryder's eyes widened in curiosity, and so did mine.

"What else?" he asked. Lina's smirk grew, and she laughed to herself.

"Something you'll love and thank me later," she replied.

He nodded but didn't question further. Instead, he looked at me and gave me a playful smile. "I didn't expect you to be here. I thought you still held a grudge against me," he told me, teasingly. I rolled my eyes and smacked his neck, making him yelp.

"Ow! What was that for?" He rubbed the spot I hit.

"I still do," I told him, "but I'm letting it slide today since you're the birthday boy. Besides, I helped Lina plan this party, so I was going to come from the start."

Ryder smiled at me and pulled me into a hug. "Thank you, thank you, thank you. I don't know what I'd do if you will never forgive me for doing such a cruel deed," he said sarcastically.

I rolled my eyes and smacked his neck again. "Ow!" he whined, pulling away. "Did you forget I'm the birthday boy?"

"No, I didn't, but don't make me remind you what I can do to you if you ever touch my food again," I told him.

He raised a brow at me. "Is that a threat?" he asked.

I smirked at him and shook my head. "No, that's a promise."

He dramatically gasped, and Lina rolled her eyes.

"That's enough you two," she cut in. "Tiana, Ryder and I will go talk to some people. We'll come back." She grabbed Ryder's arm before pulling him away.

I went to where all the drinks were and poured myself one. I chugged the alcohol down my throat and sighed. People were drinking their guts out, and I wanted to do the same today.

The alcohol barely affected me, so I decided to have some more. I was about to pour myself another glass when Mason's scent hit my nose. My breath got caught in my throat when his hand touched my waist, making sparks erupt at the contact. I felt him softly dig his nose into the crook of my neck and inhale my scent.

"You're beautiful," he whispered.

Shocked, I gently placed my drink on the table, my hands shaking. I turned around and faced him, my eyes taking in his appearance.

Damn him for being too sexy. It should be a crime.

I stared into his pitch-black eyes, as he was absorbing my look. I heard a soft growl erupt from his chest, making a shiver run down my spine. "Thank you," I whispered.

He stepped impossibly closer to me and tightened his grip on my waist. He inhaled my scent one more time before letting go. I let out a shaky breath at the loss of contact.

"You look good too," I told him as I looked him up and down.

A lazy smirk grew on his face which made my cheeks flush. "Hmm, really?" he questioned.

I slowly nodded. "Yeah."

"That's good," he muttered. If it weren't for my werewolf hearing, I wouldn't have heard it through the loud music.

I looked around, and thankfully, everyone was minding their own business, not noticing that their alpha was here. I looked back at him, and he took a step back. He then grabbed a stool and sat on it, looking around before his gaze fixed on me.

I hesitantly looked away and poured myself another drink, gulping it down. Lina soon walked up to me and smiled when she saw Mason.

"Ah, you actually came?" she asked.

Mason didn't say anything and only nodded. Lina looked at me and smirked. She grabbed my hand, and I raised a brow at her.

"Let's dance," she said.

I glanced at Mason, then back at Lina, who had a smile on her face. Seeing her excitement, I couldn't help but agree. "Okay," I muttered.

Lina turned to Mason. "Why don't you come?" she asked.

Mason shook his head and crossed his arms over his chest. "I don't dance," he said.

She smiled at him and shrugged. "Suit yourself." And with that, she pulled me to the dance floor.

My eyes widened when my favorite song started. Lina and I sang along and started dancing like there was no tomorrow.

Closer by Chainsmokers was blaring through the speakers, loud enough to make me sing with all my might without a single care that someone would hear my horrible voice. I soon grabbed another drink and gulped it down before giggling at Lina. She was singing along to the lyrics. Might I add, I was not the only one with a horrible voice.

After a while, I looked back at the place where Mason was to find him gone. I scanned the area, trying to find him. When my eyes laid on him, I couldn't stop the frown that took over my features. I was taken aback when I saw Mason leaning against a wall with Chloe standing in front of him.
My wolf growled at her and I slowly looked away, not in the mood to dance anymore. I glanced at them once again and saw Chloe touching Mason's arm. She was too close to him, but he didn't look like he cared. He was just looking around the crowded room with a drink in his hand. His eyes soon lit up once they rested on me. He then looked at Chloe, then back at me. I could've sworn I saw an amused glint in his eyes and a little smirk on his lips. I looked away only to see Lina observing us.

At first, she was pissed off, but it soon disappeared, replaced with a smirk. She leaned closer to me and whispered in my ear. "Are you jealous?"

My eyes widened at her statement. I frowned and shook my head. "No. Why would I be jealous?"

She scoffed at me. "I see the way you're looking at them." Lina nudged me. "It looks like it's working."

"What's working?"

"My brother is doing that on purpose. I can tell by the look on his face. He's either trying to make you jealous or wants to see your reaction," Lina explained.

I turned to his direction and made eye contact with Mason, who was staring intensely at me. I moved my gaze at Chloe, who was twirling a strand of her hair around her finger. Noticing that

Mason was not paying attention to her, she followed his stare and her eyes landed on me.

Chloe looked at me with pure anger and disgust, and I glared back at her. She then smirked and placed her hand on Mason's chest.

My wolf began telling me to walk over there, grab her by the hair, and pull her off our mate, so I intentionally blocked her out. But I was actually so close to doing that.

Deciding I had enough, I went to the bar area and chugged down a drink. Then I poured another one and drank it. Now, I really wanted to get drunk. I kept drinking and drinking until someone snatched the glass from my hand.

I looked up at Mason and frowned. "Hey! I was drinking that!" I pointed out.

He shook his head. "You've had enough drinks tonight."

"No, I barely drank!" I whined like a child, pouting at him.

Yeah, I can now feel the alcohol doing its thing.

"I saw you, Tiana," he said, sternly. "That's enough."

I frowned and shook my head. I was about to tell him to go back to his little girlfriend when I saw Adam walking in. I smirked at Mason and took a step back.

"Fine. You keep that. I'm going to see my friend." Before I walked away, I placed my hand on his chest and smirked. "Bye." I giggled softly as I saw him glare at Adam.

Once Adam saw me, I waved at him. "Hey!" I slurred and pulled him into a hug.

Adam grabbed me by the waist and raised a brow. "Are you drunk already?"

I giggled and shook my head. "No, I'm not drunk!" I stated.

He nodded. "Yeah, you're drunk."

I shook my head and pulled away as I heard Lina's voice through the speakers.

"Can I get everyone's attention, please?"

I looked around and saw her in the middle of the crowd with a smile on her face. I frowned when she barely got their attention, and so did she.

"I said, attention!" she screamed.

The music was turned off, and everyone stopped what they were doing and looked at her. "That's better." She coughed and smiled again.

"Now, as all of you guys know, today is my best friend's birthday. He means so much to me, that's why I wanted to make his birthday special!" she started, making everyone look at her in awe. "I got him the best present a man could ask for. Ryder, would you please come up here?"

Ryder walked to where she was with a huge smile on his face. She smirked at him and pulled a chair. "Sit," she ordered.

Ryder shrugged without a care and did as he was told.

"My present for you, Ryder, is about to come through that door right now," she said, pointing at it.

Everyone brought their attention to the big doors and waited for someone to open them. I watched carefully, wanting to know what kind of present would stand up and walk on its own. After a couple of seconds, a half-naked woman entered the room. Everyone's eyes widened, and Lina's smirk grew.

"You got me a stripper?" Ryder asked, amused.

"Yes, and she's going to give you a lap dance."

Everyone laughed while Ryder looked pleased. Of course, he would. It's Ryder we're talking about. The woman made her way to him and started dancing. From where I was, I could see him checking her out. The music started once again, and that's when everyone turned around and minded their own business.

Before Lina walked away, she said something into the microphone, which made me laugh. "She's all yours tonight."

I looked at Adam to see him watching me. I smiled at him and turned around to get another drink, even though Mason told me not to.

Mason was standing against a wall, staring at me with his arms crossed over his chest which, might I add, made him look intimidating. I gave him a sweet smile and looked away.

I grabbed another drink and drank it. I glanced back at Mason to see Chloe trying to talk to him, but he said something that made her frown and walk away with her fists clenched.

Ah, that's much better.

I gulped down another drink and was about to pour another one when it was snatched out of my hands for the second time tonight. I frowned and glared at Mason.

"Give me back my drink!" I whined and stomped my foot like a three-year-old.

Mason shook his head and wrapped his arm around my waist. "No. You're already drunk."

I pouted and shook my head at him. "I'm not drunk!"

He brought his lips to my ear. "Yes, Tiana. You are."

I shivered at the way he said my name and slowly nodded. "Okay, okay. I'm drunk. Now, can I have my drink back?" I asked, batting my eyelashes, trying to look innocent.

He let out a chuckle, making his chest rumble. "No means no."

I pouted and slapped his chest. "Why are you here? Why don't you go back to your little girlfriend!" I said, pissed.

He raised his brow at me. "Girlfriend?"

"Yeah, you looked pretty happy with her. Why don't you give me my drink and go back to her?"

Another chuckle escaped his lips, and he lowered himself to my ear once again. "Are you jealous, Tiana?"

I frowned and shook my head. "No, why would I be jealous? I'm not jealous. Nope, not one bit," I exclaimed.

My frown deepened as he took a step away from me.

"Okay, I'm going to my girlfriend then." He smirked.

My eyes widened at his words, and when he turned around, I immediately grabbed his arm.

"Wait!"

He looked at me and raised a brow, and I couldn't help the pout the crossed my features.

"Don't go to her. Stay with me," I whispered. "I don't like her around you."

His smirk fell, and he softly grabbed my hand, making my heartbeat speed up. I looked down at our joined hands and held my breath.

"I'm not going anywhere," he whispered.

I nodded and looked up at him, meeting his dark eyes.

"Good."

CHAPTER 40

I was walking towards Lina's room to invite her for lunch, when I saw Mason approaching me. I gulped when his eyes turned to a dark shade that screamed predator. I slowed down as we got closer to each other and let out a shaky breath as his eyes raked over my body.

"Tiana," he whispered.

I started playing with my fingers nervously. I didn't know what was wrong with me, but his presence made me feel different. He made me feel shy and nervous. *"Hey," I whispered back.*

"Where are you going?" he asked.

I took a step back, shaken up by our close proximity. *"I'm going to see Lina."*

His eyes darkened even more. He didn't look happy; he actually seemed upset. However, I didn't think it was because of my answer. He took a step closer and grabbed my hand softly.

"Why did you do that?" he asked.

I furrowed my brows at him and tilted my head in confusion. *"Why did I do what?"*

He moved even closer, making me step back unconsciously. *"That," he muttered. "You're backing away from me. Why? Do I make you nervous?"*

I let out another shaky breath and looked down, not knowing what to say. I knew the answer. Yes, he did, but what would he do if he knew?

"Tiana." *A shiver ran down my spine at the sound of him calling my name.*

Mother of chocolates, what is he doing to me? I thought to myself.

"Answer me," *he whispered.*

A little gasp escaped my mouth when he placed his head in the crook of my neck and then softly brushed his lips against my ear, causing overwhelming sparks to erupt in my body. I swear I felt a smirk emerge on his lips. I bit my lip to stop another gasp.

"Tiana," *he whispered again. He backed me up until I was against the wall, his arms trapping me with no room left to escape.*

I felt my wolf purr out with joy while I tried so hard to control my emotions.

"Do I make you nervous?" *he asked, this time licking my ear. I couldn't help my gasp any longer. He softly licked my ear again then kissed it.*

Holy mother of chocolates, what is he doing?

I bit my lip harder and nodded so he would stop asking.

A low chuckle emerged from his chest, but he didn't say anything. Instead, he kissed my neck. My eyes widened as he started nibbling on it, making my knees weak.

"Good," *he finally spoke after a while but his soft kisses never stopped. I felt like I would faint at any moment.*

He soon found my sweet spot, causing a moan to escape my lips without my consent. I was so shocked that I immediately wanted to dig a big hole and die. I felt him smirk against my skin again, and he continued kissing me at the same spot, guessing he knew it made my knees weak.

"Mason," I breathed out.

"One day, I'm going to mark you here." He licked it, making my eyes widen, and I gasped.

"Mark?"

He let out another deep chuckle, and my insides melted. "Yes, the werewolf term that makes you mine."

I gulped and gripped onto his shoulder so I wouldn't drop to the ground from the overwhelming sensation. "Yours?" I asked.

He nodded and pulled his face away from the crook of my neck, smiling down at me. "Yes, mine."

And with that, he crashed his lips onto mine.

* * *

A gasp escaped my lips as I jolted on my bed with beads of sweat stuck to me like second skin. I closed my eyes and placed my hand over my beating heart, trying to calm it down. Once I took a deep breath in, I opened my eyes and immediately facepalmed myself. I placed my head on my pillow and shrieked, like my life depended on it.

What in the world is happening to me? How could I dream of something like that? I shrieked into the pillow once again and hit my head against it. *Stupid, Tiana. Bad, Tiana. Perverted, Tiana. Shame on you, Tiana. How? Why?*

I rubbed my face and shook my head, trying to remove those nasty thoughts from my brain. This was bad. Why did I dream of something like that, and why was I disappointed that it wasn't real? I huffed out and sat up, looking around my room.

Darkness filled my surroundings. I looked at the clock and saw that it was barely past midnight. I sighed and got off my bed, walking to the bathroom. I washed my face and looked at myself in the mirror.

The memories of my dream flooded back, causing a blush to form on my cheeks. I ran a hand through my hair and sighed. Now I knew I wasn't sleeping any longer. I walked out of my bedroom to get a glass of water in the kitchen. Maybe then my thoughts would calm down.

I looked down the hall, wanting to know if I was the only one awake. A lot of pack members must be, but they were in their room, doing whatever they did.

I breathed deeply as I remembered the dream. Things were getting more complicated by the day. And thanks to Ryder's birthday, which was a couple days ago, I couldn't get Mason out of my head. I guessed it was all my fault for acting like a child. I was drunk and wasn't aware of my actions until it was too late.

I shook my head, getting rid of those thoughts and opened the kitchen door quietly. I peeked and sighed when I saw no one. I walked towards the fridge and grabbed a bottle of cold water, pouring myself some. As I was drinking, I saw a huge dark figure walking into the kitchen, making me spit all the water out and shriek in fear.

My thoughts went to Mason, but I immediately knew it wasn't him because his scent wasn't floating in the air and I didn't feel his presence. I soon picked up a familiar scent that I couldn't quite place.

Thankfully, Mr. Dark Guy turned on the lights, making my eyes widen after discovering who it was.

John, Crystal's mate, looked at me weirdly while I sighed in relief.

Good, it was just him. For a second, I thought it was the boogeyman.

"What are you doing here at a time like this?" he asked, opening the fridge.

I raised a brow at him. "So, the guy finally talks?" I teased.

He snapped his head at me and scowled. "Excuse me?" he said, looking fairly annoyed.

"Nothing. What are you doing here at a time like this?" I threw his question back with a sly smirk on my face. I was not sure why, but this guy annoyed me and he made me want to anger him.

I know, bad idea.

He raised a brow, not looking annoyed but amused. "So, the girl finally talks?" he teased.

A chuckle escaped my lips. "Okay, using my words against me now, are you?"

He pulled out a water bottle from the fridge and shrugged. "You started it," he muttered.

I rolled my eyes and nodded. "Yeah, you got a point."

"So, you're going to answer my question or what?" He placed his water bottle on the counter and crossed his arms over his chest.

I smirked at him. "Question?"

"You know, you annoy me," he stated, taking a step closer.

I mentally rolled my eyes at him. Like I never knew. "No shit," I muttered. "I annoy everyone."

A chuckle escaped his mouth. "I can tell." He turned away and grabbed the water bottle before taking a few steps away from me.

"You couldn't sleep either?" I asked.

He looked at me and shook his head. "No."

"Yeah, me neither." I sighed.

He raised a brow at me. "Is there a reason for that?"

I dropped my head down and felt a blush form on my cheeks. I looked back at him and slowly shook my head. "Uhm . . . no."

He narrowed his eyes, apparently not believing me. "You're lying," he exclaimed.

My eyes widened. "Okay. Yes, I am," I confessed.

"Mind telling me?"

Hell yes, I do! Of course, I'm not telling you Why would I? I thought to myself. But then I politely smiled and told him anyway. "I just had a dream."

His lips cracked into a smirk, and his eyes lit up in amusement. "Ahh, now I understand. You had a wet dream."

My eyes widened at his words, wide enough for my eyeballs to fall out of their sockets. I coughed and immediately shook my head.

What in the world was he saying? I didn't have a wet dream. I just had a tad bit inappropriate one, but not a wet dream. Straightforward much?

"What? No, I didn't," I yelled. "I just had a dream that made me wake up, and now I'm not able to fall back asleep."

By now, my cheeks were as red as tomatoes. He slowly nodded as his smirk grew. I groaned and took a step forward, wanting to walk away from him.

"Sure you did," he muttered under his breath.

I growled at him and narrowed my eyes. "I didn't."

He shrugged and I huffed, a scowl creeping onto my face.

"You're the annoying one," I muttered and started walking towards the kitchen door.

He stared at me like I was some kind of criminal. Ignoring him, I continued walking towards his spot since he was near the door.

I didn't notice there was water on the floor, and being the clumsy me, I slipped right in front of John. A shriek came out of my mouth when I landed in his arms, making his and my eyes widen in shock.

He took a step back and slipped too, causing both of us to fall to the ground. I groaned and my eyes instantly widened in shock after noticing that I was on top of a very annoyed John.

Who the hell spilled water on the floor?

I was about to get off him and apologize for my clumsy behavior when I heard someone yell from the kitchen doors, making our heads snap to that direction to see a very, very confused and angry Mason.

"What the hell are you two doing?" He stepped closer to us.

I looked down at John and immediately got off him. I looked at Mason and saw his eyes darken.

Shit.

CHAPTER 41

I gulped as I stared into Mason's eyes that were filled with fury. He looked mad, really mad. John got up from the floor, glaring at me before looking at his alpha.

"It's not what it looks like," I told him, stepping away from John.

"I know what I saw," Mason growled, walking up to me and grabbing me by the arm.

I winced at his tight grip but didn't say anything. He misunderstood, and I needed him to know that. He looked upset, like I had stabbed him in the back. But I didn't and I didn't think I ever would.

Besides, if we wanted to make out, it wouldn't be on the kitchen floor. Not like that would ever happen.

Mason snapped his head to John, looking like he was so close to punching him in the jaw and killing him on the spot. I grabbed onto his arm to prevent that from happening. John was glaring at me while I was saving his ass.

Who was I kidding? I was the one who fell on him.

"Mason," I whispered, trying to calm him down. "I slipped and he caught me. Then we both fell. That's it."

John cleared his throat and spoke, "Alpha, I have a mate. She's telling the truth. We just slipped and fell."

Mason calmed down a bit, but his eyes still held anger. He looked down at me, and I nodded. I don't know why, but I wanted him to believe me. I didn't want him to think that I'd do that with someone other than him.

Wait, what?

Mason glared at John as he wrapped his arm around my waist, making my eyes widen. "Then why are you both here?" he growled.

"It was a coincidence, Alpha. We were just grabbing something to drink. As I said, I have a mate and I would never cheat on her."

Mason let out a deep breath, tightening his grip on my waist and sending shivers down my body.

Good heavens.

"You can go now," he ordered John.

John nodded and immediately walked out of the kitchen.

Mason turned his attention to me. I glanced at where his arms were, then back at him. I let out a shaky breath and tried to pull away, but that only made him tighten his grip.

"Mason," I whispered.

He raised his brow and leaned closer. "Hmm?" he murmured as he dug his nose into my hair.

I gulped and placed my hand on his chest. "You're too close," I whispered.

"I know," he whispered back, inhaling my scent.

I let out a shaky breath and closed my eyes, trying to calm my wolf down. She was so close to tackling him to the floor and eating him all up.

Bad wolf.

I opened my eyes and tried stepping away, but he only growled and tightened his grip.

"Mason," I breathed out, "what are you doing?"

He didn't say anything and inhaled my scent once again. He placed his nose in the crook of my neck, making my eyes widened.

Goodness.

After a while, he finally spoke, "Just for a minute. Let us stay like this just for one minute."

I inhaled deeply and closed my eyes while he started running his finger along my arm. I immediately snapped my eyes open as I felt his lips touch my neck, causing sparks to erupt at the contact. My breath got caught in my throat when I felt him plant a soft kiss, making me shiver.

"Mason," I whispered.

"Hmm?" he murmured before kissing my neck again.

"What are you doing?" I asked, breathless. I gripped onto his shirt because at any moment now, my legs might give out and I would fall to the ground.

"I can't get you out of my head." He pulled away and looked me in the eyes. "What are you doing to me?"

I stared at him with wide eyes as he stared back at me with his dark ones. His wolf wanted control, and so did mine. I was left with no words. His lips turned into a smirk, and he placed his lips back on my neck, making me hold my breath.

"One day, I'm going to mark you here," he whispered against my skin.

A gasp made its way out my lips, making me push him away. I stared at him in shock as he looked down at me with a confused expression.

That dream, it is turning into a reality! Holy shit!

I backed away and ran a hand through my hair, looking down. I was so confused.

"Tiana?" he whispered, stepping closer to me.

I snapped my eyes at him, taking another step back. "I-I . . ." I breathed out. "I need to get back to bed."

And with that, I ran out of the kitchen, leaving a confused Mason behind.

*   *   *

I turned to my other side, trying to get some sleep. After a long time of attempting to catch at least an hour of rest, I finally gave up and shrieked into my pillow. After what happened in the kitchen, I couldn't sleep at all.

I didn't know why I ran away, but I was scared and confused. Breathing out, I rubbed my face and stared out the window. The sun that shone into my room made me groan and close my eyes. I didn't know how long I had been trying to sleep, but I guessed it had been hours since the sun was already up.

I groaned again once I heard someone knocking on my door.

Really? At a time like this?

"Tiana," Lina shouted, "open up!"

I scowled and dug my head deeper into the pillow.

Of course, it's Lina.

"Open up!" she screamed. "I know you're awake. If you don't open up, I'm breaking the door down."

"What do you want?" I yelled. "I'm trying to sleep. Leave me alone."

"You had enough sleep. It's time to get up. Besides, I have something to tell you!"

I opened an eye at what she said before closing it again. "What are you talking about? It's still early in the morning!" I yelled back.

"No, it's not. It's almost ten. Get up and open the door before I break it down," she demanded.

I snapped my eyes open. "Ten?" I muttered to myself and looked at the clock. Indeed, it was ten in the morning. But how? Was I awake for that long and didn't notice?

"Hello? You still alive in there?" Lina yelled.

I rolled my eyes and got off my warm, comfy bed.

Goodbye, bed.

I walked to my door so I could open it before she broke it down. I needed my door. I huffed in annoyance as I turned the lock and opened it, looking at a scowling Lina.

"What?" I growled.

Her eyes raked over my body. She then raised a brow at me. "What happened to you? You look like shit."

I rolled my eyes and backed away, jumping on my bed. I closed my eyes and hoped the Lord would have mercy on me and let me get an hour of sleep without an annoying, nagging Lina getting in the way of that.

"Rude." I heard Lina mutter. I remained silent as I welcomed my comfy bed.

"Wake up, wake up, sleepyhead. Sleepyhead, that's not your bed," Lina sang, making me groan. "I'm serious. Get up."

"What do you want?" I snapped, glaring at her

She raised her hands in a defensive manner and frowned. "Damn, girl. Chill. What crawled up your ass?"

"Lina," I growled and closed my eyes, not wanting to deal with her right now.

"Okay, okay. You have to get up so we can get ready," she answered.

"Ready? For what?" I asked.

"You don't know? Mason called for a pack meeting. He says it's important."

CHAPTER 42

"Pack meeting?" I asked. "What for?"

Lina shrugged and stood up from my bed. "I don't know. We're going to find out later. The pack meeting is starting in half an hour," she answered.

I sighed and nodded, getting up from my bed and walking to my closet. Many questions roamed in my head, wondering what the reason for this pack meeting was.

I took out a shirt and some jeans, then turned to Lina. "I'll be dressed in five minutes. Just wait for me outside," I spoke.

Lina nodded and walked out my room.

I walked into my bathroom and changed my clothes. Then I splashed some water on my face, trying to wake myself up from my sleepy state. I then brushed my hair and looked in the mirror. I sighed when my eyes landed on my neck.

Memories of what happened flooded my memory, making me close my eyes in an attempt to calm my wolf. Once my wolf had calmed down, I opened my eyes and rubbed my thumb over the spot he kissed and a shiver ran down my spine.

He said he would mark me one day. Did that mean he would accept this mate bond? My heart flipped at the thought of that.

One day.

I walked out of my room and caught sight of Lina standing by my door. She looked me up and down and then scowled.

"You look like shit," she said for the second time today.

"I know," I muttered.

Lina raised a brow at me as she looked at my appearance. "Why? Did something happen?" she asked, making me bite my lip.

Yes, something big happened.

I slowly shook my head. "No, nothing happened. I'm just not feeling well."

And that was half true. I honestly wasn't feeling too good. My head kept throbbing, which was unusual for me. My body felt weird. Maybe it was from the lack of sleep? I honestly didn't know, but I pushed that aside and brought my attention back to Lina.

Lina stopped and looked at me with concern written on her face. "You're not feeling well? Do you want to stay behind? You don't have to attend the pack meeting. I'll just tell you what it is about."

I shook my head and gave her a small smile. "As much as I like to return to bed, I'm okay. It'll pass," I assured her.

She nodded and smiled. "Then come on, let's go."

We walked towards the back where the pack meetings usually take place. As soon as we walked out, I saw everyone waiting for Mason to make his appearance. Some were standing quietly while some were talking.

I glanced at Lina to see her looking behind. My eyes followed her stare, and I soon stiffened when I saw Mason walking towards us. Everybody's eyes were on him as he walked to the front of the crowd.

Everyone was silent. Tension was present and thick in the air. Mason's eyes scanned the crowd. His eyes locked with mine, making me feel nervous on my spot. He cleared his throat, then continued to roam his stare through the large crowd. The beta and the third-in-command stood by his side.

After a minute, Mason finally spoke, "I apologize for bringing you all here on short notice. Now, as some of you know, we've been dealing with rogue problems, which are quite normal since every pack has to deal with something like that. I however noticed that it's a little more than normal, so I decided to take drastic measures for the safety of our pack. I and Alex, the Alpha of the Black Blood Pack, a pack that's not too far away from here, decided to be allies. Our pack and theirs will be stronger if we combine. These past few weeks, we negotiated and decided on this. Some of our pack warriors will move to their pack, and some of theirs will move here. We have to cooperate with them for the well-being of our pack. Any questions?"

Everyone remained silent as they processed his words. We knew that combining packs wasn't always good, especially since this pack didn't really get along much. This was for a good reason, though, and I was sure Mason wouldn't make a decision like this if it weren't important.

"How do we know if we can trust them?" a man spoke and a lot of people nodded.

"We have to if we want to work together. Remember, they're doing the same thing for their safety. We have no other choice," Mason explained.

Murmurs erupted in the air. Some people agreed, and some didn't.

"How long will this be?" another person asked.

"Until we are certain that we're completely safe. We still have a couple of days until some of them join us" Mason replied.

They nodded in agreement and stayed silent. No one else asked questions, and Mason nodded.

"Okay, you may all head back." He sighed.

Everyone started making their way back to the pack house. I glanced at Lina and she shrugged, not knowing what to say.

"Do you think this is a good idea?" I asked her.

"I don't know. Maybe," she muttered, shrugging.

I remained silent as I watched everyone leaving both of us, together with Mason, his beta, and his third-in-command in the area. Mason started walking towards us, keeping his eyes on me.

I gulped as he got closer, making me nervous.

"Mason," Lina said, "do you think this is a good idea?"

He looked at her seriously. "This is the only idea I have. I just hope it won't cause any problems," he muttered. Lina nodded and sighed.

Mason slowly looked at me and stepped closer. "Tiana, can I talk with you?"

My eyes widened. I glanced at Lina, then back at him. "Yeah, what is it?"

"Well, I'll be going," Lina spoke. "I'll see you later, Tiana." She turned around and walked away, leaving Mason and I alone. I looked at him and started playing with my fingers. He stared at me before speaking.

"Uh . . . About what happened—" he cleared his throat "—I apologize. I guess I kind of crossed the line."

My breath got caught in my throat at his words. Did this mean he regretted what he said?

He took another step closer. "But I meant what I said. One day, I'm going to mark you."

My eyes widened as I stared at him. I felt my cheeks heat up as he stared intensely at me. He meant what he said? I felt my heart swell at his words, comforting me.

"You are?" I asked.

His lips turned into a smirk, and he leaned closer to me, making a shiver run down my spine. "I promise."

I let a big breath out and looked down. I was speechless.

"Are you okay?" he asked. His smirk was gone, replaced with a frown.

I nodded. "Yes."

He shook his head. "You don't look good," he argued.

I shrugged and tucked a strand of hair behind my ear. "I'm fine. I just didn't sleep well," I told him.

Mason slowly nodded and sighed. "Okay, but if you get worse, make sure to see the pack doctor or else I'll throw you over my shoulders and take you there myself."

By the end of his sentence, a small smirk crawled onto his face. I felt my cheeks flush. "I need to go," I said in a small voice.

He muttered bye before I turned around and walked into the pack house. I placed my hand against the wall when my head started to spin. I groaned silently and shook it off.

Maybe a little sleep would help.

* * *

Lina and I headed to the field. We decided to sit on the benches and watch the warriors train. I came out so I could get some fresh air because I felt worse after I had slept. My face was hot, and my head was spinning. I figured maybe if I sat outside, I would feel a little better.

I didn't know what was wrong with me. I just thought maybe it was from all the stress and lack of sleep. Werewolves barely got sick, so this worried me a little. I sighed and felt Lina's stare on me.

"What?" I asked.

"You look horrible," she muttered.

I raised a brow at her. "Lina, I'm sure you already told me that three times today," I muttered.

She shook her head and scooted closer. "But I mean it. You look really tired. How about we take you to the pack doctor to see what's wrong?" she suggested.

"I'm fine, Lina," I assured her.

She sighed. "Fine, if that's what you want."

We observed the warriors as they trained. I caught sight of Mason talking with some pack members and glancing at us before looking away. I turned my attention to Adam once I saw him running towards us.

"Hey, Tiana," he greeted.

I smiled up at him. "Hey, how's training?"

He sat next to me and nodded. "It's going good," he answered and glanced at Lina.

"Well, hello to you too," Lina muttered, making Adam chuckle.

"Oh, sorry. I didn't see you there," he said.

Lina rolled her eyes and crossed her arms over her chest. "Yeah, that's because I'm a ghost and I'm going to haunt you for the rest of your life," she replied sarcastically.

Adam raised a brow and laughed. He soon brought his attention back to me. "So, I was wondering if you would like to have lunch with me. Since, you know, we haven't hung around in a long time."

I gave him a smile and nodded. I actually felt bad since I stopped hanging out with him. Adam's my best friend, and we used to hang around all the time, but now, we kind of stopped.

"Sure, I'd like that," I agreed.

He broke out into a smile before getting up. "Great," he said in a happy tone.

I got up and winced when the throbbing in my head grew.

Adam's smile dropped as he stared at me. "Are you okay, Tiana?" he asked, worried.

I placed my hand on my forehead and shrugged. "My head hurts so bad. I'm going inside to wash my face." I groaned and took a step back.

Lina stood up and looked at me with concern written all over her face. From the corner of my eyes, I saw Mason walking towards us. I took another step back, not wanting him to see me like this.

"Let me come with you," Lina spoke.

I shook my head and was about to tell her no when a strong wave of pain coursed through my body, making my legs give out, causing me to fall to the ground. Fortunately, Adam was quick enough to catch me and hold me in his arms.

I screamed when the pain attacked once more.

Lina gasped and placed her hands on my shoulders. "Tiana, oh my gosh! What's wrong?"

I closed my eyes as the throbbing in my head grew. I was so close to passing out.

"Tiana?" Adam asked, shaking my shoulders.

The contact between him and me only made the pain increase, making me scream again.

Lina pulled me out of his arms and into hers.

"Her scent, it's too strong," I heard Adam mutter.

"What's happening?" I heard Mason yell.

Another scream escaped my mouth as the pain came over me, making my body hot.

"I don't know," Lina said in a worried tone.

I was immediately snatched from Lina's arms and felt Mason held me tight, bringing me comfort. The pain disappeared for a split second before it came back.

"Tiana?" Mason spoke.

I whined as the pain shot all around my body.

"Tiana, please open your eyes."

"Where are you going?" I heard Lina yell.

"Where else?" Mason growled. "To the pack doctor."

My head was spinning, and my body was shaking in pain. I whined and wished for it all to go away.

Mason whispered comforting words into my ear, telling me everything would be alright. After a while, I was placed on a bed and heard a person enter the room.

"Alpha?" I recognized that voice. It belonged to Doctor Sam.

"What's wrong with her? She's in pain," Mason growled.

Doctor Sam placed his hand on my forehead, creating another wave of pain in my body.

"Oh my." He gasped. "She's going through heat."

CHAPTER 43

I snapped my eyes open once those words escaped his mouth.

My face felt hot, and my breathing rate increased. I slowly glanced at Mason to see him looking at me with wide eyes. He stepped closer and grabbed my hand, dulling the pain a bit.

"Heat?" He gulped.

I whined as a wave of pain overcame me once more, making me want to close my eyes and fall into the darkness, but I kept my eyes open so I could see what was going on.

"Yes, she needs to be marked. If her mate won't, her body will force her mate to do it or else she will have to go through this pain for a couple days until it completely goes away," Doctor Sam explained, stepping a few steps back. He placed his palm against his nose and closed his eyes for a second before opening them.

"Her scent is too strong. It will attract unmated males, so you have to keep her away from them. A touch of a male who is not her mate will only bring her pain. Only her mate's touch can soothe and comfort her."

Mason's eyes were wide as he stared at me, taking me in. I could feel the pain vanish for a split second before it reappeared. I let out a scream as the pain took over my body.

Doctor Sam took another step, and Mason snapped his eyes at him.

"Get out of here," he growled softly, not trying to be rude.

Doctor Sam nodded and immediately did as he ordered. Mason stepped closer and tightened his grip on me, making me whine. My vision blurred as tears gathered in my eyes. Mason then wiped the ones that fell to my cheeks and caressed me softly.

"Mason," I whined, "it hurts."

"Shhh," he whispered, "I know. I'm going to take the pain away."

And with that, he carried me bridal style, letting me snuggle deep into his arms. He walked out the medical room and towards his room. Thankfully, the pain decreased just a little bit.

I knew what heat was. Every female who had met their mate but wasn't marked after a couple of months would feel it. I always feared this but never really thought so much about it. It was just in the back of my mind.

Heat was when our body forced us to get marked, and being marked was the only time the pain would disappear. If it didn't happen, the pain would eventually go away after a couple of days, but it would come back after a few months.

I let out a shaky breath as Mason slowly opened his bedroom door and walked us inside. He softly placed me on his bed, and I snuggled deep into the sheets because of his scent. His scent was everywhere, making me happy and bringing me comfort.

I let out a whine as the pain came back. Immediately, Mason was next to me, holding me in his arms. I closed my eyes, liking the feeling of him around me. I was about to fall asleep when another wave of pain crashed into my body, making my body hot. I screamed.

Mason's arms tightened around me as he whispered comforting words into my ear. I let out another whine and tightened my grip on his arm.

"Shhh," he whispered before kissing my neck. "I'll take the pain away. I won't make you go through this anymore."

My eyes immediately snapped open as he continued to kiss my neck, earning a moan from my lips.

"You smell so good," he groaned before nibbling on my sweet spot.

I let out a shaky breath and gripped tighter on his arm. "Mason," I breathed out, "what are you doing?"

"I should be asking you that," he whispered. "What are you doing to me? I can't seem to get you out of my head. I think I'm going crazy." He then continued to leave sweet kisses on my neck.

I knew what he was about to do, and even though I wanted him to do it, another part of me didn't want it. This was like forcing him, and I didn't want to. I wanted him to do it on his own will, not because I was in pain.

"No," I whispered, shaking my head. "I mean, are you going to mark me?"

He let out a growl, making his chest rumble. "Yes, I'm going to mark you," he whispered into my ear huskily, making me shiver. His words made my eyes widen, and I immediately shook my head.

"D-don't," I said in a weak voice. His arms around me tightened, and he went stiff.

"Don't? What are you talking about?" he asked.

"Don't mark me," I whispered.

Immediately, he turned me around to look into my eyes. His eyes were full of worry.

"Why? Don't you want this pain to go away?" he asked.

I gripped his shirt. "I want to, but I don't want you marking me because my body is forcing you to. I want you to mark me when you truly want to," I answered as a tear fell out of my eyes.

He immediately wiped it away and caressed my cheek. "Your body isn't forcing—"

"It is." I stopped him. "Please. Marking is supposed to happen when we both are ready, and I don't want you marking me now."

I knew I was being stupid. It was like I was asking for this pain, but I didn't want him to mark me like this. I wanted him to mark me when we had fully discovered our feelings and confess them to one another.

I wanted us to be ready.

"But the pain won't go away for a couple of days," Mason argued.

I shook my head. "When you're with me, the pain goes away. Just stay close and don't leave," I whispered.

Mason's arms tightened around me, and he nodded before sighing. "If that's what you want, then I'm not going to force you," he whispered.

I gave him a smile but immediately dropped it when the pain came back. I tightened my hands around him and stiffened. He noticed and pulled his face closer to mine before kissing me.

I gasped as his lips moved against mine, making the pain go away. I wrapped my hands around his neck and pulled him impossibly closer. His arms tightened around my waist as he rubbed my exposed skin. I let out a shaky breath, and he placed a soft, lingering kiss on my lips. Once he pulled away, I opened my eyes, staring into his dark ones. He leaned in and kissed my forehead, making me sigh.

"I can't control myself when I'm around you," he whispered, making me shiver. I placed my cheek against his chest, hearing his fast heartbeat. "You make me go crazy."

That made a smile appear on my face.

He started playing with my hair, tugging on a few strands softly and massaging my back and neck. I let out a soft moan as I closed my eyes. He kissed my forehead again and whispered into my ear.

"Sleep. I'll watch over you."

I smiled as I felt the pain go away. Mason rubbed his fingers on my back, making me comfortable. He kissed my cheeks one more time before I welcomed the darkness.

* * *

I snapped my eyes open as I felt my body float on my own sweat. I looked around to see I was in Mason's room. I let out a heavy breath once I remembered everything. I clenched my fist as I felt the wave of pain wash over me once again. I looked around the room but stopped when I felt the arm wrapped around my waist tighten and pull me closer to a hard body.

My eyes widened as I realized Mason was behind me. I looked out the window to see it was dark, and I frowned.

How long was I asleep?

Mason pulled me closer to him, making the pain go away. I let out a sigh as his steady breaths fanned my neck. I smiled softly.

Who knew Mason had a side like this? So sweet. I just wanted to cuddle him, like a teddy bear.

I slowly turned around so I could face him. I just loved this side of him, a side where he showed me his true self without any care. I stared at his sleeping form. His face was so relaxed.

I was so grateful to him. He was taking care of me and didn't force himself to mark me. My eyes went down to his lips, and I had the urge to lean in and kiss them. I let out a shaky breath and did just that, kissing him softly on his lips. I then pulled away before he woke up and so I wouldn't attack him with more kisses. The pull was too strong.

I let my eyes roam down his body, and my eyes widened when I saw him shirtless. I bit my lip even harder.

Goodness, my hormones are acting up.

I had the urge to run my hand over his bare chest, but I stopped myself. This was not the time. I brought my eyes back to his face, then widened them in shock when I saw Mason smirk.

"Like what you see?" he whispered.

I gulped, feeling my cheeks heat up.

Yes, a lot.

I bit my lip as I stared into his eyes. His eyes pulled away from mine and looked down to my lips before looking back at me. His eyes darkened with lust, and he pulled me closer to his chest. I let out a shaky breath as his thumb traced my lips. He pulled himself up and hovered over me. I stared up at him, and he brought his head to the crook of my neck, inhaling my scent.

"You smell so good," he whispered, making me shiver. He placed a kiss on my neck, and I closed my eyes. He pulled away and gently kissed my lips.

"How are you feeling?" he asked.

I let out a breath and nodded softly. "I'm feeling a little better," I answered. The pain would go away and come back, but when I was in his arms, it would disappear.

"That's good," he whispered before kissing me again.

When he pulled away, I looked into his eyes. "How long have I been asleep?"

"About twelve hours." My eyes widened, and he caressed my cheek softly. "You were tired."

I cleared my throat. "Mason?" I whispered.

He raised a brow at me. "Hmm?" he asked.

"I'm thirsty and hungry," I told him.

He smiled at me and sat up. "I'll go make you something. Will you be okay alone?"

I smiled at him and nodded.

"Okay, I'll be quick."

He got up and tugged a shirt on. He then brought the sheets up to my neck and I smiled at that gesture. It felt like he was taking care of a kid. He looked down at me, and his eyes lit up.

"If you need me, scream," he whispered and kissed my lips one more time before walking out the room.

I closed my eyes shut as I felt the pain make its appearance. I gripped onto his sheets and inhaled his scent to try to calm myself down. Thankfully, that made the pain slow down. I let out a breath but whined when the pain hit me again. I breathed in and out, trying to tame myself.

My face grew hot, and my body started shaking in pain. My fist tightened against the sheets, and I let out another whine.

Breathe, Tiana.

I inhaled and opened my eyes once the door opened. Thankfully, Mason came walking in with a tray in his hands. When he saw the sight, he immediately placed the tray on his desk and came up to me.

"Mason," I whispered.

He pulled me to his body, and I let out a sigh as the pain slowly disappeared.

"I'm sorry I'm late," he whispered.

I buried my face deep into his chest as he rubbed my back. "It hurts when you're not with me," I told him.

His grip tightened. "I'm not going to leave you anytime soon," he whispered into my ear.

A smile crept onto my lips, and I looked up at him. "Promise?" I asked.

He smiled down at me and kissed my lips before pulling away. "I promise."

CHAPTER 44

I let out a scream as I felt the familiar wave of pain hit me, making my body feel hot. I snapped my eyes open to see that I was in Mason's bed. My vision blurred as salty tears formed in my eyes, then they fell to my cheek and my chin. I grabbed a fist of the sheet and gripped it tight.

As another wave of pain came, my powerful scream rang in the air. I scanned my surroundings, looking for Mason, but he wasn't here. It made me frown and more tears escaped my eyes.

"Mason!" I yelled. Without him, the pain intensified and lasted longer. *Where did he go? He said he wouldn't leave me.*

I tried to calm myself as I looked out the window. It was a bright morning outside, extremely opposite to how I was suffering inside. I snapped my head to my right as I heard the door fly open.

Mason came running with a worried expression plastered on his face. Another cry came out of my lips, and within a second, Mason was next to me, holding me in his arms.

"Mason," I cried, "it hurts! It hurts so much!"

He wrapped his arms around me even tighter, like he was afraid I would run away from him.

"Shhh, baby. It's okay. I'm here. I'll make the pain go away," he whispered into my ear.

A soft whimper escaped my lips, and he wiped my tears with his thumb. I started to hiccup from all the crying, so I dug my face deep into his chest and inhaled his scent. Slowly, the pain started fading away.

"Where did you go?" I asked, looking at him.

"I'm sorry," he whispered. "I went to the bathroom but immediately got out once I heard you screaming."

My eyes widened, and I felt guilt building up in me. "Mason..."

He tilted his head and caressed my cheek. "Yes, Tiana?"

"You don't have to... I mean, I don't want to force you to stay here with me," I said softly, looking at my hands.

He gently grabbed my chin and pulled it up, so I was looking into his beautiful eyes. I inhaled deeply as he brought his face close to mine.

"You're not forcing me," he whispered. "I'm here on my own will. I'm here because I don't want you to go through this pain alone. I'm here because I want to."

He placed a gentle kiss on my lips, making a shiver run down my spine. He pulled away and gave me a sly smile, pushing a strand of hair behind my ear. "Is the pain gone?" he asked.

I smiled at him, letting out a breath of relief. "Yes. Thank you."

His lips broke into a large smile, and he pulled me to his chest, making my heart flip. He softly rubbed my back, bringing me comfort. "Anything for you," he whispered so softly that I barely heard.

A goofy smile plastered on my lips as I listened to his steady heartbeat. After a moment of comfortable silence, I saw him gladly staring at me. "How's Lina?" I asked.

"She's worried about you. She kept asking if she could see you," he replied.

"I would like to see her. I bet she freaked out yesterday," I murmured.

He nodded and tightened his grip on my waist. "She did. She's been attacking me through the mindlink," he said. "It's already hurting my head. I had to block her a couple of times. I'll let her come see you after you're fully rested."

I raised a brow at him. "Mason, all I've been doing is rest."

He shook his head and laid me on the bed. "Well, rest some more," he ordered.

I pouted, and he immediately kissed my pouting lips, making me giggle. He pulled away and stared down at me with a soft smile.

"Sleep," he whispered in a soft voice. He grabbed my hand and started rubbing small circles on my skin, making the stinging pain slowly subside. I snuggled my cheeks deeper into the fluffy pillow as I felt my heavy eyelids shut, pulling me into a deep sleep.

* * *

I slowly opened my eyes as I felt my body grow hot and my desire strong. I gulped and tightened my fist to try to tame myself. The dim room was silent, but my fast breathing started to fill it.

I whined when I didn't see Mason. I closed my eyes to try to even my breaths but whimpered as I felt my body grow hotter, making me all the more sweaty. I opened my eyes and hoped Mason would be here before a pool of pain engulfed me.

A breath of relief escaped my lips as Mason's door opened. I was taken aback when he walked in with nothing but a towel around his waist, making my eyes darkened with lust. He stared at me and walked closer. I looked him in the eye, stopping my shameless self from checking him out.

Damn him for being too sexy.

I gulped, and I could've sworn I saw a smirk crawl up his lips.

"How are you feeling?" he asked.

I bit my lip as he leaned closer. "I . . . I feel hot."

He opened his closet and pulled out a shirt. He took the sheets off me and sat on the bed, clearing his throat. "Change into this. You're wearing too much clothes," he said. His eyes immediately widened, probably realizing what he just said. "I mean, since you're hot."

I let out a shaky breath and nodded. I sat up but immediately winced when I felt the pain hit me. I lay back down and whined. "It hurts," I whispered.

He grabbed my hand and rubbed his thumb against my skin, soothing me. "I guess I have no other choice then," he muttered before pulling me close to him. My eyes widened as he grabbed my shirt and started pulling it up.

"W-what are you doing?" I asked, flabbergasted.

He stared at me, and a smirk crawled onto his lips. He leaned against my ear and whispered, "I'm changing you into my shirt."

A gasp escaped my lips as he placed a soft kiss on my neck before pulling away. I couldn't help myself in checking him out and wishing the towel would disappear.

Damn you, hormones.

His fingers touched my bare skin as he slowly pulled my shirt up, leaving me exposed. I felt my cheeks heat up as his eyes darkened with lust, but he didn't say anything. Then he helped me out of my pants.

Dear heavens, what is happening?

I gasped as his hands gripped my waist and his eyes roamed over my body without shame. He then looked at me and leaned in, pressing his lips on mine.

He pulled away, but instead of putting his shirt on me, he started to kiss my neck and make me moan. I tightened my grip on the sheets as he continued.

"Mason," I breathed out.

"You're driving me crazy. Your scent is calling out to me. I don't think I'll be able to hold back," he muttered in his deep, sexy voice. The desire in me grew to the point that I wanted it without a single thought.

"Then don't," I whispered, feeling myself go hot.

He looked at me with dark eyes that were full of desire and lust. He leaned and placed a gentle kiss on my lips.

"You sure?" he whispered.

I nodded, and within a second, his towel was on the floor and I was completely naked underneath him.

*   *   *

Gasping, I jolted out of bed. Immediately, Mason snapped his eyes open from their sleepy state and sat up, holding me in his arms. My eyes widened as I remembered the dream, making my face grow hot.

Oh my gosh! How could I dream of something like that? I clearly have gone insane because of this heat thing. I need to calm my hormones down!

"Tiana?" Mason spoke. "Are you okay? Are you in pain?"

I looked at him and immediately shook my head. "No, I'm not. I just had a . . . a bad dream," I whispered, trying to think of an excuse. Mason calmed down and nodded.

"Were you asleep?" I asked.

He ran a hand through his hair. "Yeah. I was holding you as you slept and accidentally fell asleep too."

I felt my heart swell at the thought. "I'm sorry, I woke you up."

He shook his head and laid me on his bed, rubbing his thumbs against my skin. "No, it's okay."

He opened his mouth to say something else, but he went completely stiff and his eyes stared ahead. I frowned but knew he was talking with someone through the mind link. After a while, he brought his attention back to me, but his lips were curved into a frown.

"What's wrong?"

He let out a sigh. "I have to deal with something. It's urgent," he muttered. "Will you be alright if I leave for a while? I'll try to come back as fast as I can."

"It's okay. I'll try to hold the pain," I whispered.

He gave my hand a tight squeeze before running out the room. I let out a shaky breath as I missed his presence. His scent that engulfed the room made the situation slightly better. I gripped the sheets tight as I felt a sting of pain emerge.

I inhaled and exhaled deeply, trying to calm myself down, praying Mason would come back as soon as possible. I winced when another wave of pain hit me, breaking me into sweat. I whined and stirred as my head throbbed. I wondered when this pain would disappear for good so I could function normally again and get out of this room.

When the wave of pain reached its peak, I held back the cry that threatened to escape my mouth and bit my lip.

After a while, the door opened, and I was happy that Mason truly came fast. I was about to call out to him when my breath got caught in my throat.

"Adam?" I whispered, shocked. "What are you doing here?"

Adam ran to me, his eyes full of concern. "Tiana," he exclaimed. "I was so worried about you. No one would let me check up on you."

I pulled my hand away when he grabbed it. "You shouldn't have come here." I winced as the pain grew stronger. Him being in the room wasn't helping me at all.

"I just wanted to see you," he whispered. My scent soon hit his nose and he immediately went stiff, a low growl escaping his mouth.

"Adam," I warned, "please leave."

His eyes turned dark, scaring me. He took a step closer, which made me frown. "You smell so good," he muttered.

My eyes widened at his words. This was not good. His wolf was taking over, and my scent wasn't helping.

"Adam . . . please," I begged.

Adam was immediately on top of me, kissing my lips. I screamed in shock and pain, begging him to get off me.

"Adam, you're hurting me!" I cried.

Adam didn't stop. He continued kissing my lips and down to my neck, making the pain grow even more. I knew he wasn't the one in control; it was his wolf. All I could ever do was beg for him to knock some sense into his wolf.

"Adam!" I screamed and tears fell out of my eyes as the pain became unbearable due to his touch.

He pulled away from my neck and leaned in, about to kiss me again, when he was snatched away and slammed into the wall.

With my blurry vision, I tried to decipher the scene in front of me. Then I held the scream that threatened to escape my lips when I saw a very angry Mason—and he looked like he was about to kill.

CHAPTER 45

Mason furiously grabbed Adam by his collar and slammed him against the wall. Mason punched Adam's jaw, making him wince in pain. I tried sitting up so I could stop Mason before he ended up killing Adam but winced when the pain only grew.

Mason threw another punch to his jaw. His eyes were pitch-black, indicating his wolf was on the verge of taking control. Adam's eyes were full of guilt and fear as he stood there.

Mason growled and punched him once again, making him fall to the floor. Adam grunted but didn't try to fight back as Mason hauled him back on his feet.

"Fucking bastard!" he yelled and slammed him hard against the wall. "If you fucking touch a strand of her hair, I will fucking kill you."

I winced as I heard Mason's booming voice and cringed when I saw him raise his fist and slammed it against Adam's cheek. I opened my mouth to say something but was left speechless. The pain was eating me up, leaving me mute. I forced myself up and took a step closer to Mason.

What Adam did was wrong, but he wasn't in control. He's my best friend, and I didn't want him dead.

"Mason," I whispered. Mason didn't stop as he threw Adam to the floor and kicked him. My eyes widened and my vision blurred once again. "Mason! Please stop!"

Mason didn't budge as he continued assaulting Adam.

Adam's eyes were wide open as he stared at me with guilt. He didn't fight back and asked him to stop, he just lay there and begged me with his eyes to forgive him. A couple of tears fell out of my eyes seeing him like that.

"Mason! Stop before you kill him!" I yelled.

Immediately, Mason went stiff and turned around, facing me with pitch-black eyes that were burning with fury. His jaw was clenched, and so did his fist.

I pulled him into a hug, hoping it would calm him down. He immediately wrapped his arms tightly around my waist. He growled and placed his head in the crook of my neck, inhaling my scent. His breath became steady. After a while, he pulled away, staring at me with dark eyes.

"It's okay," I whispered.

He gulped and shook his head before stepping out of my arms. He turned to Adam and glared at him. Adam lay bloody on the floor, and I felt the urge to go to him to make sure he was okay but stayed in my place to not anger Mason.

"He touched you and brought you pain. He deserves more than this," he bellowed.

After a second, two guards frantically came running into the room.

"Take him to the dungeons," he ordered, making my eyes widen. They immediately pulled him to his feet and out of the room.

A couple of tears fell out of my eyes. I was about to say something when pain hit me, causing me to fall off my feet. Mason immediately caught me before I hit the ground. I winced and closed my eyes as I felt my body grow hotter.

"Tiana?" Mason whispered. "Are you okay?"

I let out a shaky breath. "I-I'm fine." I gulped.

Mason gently placed me on his bed and brought his hand to my face, wiping the tears on my cheeks. I closed my eyes as he caressed me softly, pulling me out of my stressed state.

After a moment of complete silence, I stared at his dark orbs. His eyes were two of the things that I liked about him. They pulled me into another world and made me feel like I was the only one in there. I let out a breath and cleared my throat.

"Mason," I whispered softly, "please don't hurt him."

His soft eyes immediately turned rough, and a growl emerged within his chest. "Tiana, he hurt you," he muttered. "He needs to be punished."

I gripped his hand tight. "He already got his punishment. You almost killed him a while ago. Please, Mason. He's my best friend," I begged him, hoping he wouldn't think of killing him. No matter what Adam did, I wouldn't want him dead. He was my first friend and the only friend I had for years.

"He fucking attacked you! What kind of friend is that?" he yelled as he stood up. His chest moved up and down as his breathing rate increased. "I should have finished him off."

My eyes widened, and I immediately sat up. I grabbed his hand as my vision blurred and tears threatened to escape.

"His wolf was in control. My scent took him off guard! He would never do that to me," I told him, gripping his hand even tighter. A few tears fell to my cheeks, and I tried to ignore the pain that threatened to emerge.

"That's no fucking excuse! Your scent is killing me over here, but I'm not jumping on you. He just found the right time to take advantage of you!" he yelled. His eyes darkened severely, making me shiver.

I shook my head and closed my eyes, trying to keep more tears from falling. "No," I whispered. "Adam wouldn't do that."

"He already did!" he growled, making me break out in sobs.

I didn't want to believe it. Adam's like a brother to me, and I didn't want to believe that he would try to hurt me.

Immediately, Mason wrapped his strong arms around my body, pulling me to his hard chest.

I buried my face into his shirt as I cried. He ran his fingers through my hair and whispered soothing words into my ear.

"Please don't cry. I'm sorry. I didn't mean to shout. I was just angry."

I shook my head and wiped the tears from my cheeks. I took a deep breath in, then looked up at him. "No, it's okay. I understand," I whispered. "I'm just sad that he did something like that to me."

Mason didn't say a word. He just tightened his hold on me and continued to rub his hand against my back. Soon, he pulled away and looked at me with slightly angry eyes.

"Where did he touch you?" he asked.

My eyes widened at his question, and I swallowed the lump that was in my throat. "W-what?" I muttered, surprised.

"Where did he touch you? That fucker, where did he lay his hands on you?" He looked at me with determination in his eyes.

Taken aback, my mouth hung open. "Why do you want to know?" I asked.

He furrowed his brows and leaned his head close to mine. "Tiana," he warned.

I bit my lip and sighed. "He kissed me on the lips and neck. That's it." I looked down at my hands.

Mason gripped my chin and made me look at his eyes. He growled lowly and sighed. He then planted a soft, lingering kiss on my lips—a kiss that made my head spin and heart flip, a kiss that left me wanting more. I softly gripped his shirt as he nibbled on my lower lip.

"No one gets to touch these lips other than me," he whispered huskily, making me shiver. His arms around my waist tightened, holding me in his strong arms.

I placed my hand on his chest and sighed into his lips. What he said next made me choke on my own breath.

"They're mine. You're mine." His lips did wonders on my sweet spot, making me feel like I was swimming in a pull of warm sensations. I closed my eyes and enjoyed it, biting my lip so my moans wouldn't escape.

"I'm the only one who can kiss you like this," he whispered against my skin.

My heart flipped, and this time I couldn't keep myself from moaning.

Mason immediately pulled away, making me snap my eyes open. He looked at me with a sly smirk, and I felt my cheeks flush.

"I better stop. If I continue, I won't be able to control myself." He took a step back and opened a drawer, pulling out a napkin and grabbing the glass of water on his desk. "Here. Drink this." He placed a pill in my hand.

I raised a brow as I looked at him. "What's this for?"

"Sam told me to give you that. It will lessen the pain and make you fall asleep," he explained.

After taking it, I felt my eyelids become heavy. All I had been doing was sleep, but I guessed that was better than having to go through the pain. I yawned when Mason lay down next to me.

"Mason, don't you have lots of things to deal with?" I asked softly.

He wrapped an arm around my waist and pulled me against his chest. "I do, but they're not important now," he whispered in my ear.

I yawned again and nodded. I was too sleepy to ask anything else. All I wanted to do was sleep and not wake up. I closed my eyes and felt Mason kiss the top of my head before I fell into the darkness.

* * *

I slowly opened my eyes when I heard people bickering. The noise stopped for a split second when I moved my head slightly.

"Dammit, Lina! Get out before you wake her up," I heard Mason hiss.

"Mason, I've been wanting to see her for a long time now!" Lina argued loudly, making him shush her.

"Be quiet," he growled. "And you'll see her once she wakes up. She needs her rest."

"She's been sleeping all day. I want to see my best friend," Lina whined.

I opened my eyes to see that it was already dark outside and wondered how long I had slept.

"She's either sleeping or in pain. Which sounds better to you?" Mason asked her in a voice laced with annoyance and frustration.

"Okay, fine. I'll come back when she's awake, but I see that you're taking the opportunity to be close to her," Lina told him with a smirk on her face. Knowing her, it wasn't a surprise that she took the chance to annoy Mason.

"What are you talking about?" he growled.

"I'm talking about how you're glued by the hip to her. You're not even leaving her side. I walked in here, and you guys were cuddling," she explained.

I remained still so I could listen more to their conversation. I just had the urge to know what Mason would say.

"Lina," Mason warned. "She's in pain, and the only person who can take that away is me."

"I know, I know . . . but you like cuddling with her, don't you?" she said the last part with a giggle.

Mason stepped closer to her, causing Lina's shriek to echo in the air. "Shhh, you're going to wake her up," he muttered.

"Okay, okay. I'll go. I get it. You're mad that I got in between your cuddling—"

"Lina!" he cut her off, causing Lina to let out another giggle.

I turned to my other side, looking at them. Mason's eyes widened, then he turned to Lina and glared at her.

"Dammit, you woke her up," he accused.

Lina raised her hands up defensively, her eyes happy. She then pulled me into a crushing bear hug. "Oh my God! I'm so happy to see you're okay! You got me so worried back there," she squealed, pulling away from me. I smiled at her but winced slightly when the wave of pain stung me.

"Sorry," I smiled sheepishly. "I didn't expect for this to happen."

"Don't worry. Just a couple more days, and it will end," she assured me, rubbing my shoulders. She then looked at Mason and smirked. "But if someone does certain stuff, then you won't be in this state anymore."

My eyes widened at her words, and so did Mason's. Lina grinned from ear to ear as she watched our reactions.

"Are you saying it's my fault?" I asked her, slightly amused.

She looked at me and immediately shook her head. "No, Tiana. I'm saying it's Mason's fault. If he weren't a pussy all this time, you wouldn't be like this."

Mason walked closer to us and glared at his sister. "Lina," he warned, "watch what you say."

Lina looked at him and smiled, shrugging. "Hey, I'm only stating the fact."

Mason growled, making a laugh escape her mouth.

"How are you feeling?" she asked.

"A little better," I whispered gratefully. I had been dying for this pain to end. Thankfully, the pain became just a stinging sensation. It was only because Mason was around, though. If he wasn't, it would be too painful to bear.

Lina rubbed my back. "That's good. I guess we have Mason to thank for."

Mason didn't even try to argue. He just rolled his eyes and crossed his arms over his chest.

"Yeah, we do," I whispered, looking at him.

Mason gave me a small smile but immediately wiped it off when Lina looked at him.

"Well, I'm glad you're okay. I'll come back to check up on you. I have to go now." Lina kissed my cheek before pulling me into a hug. "I would say take care, but I know Mason's doing that job perfectly."

I remained silent. She was right, he was.

Before Lina walked out of the room, she turned around with a smirk plastered on her face.

"Bye! You can continue cuddling now!"

CHAPTER 46

It had taken me a long time to convince Mason to leave me and see what Nick wanted. Apparently, Nick called to say he needed him for something that had to do with the Black Blood Pack, but Mason refused to leave my side. I repeatedly told him I was feeling much better, and after ten minutes, he finally gave up.

I took this time to take a shower and changed into the clothes that Lina had brought from my room. I looked at myself in the mirror, happy I didn't look bad and the heat finally went away because I was so fed up with it that I begged the Lord to have mercy on me and end it.

Actually, saying I was happy was an understatement. I was also really thankful for Mason. He was so kind to me these past few days and now I was all better because of him. I didn't know what would have happened to me if he wasn't there.

I smiled to myself as I thought of his kind gestures. He wasn't the same Mason he showed to others. I felt like it was a version of himself that only appeared in front of me, and that sort of made me happy.

My smile immediately dropped and I let out a shaky breath as my thoughts went to the day Adam had attacked me. What happened hadn't left my mind. I felt incredibly disappointed and worried about him. From what I knew, he had been locked in the dungeon for days now. I tried talking to Mason about him, but he would immediately end it, telling me not to even try.

Even though what he did was wrong, I couldn't help feeling guilty. It wasn't his fault, really. Any guy in his situation would have done the same because of my scent. It was a natural instinct.

He's my best friend, and I wouldn't wish pain upon him, ever. I let out a deep sigh, then turned my head to the door when I heard it open. Mason came walking into the room and frowned once he saw me all dressed.

"What are you doing?" he asked.

I looked at him and shrugged. "What does it look like I'm doing?"

"You should be resting," he told me.

I raised a brow. "Mason," I whispered, "I'm perfectly fine. Look, I'm all better."

His eyes turned serious and roamed my body, inspecting for any signs of pain. He then cleared his throat and brought his eyes back to mine. "You sure?"

I smiled at him and nodded. "Yes, I'm sure."

Mason took a step closer to me and dipped his head in the crook of my neck, inhaling my scent, surprising me. He then pulled away and smirked. "Okay. Your scent is back to normal, so that's good," he muttered. "Come on, let's go."

I raised a brow and looked at him curiously. "Go where?"

"To Sam. He told me that once you feel better, you should visit him so he could give you some pills," he answered.

We walked down the hall and towards the medical room. I smiled at the sight of our pack members, as if I had been locked up in Mason's room for decades. It had been torture, minus the Mason-caring-for-me part. Once we were in front of the medical room, Mason knocked on the door before opening it. We walked in to see Doctor Sam sitting on a chair. He got up and smiled once he saw us.

"Alpha," he greeted with a nod. He then turned to me and offered me a soft smile. "Hello, Tiana. How are you feeling?"

I smiled at him before answering, "I'm feeling better. Thanks for asking."

"That's good." He grabbed a box of pills out of a shelf and handed it to me. "Here, take this. It will help delay the next heat. Well, that's if you don't plan on getting marked."

Mason and I both stiffened at his words. I slowly nodded and gave him a grateful smile.

"Thanks, but do you know how long it will be till it hits me again?" I asked.

"About two to three weeks."

I sighed. That wasn't a long time, and I didn't want to go through that pain again. It's either I would get marked or I would go through that pain again.

I looked at Mason to see him staring intensely at me. He grabbed my hand and squeezed it, giving me comfort. I smiled at him before turning my attention to Sam.

"Thank you," I told him. He smiled at me and nodded.

"Anytime. If you need anything, don't hesitate to ask."

"Okay, I will."

We were walking down the hall when I noticed Mason was still holding me. I stared at our joined hands and bit my lip. When he stopped in his tracks, I stared into his dark orbs, letting them pull me into a world that only us existed.

"Tiana," he whispered, "I'm not letting you go through that again."

I furrowed my brows in confusion and tilted my head. "Huh?"

He cleared his throat before stepping closer to me. "I'm not going to let you go through that pain again. I'm going to mark you before it hits." He leaned his head close to mine.

His words made my eyes widen in shock. My breath got stuck in my throat as I stared at him. I let out a deep breath. "W-what?" I asked, surprised.

His lips curved and his eyes lit up. "You heard me. I'm going to mark you," he told me like he was just talking about the weather.

How could he say that so calmly while my mind was going haywire? My wolf purred in happiness while I tried to comprehend his words. *Holy hell.*

"Do you know what you're saying?" I asked.

He nodded, looking into my eyes. "Yes. I'm making you mine."

* * *

I paced back and forth, playing with my fingers. Sighing nervously, I ran a hand through my hair and bit my lip.

It had been a couple of days since I was completely healed and since I last saw Mason, because he had to deal with other packs and have meetings. During those days, I had planned on how to bring up Adam.

I was so worried about him, and I needed to know what was going to happen.

Mason came back today, and at the moment, I was trying to build up the confidence to talk to him.

"Deep breaths, Tiana. In and out. You can do this," I whispered to myself.

I was nervous that Mason would get mad at me, but I shook my head and pushed the negativity aside.

I went to Mason's room, and as soon as I was in front of his door, I closed my eyes and sighed before knocking on it.

"Who is it?" Mason asked.

I bit my lip as I heard his voice. It's been a long time since I heard it. His voice soothed me. "It's me, Tiana," I answered.

"Come in."

As soon as I heard that, I twisted the doorknob and opened the door. My eyes widened and the air I breathed in got stuck in my throat at the sight in front of me. Mason stood there in all his glory, staring at me with only a towel covering him.

Holy mother of chocolates!

"Ugh . . . I-I can come back later," I frantically said as I tried to keep my eyes on his face, not wanting to check out his body shamelessly.

"No, it's okay. I was just getting dressed." He smirked as he grabbed some clothes from his closet.

I gulped and nodded, closing the door behind me. "I wanted to talk to you about something," I whispered.

He raised a brow and nodded. "Let me get dressed first," he spoke.

I immediately nodded back and remained quiet as he entered the bathroom. I let out a shaky breath and closed my eyes. I was too nervous, and seeing him like that didn't help at all. Neither was my wolf. She wanted me to jump him at that instant.

I breathed deeply once the bathroom door opened. A now dressed-up Mason walked out and stood in front of me. He raised a brow and stepped closer.

"What is it that you wanted to talk to me about?" he asked.

I bit my lip as I looked at him and let a sigh escape my mouth. "Adam. I want to talk about him."

As soon as those words left my mouth, a growl emerged from his chest, making me step back. His eyes took on a darker shade. He slowly stepped closer to me, making me hit my back against the wall.

"What about that fucker?" he sneered.

I started playing with my fingers as his intimidating stare made me nervous. "Mason," I whispered, "I want to see him."

He shook his head fiercely. "No, I won't allow you to see him," he growled intensely, making me breathe in a big ball of air.

"Please, Mason. I need to see him. He's my best friend," I begged.

"Tiana, I can't! I won't allow you to see him," he yelled, his eyes darkening even more.

I cringed at his loud voice and looked down at my hands, trying to prevent my tears from building up. "Please. He's like a brother to me," I whispered as a tear escaped my eye.

Closing his eyes, Mason took a deep breath and squeezed the bridge of his nose. He soon looked at me and sighed. "Fine, but only for five minutes."

I smiled and nodded, wiping the tears from my cheek. "Thank you," I whispered.

"Let's go," he muttered.

Minutes later, we were standing in front of big doors that were guarded by two men. They nodded once they saw Mason and then gave me curious glances.

Mason walked in without saying a word and I silently followed him, scrunching my nose in disgust as the horrible stench hit my nostrils. It was the smell of blood and death, something that made my hair stand on end. I scanned the dark place and gulped when he stood in front of a cell, looking back at me. He opened it and entered.

I followed him and gasped when I saw the sight in front of me. There in the cell was a bloody and beat up Adam tied to the wall. His head snapped up and his eyes widened when they saw me. My eyes watered.

"Tiana," he whispered.

"Adam," I breathed out as I stepped forward. Immediately, Mason gripped my arm, preventing me from getting any closer. I snapped my eyes to Mason, and he gave me a warning look. I sighed and stopped before looking up at Adam.

"How are you? Are you better?" Adam asked.

I nodded and smiled softly. "Yes, I am."

Guilt glistened in his eyes. "Tiana, I'm so sorry," he whispered. "I didn't mean to do that. My wolf was in control. Trust me, I would never do that to you."

I felt my tears welled in my eyes. I stepped closer to him even though Mason warned me not to. "I know," I whispered. "It's okay. I forgive you."

I heard Mason growl, making me glance at him. He took a step forward, but I begged him with my eyes not to say anything.

"Thank goodness," he muttered. "I was afraid I had lost you."

A tear escaped my eyes, and I took another step forward, wanting to pull him into a hug. Adam had been there for me through thick and thin. He was the only person who had experienced the pain with me when I was going through the hardest moments of my life, and I didn't want to lose him. No one could ever replace him in my heart.

Before I got close, I was stopped by Mason. I looked at him and grabbed him by his shirt, giving him a pleading look.

"Mason, please. Let him go," I begged with tears streaming down my cheeks. "I forgive him. Just please release him."

Mason shook his head in anger. "No, I won't."

"Please! What are you even planning to do with him?" I yelled.

Mason growled, and his voice echoed through the dungeon walls. He closed his eyes and sighed in frustration. He then looked at me and averted his stare to Adam. Adam watched him in silence as he walked up to him.

"You have two choices to choose from," he spoke.

Adam gulped and nodded. He glanced at me before looking up at his alpha.

"You can either leave my pack and become a rogue," he said, making our eyes widen in shock, "or you can go to the Black Blood Pack and be one of their pack warriors that will stay there."

CHAPTER 47

"What?" I yelled as I walked up to Mason.

Mason snapped his head to me and gave me a warning look, telling me not to interfere.

I frowned and gripped his arm. "You can't do that, Mason!"

He shook his head and glared at me. "I can and I will."

I bit my lip as I felt my vision blurring. I forced myself to remain looking at him as I felt my heart break.

No. This can't be happening. Adam can't leave me. He can't.

Mason gave me another warning look before glaring back at Adam, who was looking at us with wide eyes.

"No," I whispered. My heart broke at the thought of Adam and I separating. We had never been away from each other. We had been glued by the hip ever since we were small. "Please, Mason, don't."

Mason growled and grabbed my arm tightly, but not enough to hurt me. "Tiana, the only other choice he has is death. I'm giving him the easy way out," he told me, making more tears fall out of my eyes.

"Okay," Adam spoke, catching our attention, and I stared at him in shock. "I'll do it. I'll serve this pack."

Mason nodded and walked close to him. I did the same, staring at those two in disbelief.

"How? He's not even ready! He's still in training. That could bring him trouble!" I yelled, worried.

Mason shook his head, a deep growl emerging from within his chest. "Nick claims he is one of the best, so he is more than ready," he argued.

"He's right, Tiana. I'll be just fine. Don't worry about me," Adam whispered.

"I don't want you to leave," I whispered, choking on my own breath as I sobbed.

Adam gave me a sad smile, and right then and there, I rushed to him and wrapped my arms around him. Thankfully, Mason didn't try to stop me.

Since Adam's hands were tied, he wasn't able to hug me back. He just placed his chin on the top of my head as I cried into his chest. I knew if it were another person, they wouldn't forgive him. I bet if someone else knew about my situation, they would think I was delusional. But he meant so much to me, and if they only knew what we had been through together, they would understand.

"It's okay, Tiana," Adam whispered, his eyes welling up with tears. "I won't be gone forever. I'll be back as soon as possible."

I nodded and wiped the tears on my cheeks. Mason grabbed me by the arm, keeping me away from Adam. I shot him a glare and pulled myself out of his grip.

"Take him down," Mason told the guards. They nodded and immediately untied Adam from the chains. Adam fell to the ground and winced. I immediately ran up to him.

"Are you in pain?" I asked.

He stood up and shook his head. "No, I'm fine." He smiled at me, giving me comfort.

"Do you have to leave?" I asked, even though I knew the answer.

"Yes, I have to. Don't worry, Tiana. You're not alone. You have Lina," he spoke as he looked at my sad face. He then cleared his throat before glancing at an annoyed Mason. "And him. You have your mate," he whispered, looking at me with a sad smile.

I glanced at Mason and breathed in deeply as I saw him staring at the both of us. I immediately looked away and nodded at him. "I hope you find your mate soon," I whispered.

He didn't say anything and just nodded. Soon, Mason walked towards us and I looked at him, sighing.

"When will he be leaving?" I asked.

Mason looked at Adam before glancing down at me. "He'll be leaving with the other warriors, on the day the Black Blood Pack warriors arrive," he answered.

I crossed my arms over my chest and raised a brow. "And when is that?"

Mason cleared his throat before replying, "Tomorrow morning. We'll be holding a ceremony for the pack warriors."

I felt my heart drop. I only had the rest of the day to spend with Adam and then he would be gone. Adam nodded and gave me a sad smile. I let out a sigh and nodded in defeat.

"Come on, let's go," Mason spoke, holding my hand.

I looked at him, then at Adam. I let out a sigh of frustration and shook my head, pulling my hand away from his grasp. "I'd like to stay with Adam today," I told him.

Mason frowned and narrowed his eyes on Adam before nodding. "Okay," he muttered before walking out of the cell.

Adam and I followed Mason towards the pack house. Mason glanced at us and turned around, walking away. Adam then took a shower and I cleaned his wounds afterwards, which caused him to wince in pain every once in a while.

"You hungry?" I asked.

He looked at me and grinned. "Yes, a lot," he answered.

"Then come on. Let's go."

We walked into the kitchen and found it empty. Adam sat on a chair, and I went to check the fridge.

"I'm going to make macaroni and cheese," I said as I grabbed the ingredients.

Adam chuckled, and I looked back at him, raising a brow.

"Because that's the only thing you know how to cook?" Adam asked.

I frowned at him and crossed my arms over my chest.

"What? No. I know how to cook," I said stubbornly.

"Oh, really? Like what?"

I bit my lip, trying to think of something. I then smiled and looked at Adam. "Cereal. I know how to make cereal."

As soon as those words left my mouth, Adam broke out in laughter, making me smile.

"Okay, you're right. I don't know how to cook," I admitted.

"Took you long enough to admit that," he muttered, staring at me in amusement.

I rolled my eyes and started with the macaroni and cheese. After a while, Adam and I sat in front of each other, eating. Out of nowhere, Adam placed his spoon on the table and stared at me.

I raised a brow at him. "What?"

He looked down at his plate, narrowing his eyes angrily at it. I frowned and placed my spoon on the table. He soon raised his head, looking at me with guilt. I frowned and cleared my throat.

"Adam, what's wrong?" I asked.

"Tiana," he whispered, "I-I don't think I can ever forgive myself."

I sighed and shook my head. "Adam, I already told you, I forgive you. Yes, what you did was wrong, but your wolf was in control. Besides, I won't let that get in the way of our years of friendship."

He sighed and ran a hand through his hair. "I know, but I can't seem to forgive myself. I was afraid you'd hate me."

I grabbed his hand and shook my head. "Adam, I'd never hate you. No matter what you do."

He looked at me, and he was on the verge of tears. "Really?" he asked.

I squeezed his hand tightly. "Really. You have been my rock all these years, and I don't want to lose you."

He let out a sigh of relief and smiled at me. "I don't want to lose you either."

CHAPTER 48

"Adam!" I shrieked as he threw a pillow to my face, making me glare at him. "Stop it. That's annoying."

His lips broke out into a huge grin as he grabbed another pillow from his side and threw it at me for the fifth time.

I ducked in time for it to miss me. I smirked at him and stuck my tongue out playfully.

"Ha! You missed—Ah!" I yelped as another one struck my face out of nowhere. I swiped my hair off my face and glared at him. He looked at me in amusement and broke into laughter.

I growled and stood on the bed, holding the pillow he threw at me. "You think this is fun?" I yelled as I hit him. He continued to laugh hysterically at my attempt to hurt him, his face turning red.

"Huh? Why are you laughing? Is this funny to you?" I hit him repeatedly with the pillow that did him no harm, while he tried to stop me.

His laughter died down, and he tried to catch his breath. He looked at me happily while I glared at him, hitting him one more time. He chuckled and shook his head, snatching the pillow from my grasp.

"So did this sleepover turn into a pillow fight?" Adam asked, raising a brow at me. I frowned and smacked his head, making him yelp.

We were in Adam's room at the moment. I had decided to sleep here tonight because I wanted to be with him before he left. I would truly miss him. I couldn't seem to get over the sadness of him leaving. Adam and I had always been together, and tomorrow would be the first time that we wouldn't see each other for a long time. It broke my heart, and I couldn't help feeling that I had taken him for granted at times. You truly didn't know someone's values until they left.

"Ow!" he gasped, rubbing the spot where I hit him. He pouted, making me roll my eyes. That wouldn't work on me. "What was that for?"

"For being stupid," I told him. "You're the one that started it."

His pout disappeared and was immediately replaced with a grin. "Okay, true, but I'm not stupid."

I raised my brow and sat in front of him. "Oh, really? Says the guy who thought Florida was in Europe."

He chuckled and raised his hand up defensively. "Hey! You know I'm not good at geography."

I nodded in agreement. "You're right. You're not good at anything," I teased him, laughing lightly.

He gasped dramatically and placed his hand over his heart. "Ouch, Tiana! Is that how you talk to your best friend who's leaving tomorrow?"

My smile immediately dropped, making me groan. "Please don't remind me," I whispered and sighed.

His teasing pout vanished and was replaced with a frown. He scooted next to me and wrapped his arm around my shoulder, placing my head on his.

"I'm going to miss you," I said.

He let out a shaky breath and nodded. "I'm going to miss you more."

I closed my eyes, blocking the tears from escaping, then looked at Adam. "Have you ever wondered what life we could have had if we stayed in our old pack and that attack never happened?" I asked.

"Yes, I do. We would be with our families right now," he whispered, a sad expression crossing his face. "I wonder where they are."

"I wonder that too, but I know they're safe. I feel it."

"I feel it too," Adam whispered.

"If that attack never happened, you wouldn't be leaving tomorrow," I muttered sadly.

He shook his head and gave me a soft smile. "If that attack never happened, then you wouldn't ever find happiness," he argued.

I removed my head from his shoulder and looked at him. "Happiness?" I whispered.

He nodded and stared forward, not looking into my eyes. "You've found your mate, someone who will make you happy," he spoke softly, "someone who will fill those empty holes in your heart." He moved his head close to me and smiled softly, making my eyes water. "You've found someone who will make you forget about your past. Tiana, I don't think I've ever seen you this happy in the last two years. I think he's healing you."

I bit my lip as a lone tear ran down my cheeks and off my chin. I let out a shaky breath as I stared at him.

"I haven't seen you that happy ever since that day . . . ," Adam whispered.

I shook my head and placed my hand on his arm, trying to push those memories away. "Please, Adam, don't remind me. Those memories haunt me to this day. I still can't get over the guilt and sadness," I whispered and rubbed my face with my hands.

Adam immediately shook his head and grabbed my hands, looking at me with a sad expression. "Tiana, how many times do I have to tell you that what happened to me wasn't your fault? You had nothing to do with it," he told me. I bit my lip again and nodded.

"I know, but it somehow was. That bastard—"

"Shhh, it's okay. What happened that day had nothing to do with you," he repeated. "It was all a misunderstanding, and in the end, you were hurt by it."

I nodded and felt my heart break at those memories. "Let not talk about this. When I remember everything, it breaks me."

Adam nodded and wrapped his arm around my shoulder again. "Sorry," he whispered. I shook my head at him.

"It's okay. Let's just focus on this sleepover for now," I said, trying to grin. He looked at me with a small smile on his lips.

"So, where were we?" he asked as he grabbed a pillow, making my eyes widen. I scooted away from him, giving him a warning look.

"Don't even dare—"

I was cut off as the fluffy pillow hit my face. I growled at him and snatched it away from his grasp. Then I repeatedly hit his face, making him erupt in laughter. I smiled, all while thinking that he was one of the best people I had ever met—and how we weren't getting any sleep tonight if we continued this pillow fight.

* * *

I groaned when I felt someone tickle me with a feather, making me scrunch my nose. I heard a deep chuckle, making me growl lowly and turn to my other side. The chuckling stopped, and I sighed and cuddled deeper into the warm pillow.

Soon, I scrunched my nose again as I felt the feather.

"Adam, I swear, do that again and I'll slap you so hard you'll have my hand imprinted on your cheeks for the rest of the day," I muttered, trying to fall back asleep. Adam chuckled again and stopped what he was doing. I sighed in relief and tried going back to sleep.

"Wake up, Tiana," Adam whispered, poking my cheek. "We have to get ready."

I groaned in annoyance and opened one eye, looking at him smiling. "Ready?" I asked.

His smile turned into a sad one. "Yes, the ceremony will start in an hour."

I frowned, remembering today's event. "Oh," I whispered.

I looked around, seeing feathers around the room from the pillow fights we had yesterday.

I know, we are a bunch of girls.

I looked at Adam and gave him a soft smile. "Let me go get ready, then I'll come back." Before I walked out of his bedroom, I turned around and looked at his appearance, smiling at him. "You get ready too. You look like shit." He laughed and nodded.

While I was doing my hair, I remembered the conversation I had with Adam yesterday. I closed my eyes and inhaled deeply.

"Stop thinking about it, Tiana," I whispered to myself, *"it's all in the past."*

I shook my head and pushed those memories aside. After a while, I went back to Adam's room. As soon as I got closer, I couldn't help the feeling that overcame me. My heart dropped as I thought that soon Adam would leave.

I let out a sad sigh.

We could do nothing about it. Maybe it was for the best.

I stopped when I saw Adam leave his room, all dressed up. He caught my stare and smiled. He walked up to me and hung his arm around my shoulder.

"You ready?" he asked.

I looked at him sadly and shook my head. "No, I'm not," I whispered.

His smile dropped, and he immediately pulled me into a hug. "It's okay, Tiana. You just have to close your eyes and open them, and I'll be back here with you."

I smiled at him, nodding. "Come on, let's go."

While we were walking, Lina came into sight. She smiled at us and hugged Adam.

"Even though you're annoying, I'll still miss you," she teased him.

He rolled his eyes and smiled. "Wow, thanks. I think that's the nicest thing you ever said to me," he said, making us laugh.

Lina glanced at me and pulled me into a hug, then we began walking to where the ceremony would be held.

"So, how many new members are coming here?" I asked Lina.

She shrugged. "I'm not sure, but I know they're a lot."

I didn't know if "a lot" was a good or a bad thing. Maybe, I guess. With more members comes more power, but at the same time, we were giving them some of ours too.

There were many people standing in the field. I stopped when I saw Mason, Nick, and the third-in-command head to the front of the pack. I gulped and glanced at Adam to see him staring at me sadly. Letting out a shaky breath, I looked back at Mason and saw him looking at me.

I was somehow hoping Mason would change his mind and let Adam stay, but somewhere in me, I knew he wouldn't do that. I knew he wouldn't give Adam another choice.

"Thank you all for being here," Mason spoke loudly, looking at the large crowd. "Today, we are welcoming some new pack members and saying goodbye to the ones who will leave. Our guests will soon arrive, but for now, I want the pack warriors who are leaving to come up here."

Frowning, I looked at Adam and hugged him. He wrapped his arms around me and tightened them. This was it. He was leaving. I sighed as we pulled away. He looked at me with a frown.

"I'll miss you, princess," he whispered, making my eyes water.

"I'll miss you too, idiot." I smiled as a tear slipped out of my eyes. "Don't be gone for long."

He nodded and wiped the tear away. "I won't. I'll come visit you once in a while."

I smiled at that and pulled him in for another hug before he walked away. Standing next to all the pack warriors, Adam smiled at me, telling me everything was going to be okay.

CHAPTER 49

I let out a defeated sigh, holding back the tears that threatened to escape as Adam disappeared from my sight, along with the other pack warriors. I felt something in me break, but I told myself to be strong. It wasn't like he would be gone forever. However, something in me feared that bad things would happen to him. I was scared that, in some way, I would lose my best friend.

I shook my head and forced these pathetic thoughts out of my head. I knew Adam. He's a strong man, and he could overcome anything. I slowly brought my attention to Mason and bit my lip hard as I stared into his eyes. His face was emotionless, but his eyes spoke something else.

They had a hint of sadness and guilt, like he knew sending Adam away hurt me.

I looked to the ground. I wasn't certain if I was angry at him. I thought about it and sighed. I would have been angry if Adam didn't want to leave and Mason forced him, but Adam did no such thing. He accepted and went without a second thought. Somewhere in me, I knew he wanted to go. He had always wanted to be a pack warrior and fight for a pack. He had always wanted to be a hero ever since he was small.

And because of that, I guessed I wasn't really mad at Mason. I knew Mason was just angry at Adam's actions and didn't want him anywhere near me. Besides, they were never really fond of each other. In some way, he wanted to protect me from him, even though Adam wouldn't ever do that again. I guessed I should be grateful that Mason didn't try to harm him or worse kill him. It's just that I was slightly disappointed, disappointed because he didn't consider my feelings.

I let out a sigh and glanced at Mason again, who wasn't looking at me anymore. His fist was clenched, and he looked angry as he shot daggers at the ground. He then raised his head and made eye contact with me. I could've sworn I saw something in his eyes, telling me he was sorry. I closed my eyes and let out a shaky breath.

Once I opened them, Mason spoke again. "Our guests have arrived. I would like to welcome our new pack members who will serve this pack until everything is back to normal. Will all of you please come up here?"

In an instant, many werewolves came into sight. They walked towards the crowd with confidence, holding their heads up in the air. They were mostly male, but I saw a couple of females too. They looked normal even though some were buff and tall.

As soon as they were in front of the large crowd, Mason spoke, "Welcome to our pack. From now on, we will consider you all as members of our pack, and we thank you for coming here to serve us. I hope there won't be any trouble as I hope my warriors I have sent off won't make any trouble. Both our packs would like to stay on good terms, so I hope we get along for the benefit of both packs."

All of us, including the new pack warriors, nodded. Mason then stepped forwards.

"Good, now someone will show you around and to your rooms. We will start with the procedures tomorrow morning, like patrolling and other important things. Your alpha and I will be in constant contact to strengthen our packs and see if we need to do anything else," he spoke and everyone nodded. "Okay. You are all excused."

And with that, everyone headed back to the pack house. There were lots of whispers about the new members. I glanced at them and noticed they weren't that much. Lots of people were talking about the new pack members and if they were going to get along or not. I glanced at them one more time and saw Mason talking to them. They nodded respectively, and I sighed.

I didn't know if this was going to be bad or not, but Mason knew what he's doing. Besides, we couldn't judge them without knowing them first. We were all doing this for the safety of both packs.

I turned around and looked at Lina. She gave me a sad smile and placed her hand on my shoulder.

"I'm sorry for what Mason did, but please don't be mad at him. You guys barely started getting along. I don't want my ship to sink," she begged, saying the last part with a pout.

I smiled at her and shook my head. "I'm not mad," I whispered. "I'm just . . . upset. I just need some time to get over it."

"Okay, that's a relief. I mean, I don't need you guys to start hating each other after you guys just started opening up." She smiled at me.

I nodded but remained silent.

She patted my shoulder and moved her head to the side. "Come on, let's go."

I nodded once again, and we started walking. I looked over my shoulders and glanced at Mason to see him staring at me. I gave him a soft smile before looking away and walking towards the pack house.

* * *

I poured myself a glass of water and drank it. Once I was done, I placed the cup on the counter and started making my way out of the kitchen doors. I ignored the people who were exiting and entering.

Even though I had been in this pack for about three months, people still stared at me, especially after those rumors about Mason and me. Those rumors had calmed down and I didn't hear about them again, but that didn't stop the stares and glances.

As I was walking to my room, I saw someone I hadn't seen in a while. I groaned and prayed he would ignore and walk past me, but of course my prayers were not heard.

"Hey, long time no see," Kyle greeted with a smirk on his face.

I rolled my eyes and completely ignored him, but he grabbed my wrist tightly. I snapped my head at him and narrowed my eyes.

"You know it's rude to walk away when someone's talking to you, right?" he said.

I growled at him and pulled my hand away from his tight grip. "Fuck off, Kyle. I don't want to deal with you right now."

His lips twitched and he stepped closer to me, making me take a step back.

"That's not very nice. I just wanted to ask you a simple question, that's all." His face seemed innocent, but I knew behind that was a wicked smirk.

"I don't want to answer any questions of yours, so leave me alone," I hissed and started walking away. Unfortunately, Kyle stepped in front of me, stopping me dead in my tracks.

"All these time, I have been wondering why the alpha stands up for you and be your little hero, but I guess I know why," Kyle started with a smirk on his face. He stepped closer to me. "All those rumors were true, weren't they? You're sleeping with the alpha. Is it because of the luna status?"

My eyes widened, and a low growl emerged from within my chest. I glared at him and clenched my fist, wanting so bad to punch him. This was getting out of hand. I had to do something about it, but before I could raise my fist and collide it with his chin, he was already on the floor.

Kyle winced in pain. He gripped his chin and stared up with wide eyes.

Mason looked furious as he stepped closer to Kyle, so I gripped his arm, preventing him from killing the guy. Mason looked at me, and the anger in his eyes faded a bit. Then he glared back at Kyle.

"Fucker. I told you not to get near her. You defied my orders. Do you really want to spend another two weeks in the dungeons?" Mason growled angrily.

Kyle stood on his feet with fear in his eyes. He shook his head immediately, and before I could stop him, Mason punched him in the jaw. Kyle fell back to the floor, and I winced at the sight.

"She's my mate. She doesn't need to sleep with me to get the luna title because it's already hers," Mason growled.

Did he just say . . .

I felt my heart flip at his words and couldn't help the happiness that overcame me.

Kyle's eyes were so wide, I thought his eyeballs would pop out of their sockets. He hesitantly got off the floor and stared at me in shock. I looked at Mason and saw him burning with anger. His chest rapidly rose and fell as he controlled his breathing.

"You're our luna?" Kyle asked, shocked.

I bit my lip and didn't know what to say. Immediately, Mason wrapped his arm around my waist and pulled me close to him.

"Yes, she is, and if I see you around her another time, I'll make sure to do more damage than I already did," Mason threatened with a growl.

Kyle nodded, looking at me with guilt. He turned around and rushed out of our sight before Mason could do anything else.

I slowly looked at Mason, biting my lip even harder. What he told Kyle made me feel weird. When I first came here, I didn't want to be a luna, but him acknowledging the fact that I was his mate and luna made me happy.

He looked at me and the anger in his eyes completely vanished. He gripped my waist tight and pulled me to his chest, hugging me. He inhaled my scent and let out a deep breath. When he finally calmed down, he pulled away.

"Are you okay?" he asked.

I nodded at him. "I'm fine."

He ran a hand through his hair and let out a frustrated sigh. "You're mad, aren't you?" he asked out of nowhere, looking at me with guilt and anger. "You're angry because I sent your friend away, right? I know you're mad, so stop acting like you're not," he growled and pulled his hair. I opened my mouth to say something, but I was cut off by his blabbering. "Dammit, Tiana! Just say you're mad at me!"

I let out a sigh and shook my head. "Mason, I'm not mad. I'm just—"

"Just what?" he asked.

"Upset," I whispered, looking down at my hand.

He gently grabbed my chin and slowly pulled it up so I was looking at his beautiful eyes. "I'm sorry," he whispered. "I just . . . My jealousy took over and . . . I-I, urgh, dammit!"

I was taken aback. He ran a hand through his hair as he averted his eyes away from mine.

"Sorry," he whispered again.

I bit my lip and nodded. "I'm going to miss him, but in some way, he wanted this, so I'm going to respect his decision." Mason nodded as I continued. "And I'm not mad at you. Just a little upset, but I'll get over it."

Mason closed his eyes, and he dug his nose into the crook of my neck and inhaled my scent. "I don't want you to hate me," he whispered in a voice so soft.

My heart flipped at his words, and I pulled away, looking at him. "Mason, I could never hate you," I told him.

His eyes lit up, and his arms around my waist tightened.

"Good," he said and placed a soft kiss on my lips.

CHAPTER 50

I pulled at my hair in frustration as I paced the room back and forth. I let out a sigh and rubbed my face with my hands. I tried to organize my thoughts, wondering what I would do. I sat on my bed and shut my wolf out because she wasn't any help. She kept telling me to stop thinking and just run out of here and jump on Mason.

Dammit, Tiana! Get your thoughts straight!

Hours after that scene with Kyle, I was still an emotional wreck. My feelings were flying in different directions, making me confused and frustrated. I kept thinking about Mason, to the point where I felt like my head was going to explode.

I wanted to know what we truly were, and I wanted the answer so bad! That question kept roaming my head. Judging by the way he was acting around me, I felt like he was slowly accepting me. And I didn't have to think twice to say I was accepting him.

Heck, I had feelings for him and I was not going to deny it. I didn't know when it started, but they grew over time. Every day, I wanted to see him more than the last, and I was hoping he felt the same way. I mean, he was acting sweet towards me, and I was sure he had some kind of feelings for me, but I couldn't stop the doubts from taking me over.

We were mates, and I felt like we couldn't hide these feelings any longer. Hell, when I first came here, I didn't want one and I was happy that he felt the same, but it was quite different now. We had gotten closer over the months, so at the moment, I needed to know what was going to happen to us. He did say he would mark me. He also mentioned I was his luna, so that got to mean something.

A goofy smile appeared on my face at those thoughts. I was quite afraid of being a luna, but I wouldn't have been destined to be with him if I couldn't handle the part, right? I sighed and stood up, forcing myself to walk out the room.

I hesitantly walked towards Mason's office. I was so nervous to the point where I wanted to abort the mission, but I mentally fought with myself and continued.

It's now or never, Tiana.

I let out a frustrated sigh and ran a hand through my hair to try to calm my nerves down. I couldn't remember the last time I was all worked up about something. I was about to grab the doorknob when I smelled a scent other than Mason's.

I sniffed the air, trying to figure out who it belonged to. It was familiar, and I was certain I smelled it before. I didn't know if it was coming from Mason's office or if it was just from someone who merely passed by. I shook my head and opened the door.

I couldn't help the gasp that escaped my lips. My eyes widened and I felt my tears threaten to escape at the sight in front of me.

Chloe and Mason kissing.

Mason heard my gasp, and he immediately pushed Chloe away and stood up, staring at me with wide eyes.

I stared at them with pure shock and sadness as I tried to comprehend what I just saw. Mason and Chloe were kissing. They were kissing. *I thought he felt something for me?* I felt my vision blur as I stared at a smirking Chloe and a shocked Mason.

"Tiana," he said, "it's not what it looks like!" He pushed Chloe away and ran to me.

I felt my head pound and my heart break. How could he kiss her? I knew we were never official, but I thought he had feelings for me.

I stared at him and took a step back, shaking my head. I closed my eyes to prevent the tears from escaping, but a lone tear fell out of my eyes. I immediately turned around and ran away.

Mason shouted at me to stop and listen to him, but I ignored him and continued running. I heard Chloe calling after Mason, so I guess Mason was chasing after me.

I ran into my room and slammed the door shut, locking it so Mason couldn't enter. I leaned my back against the wall and slowly sat on the floor, letting the tears fall out. I didn't want to be weak, but that sight broke me. I didn't like it. Mason told me he had nothing to do with Chloe, but I guessed he was lying all along. Why would he say those nice things to me if he didn't want me?

I placed my head in my hands, feeling the salty tears fall from my eyes. I let out a whimper but sucked in a breath when someone tried to open my bedroom door. I heard Mason growl as he started pounding against it.

"Please, Tiana, open the door. It's not what you think it is," he begged, banging his fist at my door.

I shook my head even though he couldn't see me. I let out another whimper and placed my head against the wall.

"Leave, Mason," I yelled. "I don't want to deal with you right now."

"Please, baby. I didn't kiss her. She jumped on me, and before I could push her away, you opened the door," he explained.

I scoffed. *Right, like that's what happened.*

"Leave," I yelled. "Go away, Mason!"

"No! I'm not going away until you open the door and listen to me," he said. "Please."

I felt my heart fall at his pleading voice. I wanted to open the door and listen to him, but my stubborn side told me not to. I saw what I saw, and I couldn't erase that image from my head.

I couldn't believe I was about to express my feelings for him.

"Leave," I whispered so softly that I wasn't sure he heard.

The banging on my door stopped. I cried into my hands as I heard him walk away. Soon, his footsteps disappeared, and I felt more salty tears fall off my chin. I felt empty and lost. I never wanted to feel something like this ever again. I was so afraid, but now I felt like I lost something. My whimpers and cries filled my silent room. I looked up from my hands and stared blankly at my dark room.

I didn't know how long I had stayed like that. It felt like hours as I stayed in the same position and let my tears fall as I stared at nothing. I was taken off guard when I heard a knock on my door, making me snap my head towards it. The first thing that crossed my mind was Mason, but the scent that filled my nose told me otherwise. I let out a shaky breath as Lina spoke from behind my door.

"Tiana? What's wrong? I saw Mason, and he was an emotional wreck. What happened?" she asked. "Open the door, Tiana."

I whimpered and shook my head. "Go away, Lina. I want to be alone," I told her, trying to hide the pain in my voice.

"What? Why? Open the door, so we can talk!" she spoke eagerly. "What happened?"

"Lina, I'm not in the mood to talk. Just leave," I said softly.

Her voice disappeared into thin air, and everything went silent. I sighed and thought she took the hint and left, but my eyes widened in shock when something slammed against my door, making a loud sound erupt in the air.

"I will open this door whether you like it or not," Lina yelled as she slammed her body against my door once again.

My eyes widened even more, and I stood on my feet and stared at my door, shocked. *Is she really doing this?* She slammed her body once again, making me gasp. *This girl is crazy.*

I immediately opened the door, not wanting her to break it. Lina stood outside breathing hard. Her eyes widened when she laid eyes on me, shocked at my appearance.

I bet my eyes were red and puffy. I must have looked horrible.

"Tiana? Oh my gosh!" She gasped and entered my room, pulling me in for a hug. She wrapped her arms around me, and so did I. A couple of tears fell out my eyes as she rubbed her hand on my back. "Come here." She pulled me into my room after turning on the lights and I winced.

Lina sat in front of me and grabbed my hand, giving it a tight, comforting squeeze. "What happened? You and Mason both look horrible."

I frowned and ran my hand over my face. Lina looked at me with concern in her eyes. I let out a shaky breath and bit my lip. I sighed and explained everything.

"What?" she shrieked. "He was kissing Chloe?"

I nodded and felt my heart drop at the memory.

"I'm going to show that bitch," she cursed loudly, getting off my bed and stalking angrily towards my door.

My eyes widened and I stood up, grabbing her hand tightly and pulling her back. "No, Lina," I whispered.

She looked at me like I was crazy and shook her head.

"I-I don't want to deal with any of them."

"Did Mason say anything? Did he try to explain?" she asked urgently.

I sighed and nodded. "Yes. He tried to explain, but I didn't listen to him," I said softly. "He did say that she kissed him and he didn't have time to pull away."

Lina's eyes widened, and she looked at me like I was crazy. "And why the hell didn't you listen to him? It's clear that she forced the kiss! Mason hates her guts, so I know he would never kiss her out of his own will!" she explained, giving me a pointed look.

I frowned and shook my head, not knowing what to say. I guessed I was afraid. I wasn't sure if I should listen to him or not, and I still didn't know until now. Something in me told me to believe her words and run off to Mason so I could give him a chance to talk, but another part of me stopped me from doing so and told me that Mason felt nothing towards me. And that broke my heart.

"I don't know, Lina," I whispered softly. "I don't know what to feel. I don't want to face him."

Lina sighed in frustration and ran a hand through her hair. "Dammit, Tiana," she muttered. "Do you like him?" she asked me with a straight face.

My eyes widened at her question, and my mouth hung open. "Why are you asking that?"

"Because I want to hear your answer even though I know it. You guys are mates, for goodness sake. You guys should have mated and had babies from the first moment you saw each other!" she answered, clearly frustrated.

I bit my lip and nodded, giving in. "Yes, I like him," I whispered.

Her eyes widened, and she broke out into a huge grin. "Finally! Someone said it," she yelled. "Now, you will go to Mason and talk things out, okay?"

I immediately shook my head at her. "No, I don't want to see him."

"Tiana, you're driving me crazy!" she yelled, getting off my bed and throwing her hands in the air.

I stared at her and shook my head. "I can't seem to get that image out of my head, Lina. I can't see him." I then looked down at my hands, and she let out a frustrated sigh. I looked at her, and she shook her head at me.

"Both of you are the most stubborn people I have ever met in my life," she muttered and backed away. "Fine. If you don't want to see him and talk things out, then okay. It's your choice. But you guys are mates, and mates need to be with each other. You can't run away from this any longer."

And with that, she walked out the door, making my eyes widen. I let out a troubled sigh as I lay on my bed and thought about her words. I felt a tear slip out of my eye as soon as I closed them. I couldn't get Mason out of my head, and I wanted him to come to me, but I knew he wasn't going to do that.

I thought of one thing before I fell asleep: how I was going to talk with Mason tomorrow.

* * *

I sighed and looked around, relieved I was alone. I lay my back against a tree, closing my eyes and listening to the nature surrounding me. I hummed in comfort as I heard birds chirping. I then admired the woods, amazed by its beauty.

What happened yesterday made me go crazy. This morning, I had decided I was going to see Mason and finally talk with him, but before that, I had to let my wolf out so I could relax a bit. I ran for a while, taking a break from all the stress. Once I knew that I ran for a long time, I shifted back.

The surrounding air was calm, and the woods were silent. It was so quiet that I could hear my feet crushing the leaves on the ground. I took my time walking to the pack house, trying to organize what I was going to say to Mason.

I stopped dead in my tracks when I heard something behind me. I turned around and frowned when I saw no one. I shook my head, thinking I was going crazy. When I started walking, I heard it again. It sounded like footsteps. I gulped and glanced behind me to see nothing. I started rushing, but someone covered my mouth with their hand, stopping my screams that threatened to escape.

I tried to release myself, but the hold on me was too strong. Whoever was holding me then took a couple of steps back.

I was about to use my angel powers, but my vision got blurry and then I felt something hard hit my head. I tried to keep my eyes open but gave up when pain engulfed me, making me fall into the darkness.

CHAPTER 51

I groaned as my head throbbed. I tried to move but I couldn't. I slowly opened my eyes and was appalled when I saw that my hands and feet were tied to a chair. Squinting, I scanned the dim room, which was a cottage of some sort with trees outside the window. I looked around and noticed that I was alone.

I bit my lip and closed my eyes to calm myself down, as many questions began popping in my thoughts.

Where am I? How long was I out? Who took me here and why?

My heart rate sped up as stupid scenarios began forming in my head. I opened my eyes and prayed that someone would save me.

Trying to release myself, I shook my hands but it was no use. The ropes were too tight. I tried shifting into my wolf but I couldn't feel her, which worried me a lot.

Where is my wolf? I whined out of fear. *Of all days, why did I get kidnapped on the day I wanted to talk to Mason?*

Mason.

I wondered if he was looking for me. Did he even notice I was gone? I should have listened to him. What would happen to me now? Would I ever see him again?

I immediately shook my head and forced those thoughts away.

Don't think like that, Tiana. Of course, you will.

The thought of never seeing Mason frightened me. I hadn't confessed my feelings for him yet, and now I was afraid I might never get the chance to do so.

I was trying to stop my tears from falling when I heard noise outside. Someone soon started banging on the door, leaving me confused. Whoever was out there wanted to get in. When the door finally flew open, a gasp escaped my lips out of fear.

"Tiana?" Mason muttered, instantly running to me.

And that's when I clearly saw his face. He looked horrible. His eyes were red and puffy, like he had been crying.

"Thank goodness, I found you." He immediately ripped the ropes and engulfed me in a tight hug.

Although I was really confused as to what really happened and how he found me this fast, I chose to push those questions aside and hugged him back.

He dug his nose into the crook of my neck and inhaled my scent, muttering stuff I couldn't understand. I rested my face into his chest as his arms tightened around my waist.

"I was so afraid that I lost you, that I would never see you again," he whimpered.

My heart broke at his voice. I embraced him even tighter. Being in his arms was perfect, and it felt like home.

"Mason, what happened?" I asked softly.

He looked at me with sadness in his eyes. "I don't know. I went to your room to see you gone, then I found a note on your bed. It said someone took you, and that's when I went crazy. I searched everywhere. Then I found this cottage and knew you were here because of your scent. I was terrified, Tiana. I thought I lost you," he whimpered.

My tears welled in my eyes after seeing him so broken.

"Don't ever leave me. I don't think I can live without you." He tightened his arms around me. "I love you so much."

My eyes widened at his words, and that's when the tears came flooding my cheeks. It was somehow hard to breathe, like the air in my lungs got stuck. Mason looked at me with sadness in his eyes, but they held love too, something I had never seen before. After grasping the meaning of his words, my heart sped up. I never knew Mason loved me. I never even knew he was capable of love. But knowing he did, made my heart flutter and made me really happy.

I pulled him in for a hug. "I-I . . ." I stuttered, unable to continue from the overwhelming emotions. "I love you too," I managed to speak in a very soft voice.

He inhaled my scent and started whispering words into my ear, soothing me. "I'm never letting you go." He looked at me with a smile and wiped the tears from my cheeks.

"Don't," I whispered, smiling.

He leaned in and placed his lips on mine, making me wrap my arms around his neck. I heard a deep growl emerge from within his chest, and I kissed him back with as much passion.

I didn't know how long we kissed, but we immediately pulled away when we heard some whispers.

"Yes, we did it," a familiar voice spoke. We then heard a smack and someone wincing.

"Shhh, be quiet!" someone else said. "I think they heard us."

"No, they are too busy sucking each other's faces off."

"Yeah, he's right," another familiar voice said.

"You idiots, they heard us. I know it."

"Hey . . . It was your idea in the first place. So if we get caught, you're the one getting into trouble."

"You guys helped me out, so if I get into trouble, then so are you two."

I looked at Mason and frowned. He had the same frown on his face, and that's when we started looking around the cottage. I knew at times like this, we should've been out of the place and not making out, but his confession made us forget about everything.

Now, we were looking where the voices were coming from. They were really familiar, so I knew exactly who they belonged to.

We saw a room behind us, and that's when Mason stalked towards it with anger, his fist clenched.

"Shit! They heard us all right. He's coming here," a voice I knew spoke.

Immediately, Mason flung the door open and glared at Lina, Ryder, and Tyler, who all looked extremely nervous. Lina waved at him as she hesitantly chuckle.

"H-hey, guys . . . W-what are you doing here?" she stuttered.

I crossed my arms over my chest and exclaimed, "I could ask you the same thing. What's going on?"

They chuckled nervously and looked at each other.

"Since it was your idea, why don't you speak?" Ryder asked Lina.

Lina scratched the back of her neck and pouted. "Okay, okay. You guys caught us. We kidnapped Tiana," she confessed. Mason growled. I grabbed his hand to calm him down. He looked at me and closed his eyes, pinching his nose. Then he glared at them.

"Explain," he yelled.

"Well . . . You and Tiana were taking forever to confess your love to each other so . . . I thought once you thought you lost her, you would regret not telling her how you feel. So when you see her, you would confess, kiss, and make up. You know what they say, you don't know someone's value until you lose them," Lina explained, rubbing her arm nervously. "But hey, it worked."

Mason let out another growl, and I shook my head. I couldn't believe she did that. This girl was indeed crazy. But I got to admit, she was kind of right. I gave her a small smile before smacking her head.

"Ouch," she pouted, rubbing the spot I hit her.

"That's for making me think I was actually kidnapped," I said. "Even though I'm not mad at you, I'm still quite upset. Please don't ever do that again."

She sheepishly smiled and nodded before looking at us. "I'm sorry I frightened you, but I found no other way for you guys to finally confess to each other. You both are so stubborn."

Mason shook his head and let out a frustrated sigh. "I can't believe you, Lina," he muttered.

She smiled and hugged him. "Hey, you should be thanking me. Now you guys are going to be a happy couple and make cute babies!" she gushed.

Mason grinned, hugging his sister back. My cheeks heated up at her words, but I tried to hide them. I then looked at Tyler and Ryder, who were smiling from ear to ear.

"Hey, don't look at us like that," Ryder spoke, placing his hands up in the air. "She practically threatened us to take part in this."

I rolled my eyes. *I can't believe this girl.*

Lina and Mason pulled away, and he wrapped an arm around my waist, making me bite my lip. My eyes then widened when I remembered what happened earlier.

"But how come I can't feel my wolf?" I asked.

"Lina was able to get her hands on something from the medical room without Doctor Sam knowing. She gave you something so you won't feel your wolf for a short period, but don't worry, it will go away soon," Tyler explained. I looked at Lina, shocked.

She shrugged and put her hands up in a defensive manner. "I couldn't let you shift and ruin everything."

"How come we can't catch your scent?" Mason asked, sniffing the air.

I sniffed and frowned. I couldn't smell their scents either. Ryder smiled and glanced at Lina, who had a goofy smile on her lips.

"I also took something from the medical room to mask our scents. I couldn't let you guys smell us. It would have blown our cover," Lina explained.

Mason ran a hand through his hair. "I have one heck of a sister," he muttered and glared at her. "Thanks to you, I made a search party and now everyone's looking for her."

Nervous, Lina let out a chuckle and scratched the back of her neck. "Well, cancel it. Tell everyone you found her," she said, smiling at us.

Mason grunted and closed his eyes. He looked like he was in a trance. After a while, he looked at us and sighed. "Come on, let's head back."

We walked out of the small cottage while I was still trying to register what happened. It was hard to believe. I looked back and frowned.

"Where did you get this cottage, Lina?"

Lina shrugged. "I don't know. It has been there for a long time. I guess it's abandoned, so we decided to keep you there."

Mason grabbed my hand. I glanced at our joined hands, then at him. He looked at me with a small smile, making me smile as well. I still couldn't get over the fact that he loved me. I thought I liked him, but when he said he loved me, it made me realize I loved him too. I didn't know how and when it started, but I knew these feelings were real.

He placed a soft kiss on my forehead, making me blush. "Come on," he whispered and I nodded.

When we arrived at the pack house, a lot of guards were surrounding it, and I noticed that the majority of them were the new warriors.

Once we entered, everyone's eyes were on us and whispers erupted in the air. Many people then shot questions at Mason.

Mason sighed and spoke, "I sincerely apologize. It was all a misunderstanding. You may go back to what you're doing."

Everyone looked at us weirdly and nodded before walking away.

Mason pulled me up the stairs. My eyes widened when I realized we weren't going to my room but to his. He pushed me in and slammed the door behind him. Before I could open my mouth to speak, his lips were on mine.

I gasped as he kissed me with so much passion. I closed my eyes and wrapped my arms around his neck. He pushed me against the wall, his arms possessively pulling me closer to him.

Once we were out of breath, we pulled away, staring into each other's eyes. I felt sparks fly from our skin contact and my heart rate went fast, real fast.

He gently brushed his lips against mine before touching my cheek with his finger. He then cupped my face with his hands, staring into my eyes again.

"I don't know how and when, but I have realized today that I love you so much and I don't ever want to lose you," he whispered, causing my emotions to go overdrive.

I sucked in a breath and nodded. Those words made my face heat up. I bit my lip and stared into his beautiful orbs. "I love you too," I whispered.

He broke out into a large grin and kissed my lips again. When we pulled away, I lay my head on his warm chest and listened to his steady heartbeat as he ran his hand through my hair, playing with them. He kissed my forehead and stared at me.

"I want to let everyone know that you're my mate and their luna. I'm calling a pack meeting tomorrow. Is that okay with you?" he whispered.

I smiled at him and eagerly nodded. I liked it. It was nice hearing it from him.

"But before that . . . ," he whispered, pushing the strands of hair away from my neck, staring at me with eyes full of lust. "I need to claim you as mine."

My eyes widened, immediately understanding what he meant. I sucked in a breath and nodded, giving him the green light.

He dug his head into the crook of my neck and started trailing sweet kisses. I closed my eyes to calm myself down, and held in the moan that threatened to escape. Making his way to my sweet spot, he nibbled, kissed, and sucked, causing my legs to go weak. I held onto his shoulder to prevent myself from falling to the floor.

He bit my sweet spot, making me gasp. He glanced at me, making sure I wanted him to continue. As soon as I nodded, he went back to the spot, kissed it, and dug his teeth into my skin.

A gasp escaped my lips due to the pain, but it was immediately replaced by one out of pleasure.

I closed my eyes and let out a sigh. He licked the blood away and started to kiss that same spot, leaving me weak. A satisfied growl came out of his mouth, and he kept muttering "mine" against my skin. He lifted me, carrying me bridal style.

I placed my head against his chest as he walked to his bed and laid me softly. Moments before I completely dozed off, I kept thinking of how Mason and I were officially together.

CHAPTER 52

I hummed in comfort as I felt warm fingers trail my cheek, leaving behind familiar sparks. Mason ran his hand through my hair and pulled me closer to his hard chest, causing me to breathe out in pure bliss. His touch slowly roused me from my sleepy state, but the familiar sparks stopped as his hand separated from my skin. I whined and opened my eyes.

The first thing I saw was his chest. I tried to pull away but he tightened his arms around me. I raised my head to see Mason smiling lazily at me, making my face flush.

Memories of yesterday flooded my head. I bit my lip but soon smiled at him.

"Morning," I whispered.

"Morning." He dug his nose into my hair, inhaling my scent. "You smell so good," he said. "My scent is all over you. Now everyone will know you're mine."

My eyes widened slightly at his words—the words that made my heart rate go fast and my cheeks heated up instantly.

Mine. I like the sound of that.

I was still surprised by what happened yesterday. It was overwhelming that I had to repeatedly remind myself that it was all real and not some kind of weird, wonderful dream.

I still couldn't believe Lina came up with a kidnapping scenario. However, I knew Lina was full of surprises, and I wouldn't expect it from anyone else except her. I was a little upset that she scared me, but what she did was hella clever. I kind of owe it to her. Who knew, if she didn't do it, then maybe Mason and I would have never confessed.

It didn't bother me that he confessed his love at that time and not over some romantic dinner. I didn't need the latter. I wouldn't even care if he confessed during a bank robbery. It was the least of my worries. What truly mattered to me was Mason's feelings were genuine.

Mason suddenly pulled me out of my thoughts when his lips touched my mark, making my eyes widen in pleasure. I closed my eyes, enjoying the feeling. It was pure bliss.

He started licking the mark, making jolts of pleasure to run down my body, something I had never felt before. It made me feel excited, and lust engulfed me in a single second. I bit my lip to hold my moan as he continued kissing my mark, making my body weak. I ran my hand through his soft hair, grabbing a handful and tugging them. He let out a groan and pulled away, making me frown.

I opened my eyes to see Mason staring intensely at me, eyes full of lust. I let out a sigh as he smiled at me.

"Beautiful as ever," he whispered so softly.

I blushed and smiled at him.

"I can't get enough of you," he said, kissing me on the lips.

I let out a soft giggle and pulled away from him. I touched my mark, surprised to feel no pain. I looked at him and smiled at his appearance. He was only in sweatpants and a shirt, but damn he looked hot!

Tiana, jump him!

I mentally fought with myself to stop myself from doing something that I might regret later . . . or not. Mason stared at me with a sly smirk, knowing I was eyeing him. I shook my head and looked out the window to see birds chirping and a sky clear of any clouds.

"What time is it?" I asked.

He sat up and grabbed his phone from the desk. I bent over to see the time but was later shocked at his lock screen. It was the picture of me blushing, the one I told him to delete. Well, clearly he didn't delete it.

I gaped at him as my mind registered what I saw. He freakin' had my picture as his wallpaper! I wasn't so sure if I should feel happy or embarrassed.

"It's nine in the morning," he answered, staring at my surprised expression and breaking out into a smirk.

"You have my picture as your lock screen?" I glanced at his phone, then at him.

He nodded and shrugged. "Yes, I do," he replied, raising a brow. "Does that bother you?"

I bit my lip and shook my head. It didn't bother me. In fact, it actually made me happy. "No."

"Good." He smiled at me before standing up. "Come on, go get ready."

"Ready for what?" I asked.

He stepped closer to me, giving me a pointed look. "Did you forget? Today, we're telling the pack that you're my mate and their luna."

My lips opened in the shape of an O and I nodded, remembering what he told me yesterday.

I felt something in me light up at his words. This really meant a lot to me. I was very happy that he wanted to tell the pack about me, but I was a little nervous that they wouldn't accept me. I mean, I was once known as "the girl who is sleeping with the alpha to get the luna title".

I wondered what they would think of me now.

Mason knew my worries since he could feel my emotions after marking me, and I could feel his. He stepped closer to me and cupped my cheeks with his hands. I looked at Mason, and he pecked my pouting lips.

"Don't worry," he whispered. "They will love you."

I broke out into a smile and nodded. Unfortunately, my thoughts went to Chloe, and my heart fell to my stomach. I really wanted her dead, and I mean, really.

> Okay, not really, but you get what I mean.

What happened made me hate her a hundred times more. I was still bothered by the fact that she kissed Mason, even though I knew he didn't want that to happen.

Mason's smile turned into a frown. "What's wrong?"

"What about Chloe? She hates my guts. I don't think she will ever stop trying to get you," I told him. I didn't really care if she accepted me as her luna or not. I just didn't want her in our way.

Mason shook his head and looked at me. "You don't have to worry about her anymore."

My brows furrowed, and I tilted my head in confusion. "What do you mean?" I asked.

"She's gone. I kicked her out of the pack," he answered. "She's a rogue now."

I gaped at him in shock and my eyes widened as his words registered in my head. "You kicked her out?" I asked in disbelief even though he just said it.

"Yes. I warned her so many times, but she still messed with you," he murmured. "I've had enough of her."

I nodded, relieved I wouldn't have to deal with her anymore. "When was this?" I asked.

Mason looked at me with sadness in his eyes. "The day she kissed me."

I cringed at that. "What about her family?"

"She doesn't have one. She was originally a rogue, taken into the pack when she was small. The old alpha took her in as she was alone," he explained.

I couldn't help but furrow my brows as he said "old alpha" and not "dad." I decided to not question it because I didn't want to ruin his mood.

I nodded in understanding and pulled away. I didn't feel bad for her. Mason did give her warnings, but she still disobeyed him. It was all her fault.

"I'll go get ready," I told him.

"I'll see you in an hour." He placed a gentle kiss on my cheek.

I was walking towards my room when I heard loud music blasting in the air. I frowned in confusion, wondering who would do such thing at a time like this. People might still be sleeping.

I was one door away from my room when I noticed that the loud music was coming from the room right next to mine. I furrowed my brows.

I thought that room was empty?

I slowly approached the room so I could see what was going on but stopped when I discovered the door was wide open. I heard a man singing along to the music. Out of curiosity, I peeked in to see a tall, buff man that I had never seen before, doing some funky dance moves.

I held back my laugh as I watched him dance his heart out. He wasn't bad but he wasn't the best either, and that's what made it funny. I continued to watch while he was oblivious of my presence.

Unfortunately, he soon did a turn and his eyes widened as he saw me by the door. However, his shocked expression disappeared in an instant and was replaced with a happy one. He turned the music off and walked up to me.

"You know it's rude to stare at someone like that," the guy teased, making me roll my eyes.

"You know people might still be sleeping and you would've woken them up," I told him, crossing my arms over my chest.

He broke out into a goofy smile and shrugged. "Oops, my bad," he mumbled and then raised his brow playfully at me. "And who might you be?"

"I must ask you the same thing," I said. "I have never seen you before, and this room has always been empty."

His lips curved into a smile, and he stepped closer to me. "Are you the person staying in the next room?"

I slowly nodded. His smile grew and he raised his hand, gesturing for me to shake it.

"It's nice to meet you. I'm your new neighbor," he stated happily and my eyes widened, a little surprised. "I'm one of the new pack warriors who moved here two days ago. The name's Ameer."

I offered him a small smile, shaking his hand. "Welcome to the pack, Ameer. It's nice to meet you. I'm Tiana."

I was thankful his behavior was friendly and positive. I didn't need a stuck-up person as my neighbor.

"Well, Tiana, I hope we can get along because I don't want someone I dislike as my neighbor," Ameer spoke with a smile present on his lips.

"Trust me, I hope too," I replied.

"I think we'll get along just fine," he said, chuckling.

I glanced at his room to see some speakers, and got reminded of his music and dancing a while ago. I looked at him and raised a brow. "Do you usually blast music and dance?"

He chuckled and shook his head. "Not all the time. Only when I don't have training."

"Just don't do that in the morning when I'm asleep. Trust me, you don't want to interrupt my sleep. I can be vicious."

Adam suddenly crossed my thoughts as I said that. We always argued because he would wake me up when I didn't want to, causing me to attack him. It was our thing. Well, not anymore, that is. I really missed that guy.

"Don't worry about that, but I can't seem to imagine you as vicious," he chuckled.

I rolled my eyes and crossed my arms over my chest. "You don't want to."

His eyes widened slightly, and he nodded. "I'll be sure to remember that when I turn on my music in the morning."

"Great," I said sweetly. "I should be going. There's a pack meeting in an hour, and I have to get ready."

"Is it about you and the alpha?" he asked.

Confused, I narrowed my eyes on him and slowly nodded. "Yes. How did you know?"

"You're marked," he replied, pointing to my neck.

I touched my mark, like a reflex. I completely forgot about it.

"And something strong is radiating off you, so I'm guessing you're the alpha's mate, the luna. Your mark is new, so it was a guess."

"Yeah. What you said is true," I murmured, smiling. "I guess I'll see you around." I took a step back and gave him a small wave. "Bye."

He smiled at me before I turned around. As I was walking towards my room, I heard him yell, which I was sure everyone heard.

"Bye, neighbor! It was nice to meet you!"

I chuckled and entered my room. Looked like I had one heck of a neighbor.

CHAPTER 53

I nervously wiped my sweaty hands to my dress and let out a sigh, biting my lips as I observed myself in the mirror. The dress I wore fitted me like a glove, and I thought it was beautiful.

I was walking towards my bedroom door when I heard someone knocking on it. I opened it and was met by a well-dressed Mason looking right at me. My lips broke out into a smile as his eyes lit up. He stepped closer to me and pulled me to his chest, wrapping his strong arms around my waist possessively. I inhaled his scent as he did the same.

"Beautiful," he muttered.

"Hey," I whispered, looking into his eyes.

He softly smiled at me and placed his lips on mine. After a second, he pulled away and dug his nose into the crook of my neck. He inhaled my scent and kissed my mark, making my eyes widen.

"Hi," he greeted back as he softly kissed it again. He then pulled away and looked at me, his eyes dark. He closed his eyes for a split second before staring at me. "You ready?" he asked.

"Yes. I'm just a little nervous," I responded, making him shake his head.

I was really nervous. I mean, what if they didn't like me? What if the rumors that flew around affected how they saw me? Many questions roamed my head, and I didn't know if I was just overthinking.

"I told you, they will love you," Mason assured me, and I let out a sigh. "Come on, let's go." He grabbed my hand and gave it a comfortable squeeze, making me smile at him.

We walked hand in hand through the hall and down the stairs. The pack house was empty, so everyone must be in the yard, waiting for the pack meeting to start. I glanced at Mason one more time and he offered me a reassuring smile, which relaxed my nerves.

Outside the pack house was a large crowd. They turned their gazes to us, stopping whatever they were doing. A lot of members had shock written on their faces as they saw our joined hands. Some were confused and started whispering words to the ones next to them, while the others had smiles on their faces.

Mason and I walked until we were in front of everyone. By now, whispers filled the air, making me nervous in my place.

"Thank you all for coming. I brought you here today to announce some great news, which should have been announced a long time ago," Mason started, glancing at me with comforting eyes before turning his attention to the crowd. "Many of you guys wonder up to this day why I spared the lives of the new members that came here months ago. Some of you already guessed it right and others created false rumors," he said the last part bitterly and his expression grew rough.

I rubbed his hand with my thumb to calm him down, causing him to sigh and tighten his hold.

"It was because Tiana, the girl who is standing in front of you, is my mate," he finally stated.

They gasped and their eyes widened as they stared at me with pure shock. Some members broke out into grins while others ducked their heads in respect or shame. I bit the inside of my cheek as I stared at the crowd in front of me.

"She is your luna," Mason declared.

By now, everyone had their heads down, a gesture of respect. A small smile crawled onto my face, and I looked at Mason to see him staring at me with loving eyes.

The pack all raised their heads, and some started blurting out words of respect.

"I want you all to treat her the same way as you treat me. Meaning, if anyone does otherwise, they will be punished," Mason ordered.

Everyone nodded, and so did Mason.

"Good," he muttered.

I scanned the huge crowd and saw Lina, Ryder, and Tyler smiling at me. Lina did a happy dance, and I had to hold back the laughter that threatened to escape my mouth. I continued looking at the crowd and saw Crystal, who I hadn't talked to for a while, smiling at me.

I completely forgot that I had spilled everything to her. I let out a sigh and smiled back. I just hoped she wouldn't say a word of what I had told her.

I glanced at Mason and he tugged my hand, pulling me closer to the crowd.

"Come. They want to greet you properly," he whispered.

I looked at the crowd and smiled as I saw their eyes light up in happiness. A luna was someone every pack wished to have. A luna was like the mother of the pack, taking care of the pack members like they were her children. No doubt they were happy that they were finally given a chance to have a luna.

We walked up to them, and everyone immediately tried to grab my attention. I smiled at each and every pack member as they shook my hand or pulled me in for a hug. I greeted many members I didn't know and many that were familiar. Some pack members apologized for believing the false rumors, which made me a little happy. At least now they knew they were false.

After a long time of talking and greeting, a smiling Mason tugged my hand and pulled me away.

"That's enough for today," he spoke, causing some members to frown. "You will get to speak with her another time, but for now we have to leave. You may all go back to what you were doing."

And with that, many turned away and left. I received waves of goodbyes, and I couldn't help the feeling of happiness that came over me. I was happy they accepted me. I looked at Mason and smiled.

"Let's go," he whispered, pulling me back to the pack house.

We walked hand in hand towards my room in complete silence. As soon as we were in front of my room, I noticed how silent he was, so I raised a brow at him.

"Is there something wrong?" I asked. He looked at me and let out a deep sigh.

"No." He shook his head and ran a hand through his hair. "I just want to ask you a question," he murmured.

"What is it?" I looked at him in confusion.

"Uh . . ." He scratched the back of his neck and sighed again. "Would you like to go out with me?"

My eyes widened, and I broke out into a smile. "You mean a date?"

"Yeah, a date," he whispered, shrugging. "I mean, if you don't want to, it's okay. I just thought that you like these type of things—"

I cut him off with a laugh. "I'd love to go on a date with you."

The stress that was clear on his face vanished, and he smiled at me. "Okay, good," he said, satisfied.

I placed a soft kiss on his cheek and asked, "When is this date?"

"I was thinking tonight . . . ," he told me, not sounding so sure.

"Tonight sounds good. What should I wear?"

He grabbed my hand and smiled at me. "Anything you're comfortable with," he murmured.

"Okay. I'll see you tonight." I slowly closed the door and broke out into a goofy smile.

* * *

I was about to get out of my room to grab some lunch when my door dramatically flew open, and a huffing and puffing Ameer appeared. My eyes widened as he ran into my room and slammed the door behind him, sighing in relief. His eyes linked with mine, and I looked at him, confused.

"What—"

"Hey, neighbor! How you doing?" he asked as a fake smile crawled onto his lips.

I frowned and crossed my arms over my chest. "What are you doing here?"

Stepping closer to me, his happy expression vanished, replaced with a troubled one. "Hiding," he answered softly, opening the door and taking a peek outside before immediately closing it again. He ran to me with fear written all over his face. "Shit," he cursed. "She's right outside."

"Who are you hiding from?" I asked, raising my voice.

He covered my mouth with his hand. "Shhh, be quiet. She might hear you," he whispered.

I pulled away from him and stared at him in confusion. "Who?"

"A monster. No. A devil," he answered before shaking his head. "No, Satan herself. She's after me."

"And why is Satan after you?"

He ran a hand through his hair and cringed when a loud voice boomed outside of my room.

"You fucker! Come out or I will drag you to hell," a familiar voice yelled, making Ameer frown.

"I told you. Satan is right outside. Please help me, Tiana," he begged.

I couldn't help but be amused. "Aren't you a pack warrior? Doesn't that mean you can fight off any Satan?"

Frowning, he shook his head. "I can fight anyone, except that creature outside," he replied, making me laugh.

I walked to the door, ready to open it, when Ameer grabbed my hand.

"What are you doing?" he hissed. "Are you going to let her take me? I thought we were best friends?" he stated dramatically, making me roll my eyes.

"We met this morning, Ameer," I chuckled.

"Still. I was ready to get those matching friendship bracelets, but you're now about to throw away our friendship." He pouted and I laughed. Then he let out a feminine scream when there was a loud knock at my door.

"Tiana? Is that fucker in there with you? I swear on my dead grandmother's life, if you don't open the door, I will drag you to hell with the both of us," the familiar voice yelled, making me wince.

I rolled my eyes, and Ameer shook his head. He looked like he was accepting the fact that he was going to die.

"Ameer, she's not going to hurt you," I said.

"She already did! She kicked me in the freakin' balls," he exclaimed, shaking his head.

I winced at him and patted his shoulder. "You're a goner," I teased.

A terrified expression crossed his features. "You're right," he whispered, making my eyes twinkle in amusement. "I'm going to die, and I didn't even cross out a single thing off my bucket list. Hell, I'm still a virgin," he cried out, making me burst out into laughter.

"I said open the damn door!" Lina shouted, interrupting my laughter and making Ameer's eyes widen in fear.

"Don't open it," he whispered. "I got an idea. Let's jump out the window and get the hell out of here. Then we change our looks and names, and move away to Canada. How does that sound?"

"You won't be moving anywhere because I'm going to kill you!" Lina yelled, slamming her fist against my door.

Woah, easy on the door!

"I need to open it before she breaks it down," I told Ameer, making him run a hand through his hair.

"I'm dead," he murmured.

"What did you even do?" I asked.

"It was an accident, I swear," he pleaded without even answering my question. I rolled my eyes at him.

As soon as I opened it, a fuming Lina glared at Ameer with pure hatred. "You bastard!" she yelled, running to him like he was her prey, ready to attack. However, I grabbed her before she could even touch him.

"Tiana, let me go! This bastard deserves to die!" My arms around her tightened, and Ameer let out another feminine scream and ran to the other side of the room. "I'm going to kill you."

"Lina!" I yelled, making her turn her attention to me. "What the hell is going on? Why are you so persistent in killing him?"

She glared at him before looking back at me, showing me her wet book, which I didn't notice until now.

"That fucker," she pointed to Ameer, "spilled coffee over my damn book!"

"It was an accident, I swear," Ameer pleaded with his eyes to save him from Lina's wrath. "I wasn't looking where I was going."

I sighed and gave Lina a pointed look. "Lina, it's just a book," I stated.

"It's not just any book, Tiana," she exclaimed. "It's my favorite book."

I looked at it, and the cover had *The Vampire Diaries* written on it. My eyes widened, and I stared at Ameer in shock. Yes, he's a goner.

> If you still haven't noticed, Lina is a huge The Vampire Diaries fan, and she will kill anyone who messes with her books.

RIP, Ameer. Even though I just met you, you will be missed.

"I'm sorry. It was an accident!"

I rolled my eyes as Lina started shouting at him, making him cringe and wince.

"I'll buy you another one," he spoke, trying to tame the beast.

Lina went silent and placed her finger on her chin, thinking. "Hmm," she mumbled. "No!" She burst out in anger and tried to escape the grip I had on her so she could attack him. I rolled my eyes at the two and tightened my arms around Lina.

For the rest of the evening, I tried to knock some sense into Lina to save Ameer's life. Keyword: tried. Let's just say Ameer ended up with a black eye. It was pathetic, honestly.

Note to self: Never anger Lina.

CHAPTER 54

I walked to the bathroom as soon as I finished dressing up. Once I was done applying some mascara and lip gloss, I observed myself in the mirror and smiled. I didn't know when Mason would come and pick me up for the date, so I just made sure I was ready.

Saying I was nervous was an understatement. I hadn't been this nervous for a long time. I guessed maybe because I hadn't been on a date for a while, and going out with Mason was something big for me.

Thinking about Mason made my smile grow. I felt like our bond was growing stronger and stronger by the minute. It was bizarre to me, especially since I promised myself to never have this feeling anymore.

It was hard for me at first, but I guessed I couldn't keep that promise to myself anymore. I knew if I kept it, I wouldn't be truly happy, so I let it go and moved on. It was better this way. Adam was right; Mason was filling the empty holes in my heart and I was slowly healing.

I let out a deep breath and slowly walked out the bathroom. I grabbed some comfortable shoes that might or might not go well with the dress I was wearing, but I didn't care honestly. He did say I should wear something I was comfortable with.

Once I was done, I noticed a small piece of paper on my pillow. I walked up to it and wondered how long it was lying there. I picked it up and smiled when I saw Mason's familiar handwriting.

I read it, and as I was doing so, I was sure my eyes were twinkling with happiness.

I'll come pick you up at eight. I'm going to make you touch the stars tonight. ~Mason

I giggled and placed the note on top of my desk, wondering what he meant by touching the stars. I glanced at the clock to see it was already eight, so I checked my reflection one more time, feeling satisfied.

After a moment, I heard a soft knock on my door and I instantly wiped my sweaty hands to my dress. I slowly opened the door to see a well-dressed Mason staring right at me.

"Hey," I whispered.

Mason's eyes roamed over my body, and I shifted in my place, nervous from his stare. He took a step closer and smiled softly.

"Hello, beautiful." He pulled me in for a hug and inhaled my scent, making me smile.

I soon pulled away and stared at him with adoration. I leaned forward and placed a lingering kiss on his lips.

"I missed you," he whispered, tightening his arms around my waist protectively.

I let out a soft laugh and shook my head. "But I just saw you a couple hours ago."

He grunted and shrugged. "Longest hours of my life," he said softly, making my cheeks heat up.

I shook my head and then stared into his eyes as he gladly looked at me. "So where are we going?"

Mason grabbed my hand, pulling me out of my room, and we started walking side by side.

"You'll see," he responded, making me pout. He glanced at me and his eyes lit up. I nudged his side with my elbow and grunted. He let out a deep chuckle, which made my pout disappear, immediately replaced with a grin.

"I want to know now," I whined, making him shake his head. He stared at me, a sly smile on his lips.

"Now that wouldn't be fun, would it?" he asked.

I groaned and shook my head. "No."

While we were strolling in the pack house, we received a couple of stares, but this time those stares were filled with adoration and happiness. We were greeted by some pack members, and I noticed the change in the way they treated me, which I was quite happy with. It made me more confident to be with Mason.

As soon as we got out, Mason led me to his car and opened the door for me. I smiled and sat inside.

"What a gentleman," I said more to myself as he sat in the driver's seat. He looked at me after hearing what I said. I laughed and he only shook his head.

"Who knew you had a side like this."

His orbs darkened as they stared right at me. "Only for you," he whispered.

I bit my lips, and I could've sworn I felt my heart skip a beat.

"You're the only one who gets to see this side of me."

Smiling, I grabbed his hand and squeezed it, and he looked at me with love in his eyes.

"I love you," I whispered with so much honesty in my voice.

With his eyes twinkling in happiness, he placed a soft kiss on my hand. He then looked at me and smiled. "I love you too."

Mason slowly let go of my hand and placed it on the steering wheel, driving off. I sat in comfortable silence as I stared out the window. We swiftly passed by so many trees, making it look like they were moving. I glanced at the sky to see the stars shining brightly down at us.

Seeing the stars made me remember what he had written in the note, and a smile crept onto my lips.

"So, how are you going to make me touch the stars tonight?"

He smirked and glanced at me before looking back at the road. "You'll see," he spoke with a hint of amusement in his voice.

I crossed my arms over my chest. "Was that all you had to say?" I grunted in annoyance. A deep chuckle escaped his mouth, making me roll my eyes.

"For now, yes," he answered.

I rolled my eyes one more time and remained quiet, looking out the window. I noticed we were now driving in some kind of woods, which was quite creepy, especially since it was nighttime.

However, I didn't say a thing, knowing Mason brought me here for a reason, and not to kidnap and kill me.

"Is this the part when I ask if you're some kind of psycho in disguise wanting to steal my organs?" I teased him.

He let out a laugh, making me smile. He glanced at me before speaking, "The only thing I'll be stealing tonight is your heart."

My eyes widened, and I felt my heart skip a beat. He smiled at me, and I let out a chuckle.

"How cheesy," I muttered, making him raise his brow. I glanced out the window and smiled. "You already did."

Mason soon parked in front of an area full of bushes. I looked around the place in confusion.

What are we doing here?

He hopped out of the car and walked to my side, opening the door for me. I stepped out and took his hand in mine. He pulled me to him and smiled before we started walking.

Mason leaned into my ear, making a shiver run down my spine, and whispered, "Close your eyes."

I did as he told, and he started leading me the way in silence. I was able to listen to the nature around me, which brought me comfort. After a while, we stopped and he stepped closer to me.

"When I said I'm going to make you touch the stars tonight, this is what I meant," he whispered into my ear, piquing my curiosity. "Open your eyes."

I opened my eyes and stared at what was in front of me. My mouth hung open as I took in the sight. It was marvelous and spectacular in many ways. It was beautiful.

It was some kind of a secret place surrounded by bushes and trees, an untouched place hidden from everyone else. There were flowers everywhere, which made the place even prettier, but that wasn't what caught my attention.

It was the fireflies.

Hundreds of them were flying around us, lighting up the dark place. I raised my hand and a firefly landed on my palm. I let out a soft chuckle and the firefly flew away. I glanced at Mason to see him smiling at me.

So, this was what he meant by touching the stars. There were so many fireflies, it looked like stars fell from the sky. It was something I had never witnessed before.

"Mason," I whispered as another firefly landed on my hand and flew again, making my smile widen. "It's beautiful. I love it," I breathed out, staring at him.

"I'm happy you do," he whispered, pulling me further into the beautiful place. I then saw a blanket lying on the ground with a basket next to it.

Looked like he planned it all out.

"I brought you here because I thought it was a nice place to sit down and eat," Mason spoke, looking around.

"It is. How did you find this place?" I asked, looking at the trees that surrounded us. "It looks hidden."

"Because it is," he replied. "I found this place when I was young. That time, I was upset and was running away from my problems. I accidentally came across this place, which isn't far away from the pack. Since then, I go back whenever I'm angry or upset. This place always seems to calm me down."

I grabbed his hand, running my thumb over his skin. His story made me wonder about his past. I never asked because I guessed it was a sour subject, but my curiosity was growing and growing by the second.

"What happened?" I asked softly.

His eyes darkened, and he slowly shook his head. "I can't say. Not now, that is," he whispered. "Let's focus on us for now."

I nodded, understanding what he meant. He opened the basket next to him and pulled out a couple of stuff before taking out the food.

Yum, food.

I felt my stomach rumble at the sight. Mason took out the plates and placed the food on it. We let the time go by as we ate and conversed a little.

I couldn't help but feel happy at his actions. I never would have thought Mason would do something like this. It was so romantic, something I never thought Mason had in him. I glanced at our surroundings and smiled as a couple of fireflies flew past us.

I looked at Mason and raised a brow as I saw him staring at me. He moved closer and wrapped his arms around my waist, pulling me to his chest.

"So beautiful," he muttered as he placed a kiss on my neck. He raised his head and glanced at my lips. I licked them and stared into his eyes. He leaned in closer and inhaled my scent before crashing his lips onto mine, making me melt in his arms.

I closed my eyes shut as Mason did wonders on my lips. After a while, he slowly pulled away and rested his forehead against mine, letting out a deep breath.

"You drive me crazy," he whispered, making me chuckle.

I looked at him to see his dark eyes staring back at me. My lips curved into a smile, and he pecked my lips one more time before pulling away. I immediately missed the contact and pouted, and his eyes sparked with amusement. He grabbed me by my waist and pulled me in front of him so that my back was facing him. He handed me my plate while his other arm remained wrapped around my waist, making me smile.

"Eat," he murmured, kissing behind my ear.

After we were done eating, I laid my head against his chest, listening to his heartbeat. I let out a sigh and snuggled deeper into his chest.

"This is nice," I whispered.

He placed his chin on the top of my head and tightened his arms around me. "We can always repeat this."

"That would be great."

We stayed like that for a long time. I felt like if we did this a little longer, I would have fallen sleep. It was so relaxing. Mason's touch and the nature surrounding us were soothing me. I let out a yawn as Mason rubbed his thumb against my waist. I closed my eyes and listened to his beating heart.

"I think it's time to go," Mason spoke.

I frowned and stared at him. "I don't want to leave," I whined like a child.

He smiled at my behavior and shook his head. "As I said, we'll come here again. But for now, we need to call it a night."

I sighed in defeat. I didn't want to leave, but I guessed Mason was right. It was kind of getting late and he was an alpha, so I bet he had lots of things to do.

Mason stood up and grabbed my hands, pulling me up. I stood on my feet and ran a hand through my hair before looking at Mason.

"Come on," he said lowly, tugging on my hand.

I looked back at the place in awe. It was truly beautiful, and it saddened me that we were leaving. I shook my head and turned my attention back to Mason. He kissed my forehead, making me smile at him. We walked side by side towards the car in silence. Mason then opened the door for me and smiled. I sat before he closed it. He walked to the other side and opened the door, but before he could even sit, he stopped and checked his pocket.

"Shit," he cursed before shaking his head.

I frowned at him in confusion.

Mason looked at me and spoke, "I forgot my phone back there. Will you be alright if I leave you to grab it?"

"I'll be fine. Go get your phone," I assured him. He closed the door before running back to the place.

I lay my head on my seat and smiled, thinking about tonight. It surely was one of the best nights of my life. I looked out the window and sighed. I didn't know what time it was, but I was sure it was late. I could hear crickets and owls, which made the place a little creepier than it already was.

I shook my head and pushed those thoughts aside. I then sighed in relief as I heard Mason's footsteps approaching but was later confused as to why he was on my side of the car. It was dark outside, so all I could make out was the shape of his body.

When the door opened, I looked up at Mason, ready to ask him what was wrong when I realized it was not him. My eyes widened in fear as I stared at the smirking man in front of me, but what made my heart fall to the pit of my stomach was his pointy fangs and his dark red eyes.

Immediately, I knew the man in front of me was a vampire.

CHAPTER 55

"What the—"

I was immediately cut off when the vampire grabbed me by my arms, pulling me out of the car aggressively and throwing me to the ground. I screamed as I tried to stand on my feet, but the vampire instantly got ahold of me, his sharp nails digging into my skin.

I let out another scream, hoping Mason would hear and come fast. The vampire turned me around so I was facing him. He smirked as I tried to release myself from his strong grip. I growled, and he hissed back.

"Finally, I got you. Alpha will be pleased," he muttered, and a chuckle of satisfaction escaped his lips.

What is he talking about? Who is this alpha?

I pushed those questions aside. It wasn't the time to ask anything. I didn't know where Mason was, but I hoped this bloodsucker didn't do anything to him.

Without a second thought, I used my powers to turn invisible, catching him off guard. I escaped his loosened grip and went behind him, immediately shifting into my wolf and taking him by surprise. He hissed at me, showing his pointy fangs. I jumped on him and sunk my teeth into his neck.

He let out a loud, painful cry as I ripped a chunk of his skin. His eyes hardened and he pushed me to the ground. He hissed at me, raging with fury. I growled at him, warning him not to come any closer. However, it didn't stop him from attacking me by sinking his fangs into my neck, making me whimper in pain.

"If he didn't want you, I would kill you right now and right here," he spoke in my ear.

He dug his fangs into my neck once again and I howled in pain while forcing my eyes to remain open. I mustered all the strength I had left to push him off me and immediately jumped on him. I growled at his face and dug my teeth into his injured neck, ending his life without hesitations.

As soon as I was sure he was dead, I backed away and shifted into my human form. I stood there naked, staring at his still body that was drowning in his own blood.

"Too bad I killed you first," I growled to myself as soon as his words registered in my head.

I glanced at the dead body one more time, feeling no hint of remorse. That vampire attacked me first, so it was self-defense. If it were out of hatred, then I would feel guilty.

I ran towards the hidden place, not caring that I was naked. Mason wasn't there, and I started to worry. Many scenarios ran through my head, making my heart fall to my stomach, but I forced those thoughts aside.

My eyes widened when I saw him unconscious on the ground, blood flowing from his side. I immediately ran up to him and kneeled. I choked on my own breath as I saw a needle sticking out of his neck, causing my heart to skip a beat.

"Mason," I whispered, shaking my head. "No, no, no, no." A couple of tears fell out of my eyes. I grabbed the needle and hissed in pain. My heart rate sped up as I comprehended everything.

The vampire had injected Mason with silver.

Holding back the sob that threatened to escape, I grabbed the needle one more time, ignoring the pain, and pulled it out of his neck. I shook his body in an attempt to wake him up somehow, but was left with a motionless Mason. I cried out in fear and immediately sent a message through the mind link, asking Nick to come and bring Doctor Sam with him.

I held Mason, trying to soothe him with my touch, as they said a mate's touch could heal anything.

"Please, Mason," I whispered. "Wake up. Please."

I closed my eyes and placed my hands on his chest. I concentrated on my angel powers. Since I used it a while ago, I didn't have much strength left, but I mustered all the remaining power I had in me to try to save Mason's life. Hopefully, my healing ability could retract most of the silver.

I kissed his forehead and lips, hoping he would be okay. Seeing him like this gave me another reason not to feel any remorse towards that vampire. More tears fell out of my eye, but I immediately wiped them away. I stood up, and with so much effort, I pulled Mason out of the place and towards the car. So when Nick and Doctor Sam came, they wouldn't take long to find us.

I soon heard footsteps running towards us. In a few seconds, I met Nick, some pack warriors, and Doctor Sam. I let out a sigh of relief, happy they finally arrived. Doctor Sam ran up to Mason with a bag in his hand and started taking stuff out. Nick came to my side and looked at me with worry.

"What happened, Tiana?" he asked.

I gulped for air, catching my breath. "A vampire," I muttered, pointing to the direction where his dead body laid. "He attacked us, but I already killed him," I told Nick and then turned to Sam. "He injected Mason with silver."

Doctor Sam nodded in understanding and explained that taking Mason to the pack house might cause more danger to his health, so he had to act fast and take care of him immediately.

Nick then ordered some pack warriors to go to where I pointed at while Ameer ran to me and handed his shirt. And that's when I realized that I was naked in front of a bunch of males. However, I was too worried about Mason to even care. I wore

Ameer's shirt before thanking him. He looked at me sympathetically and I sighed, grabbing Mason's hand.

After a while, Doctor Sam turned to me. "Thankfully, the vampire didn't inject much silver into him, and since he is an alpha, he will heal fast."

His news somehow relieved me, although I already knew that because I healed him a bit with my angel powers. I placed my hand over my beating heart.

"He just needs to stay under heavy medication," Doctor Sam added.

"That's a relief," I muttered, kissing Mason's hand.

Doctor Sam then went back to aiding Mason. "I recommend you stay with him at all times. Your touch will soothe him and might heal him faster," he said.

I nodded and remained silent. I wasn't leaving his side whether it would help him or not.

The pack warriors came back running towards us with worried expressions.

"The vampire, he's not there," a warrior said while catching his breath. Nick's eyes widened and so did mine.

"What are you talking about?" Nick growled, glancing at me before looking back at the warrior.

"We couldn't locate any vampire. The only thing we found was a pool of blood," the warrior responded. Nick cursed and sent the pack warriors to search the area. I looked at Mason in confusion.

But I'm sure I killed him.

"We should now take him back to the pack house," Doctor Sam whispered. I nodded, then two pack warriors came and carried Mason carefully. My heart broke at the sight. He looked vulnerable, something I was not used to seeing.

The warriors laid Mason in the back seat, his head on my lap. After Doctor Sam got in, Nick immediately drove off. Holding onto Mason's unconscious body, I ran my hand through his hair and kissed him softly. I just wanted him to wake up already.

His breathing was back to normal, which calmed my nerves. I gently caressed his face after noticing that he would relax under my touch. I placed another soft kiss on his lips.

It didn't take long until we reached the pack house. As the warriors carried Mason inside, understandably, many members watched us in curiosity, fear, and confusion. An unconscious alpha was something to worry about. All I could do was just smile at them.

As soon as we were in Mason's room, they gently laid him on his bed. Doctor Sam walked up to him and injected him something. He then looked at me while placing his things back in the bag.

"I was able to retract most of the silver from his system. He should be waking up soon," Doctor Sam explained. "However, he still needs healing and he should rest for a couple of days."

"Thank you so much, Doctor Sam. I'll make sure he gets the rest he needs," I said, sitting next to Mason.

Doctor Sam noticed the bite on my neck, and he walked up to me. "Let me inspect it." He touched the bite, making me wince.

"It is not deep, but it needs a few stitches," he muttered, grabbing a few things from his bag. "From the looks of it, there isn't much venom in your system. I'll just inject you with something that gets rid of the venom within a few hours," he explained.

I closed my eyes and remained silent as he injected something in me. He then stitched my wound, making me wince every once a while. After he was done, he cleaned and patched it up. He backed away with a smile, handing me a box of pills.

"Take these. They will help with the pain. Make sure you rest too."

"Okay. Thanks, Doctor Sam."

"There's no need to thank me. I'm only doing my job," he said softly before glancing at Mason, then back at me. "I will come back to give you the medication he needs." Once I nodded, he was out the door.

I let out a sigh and looked at Mason, pulling the blanket over his body. I cupped his cheek and kissed it gently.

I was so thankful he was now okay. I didn't know what I would have done if something more terrible happened to him. I went under the covers and laid next to him, wrapping an arm around his body. Inhaling his scent, I closed my eyes and thought about today.

How come someone always has to ruin our night?

I grunted and I couldn't help the weird feeling that came over me. The disappearance of the vampire's body sent shivers down my spine. There could only be two possible explanations. Either I wasn't able to truly kill him and he ran away, or someone else came and took his body.

I shook my head and pushed those thoughts aside, snuggling into Mason's chest and welcoming sleep.

* * *

I woke up when Mason stirred. I immediately sat up and stared at him. He groaned, making me grab his hand. As soon as I did that, his eyes shot open. I smiled in relief while he looked at me with confusion.

"What happened?" he hissed in pain.

I ignored his comment and hugged him, my eyes welling up. "Thank goodness you're okay," I whispered against his chest. He wrapped his arms around my waist, pulling me closer.

"It's okay. I'm fine," he whispered in my ear. "Are you okay? The last thing I remember was blacking out. What happened?"

I sighed and looked at him. "A vampire attacked us."

Mason's eyes turned a shade darker and widened, his hold on me tightening. "A vampire?" he growled lowly.

"Yeah."

"Did he hurt you—"

"I took care of it," I cut him off. "You should have seen me. I kicked his ass," I chuckled, trying to lighten up the mood. His hard eyes relaxed and the corner of his lip turned up.

"You did?" he asked and I nodded.

"Yeah. He was able to get a few bites of me though," I muttered, touching my neck. Mason's eyes hardened as he stared at my wounds. Before he could even say anything, I spoke, "I'm okay now. I thought I killed him, but the warriors couldn't find his body. That doesn't matter for now, though. I was really worried about you."

Mason sighed and cupped my cheek, leaving a soft kiss on my lips.

"I'm sorry our night was ruined," he whispered. "I'll make it up to you."

I shook my head. "Mason, you have nothing to be sorry about. I'm just glad you're okay."

He smiled softly and pulled me in for another kiss. I moved my lips against his as he kissed me passionately, making me forget about what had happened.

Mason slowly pulled away and looked into my eyes. "As long as you're with me, I will be fine."

CHAPTER 56

I stirred when I felt someone move. I slowly opened my eyes and was met with Mason's chest. I noticed it was still dark outside. I heard Mason whimper softly, and was taken aback once I laid eyes on his face.

It was red and sweaty, so was the rest of his body. He kept whimpering and growling in his sleep, making me sit up and stare at him in confusion. I placed my hand on his arm, which calmed him for a moment before he started moving again. His head shook as tears fell from his eyes. He was having a nightmare.

"Mason?" I whispered, shaking him. "Wake up."

The sight in front of me tore my heart into pieces. Never had I seen Mason like this, crying in his sleep. I shook him more and my heart fell to my stomach when he whimpered again.

"Mom," he whispered so softly that I barely heard it. My brows furrowed, and I tightened my arms around him as his breathing rate increased.

"Mason, wake up," I said. His eyes shot open and his body jolted from the bed. I rubbed his back in an attempt to calm him down. He took in a deep breath and closed his eyes. Once he looked at me, my breath was caught in my throat.

Tears streamed down his face. Right then and there, he didn't look like a strong alpha who could kill without remorse but a broken child, a child who needed a hug. And that's what I did. I embraced him without a second thought. He automatically wrapped his arms around my waist as he let out a loud cry, making me close my eyes to prevent my own tears from falling.

Him crying was the saddest thing I had ever witnessed. It broke my heart.

"Shhh . . ." I whispered, running my hand through his hair and kissing his forehead. "It's okay."

He nodded and pulled away from me. He looked down at his hands, embarrassment evident in his eyes. Frowning, I wiped away the tears from his cheeks and cupped his face.

"Mason . . ." I breathed out, placing a soft kiss on his lips. "What happened? Was it a bad dream?" He looked at me with watery red eyes, which held loneliness in them, making me want to hug him to my chest and tell him everything would be okay.

"Y-yes," he whispered hesitantly. "A bad dream."

I nodded. I knew that wasn't the only thing but decided not to question it. He seemed like he didn't want to talk about it, and I didn't want to push him. However, the word he muttered in his sleep kept running through my head.

Mom.

I guessed something that happened in his past had scarred him. When I was a kid, I heard stories that he killed his parents but I knew better than to listen to them. You never knew what was hidden deep within someone's heart, which no one else knew. Once the time was right, I would ask him about it. Right now wasn't clearly the right time.

"It's okay. I'm right here," I whispered. He nodded and pulled me to him, digging his nose in my hair, inhaling my scent. He let out a long sigh, and that's when I noticed his breathing rate was back to normal. He placed his head on my chest, closing his eyes.

I ran my hand through his hair, playing with them. He stared at me. The loneliness in his eyes had disappeared and was replaced with love.

"I love you," he whispered, tightening his hold on my waist.

"I love you too." I kissed the top of his head. He inhaled my scent one more time before I felt his breathing even out, indicating he was asleep. I softly touched his cheek and kissed his lips before laying him on the bed. I pulled the covers over him and lay next to him, snuggling my face in his chest.

Inhaling his scent, I closed my eyes and wrapped an arm around his body before I fell asleep.

* * *

The moment I opened my eyes, I was met with mesmerizing dark orbs staring back at me. Automatically, I smiled. Mason's lips turned up in a half smile and he pulled me towards him, kissing me on my lips.

"Morning," he spoke lazily, kissing me again.

"Good morning," I whispered, wrapping my arms around his neck. "How do you feel?" I asked.

"I feel much better."

"That's good. Are you hungry?" I asked, standing up.

"Yes," he responded, about to stand up. I frowned and pushed his chest gently, forcing him to lay down again. He raised a brow at me and I only offered him a pointed look.

"Don't get up," I ordered him. "You need to rest. Doctor Sam specifically told me that"

He frowned and grabbed my hand. "You were bitten, so you should rest too," he argued, making me shake my head.

"Doctor Sam was able to retract the venom out of my system, so I'm perfectly fine," I explained, kissing his lips. "You're the one who was injected with silver, so you need to rest. I'll go make breakfast, then come back."

Mason's frown deepened and he sighed. "Fine, but hurry up. I don't want you away from me."

His words brought a smile on my lips and I leaned down, placing a gentle kiss on his soft lips again. I pulled away and laid my forehead against his, looking into his beautiful eyes.

"Don't worry. I'll be right back," I told him.

"Wait," he spoke.

"Yeah?"

"Whose shirt is that?" he questioned, pointing at the shirt I was wearing.

I looked down and realized I was still wearing Ameer's shirt. I hadn't had the time to change. Mason looked like he just realized that too. His eyes turned dark, and he didn't look too pleased that I was wearing another man's shirt.

I smiled softly at him and shrugged. "This is Ameer's," I replied.

"Who's Ameer?" he growled, sitting up. I rolled my eyes and walked up to him, pushing his chest again.

"He's one of the warriors who arrived here three days ago." I looked back at the shirt, then at a frowning Mason. "He let me wear it yesterday when we were attacked because I shifted into my wolf and had no clothes on."

Mason's eyes narrowed and his chest rumbled. He didn't look too happy. He nodded and pointed at his closet. "Wear something of mine," he murmured. I raised a brow and shook my head.

"I'm going to my room to change anyway," I told him. His eyes roamed down my body before he looked at my eyes. He growled and shook his head.

"You're not going outside like that. Just wear my clothes, then go to your room and change," he ordered. I glanced at the shirt, then at his closet before nodding. "I have to move her stuff to my room," he muttered to himself, making my eyes widen. He looked at me and smiled sheepishly, his hard features fully disappearing.

I rolled my eyes but smiled a goofy smile. I opened his closet and pulled out the smallest shirt and sports shorts I could find.

I guess these will do.

I changed into his clothes in the bathroom, smiling because his scent was all over them. I inhaled his scent and sighed in satisfaction. I looked at the mirror and cringed at the sight. I just hoped I wouldn't run into someone. They would surely think differently if they saw me in Mason's clothes.

I shook my head and walked out. Mason's eyes widened once he laid eyes on me and smiled. "You look good in my clothes," he murmured, his eyes darkened with lust. I smiled at that.

"I'll be back," I spoke, walking out of his room. I sighed in relief as I noticed there weren't any pack members in the hallway. Surely if someone saw me, they would think I was doing the walk of shame. I shook my head and ran to my room.

When I got inside, I let out a deep breath. I grabbed some clothes and ran to the bathroom. As soon as I was done, I went to the kitchen.

I was greeted by Anna, Ameer, and the other pack members. I smiled at them. Ameer grinned from ear to ear and pulled me in for a side hug, a cup of coffee in his other hand.

"How's my favorite neighbor doing?" he asked.

"I'm good."

He took a sip of his coffee and shoved the cup in my face, making me frown. "Want some coffee?"

I shook my head. "No tha—"

"Ha! Too bad. It's all mine," he cut me off, making me roll my eyes. He laughed as I glared at him. "I don't share."

"I wasn't asking you to," I muttered and went to Anna. Ameer walked behind me and placed his arm over my shoulder.

"I'm kidding. Here." He raised his coffee in front of my face. "I'll share it with you and you only because we're best friends. By the way, I got the friendship bracelets in my room, but I call dibs on the pink one. You'll get the blue one." He grinned at me and I shook my head.

"No thanks, Ameer." I chuckled, referring to the coffee. He shrugged and took another sip.

"Oh, well, more for me," he murmured before chugging everything down his throat. I rolled my eyes and turned to Anna.

"Hi, Anna."

She smiled at me and nodded in respect. "Hello, Luna," she greeted, making my brows furrow.

"Please. Just Tiana," I told her. Taken aback, she nodded and smiled at me. "Can you please make Mason and I something for breakfast? Since, you know, I don't know how to cook." I smiled sheepishly and scratched the back of my neck.

"Of course," she said, chuckling.

Anna grabbed some stuff from the fridge and cabinets before she started with the breakfast. I glanced at Ameer to see him making more coffee. I raised a brow at him questioningly.

"Didn't you already drink coffee?" I asked.

"I'm addicted. I need at least two cups of this goodness in the morning," he responded, grinning.

"No wonder you're so hyper," I muttered, sure that he heard. He laughed. I looked behind once I heard the kitchen doors open. Crystal entered and walked towards me with a smile on her face.

"Tiana," she greeted, pulling me in for a hug. "How are you?" I pulled away, looking at her.

"Hey, Crystal. I'm fine. How about you?"

"I'm great," she responded and then looked at Anna. "John wants something for breakfast. Can you make something for him?"

"Yes, of course. I'm making something for the alpha, so I'll give you some too," Anna replied.

"Thanks, Anna." Crystal kissed her cheek before turning to me. We talked until Anna was done placing the food on the trays.

We grabbed them and thanked her before we walked out of the kitchen together.

We were walking down the hall when we saw Mason run out of the pack house. I looked at Crystal in confusion and shock.

He's supposed to be in bed. What is he doing?

"Mason, where are you going?" I yelled but Mason didn't stop. I huffed before placing the tray on a table and rushing to get to him, Crystal following behind. We walked out of the pack house, and I spotted him in the distance with a group of men that I had never seen before.

With my brows furrowed, I ran to him to give him a piece of my mind and then stopped dead in my tracks, completely shocked at who I was seeing in front of me. My breath was caught in my throat and my eyes widened. I felt my heart aggressively beat against my rib cage. Crystal stopped beside me and stared at me weirdly.

"Tiana, what's wrong?" she asked, placing her hand on my arm. I glanced at her before I brought my stare back to the man who was looking at me with shock evident in his eyes, eyes that were reflecting my own.

"Tiana?" he whispered, moving a step closer to me. I opened my mouth, but no words came out. I felt a lump in my throat as a lone tear slipped out of my eyes.

"Z-Zander?" I whispered, my voice cracked. Mason looked at me with confusion. Crystal's eyes widened and her mouth hung open.

"Zander?" she muttered. "Zander? As in your first mate? I thought he was dead."

I held in my breath as I turned to look at the person who I thought was long gone and forever out of my life.

"I thought so too."

CHAPTER 57

Two Years Ago

I stalked towards the pack house, angry and annoyed, while wiping away the tears on my cheeks and letting out a whimper. When I opened the door, my mom greeted me.

"Hey, honey. How was school?"

I tried to hide my overwhelming emotions and smiled. "Hi, Mom," I muttered. "It was okay." She had a confused look on her face, but I ignored it and walked up the stairs, trying to hold back the tears that threatened to escape.

"Tiana, what's wrong?" I heard her yell but I ignored her again and ran to my room. I slammed the door shut and jumped on my bed, letting out a muffled scream against my pillow. A tear slipped out my eye as I recalled how Zander treated me.

This is getting out of hand.

I sat up and ran my hand through my hair, feeling more frustrated as time went by. I couldn't believe him. I couldn't believe he was acting like this. Since when did this start? I growled and rubbed my face in frustration.

I whipped my head to the direction of where my door was when I heard it open. Adam came walking in with a frown on his face, and once he saw my state, his frown deepened.

"Tiana?" he murmured as he closed the door behind him. He sat on my bed and I immediately pulled him into a hug. "What happened?" he asked, rubbing my back. I sighed and looked down at my hand.

"Zander happened," I whispered, glancing at him. He huffed and shook his head.

"I passed by him a while ago and he gave me his hate glare, but it was more intense than usual, so I guessed something happened between you two," he said. I frowned at his words and couldn't stop the feeling of guilt that came over me. It wasn't hard to notice that Zander wasn't fond of Adam. Hell, he hated him. It was really hard to have a mate that hated your best friend.

Adam never did anything to Zander, yet he still despised him. Zander was jealous of Adam, actually not just Adam but any male who I was with or talked to. Over time, Zander grew possessive and protective, leading to problems in our relationship. And he hated that I was best friends with a man. He never directly hurt Adam. He would only throw words at him from here and there. But to the other males? Yes, he definitely would.

I guessed he never touched him because he knew Adam was very close to me.

"What happened this time?" Adam asked, catching me out of my thoughts. I looked at him and sighed.

"I'm getting tired of his behavior, Adam," I whispered, shaking my head. "I was about to leave school when a new student asked me where the exit was. So since I was leaving, I decided to walk him out. And guess who saw me with that boy?"

"Zander . . ." Adam nodded and I let out a long sigh. "What did he do to the boy?"

I winced and ran my hand through my messy hair as I remembered the scene. I huffed out, the familiar guilt I had gotten used to coming over me.

"He stalked towards us and literally punched the poor guy," I responded, clenching my fist. "I wouldn't be surprised if the boy changed schools and never showed his face ever again."

Adam shook his head and pulled me closer to him, wrapping his arms around me. "What did you do after that?" he asked.

I looked at him and lowered my head. "We had the usual. We fought, argued, and yelled at each other." I released a long breath from out of my chest. "Adam, I don't know what I'm going to do with him anymore."

Adam's arms tightened around me and he placed his chin on the top of my head, rubbing his hand on my back in a soothing manner. "Maybe you have to let him go," he whispered, making my eyes widen and my mouth hung open.

"What are you talking about?" I gaped at him. "Let him go? He's my mate, remember?"

He shook his head and sighed. "He's your angel side's mate. Since both of you are half angel and half werewolf, your werewolf mate is somewhere out there. Maybe this mate isn't healthy for you," he explained. I looked down at my hand as I comprehended his words. He was right. I did have another mate and maybe he would treat me better than Zander.

But what if I gave Zander up and never found someone else to love me like he did?

Zander was the beta's son who lived away with his mother, and months ago, they came back to stay in the pack house. We immediately knew we were mates from our scents and attraction. At first, I thought he was my werewolf mate but my werewolf disagreed. It was my mom who told us that angels had mates as well, and when the time came, we would have to choose between the two, which would be really hard.

And I wasn't looking forward to that day.

"What if I never find him?" I whispered, looking at Adam. "What if Zander doesn't give me up? You know him, he is really possessive over me."

Adam smiled at me and tucked my hair behind my ear. "I'm not sure about that, Tiana. But if you are destined to be with Zander or your werewolf mate, then you will end up with one of them. You won't know till you try," he said softly. I let out a loud huff and rubbed my face with my hands.

"What are you saying exactly?" I asked, confused.

"Reject him. He doesn't deserve you. Someone better does," he responded.

I bit my lip and registered his words in my head. It was a really hard decision to make. Should I do it? Did I even love Zander? I mean, we only met a couple of months ago and we were still young, so I didn't even know what love was. Before I could even open my mouth and reply, a booming voice made us snap our heads to the direction of my bedroom door.

Zander was standing right outside my room, raging with anger. His jaw and fist were clenched as loud growls emerged from within his chest. He roared and entered my room while Adam and I separated.

"You bastard!" He stalked towards Adam. "How dare you drill those thoughts into my mate's head?" Adam and I stood up as we stared at Zander. Never in my life had I seen Zander this hateful. Yes, I had seen him angry, but to this extent? Never.

My eyes widened in worry as he grabbed Adam by his shirt and slammed him against the wall, causing a gasp to escape my mouth. "You want her to reject me?" he yelled, punching Adam's jaw. I ran up to Zander and tried to pull him away but he only pushed me, making me fall to the ground.

"Why? So you could have her to yourself?" he roared, throwing Adam to the ground and kicking him. "She's mine! Nobody else can have her." I gasped as I saw Adam's bloody state. Since Zander was the beta's son, it meant he was stronger than Adam. Adam tried fighting back but Zander was faster than him, causing him to repeatedly hit the ground.

I stood on my feet and ran up to them. "Zander!" I cried as he continued to throw stronger punches. "You're going to kill him! Stop!"

Zander whipped his head to me, and something dangerous glinted in his eyes. He growled and looked at Adam. "That's what I'm going to do." He shifted into his wolf, catching me by surprise.

I placed my hands over my mouth as he stalked towards Adam, who was on the verge of passing out. "Zander, no!" I yelled, shielding Adam. "Don't you dare! If you lay another hand on him, then consider us over!"

Zander's eyes darkened and a loud growl emerged from his chest. He used his head to push me aside aggressively, throwing me to the ground.

I whipped my head up and all the air was stuck in my throat as I saw Zander sink his teeth into Adam's neck. It was like time stopped at that moment. Tears fell out of my eyes as I was stuck in my place, paralyzed. A muffled cry escaped my lips as Adam cried out in pain.

It all happened so fast. One second, Zander was on top of Adam and the other, a huge wolf pushed Zander away. I watched in relief as the alpha growled at Zander, making him whimper in submission. I ran to Adam and cried as I saw him drown in his own blood.

"No, no, no!" I shook my head as tears fell out of my eyes. "Please don't die! Please!"

Immediately, guards came and took Zander away. I watched as the pack doctor took Adam to his infirmary. I shook my head and cried into my hands, praying that nothing bad would happen to him.

As for Zander, I knew what would happen to him. He tried to kill a pack member, which was against the rules, and the punishment was death.

I felt my heart break at the thought of the two. I was terrified for Adam, and the thought of losing my best friend was unbearable. Zander might deserve the punishment, but I couldn't deny the fact that my heart broke knowing I would lose my mate. Or worse, I would lose both of them.

I cried in my room for hours, too nervous to check on Adam. After what seemed like ages, my bedroom door opened and my mother walked in. She immediately pulled me in for a hug, and I cried on her chest. She rubbed my back in a soothing manner. After I cried for who knows how long, I pulled away and stared at my mother.

"Shhh, darling, it will be okay. Everything's going to be okay," she whispered, wiping the tears on my cheeks.

"How . . ." I stopped to catch my breath. "How's Adam?" I asked, even though I was too afraid to know the answer.

My mom tucked my hair behind my ear. "The bite is deep, so he will be out for a couple of days," she said. "He was on the verge of death, but he is out of danger now."

My tears slip out of my eyes all over again. Hearing he was on the verge of death broke me. "I want to see him," I whispered.

"Then come on. Let's go."

We walked towards the infirmary. I sucked in a breath as I saw the alpha approaching with a sympathetic look on his face. He stopped in front of us, and I felt my heart beating violently.

"Tiana."

"Alpha," I said, bowing.

He cleared his throat and shook his head. "I'm sorry for your loss," he said. "Your mate is dead. He tried to escape the borders, and my men killed him on the spot. He was going to die anyway for going against our rules. I know it is hard. My beta is having a hard time as well, but what was done is done."

My heart skipped a beat, and a lone tear ran down my cheek. "He tried to escape?" I asked. The alpha nodded and patted my shoulder softly.

"Yes, he tried to escape his punishment," he responded. I choked on my own breath and my mother's arm tightened around my shoulder. "I'm sorry." And with that, he walked past us, leaving me standing there in pure shock.

"He tried to escape his punishment," I repeated it to myself, tears escaping my already red eyes. "What a coward." I shook my head and wiped the tears off my cheek. I couldn't believe him. I couldn't believe he tried to kill my best friend, and I couldn't believe he tried to escape and think of never returning.

I thought a mate was supposed to understand you and never leave your side? I thought a mate was supposed to accept you and the people around you? I thought a mate was supposed to love his other half no matter what happened and sacrifice his emotions, even if it was jealousy or hatred?

If this was how mate bond worked, then I didn't want another one.

* * *

Unwanted memories flashed in my mind, hitting me like a slap to the face. It was like time stopped as I stared into Zander' eyes, eyes I thought I would never see again. My head started to ache as questions began piling up and as I tried to comprehend everything.

Zander is alive. He never died.

Mason stared at us in shock and anger after hearing what Crystal had said. I looked at him, knowing he was feeling many emotions all at once. His fist was clenched and his eyes were wide.

Zander took another step closer to me, making me step back. "Tiana," he breathed out.

"You're supposed to be dead," I hissed, my eyes welling up in anger. "How are you alive?" I yelled. He winced at the loudness of my voice and bowed in shame.

Mason came close and I looked at him, my vision blurry. He looked angry and confused, yet he still grabbed my hand to comfort me. I looked at Zander to see him glaring at our joined hands, making me want to scoff. He brought his eyes to me, which was filled with guilt.

"I'm sorry, Tiana. The alpha let me go that day so they wouldn't have to kill me. My dad didn't want me to die, and neither did I."

I sucked in a breath and took a step away from everyone, shaking my head in disbelief.

Everything was a lie.

A tear slipped out of my eye. I ran away from them and entered the pack house, my heart beating aggressively against my ribcage. I slammed my door and locked it. I leaned against the wall and let my tears fall freely. Everything hit me, and it was difficult to take it all at once.

I cried for the days when I thought I lost my mate, and I cried for the days that I blamed myself for Adam's injuries. I cried as my memories haunted me all over again. I couldn't believe he ran away and left me on my own to suffer.

A loud knock on my door brought me out of my thoughts, and the scent told me it was Mason.

"Tiana, please open the door," he said. I shook my head, even though he couldn't see me. I couldn't face him. I was too ashamed. I never told him the truth. Only God knew what he was feeling right now.

"M-Mason, leave," I stuttered as more tears fell out of my eyes.

"No, Tiana. I won't leave," he argued. "Please open up so we can talk."

I cried unceasingly and wished Adam was here. He was the only one who helped me go through this in the past. I needed him here, more than anything. I wiped my tears as Mason kept begging me to open the door. I sucked in a breath and felt my heart break at his weak voice.

"Get me Adam," I said and everything went silent for a second.

"Adam?" he asked, sounding disappointed by the fact that I chose to have Adam by my side instead of him.

"Yes. Please get me Adam."

Mason was hurt, and I know it. I didn't want him to feel that way, but I had to see Adam. He was the only one I could talk with. I needed some time before I could face Mason, before I could explain everything to him.

"If I get Adam, w-will you talk to me?" he asked, his voice cracked. My heart fell to my stomach and I closed my eyes, leaning my head against the wall.

"Yes I will," I responded.

He went silent again before he spoke, "Fine. I'll get him."

CHAPTER 58

I stared at the blank wall for hours and sat on the floor doing nothing. Everything around me was silent, the only thing I could hear was my slow breathing. I kept zoning out, not concentrating on anything, even the people outside my door that checked up on me every once in a while. Everything was a blur.

Ameer and Lina came by, trying to convince me to open the door but I didn't budge. I just stayed silent and ignored them, crawling deep into my little world.

I felt numb. It seemed like I was in some kind of a nightmare, where the dead came back to life. That's how I was feeling. When Zander reappeared, it was like all my nightmares had awakened, hitting me like a splash of cold water.

The pain of the memories that I had locked in my heart for two years came back—the memories of when Adam was attacked and the guilt that would devour me every time I remembered it. I blamed myself for every injury Adam had got. I blamed myself for his coma that had lasted a week. Even when he had woken up, I still blamed myself.

The pain of the heartbreak that I went through for losing my mate seemed fresh in my heart. I hated him because it was like a piece of me had been killed at his betrayal. It felt like he had stabbed me in the back for harming someone so dear to my heart. I felt even more betrayed that he had lied to everyone, especially to me. Because of him, I had gone through hell.

How was he able to live for two years knowing I thought he was dead? How was he able to stay away from me that long, and why? Did he care more about his safety than his mate's feelings? Clearly yes! I loathed him then, and I loathed him even more now. I wanted him out of my life.

I now realized how stupid I was for trying to resist my mate bond with Mason, due to my fear of getting stabbed in the back, the same way Zander had done. I was pathetic for believing that. Mason was nothing like Zander, and I realized that too late. If it weren't for my stubbornness, we would have been together a long time ago.

Someone aggressively knocking on my door tore me away from my thoughts. After taking a whiff of air, I knew it was Adam.

"Tiana," he called. "I'm here. Please open the door."

I stood up immediately, balancing myself with the wall as my head started to spin. I shook my head and opened the door to see Adam looking at me with nothing but worry in his eyes. He engulfed me in a huge bear hug.

I wrapped my arms around his body and felt my eyes water by his presence. I missed him, even though it had only been three days since I last saw him. I held back my tears as he pulled away from the hug and stared at me. He gently tugged me into the room and closed the door behind him.

"Tiana," he whispered, holding my hand. "I missed you, princess."

I sucked in a breath and nodded. "I missed you too," I croaked, my voice raspy.

Adam pulled me towards my bed and we sat down. "Mason told me everything," he said, clenching his fist as his eyes darkened severely. "He also said you wouldn't speak to anyone, so he ordered me to come."

I looked down at my hands and bit my lip, my eyes began to blur due to my tears.

"Adam . . ." I whimpered. "He is back. He never died." By now, my tears fell out of my eyes. Adam wiped them off my wet cheeks, a low growl emerging from within his chest.

"I know," he said. "I'm so sorry, Tiana. I'm sorry this is happening to you. I wish he died that day so you wouldn't have to go through the pain all over again." He pulled me so I was laying my head on his chest. I whimpered and shook my head.

"What is he doing here? What is he back in my life?" I cried. "Why did he have to show up after everything?"

"Shhh. It's okay, Tiana," Adam whispered as he held me tighter. "He won't come back into your life, if you don't want him to."

I looked at Adam and frowned. "Of course I don't want him back in my life, not after I found Mason, not after everything," I exclaimed, making him smile softly at me. He tucked my hair behind my ear and nodded.

"Don't let him get to you. If you're happy with Mason, then don't let him affect your relationship, dead or alive." He stared at me comfortingly. I nodded, wiping my tears away.

"You are right," I agreed but looked at Adam in confusion, my brows furrowed. "Did Mason tell you why he came to the pack?"

"Yes. Zander is a member of the Black Blood. Alpha Alex sent him here to check on Mason after he heard that he was attacked by a vampire," he explained, making my eyes widen.

He is a member of our allied pack? I thought to myself.

"But don't worry, he is gone now. I'm going to make sure he doesn't step foot in this pack ever again." Adam smiled at me, making me return it.

I soon frowned as I thought about Mason. I bit my lip and then sighed. "How's Mason?" I asked sadly.

"He looked horrible when I saw him. I believe he thinks you are going to leave him," he responded, making my mouth hang open.

"What?" I gaped. I would never leave Mason. He was the best thing that had ever happened to me. "Why would he think that?"

Adam nodded with a sad gaze. "Yes. What else do you expect him to think? You never told him you had another mate, and then out of nowhere, he showed up. You just got together, so he thinks you will leave him without a second thought. Well, that's what I assumed when I saw his face," he explained.

I frowned and stood up, staring at Adam in shock. "I . . ." I stammered. "I can't let him think like that."

Adam smiled and nodded, standing up as well. "Then don't. Go tell him everything," he said. "Go tell him you love him."

I smiled at him and nodded, pulling him in for a hug. We soon pulled away and I could've sworn I saw a sad glint in his eyes, which made me confused. Ignoring it, I stepped back and gave him another smile.

"Thanks, Adam. I knew I would feel a lot better once I talked to you."

He gave me a boyish grin. "Of course you would. Did you forget we're best friends?"

"How could I? I'll see you later. I'm going to find Mason."

Adam chuckled, shooing me with his hands. I gave him one last smile before I ran out my room and towards Mason's.

As soon as I was in front of Mason's room, I heard a soft whimper. My eyes widened. I felt my heart fall to my stomach and my heart skip a beat. Gulping, I was about to twist the doorknob when I heard Mason say something.

"She's going to fucking leave me." His voice cracked at the end, then things drastically dropped to the floor. "She's leaving me . . ." His words turned into soft whispers.

I felt a lump in my throat as I opened the door. His room was a complete mess. The curtains were shut, preventing any light from entering.

I was taken aback as I laid eyes on Mason. His head snapped to me, making me see his puffy red eyes, which were filled with tears. My heart tore at the sight of him. He immediately stood up, staring at me in shock. I entered his room silently, closing the door behind me.

"Mason," I whispered, stepping closer to him.

"Tiana . . ."

Within seconds, he wrapped his strong arms around my waist, pulling me close to his chest. He automatically dug his nose into my neck as he let out muffled whimpers.

"Tiana . . ." His voice cracked.

Something dampened my neck, making my eyes widen. I held him tight as he cried.

"D-don't leave me," he whispered. "Please. I'll do anything." Tears fell out of my eyes. Him crying broke my heart, a sight I couldn't handle. I would never want to see him like this ever again.

I never once thought Mason was capable of crying, but it looked like even the toughest people in this world shed tears. And it isn't something to be shameful about.

"Shhh . . ." I ran my hand through his hair. "I won't leave you. I never will." His soft cries muffled, and he raised his head so he was looking at me. His eyes were filled with unshed tears, and his cheeks were wet. I gently wiped them, staring into his beautiful orbs.

"You won't?" he whispered. I smiled softly at him and nodded, placing a kiss on his lips. He reminded me of a broken child who was seeking comfort and someone to love him.

"I won't. Mason, I love you and I'm never leaving you," I answered. He closed his eyes, taking a deep breath. Once he opened them, he pulled me towards him once again, tightening his arms around me.

"I-I thought you would leave me," he croaked as he inhaled my scent. I shook my head and placed another kiss on his lips.

"I would never do that," I whispered. He looked at me with sadness and relief.

"What about your first mate?" He frowned. "You would pick me over him?" I bit my lip and nodded.

"Yes, I would. I'm sorry I never told you about him. I just didn't think I was ready," I explained. "Zander is my angel side's mate. And two years ago, he tried to kill Adam. I always felt like he was crazy. The alpha lied to us, saying he was dead, but it turned out, he never died. The alpha sent him away to Black Blood since he was the beta's son."

Mason looked at me with wide eyes. I sighed and ran my hand through his hair, looking at him. "I'm sorry I shut you out and didn't talk to you sooner. I was just in a state of shock. I don't ever want to see him again. He wasn't the mate he was supposed to be, and he ruined my life," I explained. "And I love you, not him."

Mason nodded. "I won't let him step foot into this pack ever again. I won't let him take you away from me," he promised, clenching his jaw as he said those words. "I love you beyond words, and I'm not going to let someone take you away from me."

I smiled at him, kissing him on the lips. "Don't," I whispered.

His hands tightened around my waist as he kissed me again, but full with passion this time. As soon as we were out of breath, we pulled away and he stared into my eyes, smiling at me.

"I love you, Tiana," he whispered softly.

"I love you too."

CHAPTER 59

"Do you have to leave?" I muttered, looking at Adam with a pout on my lips. He chuckled and pulled me in for a hug.

"Yes, Tiana. I have to," he responded, making me sigh in defeat. We pulled away and he offered me a sad smile, placing his hand on my shoulder. "Don't be sad. I'll come back to visit." I smiled at him, punching him softly on the chest.

"Thanks for everything, idiot," I joked. He raised a brow at me and pouted, a sad expression on his features.

"Idiot? Is that what you say to your best friend who's leaving?" he asked. I nodded and giggled once he started tickling me, making me beg for him to stop.

"Okay, okay! You're not an idiot," I gasped. He stopped and smiled goofily, making me laugh out loud. I ran my hand through my hair and breathed in deeply. Adam pulled me in for another hug and I sighed against his chest, wrapping my arms around his body.

We were out in the yard, ready to say goodbye to Adam. Unfortunately, he couldn't stay longer. I frowned as I thought of that. If only he could stay for a couple of days.

I sighed again as I thought about today. Today was something I would like to erase from my memory. I was still overwhelmed and shaking, but thankfully Adam and Mason calmed me down.

Someone grabbed my hand and pulled me away from Adam, making us break the hug. From the sparks, I knew it was Mason. I looked at him and smiled. He smiled back before looking at Adam and frowning. Adam let out an awkward cough and took a step back.

"I'll see you later, Tiana," Adam whispered as a couple of guards walked up to us to accompany him back to the other pack. I waved at him, upset.

"Bye, Adam."

Adam smiled at me one more time before walking away.

"Adam," Mason called out, making him stop and turn around. I furrowed my brows at Mason in confusion. He cleared his throat and glanced at me, then at Adam. "Thanks for everything," he said lowly.

Adam's eyes widened and his lips broke out into a grin. "Anytime, Alpha," he spoke before he continued his way.

I smiled at Mason and he looked at me, placing a gentle kiss on my lips. We soon pulled away and stared at each other.

We were pulled out of our gaze when a guard came running towards us. Mason snapped his head at him and furrowed his brows.

"Alpha," the guard breathed out, catching his breath. He stood straight and looked at Mason.

"What is it?" Mason asked, looking serious. The guard glanced at me, then back at Mason before speaking.

"There is a man from the Black Blood Pack who demands to see the luna," the guard said, making my eyes widen. "He's right outside the borders."

Mason's eyes narrowed and a low growl escaped his lips. I grabbed his hand to calm him down. Mason opened his mouth to say something but stopped when we heard someone shouting.

"Come back here," a man yelled. "You're not supposed to be here without the alpha's permission!"

Mason and I whipped our heads to where the yell was coming from.

"Fuck off," someone shouted. "I'm here to see my mate!"

My eyes widened as I recognized the voice. My grip on Mason's hand tightened and Mason immediately wrapped his arm around my waist, pulling me close to him.

Out of nowhere, two guards came out from the woods as they tried to pull an angry Zander away from us. My mouth opened as I stared at him. His and my eyes locked, something in his eyes glinted. Mason's hold tightened, making me glance at him.

He was glaring at Zander with pure hatred. I looked back to see Zander yelling at the guards before he glanced at me. His eyes went to the hold Mason had on me, a growl escaping his chest. Zander's eyes darkened, and he pushed the guards off him before stalking towards us in fury.

What is he doing here? Who does he think he is, walking into this pack like he owns it?

"What are you doing on my land?" Mason growled as Zander walked closer to us. Zander's eyes darkened, and he stared at us, another growl escaping his lips.

"What are you doing with my mate?" he yelled, glaring at me. I furrowed my brows in anger.

Who does he think he is? I opened my mouth, ready to say something when Mason beat me to it.

"She's not your mate," he roared, pushing me behind him as he stepped closer to Zander. "She's my mate."

Zander's eyes widened, furrowing his brows in anger. "Your mate?" he growled. "She's not your mate! She's mine!"

Before I could stop him, Mason took a step forward and threw a punch to his jaw, making him fall to the ground. Growling, Zander gripped his jaw as his eyes darkened severely.

"She's mine," Mason growled, stepping closer to him. "She will stay mine, and don't even think she'll ever be yours."

Zander stood on his feet, staring at the both of us in anger. He growled and looked at me. "How could you do that? You're supposed to be mine!" His eyes darkened once he laid eyes on my mark. He let out another growl.

"Do what?" I yelled, narrowing my eyes on him in anger. "You're the one who left me. You're the one who betrayed me. Do you really expect me to come running back into your arms after finding out you're alive?" I growled. Zander's eyes widened and he took a step towards me, making me step back. "I have a mate, and it's not you. So leave us alone and stay away from our lives."

Zander looked at me in disbelief before he glanced at Mason. "This is your mate?" he growled, pointing at Mason. "He's a monster," he yelled. "You'd choose a monster over me?"

I growled in anger and stalked towards him, but Mason's grip on me prevented me.

"The only monster here is you," I hissed, glaring at him. "You ruined my life, and the only thing Mason did was make my life better. So fuck off, Zander!"

Zander's jaw clenched and he took a step forward, looking into Mason's eyes. A growl emerged from within his chest before he looked at me. "Your mate over here," he spoke, pointing at Mason, "is a monster. Have you forgotten what he does? He kills people. He killed his fucking parents."

My eyes widened as those words escaped his lips, and before I could comprehend it, Mason leaped at him and threw a punch to his face. Zander fell to the ground for the second time today, groaning in pain.

Mason threw a couple more punches before he got up and glared at the guards. The guards immediately grabbed Zander, pulling him away. Zander looked at me before looking at Mason. His eyes went back on me and they darkened with rage.

"I'll get you back," he yelled. "I won't let anyone else have you."

I cringed at his words and Mason wrapped his arms around me, pulling me to his chest. When Zander was out of sight, I let out a big sigh and closed my eyes, inhaling Mason's scent.

"Don't worry, Tiana," Mason whispered in my ear, making my nerves relax. "I won't let him touch a strand of your hair."

I smiled softly and nodded, looking at Mason with adoration. His eyes sparkled with love and his hands tightened around me.

"I know," I spoke. "I believe in you." He leaned in and placed a gentle kiss on my lips. I sighed as I wrapped my hands around his neck. Before we could deepen the kiss, he stopped and pulled away abruptly. My brows furrowed as I stared at him in confusion.

Mason's eyes hardened before they softened with a sad glint in his eyes. I frowned as I stared at him. Mason avoided my eyes and stared somewhere else. My frown deepened and I cupped his cheek, pulling his attention towards me.

"Mason," I whispered, "what's wrong?" He looked at me before he sighed.

"Tiana, I don't want you to think badly of me," he finally spoke. "I don't want you thinking of me as a monster." My eyes widened when I caught on to what he was trying to say.

"No, Mason. I would never think badly of you. I don't care about the rumors," I exclaimed, shaking my head. His eye softened and his arms around me tightened.

"But some of those rumors are true," he whispered. "I've killed people before. Maybe I am a monster." I shook my head and cupped his face in my hands, pulling him closer to me.

"I don't care what you've done. Those are all in the past," I argued. "And even if you are a monster, you're my monster." I grinned. His pouting lips turned into a grin, making me smile. I pulled him towards me and kissed his lips. His lips moved against mine perfectly. He sighed before pulling away.

"I think it's time for you to know everything, everything about my past," he whispered.

I shook my head and frowned. "Mason, if you're not ready, then you don't have to."

"No more secrets. I don't want anything between us," he said gently. I bit my lip and nodded, running my hand through his hair.

"Okay, no more secrets."

"Lina and I didn't have a great childhood," he started, looking at me with a sad expression. Guessing the memories wasn't something he would like to remember, I held his hand.

"My father wasn't the mate he was supposed to be to my mother. In front of everyone, he was perfect, but behind doors, he was a whole different person. He was abusive, not just physically but mentally. My mother didn't deserve all that, neither did Lina and I. My mother was the main target, but once in a while, it was us," he continued, his eyes darkening.

"One day, my father turned all his anger on Lina. He beat her to the verge of death. I tried to stop him, but I wasn't strong enough. My mother grabbed a chair and hit him with it, saving Lina's life. He got angry, really angry so he . . ." He stopped, closing his eyes before staring at me with a sad, broken expression. A lone tear fell to his cheek.

"He killed her," he whispered and my eyes widened.

"I was always a mommy's boy. She was my everything, along with Lina. That day turned me into a different person, and on that night, while he was asleep, I mustered all the strength I had and tried to kill him. But in the end, I didn't have the courage. He then started to weaken since he lost his mate. Even though he never cared about her, his wolf did. So I was able to claim the alpha position," he explained. "Those rumors that I killed my parents are false. I didn't kill them."

I felt my heart drop. I couldn't imagine him and Lina going through that. "What happened to your father?" I asked. He sighed, gulping.

"Here, I'll show you," he whispered, tugging my hand. I frowned but walked beside him. We stopped in front of the dungeon and he turned to look at me.

"I threw him here. I knew killing him would be an easy way out, so I made him suffer," he spoke. "I wanted him to wish he was dead, to wish he was not the man he was." I nodded slowly, registering everything in my head.

All I wanted to do right now was pull him in for a hug. What he was doing to his father didn't make me feel any different about him. His father deserved it all.

I held his hand and gave it a tight squeeze. He smiled at me and turned around, pulling me away from the doors. I frowned and shook my head, pulling him back. "I want to see him," I spoke gently. His eyes widened and he immediately shook his head.

"No. I can't let you see him," he whispered.

"Please. I want to know everything about you. I want to see the man who made you go through hell." Mason sighed and then nodded.

"Fine, but only from afar. I don't want you near him." He opened the dungeon, pulling me inside. I gulped as the smell of blood and death filled my nostrils. Cringing, I ignored it and walked behind Mason. He stopped and I stepped beside him.

His eyes were pitch-black. I followed his stare and looked at a dark cell. Squinting, I saw a skinny body lying on the floor. I looked around, and that's when I noticed it was the cell I had been locked in.

The man started to groan. Mason wrapped his arm around my waist and pulled me close to him for comfort. Out of nowhere, the man started screaming. "Someone get me food! I'm starving," he yelled.

I heard that voice before.

And that's when it hit me. He was the man that Adam and I had talked to when we were here. The man was Mason's father.

"I've been here for years, but I have never found a way out. I know the pack like the back of my hand, yet I never managed to get out."

Now it all made sense. He was the alpha yet he couldn't get out, so he had discouraged us from the thought of escaping.

Mason tugged my hand as the man in front of us continued to scream. I looked at him and nodded, tightening my hold on him. I glanced one more time at the cell before we turned around and walked out the dungeons. I deeply inhaled before looking at Mason with a sad expression.

"I'm sorry you had to go through all that," I whispered. He smiled at me and shook his head.

"Don't be. Now that you're in my life, I'm extremely happy."

I smiled at his words and kissed him. "Me too," I whispered. He placed another gentle kiss on my lips before we walked hand in hand towards the pack house.

CHAPTER 60

Hearing a knock at my door, I got up and opened it to see Mason. I smiled and he pecked my cheek. He stared at me, a small smile crawling onto his face.

"Good morning," he greeted, grabbing my hand. "Are you hungry?"

"Yes. Actually, I'm starving," I responded and he chuckled.

"Then let's go. I'll make us breakfast," he said, pulling me out of the room. We walked hand in hand towards the kitchen in comfortable silence.

It's been a week since I last saw Zander and since Mason told me about his past. Things had grown stronger between us, and I couldn't wish for anything better.

In the kitchen, we were greeted by a couple of pack members. I gave them a smile before I sat on a stool and Mason walked towards the fridge.

"What does my luna want to eat today?" he asked, making me giggle. I could've sworn I heard a couple of *awws*, which made my cheeks heat up. Mason's lips curved up. I shrugged, tucking my hair behind my ear.

"I don't know. Pancakes?"

He nodded and walked towards the cabinet, pulling out a couple of stuff. I watched him make the batter with a small smile on my face, making my stomach rumble. Watching him cook became my routine since I didn't know how.

As soon as he was done with the batter, I watched him flip the pancakes in awe. He didn't look like an alpha at the moment. He looked like a cute, cuddly bear who loved life.

"You never told me. Who taught you how to cook?" I asked, stepping closer to him. He glanced at me, smiling sadly. He sighed and looked back at the pile of pancakes that were now on a plate.

"My mother," he whispered. I frowned and grabbed his hand, squeezing it. "She loved to cook. I always watched her, and that's how I learned." I nodded and placed my head on his shoulder. He smiled at me and placed a kiss on my forehead.

"She sounds lovely," I whispered.

"Yes, she was."

I cupped his face and pulled him towards me, placing a soft kiss on his lips. "Mason," I whispered. "You can always talk to me about anything. I'm here for you." His lips curved into a small smile and he nodded.

"I know," he whispered. "Thank you."

Placing one last kiss on my lips, he turned around and grabbed the plate of pancakes. We sat down and started eating in silence. I was enjoying my pancakes when Mason placed his fork on the table, staring forward. Furrowing my brows, I looked at him in confusion.

His eyes hardened as he stared into space. After a couple of seconds, he snapped out of it and stood up within an instant. My eyes widened as a low growl emerged from his chest. Standing up, I grabbed his hand.

"Mason," I spoke, "what's wrong?" He looked at me and turned around, rushing towards the kitchen doors. I ran behind him and placed my hand on his arm. "Mason, what's wrong?"

He snapped his head at me. "My men found a vampire right outside the borders. They were able to catch him because he was weak from sun exposure," he answered. My eyes widened as my mouth hung open.

What's up with all the vampires?

"Where are you going?" I asked.

"I'm going to question him," he responded, looking at me. "You stay here." I shook my head and tightened my hold on his arm.

"No. I'm coming with you," I argued.

"Tiana, stay here," he growled lowly. I shook my head again and gave him a pointed look, telling him I wasn't going to budge. "Did you forget I'm the luna? I have the right to come with you and witness what's going to happen. I want answers too."

He sighed in frustration and ran a hand through his hair, shaking his head. "You're impossible," he muttered under his breath. He then turned around and started walking. "Let's go."

We walked towards the dungeons in silence. As soon as we were in front of the doors, the guards nodded and opened them.

The familiar stench of blood and death hit me. Shaking my head, I ignored it and went further into the dark dungeon with Mason by my side. Groans and whimpers echoed inside.

I stopped dead in my tracks as soon as Mason stopped in front of a cell. I winced once I heard hissing. Mason wrapped an arm around my waist and pulled me to him, bringing me comfort. The people guarding the cell nodded at us before opening it.

My eyes widened as I saw the vampire in front of me. He was chained to the wall, hissing and groaning. Mason let out a loud growl and stalked towards him, causing the vampire to snap his head at us. His eyes widened, especially after he laid eyes on me, then he hissed at us. Mason grabbed his neck, slamming his head against the wall.

"P-please let me go," the vampire croaked in fear. "I-I didn't do anything."

"Why were you outside my borders?" Mason sneered, tightening his grip on the vampire's neck.

"I wasn't doing anything," the vampire responded, making Mason growl.

"I'll repeat myself one more time. Why were you outside my border?" Mason yelled, making me cringe. The vampire closed his eyes before glancing at me, then back at Mason. "He . . . he sent me here." My eyes widened and so did Mason's. Mason sneered and let out a low growl.

"Who and why?" Mason questioned. The vampire shook his head, looking scared.

"I-I can't say," he stuttered. "He would kill me if he found out I told you." I furrowed my brows in confusion and Mason slammed his head against the wall again.

"I will kill you if you don't tell me," Mason threatened. "And I'll make your death slow and painful." The vampire's eyes widened in fear and nodded.

"I'll tell you. I'll tell you everything. Just please don't kill me," the vampire begged. Mason nodded for him to continue. "My alpha, he is the one sending us here."

Mason furrowed his brows. "Alpha?" he asked.

The vampire nodded. "Yes. He is an alpha of rogues and vampires combined. He started the pack a long time ago, and it slowly grew. He's sending us here because he wants her," the vampire spoke, gesturing his head at me, making my eyes widen.

An alpha of rogues and vampires wants me?

"Why?" Mason growled, tightening his hold.

The vampire struggled but continued, "I don't know. All I know is he wants her because she's half angel."

Mason hissed, and the vampires pleaded for his mercy.

"I swear. That's all I know. Please don't kill me."

"What is your alpha's name, and where does his pack live?" Mason questioned. The vampire shook his head, making Mason growl at him and slam his head against the wall.

"His name is Alpha Roy. His pack is far from here and it is surrounded by many rogues and vampires, so they can take you down easily," the vampire responded.

Mason's jaw clenched. "Where is his pack?" he asked lowly. The vampire gulped and nodded in defeat. The vampire told him where the pack was, which lay in a deserted land that everyone thought was abandoned.

Frustrated, Mason let go of his neck and let out a loud growl. I ran up to him and grabbed his hands. Mason looked at me and his dark eyes softened. He wrapped his arm around me and pulled me out of the dungeon. He looked mad, very mad. I didn't know what to do, so I just stayed silent. After a while, we walked back to the pack house. I looked at Mason to see him looking forwards, his eyes pitch black. Frowning, I grabbed his hand.

"Mason," I whispered, making him look at me. "What are you going to do?" His eyes softened and he ran a hand through his hair, letting out a deep sigh.

"I don't know, Tiana," he whispered. "I don't know. For now, I'm going to send a couple of my men to investigate that pack. There isn't much I can do. I already tripled the security, yet they still manage to get to us. I don't know anymore."

I bit my lip and looked down. He was right. We had high security yet we still encountered rogues and vampires. And what's more confusing was that they knew when we left the pack or not, like they had eyes following us wherever we went.

Realization hit me, making my eyes widen. My head snapped at Mason, seeing him looking at me intensely.

"Mason," I whispered.

"What is it?" he asked.

"What if someone in the pack has been telling them our every move?" I asked, making his eyes widen. "Think about it. Whenever we get out of the pack, we encounter a rogue or a vampire."

Mason's eyes darken and a low growl escaped his lips. He turned around and stalked towards the pack house. I frowned and followed him.

"Mason," I yelled. "Where are you going?" He glanced at me but continued to walk.

"To my office. I need to think," he whispered.

We walked in the pack house and up the stairs. As soon as we were in front of the office, I smiled softly at him and he sighed, pulling me towards his chest.

"Don't worry," I whispered. "Everything will be okay."

Letting out another sigh, he nodded. "I won't let anything happen to you. I swear," he promised, running his hand through my hair.

"I know," I whispered before pulling away so I could look at him. He nodded and opened his office door.

"I need to be alone for now so I could think. I'll stop by your room and see you."

"Okay," I breathed out. "Let me know if anything happens."

Smiling one last smile, I was walking away when someone ran towards us. A guard walked up to Mason, catching his breath. Mason looked at him questioningly and then the guard stood straight before saying something that made my heart rate speed up.

"Alpha," the guard breathed out. "There are five people outside the pack borders, and two of them claim to be the luna's parents."

CHAPTER 61

"My parents?" I whispered, shock laced my voice. Mason's and the guard's heads snapped at me as I ran to them, their eyes wide in surprise. Mason grabbed my hand in comfort.

"Let them enter," Mason told the guard. The guard nodded and ran off. I stood in my place, shocked. The man's words circled my mind, making my head spin with confusion and many unanswered questions. I always knew my parents were alive, but hearing they were actually here made my heart rate speed up.

I felt my eyes water at the thought of finally seeing my parents after three months. Those three months felt like a year. I just wanted to run into their arms and never leave. At this moment, I realized how much I missed them.

I looked at Mason to see him staring at me. He tugged my hand and started walking. "Come on. Let's go," he whispered gently at me.

Nervous, my body began to shake. What if it wasn't them? What if I was only getting my hopes up? Where were they all this time? Are they okay? Many questions hit me like cold water, making me more nervous by the minute.

While we were walking towards the entrance, Lina came running and immediately pulled me into a hug. I smiled at her softly, but Mason snatched me away from her and gave her a pointed look.

"Not now, Lina," he murmured. "We have to go."

She raised a brow and looked at me. "Where?" she asked.

"Outside," I responded. "I think my parents are here." Her smile grew after an expression of shock crossed her features.

"Oh my gosh! Really?" she gaped. I shrugged, not knowing what to say. Mason tugged my hand and I gave her one last smile before we continued our way. In an attempt to calm myself down, I kept biting my lip.

We walked outside but stopped in our tracks when we saw five people emerging from the trees with several guards by their side. My breath got stuck in my throat and my eyes widened as I realized who they were—my parents, Adam's parents, and an old lady I had never seen before.

My heart sped up as I ran to them. A couple of tears fell out of my eyes as my parents finally engulfed me in a tight bear hug that made me gasp for air. I tightened my arms around them as I buried my head on their shoulders.

"My sweet baby," my mother cooed, trying to hold back her tears. "It's okay. We're finally here."

"Tiana," my father cried. "I missed you, baby. I missed you so much."

I looked at them and their faces held so much happiness, which made my heart full. I wiped the tears from my cheek and smiled at them. "I missed you too," I whispered. "I was so worried something happened to you two."

My mother rubbed my back to comfort me. "Don't worry. We were fine all this time." She smiled, glancing at my father.

My father wiped his tears and nodded. "We'll tell you everything."

I was thrilled I finally saw them. It felt surreal, like this was a nice dream and I was about to wake up any minute now.

Mason came walking towards us. My parents looked at him and nodded in respect, knowing he was the alpha.

"Alpha," they greeted, "thank you for letting us in."

Mason nodded before wrapping his arm around my waist, making my mother's eyes widen. "There is no need to thank me," he spoke, glancing at me before turning his attention back at them. "You are my mate's parents, so you are welcome to stay here."

Their eyes widened and my mother gasped in joy. My father stood there, staring at us in shock, as my mother pulled me in for a hug.

"Oh my gosh! You finally found your mate," she gushed before pulling away. I smiled at her, happy she was accepting us. I glanced at my father, seeing his lips curve up in a smile.

"Who knew the man I told my daughter about would be her mate?" he muttered under his breath before hugging me. I laughed, happy he felt the same.

"I would give him the 'break my daughter's heart, I'll break your face' talk, but he's an alpha," my father whispered in my ear, making me laugh once again. I pulled away and stepped next to Mason as he wrapped his arm around me. Adam's parents stood next to my parents, smiling at us.

"I'm so glad you guys are okay," I whispered, embracing them.

"Oh, honey, we are happy you and my son are okay," Adam's mother spoke before pulling away and looking around. "Where is he? I want to see him." I smiled sadly at them and glanced at Mason. I opened my mouth to speak, but Mason spoke before I could.

"He is a pack warrior serving in our allied pack. I've already contacted him and he is on his way," Mason responded, making my eyes widen. I smiled at him as he kissed my head.

Adam's parents let out a sigh of relief and nodded. I looked at my parents to see them staring at us in awe. I then glanced at the old lady who had remained silent this whole time. I furrowed my brows in confusion and took a whiff of her scent. My eyes widened.

She wasn't a werewolf. She's a witch.

Mason seemed to notice as well as he tightened his arm around me. My parents saw us eyeing her and they took a step closer to us.

"Who's she?" he questioned. "What's a witch doing on my land?"

The old lady remained silent and my mother stepped closer to me, grabbing my hand.

"Can we go inside so we can talk? There is something important she has to tell you both," my mother asked.

The seven of us walked into Mason's office, and before Mason could close the door, Lina came walking in. I raised a brow at her and she shrugged, sitting in front of me.

The witch eyed Lina, her eyes widening but not saying anything.

"What's going on?" Lina whispered to me.

"I don't know," I responded.

"I'm happy you and your parents are reunited," she whispered, glancing at my parents.

I thanked her and turned to my mother, and that's when she started to speak.

"This is Gia, a friend of mine since I was little. Gia can see glimpses of the future since she is a witch. Months ago, Gia saw our pack being under attack so she warned us. We informed the alpha, but he didn't believe it and did nothing. We wanted to inform the pack, but the alpha refused to let us as it was something he thought wasn't going to happen. So Gia gave us an invisibility potion. The day when our pack was attacked, the four of us took it and we managed to escape," my mother spoke, glancing at all of us.

Mason's eyes were wide with surprise and so were mine. I never even knew my mother was friends with a witch.

"We went to her house and stayed there for months. She tried helping us find you, casting a tracking spell. It took three months to track you and Adam down, and when we knew you were here, we came as soon as we could," my mother explained, smiling at me. I smiled at her and glanced at Gia, who looked serious.

"But there's more." My mother glanced before she continued, "Since Gia can see the future, she knows who attacked us that night and sees some glimpses."

Gia then broke her silence. "There is an alpha who owns a pack of vampires and rogues. The alpha's name is Roy. He isn't a werewolf, but a vampire. His son, who is around your age, is a hybrid—half vampire and half werewolf. His name is Asher. A prophecy claims that two hybrids of different kinds can breed the most powerful offspring.

Roy knows this and is looking for a hybrid who is different from his son. As a result of the breeding, the family may grow to be the most powerful supernatural family in the world. So when he found out Tiana is a hybrid, he attacked the pack. He wants you, Tiana." Gia pointed at me. My breath got stuck in my throat and my eyes widened. "Not for him but for his son. He knows where you are. That's why you keep encountering vampires and rogues. They're trying to get you."

Mason let out a loud growl, but the witch shushed him, glaring at him. "I see a big war right around the corner. They will stop at nothing to have her," she croaked.

My parents looked at me with worry, Lina was taken aback, and Mason was furious.

"But it can be prevented," Gia spoke after a while, making us snap our heads at her.

"How?" I asked, my voice laced with hope.

"One person can prevent this war from happening," she whispered. Mason stood up and glared at her.

"Who?" he roared.

Gia glanced at him before her eyes moved across the room and stopped at someone. I followed her gaze and my eyes landed on Lina.

Gina pointed at her. "Her. She can prevent the war."

CHAPTER 62

Surprised, everyone stared at Lina, whose mouth hung open, welcoming any fly that flew in. She reflected the same expression everyone had on their faces.

"What?" Lina questioned, sitting up straight as she stared at Gia. "Me? What do you mean, me? I don't understand." Gia nodded and stood up, walking up to Lina.

Mason's eyes were wide as he registered what Gia said about his sister. It was confusing.

How could Lina prevent the war?

Gia stepped in front of Lina and nodded, staring into her questioning eyes. "Yes, you are the one who can prevent chaos from happening," Gia confirmed.

Lina's eyes roamed the room as everyone remained silent. She then looked back at Gia and gulped. "How?" she asked.

Gia sighed and backed away, shaking her head. "I don't know how. All I saw was you, that's it," she answered. "On the night of the war, you have to be present to prevent it from happening."

Mason stood up, glaring at Gia. "I won't let my sister take any risks of getting hurt," he growled. "She won't come."

Gia glared before walking up to him. "She has to," she hissed. "If you want your people to live and your mate to remain by your side, she has to come."

Mason's eyes softened before they laid on me. I smiled at him to give him reassurance. He then glanced around the room before stopping at Lina, who had a mixture of feelings plastered on her face.

Mason then looked at Gia and his soft eyes hardened. "I won't allow anything bad to happen to my sister," he whispered. Gia sighed and shook her head.

"Nothing will happen to her," she assured. "She'll be fine and safe. The safety of your pack is in her hands."

Mason looked hesitant. "It's her choice, not mine," he whispered. Everyone's eyes turned to Lina, who was staring at Gia.

"I'll do it. I'll go," Lina claimed.

"When will this war happen?" he asked. Gia shrugged and sat back on her chair.

"I don't know. I still haven't seen that yet, but when I do, then you all should be ready," she replied. We all sighed and Mason nodded, walking from behind his desk.

"I'll make sure to have my men ready for the time being," he spoke, glancing at me before he looked at Gia and my parents. "There are plenty of empty rooms in this pack house. My men will show you to your rooms." He looked at me and I offered him a small smile. He nodded and walked towards the door, letting out a sigh. "I need to take care of my men. If anyone needs me, then I'll be out in the yard."

We all nodded and he was out the door, shutting it behind him. I looked at Lina to see her staring at the floor. I sighed and stood up, sitting next to her. She looked at me and I offered her a reassuring smile.

"You do know if you feel uncomfortable or threatened, then you don't have to do this," I whispered. She immediately shook her head.

"No, I have to do this. I want to," she whispered back. "You heard what she said." She glanced at Gia. "War will break out if I'm not there. It would be selfish of me to not come. I have to go for the safety of the pack. Besides, she did say nothing would happen to me."

I placed my hand on her back, patting it. "That's very brave of you," I whispered. She chuckled at me.

"I guess I'm not that useless after all," she joked.

I looked at my parents, who were staring at me with adoration. I smiled at them and was about to walk to them when the door slammed open, revealing a shocked Adam.

"Mom? Dad?" he whispered, running to them. They stood up, engulfing him in a tight hug. He whispered some muffled words as his mom cried in happiness. They soon pulled away, smiling at each other. Adam's eyes watered with emotions.

"I missed you both," he whispered.

His mother cupped his cheek. "We missed you too, honey. We're so happy to have you back." H

His father's eyes widened once he looked at his clothes. "You're a pack warrior?" he asked.

Adam smiled and nodded. "Yes, I am," he responded. "But I'm not working here. I work with our ally."

"Wait, does that mean you're not going to stay here?" his mother asked, frowning.

"No. I'm going to start training here, in this pack," he answered.

"Really?" I asked, shocked. His head whipped to me and he smiled, nodding.

"Yes. The alpha allowed me to stay," he responded, making my smile widen. I happily pulled him in for a hug and he hugged me back. I stared at him and raised a brow.

"But what changed Mason's mind?" I asked.

He answered, "It is because my parents are going to stay here."

The office door opened again and three men walked in. They nodded at me in respect and I smiled at them.

One directed his attention to our parents and Gia and said, "We will show you to your room. Please come with us."

I hugged my parents before they went with them. I was left alone with Lina and Adam. Lina smiled at Adam and pulled him in for a hug.

"I'm happy you're back. I had no one else to annoy while you were gone. Instead, I had to handle a really annoying Ameer," she spoke, pulling away. Adam chuckled and rolled his eyes, raising a brow.

"Ameer? Who's that?" he asked.

I stepped up and spoke, "He's one of the pack warriors who came from the allied pack. He and Lina are enemies." I chuckled. "They despise each other."

Lina rolled her eyes. "He keeps blasting music, which annoys the hell out of me." She crossed her arms against her chest. "He also keeps spilling his damn coffee on me and acts like it's an accident. You might think that he is all brave and all since he's a pack warrior, but he's a pussy that screams like a girl when he lays eyes on me."

Adam laughed out, and I rolled my eyes.

"He's not bad. He's really friendly, but he gave Lina the wrong first impression," I defended, making Lina glare at me. "You should meet him, I'm sure you'll like him."

Lina shook her head, but when I looked at her, she stopped and offered me an innocent smile. I rolled my eyes and Adam nodded, smiling.

"I'd love to meet the person that annoys the hell out of Lina," he joked, teasing Lina. She growled at him and huffed before they broke out into an argument.

"I'm going to see my parents. You both keep bickering like the usual," I said, laughing. They both rolled their eyes but paid no more attention to me and continued arguing. I opened the door and stepped out, shutting it behind me.

I walked down the hall, figuring out which room my parents would stay in. On the way, I saw Ameer rushing towards me.

"Hey, best friend," he greeted, pulling me into a hug.

I pulled away and stared at him, smiling. "Hey. Where are you going? You look like you're in a hurry."

"Yeah. The alpha called us out to the yard. He says it's important," he answered. I nodded, guessing it had to do about the war that Gia had warned us about.

"Okay. You should go before he gets angry," I spoke. He said goodbye before he ran off. Then he stopped and came back. I raised my brow as he was catching his breath.

"I almost forgot," he breathed out, pulling something out from his pocket. "Our friendship bracelets."

I saw a blue bracelet in his hand that had "Best Friends" on it. I laughed out loud and grabbed it. Ameer raised his wrist and wiggled it, showing the exact bracelet but pink. I chuckled and wore mine.

"You were serious about the bracelets, huh?" I questioned, amused. He raised a brow and plastered a fake offended expression on his face.

"You were doubting our friendship?" he asked. I rolled my eyes and shook my head.

"No. I just thought you were kidding," I spoke. He shook his head and wrapped an arm around my shoulder, pulling me towards him.

"I sure wasn't," he said. I nodded and smiled. "Don't take it off. It symbolizes our amazing friendship." He cheekily smiled at me. I chuckled and nodded.

"Okay, I won't."

His smile widened, and he hugged me before pulling away. "Great. Now I have to go before the alpha gets angry."

Chuckling, I nodded before he ran away. I shook my head at him and walked off, glancing at the blue bracelet.

He is one heck of a person

*   *   *

"You ready?" I asked, walking into Adam's room.

"Yeah. Training just ended and my wolf is begging to be let out," he muttered.

We walked out of the pack house, side by side. It had been a week since Adam came back. We had been spending time with each other and our families. It felt nice. Them being here made me realize that I truly missed them.

We also had been on high guard lately, many warriors surrounding the pack house and borders. I checked on Lina many times, wanting to see if she was okay. She seemed pretty fine, not really thinking about what Gia had said. However, I knew she was confused as to how she would prevent the war. We all were.

Shaking those thoughts aside, I walked towards the woods with Adam. As soon as we were deep in the woods, I looked at him.

"I'm going to change," I spoke, pointing at a large tree in the distance. He nodded but stopped, staring straight forward.

I raised a brow at him and he shook his head, letting out a sigh. "What's wrong?" I questioned. He looked at me and softly smiled.

"The alpha called me," he responded. "I have to go. You run without me." He offered me one more smile before he walked away.

I shifted into my wolf and began to run, the soft wind hitting my face and my fur dancing in the air. I ran and ran, all while making sure I was only near the pack house in case of emergencies. After a moment, I realized I shouldn't be out of the pack house for long without someone else.

I shifted back to my human form and wore my clothes. I was ready to return when a familiar scent hit my nose. I stopped dead in my tracks as my back stiffened. The leaves crunching indicated someone was walking towards me.

Whipping my head behind me, I was met with the last person I never wanted to see.

Zander.

I took a step back, glaring at him. "What are you doing here, Zander?" I asked. He stalked towards me, his fist clenched. "You're not supposed to be on this land."

"Did you forget I'm one of Alpha Alex's men?" he questioned, making me frown. "That means I can enter because we are allied packs after all, aren't we?"

I growled at him. "I don't care about that," I hissed. "Mason warned you not to come here."

He let out a growl. "I don't care about that bastard," he sneered, gripping my arms. "You're mine, and he took you away from me."

I cringed at his hold, trying my best to pull away. I glared at him, feeling my anger rise by the minute. "He took me away from you?" I asked. "Are you serious? It's your fault, not mine and not Mason's. Don't blame other people when it is completely you. You're the one who tried to kill Adam and who left, Zander. It was your fault."

He growled at my words and I felt his nails dig into my skin. "If I didn't leave then, I would be dead right now," he hissed. "And I'm not going to let him take you away from me."

I narrowed my eyes on him before speaking, "He already did."

His eyes darkened severely and a threatening growl emerged from within his chest. He slammed me against the tree, making my eyes widen. His grip on me tightened and he looked angry, really angry.

"Zander," I warned, "just leave. I don't want you near me ever again."

Growling, he let go of my arm. "If I can't have you, then no one will." He pulled out a gun from his pockets and pointed it at me, making me stiffen and stare at him in shock.

"You're crazy," I whispered. "You're insane."

He let out a laugh and shook his head. "You made me like this, Tiana," he hissed. I glared at him and shook my head.

"No, you were always like this," I whispered. "I wish you actually died that day." His eyes widened before they hardened.

"Too bad you're going to die before me," he sneered. I stood there, ready to shift when a large silver wolf jumped onto Zander. The wolf, which I recognized as Mason, dug his teeth into Zander's neck. He let out a loud growl as Zander's cries filled the air.

I watched in shock as Mason tore chunks of flesh from his neck, leaving him still and lifeless on the floor. My eyes widened as I registered the scene in front of me.

Mason killed Zander.

And this time, Zander was actually dead.

CHAPTER 63

The tension in the air was thick, knowing we would be under attack at any moment. The clock ticked very slow. A week had gone by, but it already felt like a month to me.

Zander was finally out of my life. I had wished that things would end in a civil manner, yet blood still poured. I didn't blame Mason. Not one bit. I knew his protective side kicked in as soon as he saw the gun pointing to me.

After he ended Zander's life, we didn't argue and split apart; instead, we got closer. I knew if it was the other way around, I would have done the same thing.

This week, Mason didn't allow me to be out of his sight. He had moved all my stuff to his room, persistent in keeping me close in case of emergencies. I knew he didn't let his guard down even for a second. The pack warriors surrounded the house and borders, as if waiting for something to happen. As for what that something was, I didn't know. I guess, a sign or a move.

Mason sent his warriors to the place the vampire had told us about, but they found no signs of existence. The only explanation was they fled once they had noticed one of their vampires was with us. To where? I didn't know, and neither did Mason.

I didn't know what Mason did to that vampire in the dungeons. For all I knew, he could be dead.

I was drastically pulled out from my thoughts when Mason played with my hair. I looked at him and frowned, seeing the bags under his eyes. He looked tired, very tired. His dark orbs looked at me and a lazy smile crawled onto his lips. I sighed and shifted closer to him, grabbing his hand.

"Mason?" I whispered.

"Hmm?" he murmured.

"When was the last time you slept?"

His lazy smile slowly dropped into a thin line. He shrugged and twirled a strand of my hair around his finger. "Doesn't matter," he muttered, digging his nose into my hair. "You're all that matters."

I stopped myself from getting swept on my feet and narrowed my eyes on him. "Mason," I breathed out, "you look so tired. Sleep for an hour or something."

He shook his head and placed his nose in my neck, inhaling my scent. "No, it's okay. I can handle everything without sleep."

I shook my head and held his face in my hands. "Please, for me? You worked all week. You need a little rest," I pointed out, pouting to convince him. He concentrated on my face before he let out a long, defeated sigh.

"Fine," he murmured.

"Great," I exclaimed happily, making him lie on the bed. "Sleep."

"Bossy," he muttered, the corner of his lips twitching.

I narrowed my eyes on him. "Thick headed," I shot back.

"Stubborn," Mason said.

"Possessive."

"Impossible."

I raised a brow. "Impossible? Is that all you say?" I asked. He shrugged, grabbing my hand and pulling me towards him, making me fall onto his chest.

"Yes, I'm only speaking the truth," he answered.

"Maybe you are. Now sleep," I ordered, pulling myself out of his arms and standing up. He slightly pouted at me, making a small smile appear on my lips.

I opened my mouth, ready to say something, when the door opened and Adam came walking in.

"Gia wants you both. She says it is urgent," Adam spoke, causing me to furrow my brows and Mason to immediately stand up. We followed Adam to the office. Then Adam offered me one last smile before he walked away, leaving us alone.

Soon, Gia came in and sat down. "We need to talk," she said.

"What is it about? Did you see something?" Mason asked.

Gia nodded. "Yes, I did."

"What did you see?" I asked.

Gia took a deep breath before she spoke, "Have you ever wondered how the rogues and the vampires know your every move?"

"Yes, we did," Mason responded. I narrowed my eyes on Gia.

"There is someone in your pack who has been stabbing your backs," Gia claimed.

"Who is it?" Mason asked lowly. Gia dropped her head down before looking back at Mason.

"Before you find out who it is, you should know this person isn't doing this on their own will. They were forced," she explained, sparking my curiosity. Mason furrowed his brows and nodded.

"Just tell me. Who is it?" Mason questioned aggressively. Gia stood up and walked to the door, opening it. My eyes widened as I saw Kayla. Gia offered her a small smile before patting her back. Then she walked away, leaving us confused.

Kayla walked into the office, closing the door behind her. Her eyes were filled with guilt, especially after she looked at me. Mason drastically stood up, narrowing his eyes on her.

"Kayla?" I whispered.

"I'm sorry, Alpha," she whispered, looking down. "I'm sorry."

Mason was furious as he took a step closer to her. "You're the backstabber?" he asked, a low growl emerging from his chest.

I grabbed his hand, trying to calm him down, as I comprehended what was going on.

Kayla looked at us sadly. "Yes, but it was never my intention. I was forced to do it," she whispered, begging me with her eyes to believe her.

I frowned as those words came out of her mouth. Kayla and I weren't best friends, but I did consider her as a friend. I began to wonder whether everything was a lie from the beginning or not.

"What do you mean?" I asked. Her eyes were filled with unshed tears that were threatening to escape. She opened her mouth, but nothing escaped it.

After a moment of mustering up her courage, she finally spoke, "They took him and threatened me. If I didn't inform them about your every move, they would kill him. They made me cross your borders, knowing Tiana would make you spare my life. Then I would have to tell them everything. Please believe me." Her tears began falling to her cheek. "If you don't believe me, ask Gia. She saw it all. I'm not lying."

"Who did they take?" Mason asked. She inhaled deeply and wiped her cheeks.

"My mate," she answered. "He has been a prisoner for three months. I was left with no choice. I would do anything for him. I was worried that if I told you, then they would kill him."

"Is he still with them?" Mason questioned.

Kayla let out a sigh and shook her head. "No. He was able to escape. He is now in his secret house, so the rogues and the vampires won't find him."

Mason let out a sigh and ran a hand over his face. I knew Kayla was telling the truth; I could tell by the sincerity in her eyes. They were glimmering with pain and sadness.

I understood how she felt. She only wanted to keep her mate safe. If I was in her place, I would do the same. Besides, Gia would know if she was lying. Even though, I was overwhelmed with shock, I smiled sympathetically at her.

"I won't forget what you've done," Mason narrowed his eyes on her. "However, I won't punish you because I understand why you had to do it. I would have done the same." His eyes flickered to me before looking at Kayla. "So I want you to go back to your old pack with your mate," he finished. I frowned but Kayla nodded.

"I know now that my mate is back, I have nothing to do with this pack any longer." She glanced at me. "Thank you and I'm sorry for everything. I will go back to my normal life now," she said, hugging me. I was caught off guard, but I returned her embrace.

She must have gone through hell. I didn't blame her, I would be too cold hearted if I did.

Kayla pulled away and smiled at Mason, who nodded at her and wrapped his arm around my waist.

"Will you and your mate be okay?" I asked.

"We will be fine. Thank you," she said, taking a step back. "Please excuse me. I'm going to start packing."

"I'll have my men take you to your pack," Mason said.

"Thank you, Alpha." She smiled gratefully at him, but before she could even place her hand on the door, it flew open and a worried Gia came rushing in.

I frowned as my eyes rested on her, and Mason tightened his hold on my waist. Even though we sort of knew what was happening, Mason still asked, "What's wrong, Gia?"

She took a deep breath, closing her eyes for a moment. Her eyes were filled with fear and worry, something that made a shiver run down my spine.

"Tonight, they're coming tonight."

CHAPTER 64

"No," Mason growled lowly, narrowing his eyes on me. I ran my hand through my tangled hair and crossed my arms against my chest, shaking my head.

"I'm coming whether you like it or not," I argued, making him growl again. He grabbed my arms tightly and pulled me to his chest, his eyes turning darker by the second.

"I said no, Tiana. You are not coming with us tonight. It is too dangerous," he shot back, making me huff in frustration.

"I want to come. I am the luna of this pack, so I have every right to come with you," I said, not giving in. "I need to, Mason. Please let me."

He looked at me with confusion in his eyes and shook his head. "No," he whispered. "I can't risk it. I won't risk losing you." His hard eyes turned soft at this moment, sadness present in his dark orbs.

I cupped his cheeks, pulling him to me and placing a gentle kiss on his lips. I stared into his eyes, wanting the sadness to vanish completely.

"Mason," I whispered, "I'll be fine. Trust me."

He looked hesitant for a moment and then said in defeat, "Fine." He slumped his shoulders as he let out a sigh. I smiled and pulled him towards me for a hug. He immediately wrapped his arms around me, digging his nose into my hair.

"Thank you," I whispered and he just nodded. "I love you."

He placed a kiss on my forehead and stared at me, adoration and love evident in his sparkling eyes.

"I love you too, Tiana, more than you can ever imagine."

* * *

After a couple of hours, I went to the yard to see how the pack warriors were doing and to check Adam and Ameer before we had to leave soon. Gia had mentioned we had to meet the enemies along the borders for the pack members' safety.

I was really nervous but I had to go. It was me they wanted, so it would be cowardly of me if I stayed hidden while they fought. I was the luna, and as their luna, I had to go.

Everyone knew what might possibly happen, so they all had their guards up. I could see Mason in the distance, monitoring the warriors strictly. They looked stressed as they trained.

I went to them, and as soon as I was near, Mason gave them a short break. I smiled at him and he placed a gentle kiss on my cheek before he pulled me away.

"I have some work to do," he spoke. "I'll see you later."

I nodded, and he kissed me one more time before walking away. Looking around, I spotted Adam and Ameer talking to each other and laughing.

When did they meet? I wondered, curious.

As soon as I was in front of them, they smiled at me and greeted me with a hug. Then I stared at them with my brow raised.

"Hey there, best friend," Ameer gushed, pinching my cheek. I slapped his hand and rubbed my cheek.

"Hey," I muttered before looking at Adam. "When did you guys meet?" I asked.

Adam gave me a look before he shook his head. "Tiana, did you forget that we are both pack warriors? We were bound to meet," he pointed out.

"Oh," I muttered. "Well, you guys seem to get along."

Ameer smiled and nodded, wrapping his arm around my shoulder. "We do but don't be jealous," he mused. "You are still my first best friend." He raised his wrist in front of my face and wiggled it, showing the pink bracelet that wrapped around it.

I narrowed my eyes on him and smacked his neck, making him yelp and rub the spot. "I'm not jealous." I crossed my arms against my chest. Adam gave me a look that said he didn't believe me.

"Sure you're not," Ameer spoke, making me smack his neck for the second time.

"Ouch," he muttered. "You're such a violent woman."

Nodding, Adam looked at Ameer. "That's what I always tell her, but she never believes me."

They both laughed while I rolled my eyes and let out a huff as they continued to joke around. After a while, Mason called them back to resume their training. I said my goodbyes before I returned to the pack house and went to Lina's room.

*   *   *

"Mason just mind-linked me," Lina spoke, breaking the silence that filled the air. "He wants to meet us outside the pack house, together with the warriors. They are about to depart."

I sucked in a shaky breath before I nodded and stood up. *I guess it's time*, I thought to myself.

I glanced at Lina as we exited the office, and she had a serious look on her face. When we reached the stairs, I saw my parents by the front door and ran to them, pulling them for a hug.

"Honey, do you have to go?" Mom asked, her eyes glimmering with worry. "It is too dangerous. I don't know what I will do if something happens to you."

I grabbed my parents' hands before smiling at them, trying to give them reassurance. "Mom, Dad," I whispered, "don't worry. I'll be fine. Mason is with me. He will keep me safe."

They looked at one another, and with a defeated sigh, they nodded. I pulled them in for another hug.

"Okay. Just please stay safe," Dad whispered, his eyes filled with sadness.

"I will."

And with that, Lina and I exited the doors, meeting Adam, Ameer, Mason, and a couple of pack warriors. I offered Ameer and Adam a soft smile before Mason pulled me for a hug.

"Everything will end tonight," Mason whispered in my ear. I looked at him and nodded, his eyes giving me comfort.

"Don't worry, Tiana," Ameer spoke, placing his arm around my shoulder. "I'll protect you with my life."

I smiled at his words, happy he was optimistic at a time like this. Adam nodded and placed his hand on my other shoulder. "Me too," he added.

I was about to say something when Mason cut in, "The others already did a head start. Let's go and catch up with them."

We started walking towards the pack warriors. I whipped my head at Mason as soon as he tangled his hand with mine. He raised it up to his lips and gently kissed it.

I smiled softly at him and gave his hand a squeeze, stepping closer to his side. I gulped as soon as I felt the tense atmosphere. The closer we were to the borders, the more the tension grew.

Adam and Ameer had serious expressions plastered on their faces while Lina gave me a crooked smile and patted my back.

"Everything will be fine," she whispered.

I didn't know what would happen tonight, but I prayed no one would get hurt and Lina could actually prevent the war.

How? I still didn't know.

I was pulled away from my thoughts when Mason's hold on me tightened. His eyes shifted into a dark shade of black, his expression turning aggressive by the second. We almost reached the borders, and in the distance was a long line of pack warriors, ready for action.

We eventually joined them, staring at the trees that surrounded us, waiting for an appearance. I kept my head high, trying to be brave for the members of my pack and hoping what Gia had said was true.

The air around us was quiet, but that all changed when we heard footsteps from afar—footsteps of many people. I sucked in a breath while Mason took a step in front of me and nodded to the warriors, signaling them to be ready.

The footsteps grew louder and louder by the minute, causing the tension in the air to grow. I held in my breath as rogues and vampires slowly came into sight, causing a couple of our warriors to growl. The enemies growled and hissed back, which urged Mason to throw the warriors a warning look.

We all remained silent as we waited for the rest of them to make their appearance. After a long dreadful minute, numerous rogues and vampires were now standing in a long line, but what caught my attention was the two men in front of the large group.

One was old, and the other one was around my age. The old man who was directly in front of us stared at me with a smirk on his face, making me step closer to Mason in refuge. The other one gave the impression that this was the least place he wanted to be at, looking extremely bored.

"Well, ain't this a surprise," the old man, whose name I knew was Roy, spoke. "You saved us time and work, how thoughtful of you. But I wonder how you knew we were coming."

Mason let out a low growl, stepping forward.

"Although that's not important," Roy continued before Mason could even say anything. "You must have known our reason." His eyes slowly rested on me, making me narrow my eyes on him.

"You aren't taking what's mine," Mason growled loudly, causing Roy to smirk. "Leave before any blood is shed."

I caught a glimpse of Lina and saw her eyes go wide. I followed her gaze to see a shocked Asher staring right back at her.

What the . . .

"Is that a threat?" Roy hissed, snapping me out of my thoughts.

Before Mason could reply, Asher growled, "Father, I told you many times that this is not what I want."

Roy brought his attention to him, hissing. "Shut up, Asher! Don't get in the way of my plans! I'm doing this for the future of our family!"

Asher clenched his fist. "I could care less," he sneered. "I don't want your plans. I want my mate."

Roy's eyes went dark as he stared at his son. Growling, he stepped closer to him and shook his head.

"Your mate is the person I choose for you," he spoke lowly. "And that's her." He pointed right at me.

"No, she is not. She is my mate," Mason roared.

"You can't control my life," Asher hissed, growing angrier by the second. "I will live the way I want to. I am tired of your bullshit. I won't accept any mate other than my real one."

Mason's hold on me tightened as they continued to argue. I looked at Lina to see her staring at Asher, her mouth open and her eyes dark. Before I could even question a thing, I heard Roy yell.

"You will obey my orders!" He looked at his men. "Get her!" He pointed at me, making our men immediately leap and shift in the air. My eyes widened as vampires and rogues came running towards me. Mason immediately shifted and started to take them down one by one.

Everything went by like a blur. Growls and hisses erupted in the air. Wolves and vampires ran past me and many of them were down on the ground. I was immediately snapped out of my trance as soon as I saw a werewolf running towards me, but before I could even react, Adam pushed me out of the way, making me fall.

Adam and the rogue fought, digging their teeth into each other's neck. Then another one jumped on Adam, biting him. He let out a howl in pain. I was running to him, ready to shift, when one of our pack warriors pushed the rogues off him.

Adam shifted back into his human form, a pool of blood leaving his still body. I kneeled as my vision blurred.

"Oh my gosh, Adam," I exclaimed, starting to panic. Adam, say something."

Adam looked at me and winced in pain. "T-Tiana . . ." He grabbed my hand as blood kept flowing out of him. Tears fell out of my eyes. Everything around me—the fight, the growls, and the yells—stopped. All my attention was only on Adam.

"I need to tell you something that I should have told you a long time ago," he managed to say, closing his eyes for a moment. I shook my head and tightened my hold on his hands.

"Shhh, tell me later," I whispered, tears streaming down my cheeks. "We need to get you to a doctor." As soon as I said that, I immediately mind-linked Doctor Sam, telling him to come immediately with more men.

Adam only shook his head. "No, I need to tell you now." He smiled at me and raised his hand to my cheek, wiping a tear away. "Tiana, I love you so much," he managed to say. "I have always loved you. I never mustered the courage to tell you, but I wanted you to know that before I die."

I immediately shook my head and stopped him. "Don't say that," I whispered. "We will talk about that later, once you are up and healthy."

He slowly shook his head. "I never told you because I knew I had no chance. You mean so much to me, and I truly hope

Mason can make you happy," he croaked as his eyes slowly closed. I cried, repeatedly shaking my head.

"No, no, no. Please, Adam," I whimpered. "Keep your eyes open. I beg you." I sobbed as I held my best friend in my arms. I tried my best to heal him with my angel powers as I waited for Doctor Sam to appear. Then I heard a booming voice in the air.

"Enough," Asher roared. I whipped my head to where he was to see him leaping onto his father, ending his life within a second. "Everyone, stop this instant!"

All of Roy's men stopped and stared at him, shock crossing their features as they saw their old alpha lifeless on the ground.

"I'm your alpha now," he yelled. "I demand you all to retreat this instant!"

The rogues and the vampires slowly walked towards him in defeat while our men still had their guards up. After a moment, his men were back to their positions. Asher looked at Mason, who immediately came to my side.

"This was never my intention." He looked at the injured men that filled the area. "We will retreat. I apologize sincerely. However, I will come back," he yelled, making Mason growl threateningly, "for my mate."

His eyes landed on a shaken Lina. My eyes widened as everything registered in my head. And with that, he and all his men were out of sight.

I immediately looked back at Adam, and that's when Doctor Sam and the others came running to us. I checked his pulse and let out a breath as soon as I felt it. However, the blood didn't stop. Doctor Sam immediately came to aid him and then a voice from the distance caught me off guard.

"Mate," a feminine voice yelled. I whipped my head to the source of the sound to find a rogue running towards us. Mason let out a growl, standing up. Without even sparing us a glance, the rogue kneeled to Adam and pulled him out of my arms and into hers.

"Mate," she whispered, hugging him to her chest. My eyes went wide as I witnessed what was in front of me. Mason took a step closer to her, but Doctor Sam stopped him, shaking his head.

"Let her be with him. A mate can heal their mate's pain," Doctor Sam whispered. I immediately nodded, surprised that Adam's mate was a rogue from Asher's pack.

"Take all the injured back to the pack house so we can aid them," Mason yelled. The warriors instantly did as he ordered. I watched as they carried an unconscious Adam away, with his mate by his side.

Mason pulled me in his arms and whispered soothing words into my ear, calming me down. "He will be okay, especially since his mate has found him."

"Alpha!" A warrior rushed to us, his face pale as he was catching his breath.

"Yes? What is it?" Mason asked.

"One of our men died. A vampire was about to inject the luna with silver, so he protected her and got injected. He was also bitten several times," he spoke, sadness lacing his voice. My eyes widened as I heard he died trying to save my life.

Mason stood silent for a moment before speaking, "Who is it?"

"Ameer."

EPILOGUE

I opened my eyes and the white ceiling that I usually stared at whenever a thought crossed my mind greeted me. I looked out my window, seeing the sun shining right through it, lighting up my boring room.

Rubbing my eyes, I sat straight and looked at my clock. As soon as I saw that it was nine in the morning , a sigh escaped my mouth. Getting up, I ran my hand over my hair and face as I thought about what would happen today.

Today is the day.

I opened my closet, picking out something that would go well with today's event. I placed the dress on my bed and stared at it for a good five seconds before shrugging.

"I guess this will do," I muttered to myself before entering the bathroom. I stared at my reflection and noticed how tired I looked.

The dark bags under my eyes, due to my sleepless nights, wouldn't go unnoticed. I guessed the stress the luna role entailed was slowly eating me up. I had insisted on helping Mason in leading the pack since, you know, I was the luna and should act like one. Then the outcome of that was less sleep.

I wasn't complaining though. I wanted this and I wouldn't go back on it.

I glanced at myself one more time and shrugged. "There's nothing makeup can't do," I murmured, splattering water on my face.

After doing my business and cleaning up, I walked out the bathroom and changed into the dress. Then I fixed my hair and looked at the mirror on my wall. Feeling satisfied, I grabbed and wore the blue bracelet that had "Best Friends" on it.

I wore the bracelet every single day and took great care of it, as it was a reminder of my friendship with Ameer, which he never lied about.

There were barely any pack members in the hall, but whenever I walked past one, they would smile respectfully and I also did the same. I then saw John and Crystal cuddling on the couch as they watched whatever was on the TV. Crystal and I waved at each other while John only nodded in respect before turning his attention back to the TV.

I smiled softly, knowing John didn't quite hate me anymore. The past few months that went by, I had gotten closer with Crystal since Lina wasn't here anymore. Because of that, John had to accept the fact that I was her friend and his luna. I could tell behind that grumpy face of his was a softie, which he only showed his mate.

I still hung out with Tyler and Ryder, but it just didn't feel the same anymore without Lina. However, they always tried to make it seem like nothing had changed. I knew deep down, they were very happy for Lina.

After greeting Anna and drinking water in the kitchen, I walked down the hall, making my way towards Mason's office. I then saw a man running towards me, looking frantic and scared. I furrowed my brows as I saw his sweaty red face.

Stopping in my tracks, I faced the man not too far away from me and tilted my head in confusion. "Ameer? What are you doing?"

"What does it look like I'm doing?" he asked, running his hands over his face. "I'm getting the hell out of here." And with that, he ran past me and down the hall, slowly disappearing from my sight.

Feeling curious, I went after him. Curse words echoed from his room. Furrowing my brows, I peeked inside and frowned as soon as I saw him shoving his clothes in a suitcase.

Slowly, I walked into his room and crossed my arms, clearing my throat to grab his attention. However, he didn't acknowledge my presence and continued his business.

I coughed this time, but he still didn't spare me even a single glance. I rolled my eyes and walked up to him, placing myself in front of his sight.

"Ameer," I spoke lowly but he still continued what he was doing. I stood there, feeling like I was transparent. "Ameer," I spoke louder this time, poking his back.

No response.

Shaking my head, I ran a hand over my face. "Ameer," I yelled, making him jump back from shock and look at me weirdly.

"What?" he asked, standing straight. "You're wasting my time, Tiana," he groaned. "The devil is going to be here soon, and I need to be 100 miles away from her."

I look at him in disbelief before shaking my head at his dramatic behavior. "Seriously, Ameer?" I breathed out, stepping closer to him. "You're still afraid of her?"

"I'm not afraid of her," he argued, crossing his arms. "I just don't want to be anywhere near her. The last time I saw her, she gave me a goodbye kick in the balls as a farewell present."

I rolled my eyes and shook my head once again.

"She's a devil, I tell you. I'm still shocked over the fact that a devil like her has been granted the chance of having a soulmate."

"Aren't you an angel now?" I asked, raising a brow. "Doesn't that mean you can fight off any devil?" His features dropped before he placed his finger under his chin and thought.

After a moment, he placed his hand back to his side and shook his head drastically.

"No, that doesn't mean shit," he spoke, running his hands over his face. "I take that back. She's not a devil. She's Satan herself, and this angel cannot fight off Satan." He went back to shoving his clothes into the suitcase, making me roll my eyes for the hundredth time. I gripped his shoulder and made him look at me.

"Where do you plan on going then?" I questioned.

He stopped and shrugged. "I don't know. Anywhere away from here," he responded. I gripped his ear, making him yelp in shock.

"Listen, Ameer," I said threateningly. "You will stay and make amends with Lina. Do I make myself clear?"

He dramatically shook his head. "But—"

"No buts," I cut him off. "You will stay or else I will make Lina track you down and give you a hello kick in the balls as a greeting present."

He sighed in defeat. "Fine," he grunted. "I will stay, but she ain't getting anywhere near me." His frown turned into a smile when I nodded. "Great," he mused before pulling me for a quick hug. "How are you, best friend?" he asked.

"I'm good," I responded, chuckling. "How about you? Are you still facing troubles with the angel side effects?"

"Thankfully, no," he answered. "I felt weird at first, but three months went by fast. I guess you can say I'm used to it now."

"That's good." I breathed in relief. "I was afraid you would never get used to it and blame me." I frowned with my head down. Ameer immediately made me look at him and shook his head, giving me a small smile.

"Tiana, did you forget that you saved my life? If it wasn't for your angel powers, then I would be six feet under the ground," he stated.

"Well, if it wasn't for me in the first place, then you wouldn't have gotten injected with silver," I pointed out before sighing. "I'm just glad you are okay, even though I completely lost my angel side."

Ameer placed his hand on my shoulder, squeezing it in a comforting manner.

Three months had gone by, but it felt like everything happened just yesterday. It was also the day Ameer became a member of our pack for his courageous act. Everything went by so fast and I still cannot believe what happened.

I could still remember everything in detail.

* * *

"Let me go," I cried, trying to release myself from Mason's tight grip. "I need to see him. Maybe I can still save him," I begged. Mason looked at me with sadness in his eyes and slowly shook his head.

"Tiana," he whispered softly. "You can't. He is already dead."

I drastically shook my head in disbelief as I processed his words. "No, he isn't dead," I argued, a tear falling to my cheek. "I won't allow it." I pulled myself out of Mason's grip and faced the guard that announced the news.

"Where is he?" I asked. He glanced at Mason, who took a deep breath and nodded. The guard told me to follow him, and we immediately ran to where Ameer was. I inhaled a sharp breath as I saw his still body lying in the distance.

I rushed to him and kneeled, tears falling from my eyes. I shook my head as I saw his pale features. "You won't die," I whispered before placing my hands on his chest and concentrating to direct all my energy to him.

After a moment, I felt like passing out and my heart skipped a beat when I saw that nothing changed in Ameer. I slowly pulled my hands away as a lone tear fell on his face.

I closed my eyes and slowly opened them to see a conscious Ameer right in front me. My eyes widened, but before I could say anything, Doctor Sam came running towards us. I glanced at Ameer, who had his eyes open but his body was still.

"Ameer?" I breathed out, hope lacing my voice. He remained silent, not even looking at me. I whipped my head to Doctor Sam, who was by my side at the moment, aiding him.

"Doctor Sam, what happened?" I asked, worried. "What's wrong with him?"

Doctor Sam stood silent for a moment before looking at me with wide eyes.

"What?" I asked, getting nervous.

"He is alive," he whispered, making me smile. "But he is not a werewolf anymore. You transferred all your energy to him, and now he has your angel."

* * *

As I was heading to Mason's office, someone covered my eyes with their hands, making me stop.

"Who is it?" the person asked, making me smile.

"Umm . . ." I murmured, placing my finger under my chin. "Let me guess, the Queen of Britain?"

"Ah, ah, but you are close though."

I started tapping my finger on my chin and acted as if I was thinking. "The Queen of Stupidity?" I shot. "I'm sure that's the right answer."

The hands that covered my eyes disappeared and an offended Adam came into sight.

"What's that supposed to mean?" He crossed his arms and I let out a laugh before shaking my head. "Are you calling me a woman? Correction, Tiana. It's the King of Stupidity."

Another laugh escaped my lips as Adam's lips curved upwards. "Well, at least you finally admitted it," I pointed out, making him roll his eyes.

"Yeah, yeah, whatever," he muttered before hanging his arm around my shoulder. "What are you up to?"

"I'm heading towards Mason's office so I could force him to get ready," I responded. "Since, you know, he isn't too fond of the fact that Asher and him are going to be having a family dinner."

"I understand where he is coming from," Adam said. "The poor guy had to hand his sister over to a vampire alpha. That's nothing to be happy about. And, you know, since vampires and werewolves are mortal enemies, he wouldn't want one sitting at his dinner table."

Rolling my eyes, I slapped his arm. "Did you forget this vampire is Lina's mate? Mason has to deal with it," I spoke. "I would've expected you to understand since, you know, you have a mate of your own."

Adam's lips broke into a smile before he nodded. "Yeah, yeah," Adam muttered.

"So how are you and Cara getting along?" I asked.

"We're doing great. Getting stronger and stronger by the day."

My smile grew as I heard his response. Thanks to Cara, Adam survived that day. They immediately clicked, so Mason let her join our pack even though she was a rogue. I was sure that as soon as Adam laid eyes on Cara, everything he felt for me disappeared and Cara became his first priority.

I wanted Adam to stay happy, and I was sure Cara could provide him many reasons to feel just that.

"That's good," I told him before stepping away. "I need to go now, the sooner the better."

After a while, I was in front of Mason's office and I could smell his scent from behind the door. When I entered the room, a grumpy Mason looked at me and he sat straighter on his chair.

"Aww, is my little bear grumpy?" I cooed. He raised his brow before pulling and engulfing me in a hug. A low growl escaped his chest before he dug his nose into my hair, inhaling my scent.

"Yes," he muttered, pulling away. I smiled and shook my head, cupping his face in my hands and giving him a small peck.

"Don't be. You are seeing your sister today," I pointed out. He huffed and shrugged like a three-year-old.

"I'm seeing my sister with a man," he grunted. "A vampire, to be exact."

"A half vampire," I pointed out.

"Same thing," he muttered, looking displeased.

"It's okay, honey. It's only for dinner." I smiled at him.

"I know," he muttered. "Just don't blame me if he ends up with a broken nose."

Taken aback, I immediately shook my head. "No, no, no!" I shook my point finger in front of his face. "No one's ending up with a broken nose today."

Mason's lips twitched upwards as he looked hesitant. "I can't promise anything," he grumbled. "As long as you are by my side, I am calm."

"I would never leave your side," I whispered, making him smile.

"You better not."

Smiling, I rested my forehead against his. "I love you," I said softly and he placed a gentle kiss on my lips.

"I love you more."

* * *

"Mason?" I called out, knocking on our bedroom door. "You ready? I swear if you're not, then I won't hesitate to come in there and dress you myself."

All of a sudden, the door flew open, catching me off guard. A well-dressed Mason smirked at me.

"I wouldn't mind," he mused, making me roll my eyes. I crossed my arms against my chest and shook my head.

"Let's get downstairs already," I muttered. "They will be here any minute now."

Mason nodded and grabbed my hand gently, pulling me towards the entrance. The pack house was quiet, the members staying in their room or somewhere else to give our family privacy. When the doorbell rang, we immediately knew that the couple had arrived.

I could smell Lina's scent from behind the door. Smiling, I opened it to see a well-dressed Lina next to a natural-looking Asher, who had his hand on her waist. Lina's lips curved up into a smile as soon as she saw me. She pulled me into a tight bear hug that left me gasping for air. Chuckling, I moved aside, letting her greet her brother.

"Hello, Asher. Thank you for coming along."

Asher nodded in respect and pulled Lina to his side. I smiled at them and couldn't help thinking how cute they were.

Lina had always wanted a mate, and now she got one.

"Come in." I stepped aside to let them enter.

"Goodness," Lina whispered as we were walking down the hallway. "I truly miss this place."

"We miss you, Lina, especially Ameer. He misses you a lot."

Her eyes narrowed before a smirk crawled onto her lips. "That better be sarcasm because if it isn't, then the feeling isn't mutual," she muttered, making me chuckle.

"The poor guy was so close to packing his bags and leaving as soon as he heard you were coming," I stated. Lina laughed out loud and shook her head.

We entered the dining room, where the table was already set up, but before we even got the chance to sit, Ameer entered, sipping coffee out of a mug. We all looked at him while he was unaware of our presence. Ameer, all of a sudden, went stiff as he slowly turned his head to us.

"Shit," he cursed, his eyes wide as soon as he saw Lina. "I completely forgot!" He exited the room frantically.

"See what I mean?" I whispered to Lina, making her smile.

"I see."

I glanced at Asher to see him looking curiously at Lina, who just smiled at him and grabbed his hand. Mason cleared his throat, indicating we should all sit and begin.

"I'm starving," I said.

During the meal, Lina and I were having small talks, trying to ignite a conversation, while Asher and Mason were just glaring at each other, remaining silent.

Thick tension spread in the air, and I knew Lina was aware of it too. She then whispered something in Asher's ear that made him scowl. I turned my attention to Mason to see him looking annoyed.

Narrowing my eyes on him, I pinched his hand, which made him turn his attention to me.

"Say something," I whispered. He huffed and sat straight, facing Asher.

"So . . ." he started, narrowing his eyes on him. "Are you treating my sister well?"

Lina and I rolled our eyes as those words left his mouth, making me mentally face-palm myself.

Asher stiffened and scowled at him. "What are you trying to imply? She is my mate. I'm treating her the best I can."

Mason slowly nodded and muttered lowly, "That's what I thought."

Asher seemed to have heard because he stood up and glared at him, a low growl emerging from within his chest.

"If you got something to say, then say it in front of my face," he spoke lowly, making Mason stand up as well. I gripped Mason's arm as Lina did the same to Asher.

"The same goes for you," Mason told Asher.

"Hey, hey, hey," Lina interrupted. "Can we all sit and continue with our dinner in a civil manner?"

Asher and Mason snapped their heads to her before looking back at each other.

"Not until he stops with that shitty attitude," Asher said lowly.

Mason growled, "Watch your mouth, bloodsucker. You're in my territory."

"Did you just call me a bloodsucker, mutt?" Asher hissed, gripping the table tight. Mason growled at what Asher said. My eyes widened, and that's when Lina and I both grabbed them by the ear and pulled them towards us. Lina whispered something in Ashton's ear, making his eyes widen.

"Behave, Mason," I hissed into his ear, making him huff. "Don't anger me."

Mason nodded, and that's when Asher and Mason slowly sat back down on their chairs, glaring at each other like grumpy three-year-olds. I slowly shook my head and went back to eating, hoping no one would end up with a broken nose tonight.

* * *

"I was this close to breaking his nose," Mason grumbled, jumping onto our bed and lying down, running a hand over his face. "Did you see how he was holding her? He clearly did that to piss me off."

Rolling my eyes, I sat on the edge of the bed. "Aren't you thinking a little too much of it?" I questioned, making him look at me. "He's her mate, so of course he will hold her the way he did."

Mason sat up and huffed, running a hand through his hair. "I know," he whispered. "I just can't accept the fact that my little sister has a mate. It's too hard."

I smiled and grabbed his hand, giving it a comforting squeeze. "You will get used to it," I told him. "She is happy now, and that should make you happy too."

Mason pulled me to his chest, digging his nose into my hair and inhaling my scent. "I am, but what makes me truly happy is having you by my side," he whispered lowly, making my heart melt. "My life is nothing without you. I love you and everything about you."

I slowly pulled away and looked at his dark orbs, smiling at him. "Even my flaws?" I asked. He smiled at me and started playing with a strand of my hair, twirling it around his finger.

"Yes," he answered, "even your stubborn side."

I let out a small laugh. "I'm not that stubborn though," I mumbled. Mason shrugged and wrapped his arms around my waist, pulling me to his chest.

"You are. You are like my prey who I can never let go of," he mumbled against my ear, "who I will run after till the day I die."

"Prey?" I stared at his dark eyes. He placed a gentle kiss on my lips before looking at me with love in his eyes.

"Yes," he whispered, "my impossible prey."

THE END

Do you like werewolf stories?
Here are samples of other stories
you might enjoy!

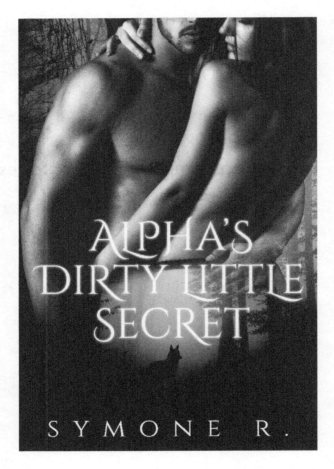

CHAPTER I

AMIRA

Gazing at the several unknown faces, I began to feel as if I was living in the shadows once again. I was left bearing a secret that made me feel like I was living in a lie.

Innocent humans watched as our college professor continued to lecture about Accounting and Finance. I looked to my left; beside me was a girl. Her blonde hair was draped over her brown eyes as she continued to scribble insignificant pictures on her notebook. What amazed me the most was how unaware she was of the nonhuman creature seated only inches away from her.

She sighed. My useful heightened senses allowed me to listen to her heartbeat and breathing that would accelerate every time the professor searched for a student to answer a simple question. Her heart rate would regulate once the professor called someone else. She slouched in her chair, her eyes occasionally wandering off from her work to a boy sitting in the far corner of the room.

"Amira? Are you paying attention?" I looked to my right, finding the eyes of my friend, Eric.

Eric and I have been friends since we were thirteen. Six years later, we were still going strong. We had a lot of classes together over the years, so our friendship continued to grow. However, despite us being friends, I could never find it in myself to tell him who I really was. Or should I say, *what* I was.

"Yeah…no," I admitted before we both shared a low snicker.

"Eric, you know I got all of this stuff already," I reassured him, slouching down in my chair.

I was known to be very intelligent in school. Unlike most, it was very easy for me to remember and comprehend any given task. This skill has been very helpful to me.

"Well, then, if it's so damn easy for you, you can teach it all to me because I'm lost as hell." Eric sighed. His eyes narrowed in on the textbook in front of him as I chuckled at him.

"Okay, ladies and gentlemen, class dismissed," the teacher announced as she wrapped up her lecture. I stood from my desk. Students began gathering their things before everyone scrambled out of the door.

"So, lunch on me today?" Eric offered.

"No, sorry. I have to help my mom prepare for this dinner we are having tomorrow. Just a few out-of-town guests." I sighed heavily.

"Okay, cool. Well, I'll text you tonight?"

"Sure."

* * *

The appetizing smell of food danced its way around me, clouding my nasal passages with the mouth-watering aroma of my mother's home-cooked meal.

I walked into the kitchen to see my mother running back and forth. She was cutting vegetables, stirring food in the pots, and measuring the temperature of whatever she was roasting in the oven.

"Mom, is it this serious?" She was acting as if the president was stopping by for dinner.

"Yes, sweetie. This is when you'll see your new alpha for the first time." My mother was more cheerful than the rest of us were.

It was amusing how my mother cared about the alpha's arrival more than the actual werewolves that lived here. I expected her to feel uncaring about his presence as if he was just another regular visitor, her being a human and all.

I guess being married to and being the mother of a werewolf really had her interested in the supernatural world. Unlike her, I couldn't care less about the werewolf society. I found human life to be much better. Accepting. I enjoyed not living under the command and authority of some male who was determined to show his dominance over everyone because of a title.

That was why I loved living in the city. Majority of our pack, including the alpha and beta, lived far out in the country somewhere.

Honestly, that's how I liked it. I loved being away from the group who allowed their title to get to their overgrown skull.

I preferred the distance. However, my father seemed to not feel the same way I do. Recently, he had invited the previous alpha and luna, and their son—the new alpha—over for dinner. Only my father could ruin such a beautiful thing.

"But Mom, they aren't coming until tomorrow," I reminded her again.

"I know, I know, but I prefer to get things done now."

I sighed. Looking over everything, I could see how she had handled things.

"You seem to have everything done." The chicken was roasting in the oven; the vegetables were boiling in the pots; and she seemed to be starting on dessert. "Call me if you need anything then."

I snatched up my bag from the kitchen counter. Reaching into the cupboard, I pulled a granola bar from the box before I left the kitchen.

I silently cursed my mother and father again. I don't even know why I have to be here. If I could, I would disappear before the guests even made it to town. Sadly, my father requested that I should be present for the attendees.

Why did I seem so against the presence of the new alpha? I would say our past was just a tiny piece of the reason that I wanted to disappear. Even though my mother said it's the first time meeting the new alpha, it's actually not. We had already met before he had taken over the title, alpha.

When I was about eight years old, my father and I would visit the main pack house for some business. Since my father was one of the strongest warriors of our pack, the previous alpha would need him by his side during decision-making.

That's when I had first met eleven-year-old Xavier, the soon-to-be alpha.

My father said—to keep us busy and out of their hair while he helped the alpha—Xavier and I should go play, and we did. Honestly, I thought Xavier was cute. I was actually very fond of him. Stupidly, I asked him if he felt the same way. Let's just say it was not the answer I hoped for.

To impress his friends, who were the children of other higher ranked members, he knocked me off the swing. I remembered crying on the ground as he and the other kids laughed before they left me soaking in my own tears.

That fucking bitch.

Yes, I knew that it happened many years ago, but for some reason, I just couldn't forget and forgive. I guess I just didn't take rejection or embarrassment too well. I still don't.

Luckily, after that, I never saw him again, and I was perfectly fine with it.

I quickly shook the thoughts off before I disappeared into the bathroom.

I stood in front of the mirror in my room after I finished taking a shower. I ran my hands down my hips as I stared at my reflection. I adored my frame. I didn't consider myself fit or slim like the other female werewolves I had encountered. Other she-wolves had a fit and athletic physique, the type of body that would look exceptional in anything. I, on the other hand, did not have that. I was a curvaceous woman—full breasts, thick hips and thighs without such a slim waist. I would always assure myself that I would soon diet. At least, after I finish off the pizza I was enjoying.

I began to smile. My full pink lips looked well with my silky smooth skin and brown eyes.

I pulled out my blow dryer and started drying my shoulder-length black hair. When my hair was already dry, I pinned it up and leaped into my bed. Turning my television on, I searched through various channels until I finally landed on a show I could finish my night with.

* * *

Wrapped up in my comforter, I felt at ease. No classes. No early morning wake-up calls. Just the perfect time to oversleep.

"Amira, wake up. Let's go the mall." I heard my mother's all too familiar voice as she pushed through my bedroom door.

"No, thank you," I rolled away from her. "It's too early."

"Too early? It's 12:30 in the afternoon. Now, get your butt up."

I turned to my mother and an annoyed snarl escaped me. She narrowed her eyes and shot me a warning glare before walking away. It was a warning, convincing me that her wrath was more powerful than my teeth.

"Make it an hour, or I'm coming back."

"Fine." I sighed.

I stayed in bed for another fifteen minutes; I just did not want to get up. Mustering up some energy, I swung my legs and sat up from the bed. Tired and drained, I dragged myself to my bathroom.

After finishing my routine, I picked up my bag and made my way downstairs.

"Hey, Dad," I greeted my father as I walked into the kitchen. He glanced up from his paper to meet my gaze.

"Hey, where are you two headed?"

"She's dragging me to the mall." I slipped into a chair beside him. I reached for his paper and pulled the comic section from the crumbled pile.

"Oh, good luck." I could sense the humor in his comment.

My father knew how things went when it involved accompanying my mother to the mall. He had found a way to get out of it. During their mall trips, he would make her shopping experience hell. He complained, dragged his feet, and gave opinions my mother found useless. Occasionally, he would become 'ill' during their mall runs.

I could only admire his tactics for escaping.

"Okay, sweetie, I'm ready."

"Okay." I sighed and stood up from my chair.

I followed my mother out to the car and got in. I slumped down in my seat as I listened to the vehicle's engine roar to life from under the hood. I slipped my earbuds on and drifted into my own thoughts the entire ride.

* * *

We roamed the mall for hours, not looking for a specific item. My mother just wanted to buy random things. With the help of my complaints, my mother wrapped up her shopping journey, and we finally left the mall.

"Sweetie, can you tell your father to come help with the bags?" I scowled at her. *What am I? A personal beeper?*

Reaching into our mind link, I urged for his assistance. A few seconds later, my father emerged from the front entrance. He grabbed my mother's bag, refusing to have her carry her own.

He should have joined us in our mall run then. With his petty whining, I would have been home already.

By the time we arrived home, I made my way to the kitchen and walked over to the refrigerator, pulling a bottle of water from the shelf. As I turned to leave, I witnessed my parents sharing an intimate kiss in the living room. "We all have rooms for that, people."

"Sorry, honey." My mother's cheeks flushed red as she pulled away from my father.

"You will understand once you find your mate," my father explained.

A mate. To us werewolves, our mate would be someone the moon goddess has blessed us with. A mate would be someone we plan to spend the rest of eternity with.

Love. A destined bond that was almost unavoidable and hard to break. My mother and father were mates. He shared his secret with her, and she accepted his life and him as well.

However, some weren't that blessed. Some were cursed. Some were given a mate who could be careless, cold-blooded, and downright disgraceful.

There could be some who don't want a mate. Some who would rather remain unrestricted than fall into the spell of the mate bond.

Rejection. Some would rather reject their mate; it's their way of freeing themselves from the world they consider a prison. However, it's not always accepted by the other. The rejected mate may not fully accept it, leaving them with a broken heart and the feeling of desertion. Some would begin to feel as though it's their own actions that caused the rejection, and feel self-loathe and hatred for their wolves. Finally, another dangerous aspect was pain, hatred, and even suicidal ideation.

Honestly, I didn't care about finding my mate. I didn't want to find some wolf who probably believed that I my only purpose was to bear his children and sleep with him. A man who would probably only use me as his chew toy. I couldn't allow someone to have so much control over me, so much power. And then give me so much heartache.

"No, thank you on the mate thing, Dad." A waved my hands frantically. I didn't want that curse.

"Honey, go, get dressed. Our guests should be arriving in about an hour." My mom pressed.

Shifting my eyes toward my father, I shot him a venomous glare once again.

"Oh, honey, you will love them. They are nice people, so relax."

Disagreeing with him, I picked up the small bags I had gotten from the mall and ran up to my room to prepare for an unwanted arrival.

If you enjoyed this sample, look for
Alpha's Dirty Little Secret
on Amazon.

THE ALPHA'S UNKNOWN *Son*

SKYLAR THOMAS

PROLOGUE

ROSE

"Come on, Rose. Go!"

I sigh and lean back on my bed, ignoring my best friend, Marcus.

"Rosealine Washington, get up. We're going to that party," Marcus says as he pulls the covers off of me.

"Marcus, I don't want to go. I don't do parties, and Nick barely knows my name anymore, so I don't think he'd be sad if I don't show up." Marcus ignores everything I say. He rummages my closet and pulls out a tight black dress, the one he bought me for Christmas and I've yet to wear.

"He knows your name! You're the beta's daughter. You literally grew up with him. And even if he doesn't know your name, it doesn't matter. It's not like it's a private birthday and he's the only one going. The whole pack will be there!" he says as he takes out my only pair of heels that are, unfortunately, six inches in length.

"Do you know how much trouble I will get into if Jake sees me drinking? And I know that is the only reason you want to go because you don't even like Nick."

"Yes, I know how mad your sexy brother will be if he sees us drinking, but he won't! There will be tons of people there, and they will be so drunk, all we will be is a blur to them, so get dressed."

I groan knowing he's right but still not wanting to go. I haven't been out in a while, but I think this might be good for the soul.

I change into the tiny dress and want to crawl back into my sweats immediately. After a short argument with Marcus, I change into some sandals, and NOT the ankle-breaking heels.

The soon-to-be-alpha, Nick Rollins, is having a birthday party tonight. The whole pack is invited, and some others from neighboring packs. My brother, Jake, the future beta, specifically told me not to touch the alcohol tonight. He knows how I can get when I'm drunk—emotional and vulnerable. Even though this is my pack and I should trust them, Jake and I know there's a few of them that would risk their lives to get a piece of...well, anything, really.

Jake's always been a protective brother towards me. There's been way too many times in my fifteen years of living that he's had to pick me up and put me back on my feet after a guy has broken me down to barely anything. Relationships are never really my forte. They always end up with me falling too hard for a guy that just wants what's under my clothes. But I don't realize that until it's too late. I never gave in to the douchebags, mostly because my parents wouldn't let their fifteen-year-old daughter have a boy in her room, but that didn't stop the bastards from trying something when we were away from the house. Thankfully, I'm a beta's daughter, so I have enough strength to get away from them. I haven't had a boyfriend since the last one though. I took the broken arm he gave me as a warning that the moon goddess didn't want me to date before my mate.

"Ooooh, looking like a whole meal, girl!"

I just shake my head at Marcus with a smile on my face. He always knows how to boost my ego at just the right amount.

"Well, if that wasn't a confidence boost, then I don't know what is."

We laugh, and Marcus starts talking about finding our mates, a topic Marcus always brings up. He's a hopeless romantic and constantly talks about how he wants his mate to sweep him off his feet. I try to tell him that maybe he shouldn't put his standards so high so he doesn't get let down, but he never listens.

Marcus is gay, so finding his mate in a pack with less than ten gay wolves is a hard thing to do. Most guys don't find their mates until they're eighteen, but luckily, or not so lucky for me, us girls find them at sixteen. My birthday is in two months, so wolf and I have been anxious. She's happy anxious, and I'm more dreading anxious. I don't *not* want a mate but just not right now.

After curling my hair and putting some lipstick and mascara on, Marcus and I head out the door. I love the look of a full-face of makeup, but I just don't feel up to it tonight.

With my father being a beta, we live pretty close to the pack house, so as soon as we step out, we can hear and see the party. Music is blasting through the speakers, and there are multi-colored lights going off. Kids are grinding on each other while others sit and talk at the bar.

We make our way to the backyard but stop when we spot my brother and Nick. They're talking to two of the girls from the pack, Amber and Ashley. I nudge Marcus and tell him to go the opposite direction.

We finally make it out to the backyard and to a small corner without being caught. If Jake knew I was here, he'd sober up real quick and watch my every move. He deserves not to be my babysitter for a night, so staying hidden is for the best.

"If you see or sense them, let me know. I don't want them seeing us."

Marcus nods in agreement and runs to the bar, grabbing whatever they have available. It's beer, and I grimace at the cup, hating the taste but loving the feeling that comes with it. Being drunk or at least a little tipsy lets me escape from all the thoughts in my head.

Werewolves don't get drunk or high easy, so it takes a few cups before I'm even tipsy. I stay in my corner for most of the night, Marcus having disappeared to talk to some guys in the opposite corner of me.

Taking a drink, I look around the backyard. They really did invite the whole pack, even the adults and elders. I spot Nick's younger brothers in the corner. Nick is turning eighteen tonight, but his brother Noah is two years younger, closer to my age at sixteen.

As if catching me staring, Noah turns to me and grins. I grin back at him and motion him to come over to me. Noah and I have always been close, and even though we haven't talked in forever, I still like his company. He was always right there with Jake, helping me to get over this week's loser I fell in love with. Maybe I am a hopeless romantic.

"Hey, Rosie Posie!" he says as he comes to stand by me. I glare at him for using the nickname he gave me. He totally stole it from my dad, but at least my dad stopped calling me that when I was twelve.

"Aww, come on, you love that name!"

I just shake my head at him. He smirks back at me, grabs me by the waist, and pulls me closer to him. I squeal at the sudden movement and look up to see that his smirk had widened. I pull back from him, hitting him on the chest. He's always been a touchy-feely person. He always used to say when we were kids that we'd grow up to be mates. I knew we would never; I feel nothing towards him besides brotherly love.

"Well, aren't you two just the cutest!" Marcus says in a high-pitched voice.

I roll my eyes and look at my best friend as he stumbles over to us. He is way too drunk for his own good. He almost falls into Noah's arms but catches himself. I grab ahold of him, keeping him steady.

"I'm surprised to see you here, Rose; you never come to these things," Noah says, that stupid grin still on his face.

I glare at Marcus when he busts out laughing.

"Well, I wouldn't be here if it wasn't for Miss Thang over there," I say, pointing to Marcus who smiles.

I set him down in a chair and turn back to stand next to Noah.

"So Rosie Posie, you wanna dance?" Noah asks, bowing and extending his hand. I roll my eyes and shake my head no. I'm not a big dancer.

"It's a party, Rose; just dance with me, at least right here." He doesn't wait for my answer. He grabs me close to him again, and we move to the slow song. I laugh as he spins me in circles, bringing me back to his body as we sway in unison. The song ends, and I smile up at him and kiss his cheek. He smiles down at me, not one ounce of lust in his eyes, just love—the kind I see in my family's eyes when they look at me.

"You know I love you Rose, right?"

"I know, Noah. I love you too, and I also know that Jake sent you over here to babysit me."

"How did you know that?"

"Well, I wasn't sure, but you just confirmed it, plus you smelled just like him when you came over here."

He glares at me but then breaks out into a grin.

"Should've known you'd figure it out, but hey, I wanted to talk and the dance was ni..."

"Noah, get away from her."

We freeze and stare at a very pissed-off looking Nick. Jake comes to his side, a confused look on his face.

"Why?" Noah says.

I look at the brothers. Both their faces are in a glare. Noah eventually lowers his eyes as Nick bears into him, and his alpha demeanour radiates off of him.

"Maybe we should have this conversation in the house, Nick. People are staring," Jake says in a low voice as he looks around.

Sure enough, several people are staring at us. We all head into the pack house. Stopping in the living room, Marcus stumbles in last, falling into Jake's arm as he tries to close the door.

Oh, if he only knows where he is, he'd be in heaven.

"Can someone please explain what's going on?" Noah asks as he and his brother gets into another glaring match.

"You need to stay away from her." Nick grits out of his teeth.

"She's my friend. I can hang out—"

Noah doesn't get to finish as he is pinned against the wall with Nick's hands around his throat.

Jake forces Nick off of Noah, the latter's body dropping to the floor immediately. I rush over to him, but I am stopped by a voice.

"Don't you dare touch him, mate."

My eyes snap to Nick's, but those aren't Nick's eyes; his wolf is in control.

"M-mate?"

"Yes, my love, you're my mate." His voice is deeper, and it doesn't take him long to reach me. He strokes my cheek with his hand, and I feel sparks all over my skin. The room is silent; everyone is pretty surprised, me included.

"This can't be happening." I take a step back from him, gaining a growl from him. I can tell he's fighting for control of his wolf again, and soon, his eyes return to their normal color.

"Rose…"

"Let's give them some time, Noah," Jake says as he picks up a half-conscious Marcus.

Noah nods, gets up, and heads out the door. Jake pauses before he leaves, turning to look Nick directly in the eyes.

"I'm happy for you, guys, but if you hurt her, Nick, alpha or not…she's my sister, and I will protect her." He leaves without getting a response.

I turn to Nick, a look of lust and confusion in his eyes. He grabs my hand, and we head upstairs. I try to tug my hand free but he doesn't let me. We reach his room and he drags me in. I finally pull my hand free and put some space between us.

"Nick, what are we doing up here? We need to talk."

"What's there to talk about? We're mates. People need to know that."

I don't have time to respond before I'm pushed against the door, and he crashes his lips on mine. Unlike all the other boys, who I would have pushed away, I do nothing, and it's like all my limbs have gone numb. My body melts into his, and I enjoy the feeling of his lips on mine. It's not like all the other kisses I had. This is better—much better.

He traps my hands above my head with one of his arms while the other explores my body.

He reaches behind my back and unzips my dress, letting it fall to the ground. I feel like I should stop him but I don't. I enjoy it and my wolf does too. She's itching to get out, and with the way Nick's lips feel on my neck, I fall into a state of bliss. My wolf takes it to her advantage and takes control.

My hands roam his body, and next thing I know, we're both naked, and my precious virginity is about to be gone.

Nick enters me with one quick thrust and I cry out in pain.

"Ahh, so my little mate is a virgin…even better." Nick chuckles as he thrusts into me roughly.

My virginity is soon taken away multiple times that night: on the wall, the couch, the kitchen counter, and the bed.

Oh, how I wish I stayed home.

* * *

Waking up the next morning, I feel a sting come from my shoulder. Putting a hand to it, I feel tingles rush through me, and I look down to see a bite mark.

Nick Rollins marked me last night. Or so I thought. Looking closer, I see it's just an ordinary bite mark, not deep enough to be a mating mark.

Speaking of my mate, I get up to go look for him. I feel a strong burn in my lower region, and the thoughts of last night flows back to me. Not once did my wolf let me take back control. Her and Nikolai, Nick;s wolf's name, were having way too much fun. Nick's smell is faint in the room so I know he's been gone for a while. I look around the house. I can't seem to find him anywhere, so I check the last place in the house where I could possibly find him.

His office door is closed shut, so I position myself to knock, but I am stopped as the door flings open. Nick stands there with a glare on his face.

"You need to leave." He says coldly and then brushes past me like I was nothing. The similar feeling creeps in, this time with a lot more regret.

"W-what do you mean Nick? You said we were mates last night. You took my virginity."

"Yours is not the first virginity I took. Now get out of my house before I force you." He doesn't even spare me a glance, disappearing into his room, the door slamming behind him.

I stand there for a minute, shock and hurt. I squeeze my eyes shut, hoping to open them for all of this to be a dream. But I open them and it isn't. I don't know how but I force myself to leave the room. My heart feels heavy, and it physically hurts to move. My wolf begs me to go back and beg for him to take us back. But I won't be humiliated, not by him.

* * *

I stare at the thing with an emotionless look on my face, hiding all the emotions that stir within me. Three minutes—that's all I have to wait. I look at the clock, ticking. Time seems to go by slowly. The clock hits 6:47—the time I've been waiting for—but it seems like I can't pry my eyes away from looking at the stupid stick.

Two lines.

That's all it took for my heart, with its little pieces I've tried so hard to put back together, to break. It has been a month since that night. Nick left with his family and the rest of mine the very next day to do pack business.

My parents question me as they see the sadness on my face that they know all too well. I blow them off by telling them it's just my period.

Jake knows though. He knew the second he saw me. It took everything in me to convince him not to kill Nick. If he dies, I would too. That is the only thing that's stopping him. I'm sure they have made up by now though. I hope they did; my brother doesn't deserve to lose his best friend because of me.

"By the sound of your heartbeat, I'm guessing it's positive?" Marcus' voice comes from the outside of the bathroom. At his question, I break down. I can't be a mom. I couldn't even be a good mate. How am I supposed to be a good mom?

I don't even realize that I had spoken out loud until my best friend speaks to me.

"Rose, you were a perfect mate, and any other man would have been happy to have you as theirs! You'll be a great mom. I know that for sure!"

I break down all over again, the emotions becoming too difficult for me to control.

I'm going to be a mom.

"When are you going to tell everyone?" Marcus asks when I finally stopped crying.

"I'm not." The words come out firm. I will not allow my child to be humiliated or rejected.

"You're gonna leave?" Marcus asks, a look of sadness on his face.

"You know I have to. I can't go through this pregnancy being sad all the time, and being here makes me so sad, Marcus. My baby doesn't deserve that."

He nods and takes me into his arms. We stay there for a while. I can't seem to let go as I hug him for what would be the last in a while. He tells me he has a few cousins in other packs and might get them to take me in. I nod, thankful I have him as my friend.

Later that night, he lets me know his cousin, Zayne, would allow me to be in his and his mate's pack. I'm happy I can get away—away from the constant pain.

Marcus' voice brings me out of my thoughts as he sticks some papers out to me. "Okay, so this is a bus ticket to take you to my cousin Zayne's town. He said he will meet you at the bus stop and let you stay at their pack house. You will leave tomorrow morning and should get there before dark."

I nod and take the bus ticket from him. I take a long look at my best friend and see him smiling a sad smile.

"I will miss you so much, Marcus. You don't even know."

"I will miss you too, Rose! But I have all night with you so we're going to get a bunch of junk food and watch Law & Order until we fall asleep, ok?"

I nod and grab him for a long hug. Wiping my tears, I tell him to go downstairs and grab the snacks while I pack a few things. I don't pack much, just enough to not have to do laundry for a while. I write my parents and brother a letter; letting them know I'm okay and I just need time away from this place. I know my parents will flip, especially with me being so young. I give them the information of where I'm going and ask them to keep it secret. I left out the pregnancy part though.

Marcus comes back into the room, arms filled with snacks. We lay down and start the show we've watched for years.

"I think it's a boy," Marcus says out of the blue.

"Maybe…" I trail off, thinking if it is a boy. If it is, I'd be taking the pack's future alpha away.

"Oh, I know it is. I've never been wrong in my guesses."

I laugh at him but drop the subject.

We do just as he had said; both of us are passed out until my alarm goes off.

I get up and gather my stuff, waking Marcus up to say goodbye. I hug him goodbye and head to my parents' room.

I leave the letters and quietly make my way to the door.

I say one last goodbye to my home. I head for the one-way bus to my new home with the only important thing I take with me.

The alpha's unknown baby…well, at least, that's what Marcus said.

If you enjoyed this sample, look for
The Alpha's Unknown Son
on Amazon.

A ROYAL'S TALE

BEASTY

JENNISE K

CHAPTER ONE

They said life was wonderful.

"The possibilities a person can have are endless, the tales their lives can spin—countless."

That was what everyone around me said.

And every time they said that, every time they mentioned peaches and sunshine and candies and perfection, I couldn't help but laugh.

After all, they were all optimists—my mother, my dad, my sister. Hell, even her self-proclaimed nerdy accountant of a husband shared the same perspective as them.

But what had the glorious life they spun given them in return?

An untimely demise.

What optimists always forget to realise was the ultimate hard fact that life wasn't all peaches and sunshine. There was only a limit to where all the plan Bs, Cs, and Ds actually work until something goes wrong again. It was a game.

It wasn't like I was a pessimist. I had seen the joys of life. I had walked through fields of flowers. But I knew that that has never stopped the fields from drying—turning barren—when seasons change. Growing up, even I knew that sometimes life's game could rival that of *The Hunger Games*. But dammit, I wish life would realize I was no *Katniss Everdeen*.

Cringing at even comparing *The Hunger Games* to my own life, I shut my eyes for a minute before I did another sweep around my workplace. Midday Wednesday found me behind the counters of a very posh and fashionable boutique situated just near my college campus.

I was employed because I wanted to have a few extra bucks in my pocket besides the allowance that my scholarship offered. Another reason I preferred to work? I didn't want to be a burden on my aunt. I've been lodging in her home ever since I moved to Berlin after all.

In the professional world, Aunt Prue—her real name being Prudence—was a high-end and independent career woman. She was one of the most talented lawyers Berlin had.

Besides my mother and my grandma, she was my only living relative left that was within considerable distance since Grandma Primrose lived all the way around the world in Australia. Aunt Prue had insisted—no, in fact, ordered—that if I were to study in Berlin and not in London, my home city, I would have to live with her.

It had taken a few weeks of convincing, but in the end, I gave in. It wasn't such a bad idea. After all, I did need a new environment to take my mind off of my family's tragedy.

"Erm . . . excuse me?"

My eyes immediately darted up and met with warm ones. I gave its owner a genuine smile. "Hello! How may I help you?"

The red-haired girl, who looked about thirteen, fidgeted on her feet before extending a dress towards me. My eyes moved over to the dress and stopped.

It was skimpy de la skimpy. Definitely not the kind that thirteen-year-old girls would wear on the daily.

"Going to a party?" I suggested lamely, not at all judging the poor girl for wanting to wear that piece of rag. I bet my woolly socks that it could barely cover anyone's posterior, if at all.

"Yeah," the girl mumbled out shyly. I nodded, smiling, as I reached out and took the dress from her extended hands.

"It's beautiful. Impressing a date?" I asked, eager to make small talk.

Her eyes fidgeted to mine and back to the dress. She nodded. "Kyle likes . . . girls in these sorts of . . . clothes."

My fingers froze just before touching the register's keypads. I looked up at her. "How old is this Kyle?"

The girl fidgeted again. "Twelve." At my frozen expression, she quickly added, "I'm twelve too!" as if that alone justified her wardrobe choice. I kept my composure so as not to hurt my customer's feelings, but in my mind, I was screeching: *Girl, where your parents at?*

I shoved *Jiminy*—or my conscience—down as I looked at the nervous girl, "What do *you* want to wear to the party?"

Her eyes sparkled. "Honestly?"

I smiled. "Honestly."

"I'd rather wear that." She pointed towards a pretty pink dress. I smiled. *So she preferred classic style dresses. Good taste.*

"Well then, let's get you that dress!" I grinned, but she only stared at me. "Well, bring it over then!" I urged her.

As if on automatic—like something was activated inside her—the girl moved almost instantly towards the dress and brought it over. I took it from her.

"B-but what about that dress?" the young girl blurted out, desperately hoping I'd still opt for her to take the rags instead of the classic pink one that I just pulled.

"Can I tell you something?" I spoke softly as I held onto the dress, the bright red one completely forgotten on the counter. The girl nodded.

"If Kyle really liked you, he wouldn't make you change who and how you are. You're already good and pretty. In fact, I love your taste. Don't change it for someone who doesn't see the beauty here." I tapped a finger on my chest and smiled when I saw the girl crack a small smile, understanding flooding over her face.

Her helpless eyes met mine, and she wailed, "B-but I like him!"

A small movement on the far corner of the shop caught my eye, and I looked up to see a young boy standing in the dark, waiting. His soft gaze directed at the girl before me.

"Who's that?" I cocked my head in the boy's direction.

The girl turned then smiled. "Oh, that's my best friend, Hugh."

My gaze moved back to the boy, and a smirk formed on my lips.

"Does he ask you to change your style?" I asked the girl, thankful that there wasn't much traffic in the boutique today. *Not that Madame Crawfort would be happy about that, but eh!*

"No." The reply was instant, and I felt my smirk increase.

"That's because he really does like you. In fact, I think he's really cute, don't you?"

"But he's my best friend!"

I shrugged. "So?"

The girl froze. She looked up at me. "You mean . . ."

I shrugged again. "Hey, like Olaf said, *'Some people are worth melting for!'* Take a chance. Go to the party with Hugh."

"But—"

"Better a guy who likes the real you than the one who makes you be someone else, aye?"

I watched as the guy's eyes moved from the girl to me, clearly confused. So was the girl.

"Think about it!" I shrugged as I smiled at the very confused girl in front of me. Pressing on the keyboard, I keyed in both the dresses and put both on my card. I handed the bag out to the girl.

"But you didn't—"

I waved a hand in the air, dismissing the girl. "It's on me! Think about what you want. Any choice that makes you happy is *the* right choice."

The girl gulped, and tears suddenly formed at the edges of her eyes. Suddenly, I felt like running away. I didn't know how to deal with people crying. Heck, I didn't even know how to comfort myself because I couldn't cry anymore. No more.

"T-thank you!" the girl croaked, and I blinked, reaching out to her like how my mother used to do every time I cried. Only I was sure that I did it more awkwardly.

I patted her cheeks. "It's okay! Now go. Hugh's freaking out."

Looking back, the girl giggled and confirmed my remark; the kid really was freaking out. She looked at me with her eyes bright and said, "I'm Lessie by the way."

I grinned, secretly glad that she wasn't going to cry anymore.

"It's nice to meet you, Lessie. I'm Olivia."

*   *   *

"I am so glad you didn't *av* any classes today, *ze* boutique *vas* quite—*ow ze* say *eet*—busy!" Madame Crawfort, the owner of the boutique, said in obvious satisfaction.

Handing over her pair of the store keys, I smiled at my employer. "To be honest, I do have a class in a few minutes."

"*Zet* is disastrous! You must not go! Oh, you must not! You look *seemply* tired beyond any good point!" she said indignantly, shaking her head as she did so.

I shrugged then sighed as I pulled on my coat. "I understood the consequences when I decided to work while I studied, Madame Crawfort."

"Aw, you poor child! *Vell*, you can, take—*ow ze* say *eet*—tomorrow off! I *vill* tell Mary to cover for you." With the way she clucked at me, one would never think she was my employer. I gave her a very thankful smile as I made my way towards the door, keys and bag both in hand.

"Thank you, Madame Crawfort. You're too kind! Have a good night!" I called out, stepping out of the front door and closing it behind me.

Walking towards the elevator of the mall, I counted on all the lucky stars I had to help me get into class before Professor Hern showed up. No one really liked being late to his lectures.

* * *

"And that is all for today. Please don't forget to hand in your assignments by late next week. Good evening, everyone."

At that, the whole hall instantly jostled with excitement as tired people—meaning all of us—hurriedly and lazily shoved our books into our bags and tried to make it first to the exit.

"Please tell me you're not going to the library now," Abigail, my best friend and personal psychologist, asked. She looked like she was close to dropping unconscious.

"You know I have to, Aby. I'm dead for the day as well, but I have to get some books first. This assignment won't finish itself." I sighed as I flung my backpack on my shoulder and made a move towards the door. Aby and Jaydin, my other best friend, followed behind.

"It won't kill you to search online for once, you know?" Jay teased me, nudging my side.

I stuck my tongue out. "Shut up." Jay was unperturbed and responded in kind.

"You guys heading over to the pub downtown, again?" I asked as we walked towards the library with Abigail close behind; she had a tendency to bodyguard me. I couldn't deny that both she and her instincts were always correct, though.

Our feet pounded against the cobblestone floors, echoing back our urgency to the cold walls as we made our way through the corridors that led towards the massive library.

Smiling and nodding at a few students who passed by us in the halls, Jay returned his attention to us to answer me. "Yes! And you can come too, you know?" he tempted us as he slung his arms around both Abigail and me.

"Getcho hands off me, boy!" Abigail hissed immediately, shoving Jay's hand off her and moving away as quick as a flash.

Aha, a clear sign of Aby being nervous.

Grinning, Jay looked at me and declared, "She wants me."

I scoffed and rolled my eyes for good measure. "Sure, she does! As for the pubs offer, I can't. You know I have Lolette's file to read through. My three-week-old niece is under my custody, and I don't know what to do, Jay. I'm only twenty!"

"I thought her grandparents refused to give her up?"

I sighed. The library was now in sight. "Well, ever since Elizabeth and Gerard . . . the car crash . . . it's been hard. It has made everything harder."

"You don't want Lolette?" Abigail whispered, moving in closer as we finally caught up to her and went into the library.

I sighed again. This time a tad heavier. "I do. Of course, I do! She's the last part of Liz that I have left! First, Mum and Dad . . . and just five years later, Liz and Gerard! It's not fair."

"We get it," Abigail assured me as I walked towards the bookshelves. She understood I was still a bit reluctant to divulge on such a topic.

I picked out a couple of books on Behavioural Psychology then headed towards the fiction section.

"I think I'm allergic to this place." Jay shuddered as he followed Abigail and I going over the books. We carefully read the descriptions and took a second to decide if it was to be included as one of our resources for this week's book review. I shook my head at the green paperback in my hand and placed it back on the shelf. Tonight was not the night for knights.

"It's a library, Jay. Say it, acknowledge it, and you'll feel better!" I mumbled while my eyes busily scanned the many spines

aligned along the shelves. One grey spine—whose frayed edges beckoned to me—stood out among its neat neighbours.
The Hellion's Fate.
Bleak, cold, and dark.
"Perfect." I turned towards my best friends, smiling and feeling very accomplished.
Jay's eyes caught mine, and he winked mischievously. I immediately knew the boy was up to no good. Moving between Aby and the bookshelf in record time, he wiggled his eyebrow at her. I bit my lip to stifle my giggle.
Leaning in closer to Aby, Jay spoke out in a husky voice, "*Te amo.*" My eyes widened, and my bite on my lip tightened.
Abigail just rolled her eyes and moved away. "Yeah, yeah, *chow mein* to you, too."
I couldn't help it. I barked out laughing but immediately covered my loud mouth with my palm.
Jay groaned dejectedly. "I can never win!"

* * *

"Reckon I'll stick around here for a bit guys," I told Jay and Aby as I placed my books on the tiny table. Sinking down on the sofa beside it, I let out a happy sigh.
Aby cocked an eyebrow up in all her superior judgemental splendour, and I scoffed.
"I'll get home safely, Mother. Now shoo! Have fun you two!"
Her lips quirked up at the edges as she rolled her eyes and looked away. "Alright, if you say so. We'll see you tomorrow!"
"Laters, baby." Jaydin winked before he turned around and followed Abigail out.
A hopelessly wide smile spread on my face. Not only was I going to be left alone with my reading, I just gave Jay more opportunity to take his chances with Aby. I shook my head before I

got caught up with my imagination. My fingers stroked the book I was itching to begin reading.

I turned to the first page.

"I knew there was heartbreak in the future. But I couldn't give up today's smile for tomorrow's tears. I couldn't."

* * *

"It's already quite late, you know."

I looked up to see who it was, sighed, then looked down at my book again. "Go away, River."

River Welshnit—the university bad boy and the forever persistent flirt—frowned as he sat down on the couch opposite mine. "No, I'm serious. Go home, Olivia. It's late."

I ignored him.

A few minutes passed, and I could no longer bear his stare boring holes into my forehead. Looking up at him again, I gave up and peeked at my wristwatch.

10:35 PM

He was right; it was late. I needed to get going.

"Well . . . good night then," I mumbled as I picked up the books and began walking towards the librarian's desk. I felt River follow.

"No thank you?" I rolled my eyes and resumed my business with the staff, checking out the books I needed for our assignment and *The Hellion's Fate*. A few scribbles after and I was good to go. I began walking towards the exit.

I was already outside, but still, River followed. Could he not take a hint?

"Thank you," I blurted out. It was one of those cold nights, and as I spoke, my breath came out heavy in the night air, I could almost see it.

Beside me, River shrugged. "It's okay. I'm just taking care of you—for Lolette. We both love her a lot. You know that." I nodded. Slumping, we walked towards the parking lot. River was right. We both loved her a lot.

River. My dead brother-in-law's breathing, walking, younger sibling.

Thankfully, we reached my car. Sensing my discomfort despite my best efforts to mask it, River asked as I opened the door and shoved my bag pack inside, "Do you want me to drive you over?"

He knows...

I turned, my arm bracing the door. "It's fine, River. I'm a big girl. I can take care of myself."

Can you?

Our eyes stared at each other for a while before he finally nodded. He put his hand up in defeat. "Okay then. Good night."

Smile.

I beamed up at him. "Good night!" I chirped then went inside the car.

* * *

The ride seemed to be going too slow. It was quieter, longer than usual. I was feeling more than the normal amount of reluctance of getting home.

Just then, the song slipping out from the car's speakers changed into one of the more upbeat songs I had in my iPod, and I immediately straightened in my seat, already feeling more than energetic enough about getting home.

Music therapy always worked.

Suddenly, the loud blast of my offensive ringtone replaced the song and surrounded the entire car, and I, shocked for a second, blinked before I looked at it on the passenger's seat.

Prue calling...

I didn't bother to answer the call. *I'll get home in fifteen minutes anyway*, I reasoned with myself and looked back up at the highway.

Out of nowhere, a guy in a dark hood stood in the middle of the road directly in front of my car.

A loud shriek ripped out of my throat, and I swerved the car sideways, hoping that I did no harm to the man. I felt my car go out of control as it swerved off the road and move towards the darkness. I was so shocked; I couldn't stop as my head hit the steering wheel with a hard bang. Everything went black for a second.

That's it. First, it was your family. It's your turn now! I screamed in my head as I tried to gulp down my heart, which was beating crazily fast. In the blackness of the night, my eyes adjusted and my sight came back.

Warm blood gushed down the side of my head, and I fought a blackout from engulfing me as my feet hit the brakes. But that didn't work, and now, I desperately tried to turn the wheels around, crying out helplessly when it rotated towards the other direction.

I'm dying. I'm dying.

Tears leaked down my face as I turned around to look at the road. My eyes widened when I found nothing.

No hooded man.

No man at all.

Nothing.

I tried working on opening the windows when I felt the car turn over. My heart stopped in my chest.

I don't want to die yet. I don't want to die!

As I sat there—thanks to the seatbelt—suspended in the upended car, tears kept rolling down my face. I thought about my mum and dad, then my sister and her husband—who all died in a similar fashion. They were all gone.

Dead.

Just like how I will be.

The car gave an ugly screech as a large dent made through the driver's door, pushing the metal inwards. A final jolt and the car reached the bottom with a big drop. With no control over myself, I felt my head hit the dented roof as the final strains on my life began to loosen.

Want . . . to . . . li . . .

A loud sound of ripping metal shrieked in the dead silent night, and I felt light seep through me again. Hanging by a thread, I cracked my eyes open just in time to see a pair of golden eyes shining back at me.

Dying and delirious, I giggled, then sobbed as I felt the darkness coming over again. My mind desperately clutched back to the image of the golden-eyed creature. *What was that?* I heard myself groan again, and my lips moved up to form a smile.

My eyes cracked open, and I saw the golden eyes still staring at me. Was this the grim reaper? Was this it?

I felt a strong grip working around me, but it was too late. Still looking at the golden eyes, I realised I was still smiling. It was then when I realised *it* was finally here. Without knowing it, a singular name rose up in my mind and came out of my mouth in a whisper.

"Beasty . . ."

Death . . .

Everything around me began turning bleak again, and I almost didn't even notice as I was pulled out of the now ruined car. I felt something warm caressed my neck—soft, slow, soothing.

Then it turned into something sharp.

A scream ripped out of my throat as I felt an intense pain in my neck.

I heard my scream fade away in the distance.

And then my entire world went black. The darkness—it had come.

Beasty . . .

If you enjoyed this sample, look for
Beasty
on Amazon.

ACKNOWLEDGEMENTS

I'd like to acknowledge and give a huge thanks to Le-an Lai Lacaba who once told me that she had faith in me and knew that I could do it. If it wasn't for her, then I wouldn't have been able to do this. Thank you for looking past my flaws and helping me accomplish something I've never thought I could ever do.

A big thank you to my twin, Rua Hasan, and my close friends for supporting me from day one and motivating me to not give up. I don't think I could have done it without your support.

Thanks to the website that helped me begin this journey. Thank you, Wattpad, for allowing me to write and meet amazing authors who made me who I am today.

And lastly, thank you BLVNP for giving me a chance. I wouldn't have done it without your support!

ABOUT THE AUTHOR

Raneem Hasan is a Palestinian girl who was raised between California and Jordan. She started writing at the age 15 with her first book and has since then loved to write. Her dream is to one day become a well-known published author, bring smiles on others faces as they read her work, and to inspire people to achieve their goals like what she did.

Made in the USA
Monee, IL
16 February 2024

53625935R00340